To

TH
THE POET AND THE PIMP

with best wishes

First published in UK 2024

www.malcolmeva.com

Liberties have been taken with some featured locations, in the cause of the fiction.

Typeset by Megan Sheer: sheerbookdesign.com
Cover artwork by Karina Gabner

ISBN 9781068537004

THE PRIEST, THE POET AND THE PIMP

MALCOLM EVA

'The Priest loves the Dancer
The Dancer loves the Drummer
And the Drummer loves his drums,
And they'll all be alone
When Winter comes.'

The Priest, The Dancer and The Drummer by Bob Pegg

CHAPTER 1

Growing out of Lillie Road, behind Earl's Court and beside the bus depot, the tall blue office tower kept its watch, always. Part of this block was used as the eyes and ears for the country's defence during the recently ended Cold War. The rest of it helped manage other defence efforts. There were always a few lights on in this building, whatever time of the night, whatever day of the year. Cold War or not, it still never slept.

And so, when work was too routine for too many hours, workers in the offices might wander to a window, coffee in hand, and look out over the neighbouring areas of London.

At this moment, on an autumnal late afternoon, a viewer standing at a window on the twenty-second floor might have seen a bearded giant in a tattered combat jacket striding hard along the street in front of Brompton cemetery: Arnold Gill.

Arnold was in a hurry to get back to his flat in Philbeach Gardens. It wasn't long until the next reading in the cafe and his new poem had just started to take shape. He knew from years of experience that if it were to be finished in time for next week's reading, he had at least one late night's seclusion ahead of him, maybe more; he was unlikely to collapse into bed until at least two. But the images were there, hammering at his door, and he must get back to the flat and put them down on paper before they melted again, leaving him with the faint echo of yet another forgotten dream.

He held his evening meal, such as it was, in a paper bag under his arm, the edges of the tins poking his ribs as he strode on. He didn't notice the incipient bruising; all of his mind was on the three lines that he chanted over and over to himself lest they desert him before he found a pencil. Pen and pencil were still easier to use to capture his thoughts than a dictaphone, if only he could hang onto them long enough

When he sat down at his table, he noted with mild surprise that he was bleeding slightly from his thigh. He vaguely remembered falling against a shopping trolley as he bustled past a woman in Penywern Road. No matter, that was not important – although, of course, it might open up into a theme later on. He made a note of the incident, just in case.

Or if our viewer had instead been looking towards Fulham, he might have seen Jez Kaplan, 31 going on 55, smiling beatifically as he meandered towards the tube station. He was smiling now because for a few hours, he was happy. Then the illness would start again, and the panic. He dreaded the panic, because he allowed himself to do such degrading things to alleviate it. His was only a chemical happiness, after all, but it still made him smile. Jez was going to see his friend at Piccadilly; it was not necessarily safer, but he preferred it to buying the stuff on his own home patch. He didn't have many standards left, but he tried to hold onto the few that remained.

He found it hard to get into the station. For some reason, walking straight through the door didn't work; he had to sidestep many hurrying commuters and found his steps leading him straight out again. He didn't know whether to laugh or panic. Few commuters noticed him, with his straggly black hair and wasted-looking face. After all, there were too many like him along their daily journey.

If our idle watcher were looking down towards Earl's Court itself, much of the High Street would in fact be masked by intervening buildings, so he wouldn't be able to see the girls clustering by the station entrance, or by the lamp posts further down. It was the start of the shift for many of them, so they were barely yet looking for customers. Perhaps they held an eye open to the passing men, but they were not trying. Instead, like most workers they chatted as they started the evening's work, laughing in twos and threes, or commiserating on a day's misfortune. There was no sign yet of Mahmoud or Dave, so they were relaxed enough to enjoy each other's company for a few minutes. Only gradually would they break off and find their own spot to stand and offer business. There would be little custom for them until the rush hour was past, and men could take the time to look at them before making a choice.

The girls recognised most of the different classes of customer that chose them. There were the hungry and lonely, many of those in this area of transients. After their first self-conscious visit, they seized on the girls as friends and spent as much time talking to them about life as they did wrestling horizontally with them.

Most of their custom came from businessmen up in town on a course or conference, perhaps, and taking advantage of a break in domesticity to visit the wild side. If they really wanted the wild of course, Earl's Court and London could offer them far more variety and risk than the young girls by the station. But then, most of these respectable punters were only playing at being wild for the night.

There were also the tourists, young backpackers from around the world, especially Australia, who for some reason seemed to be drawn to this area more than any other part of the UK. Soon after arrival many of the young men, having found a bed and unloaded their backpacks, liked to celebrate the end of this stage of travel, and the girls helped them feel even better about being here. Those who stayed awhile usually found other, more settled company and left the girls alone again.

There were others, too, like Arnold, who treated them with courteous disinterest, purchasing a commodity, but who rarely needed to notice a human being behind the skin.

Then there were the dangerous ones who maybe carried knives or razors, who wanted what the girls hated to give and were frightened to refuse. If one were seen on the street, the girls redoubled their efforts to find a safe customer before the sadist picked them. There was no refuge in numbers here; as often as not they would take two at once. The girls soon learned to recognise the dangerous ones, even though they didn't follow a clear pattern. Some were noisy, others alarmingly quiet, but they were unmistakeable – once a girl had experienced it she recognised it coming again. But they could not refuse; Mahmoud would not let them refuse a customer, ever. It was bad business if a girl was too marked or bruised for work, but it was worse business to refuse.

Kate hadn't been on the street long enough to experience this, but she was experienced enough to fear Mahmoud. She was still only young and hadn't any other way to pay for her room. Indeed, were it not for Mahmoud, she would still be living on the pavements. She hadn't been frightened of him then, not until she realised he had lied, and she couldn't leave after all.

Our watcher wouldn't see Kate from his vantage point, or her friends. He wouldn't know of Mahmoud and his little empire, and if he did see the girls, the scarring of one or two of them wouldn't seem significant enough to draw his interest for long.

He would be able to see Knightsbridge and the top of Harrods. At this hour in a few weeks, with the Christmas windows complete, it would look like a magical galleon, outlined in light and moored in the heart of frantic shoppers. For now, it was just a large bump in the late afternoon skyline, the clouds behind not yet quite ready to turn pink.

He could have seen where South Kensington station was, but it was too far away for him to see Gerard Tisserant emerge this evening onto the pavement. That was a shame, for although Gerard wanted quiet and anonymity, this felt for him like such an enormous step that he was sure the whole of South West London could see him and recognise him as the newly-lapsed priest that he was. He was mistaken of course, for hardly anyone noticed him as he apologised his way past clusters of sightseers and shoppers.

Gerard lugged a large, square suitcase with him, increasing his sense of clumsiness and conspicuousness. The wheels didn't ease his passage through the evening crowd but rather caused more bumps and collisions behind him.

'Sorry, I'm sorry,' he muttered breathlessly to the young executive-suited woman who rubbed her knee painfully as he passed her. She ignored his apology and glared at him. He felt himself to be sometimes swimming against the current of home-goers and sometimes drowning. Perhaps it would be easier to carry it rather than wheel it through the crowds.

He remembered the address he was seeking, though not the directions, and stopped with relief every few yards under the pretext of looking at his makeshift map once again. Even those seven or eight seconds were a welcome break each time for his palms and upper arms.

Gerard's few years as a parish priest in semi-rural Derbyshire had not been good for his physical stamina and physique. Parochial and pastoral duties made demands on his compassionate ingenuity and moral strength; they did not encourage muscular power. He was still only in his thirties, and his metabolism had not yet slowed on him, but his muscles were out of tone and his lungs held less than their full power, so his manoeuvres with the suitcase through the crowds reduced him to just one breathless ache.

It didn't help that he had not expected this early autumn evening to be so warm. He was dressed in heavy dark clothes, which combined with his exertion to drench him with perspiration. At least, he thought wryly, his coat had pockets deep enough to hold his walkman and the cassettes of Bach and Mozart that he'd listened to on the journey from Derby, though their bulk added to his discomfort.

Nick and Jenny were expecting him at half past six; he would not be very late if only he could track down the road where they lived. Would they have changed much? He had only seen them twice since graduation, and for over ten years now Christmas provided their only communication – until his plea for help last week.

In fact, he turned up on their doorstep at five past seven. Gerard was a strong believer in 'guestpitality' as much as hospitality, and his first words to Nick and Jenny were of remorse and great apology.

'Stop it, Gerard, at once!' snapped Jenny, with a laugh that showed her pleasure at seeing him again after so long. 'Good God, man, sorry – Father. I mean do you really think that after living in London so long we actually expect London Transport to get visitors here on time?'

They drew him in from the step, and he let his case fall to the ground with intense relief and a laugh, as he relaxed at last. Fear of being late and rude, fear of shyness, and fear of morbidness all fell from him with his coat, and he was home again.

They had not grown old. Jenny's hair, still long and ginger, swung with a turn of her head, just as he remembered seeing it all those years ago. Nick betrayed slight signs of years passing: his brown hair was greying a little and drawing back from his temples, but not enough to age him too noticeably. He had thickened out, Gerard noticed. Their clothes were as smart as always, although much more expensive. Gerard became painfully aware of his cheap, nondescript suit and old coat. Once they all were as poor as a student grant could force them to be. Only he seemed to have kept the habit, despite his sudden and regretted wealth.

He wondered if they too were looking at him for signs of the passing years. He had kept his light brown hair, not yet greying or thinning, but that felt like a minor miracle after the last year. He was still thin and had not bulked out yet with early middle-age, but he did not look a contented man – the shadows under his eyes had grown too big to be hidden by his brown-rimmed spectacles. Frown lines were starting to carve into his forehead. But he had arrived, he was once more with his friends, and he could not stop the smile across his face, even if he had wanted to.

Nick and Jenny's house was part of a Georgian terrace off Kensington High Street. Successive owners had removed more and more parts of the original; the interior stucco had all vanished decades earlier, panelled doors had long since given way to plain wood veneer, ceilings had been lowered and walls built to give more rooms. It was still large, though, and it was still the home of patricians who prided themselves on their immaculate taste. Gerard himself did not share their inclination for glass-and-clipped posters advertising impressionist and post-modernist exhibitions in New York and Bonn, but Nick and Jenny were happy surrounded by them. Similarly, he was not at one with their reproduction Victorian mahogany tables and dressers underneath the posters, but the wood shone with a high polish that showed how much they were loved.

He took in the photographs along the mantelpiece over the dummy fire, as well as the full bookcase by the adjacent wall. He was glad to see that even with their busy work lives, they seemed to make time to read. They hadn't changed that much, then.

What Gerard did see with pleasure was their delight at his arrival. No matter how their lives had diverged, their warmth allayed his depression and uncertainties for a few hours and took him back to their younger days together.

When he came downstairs again from unpacking, Nick handed him a large glass of scotch like his own, and smiled as he watched Gerard taking in the house.

'Bit of a change from Crosby Avenue, eh?' he said.

'Yep, you've come a long, long way,' Gerard replied, mirroring the amused smile. 'How long did we all live there, eh?'

'A good two years – it took us right up to Finals.'

'That's right. Oh no, do you remember that revue we did for Rag Week? We wrote it in three days, rehearsed it in four and died the death in front of an audience for three nights.'

'That was dire!' Jenny joined in. 'Positively the worst theatrical experience in the world anywhere. And we were so proud before we performed it!'

'Hey, Ger,' Nick said, 'what was that tongue twister song you wrote for it? Nan, Stan, Fran on the sand … How did it go?'

'Aargh, please! I went to five years of therapy to get over that – why did you have to remind me, why? Erm, what was it?

'Meet your Nan by the bandstand, Stan, not the grandstand, Stan, but the bandstand on the sand, Stan.'

And Gerard laughed with them as he stumbled over well-forgotten words from years past.

'Happy days, though, weren't they?' sighed Jenny, 'I mean, it was a good time, come on.'

'Apart from that revue? And all the angsty evenings in the run up to Finals. Yeah, it was a bloody good time,' said Gerard, 'the best. Before real life caught up with us.'

'Come along next door, dinner's ready now,' and Jenny took his arm in the old familiar way, leading him through to the dining room. Her cooking was as good as he remembered it, but now far more cosmopolitan. Nick poured the wine as she set the plates on the table, then when they were all seated raised his glass in a toast:

'To friendship! And always remember, in wine there is wisdom, in beer there is fellowship, in water there is bacteria. Health!' And he laughed and drank the glass straight back. Gerard and Jenny raised their glasses in turn, but sipped more decorously.

Gerard ate all four courses with pleasure and listened to them describe their jobs in their respective companies. He didn't understand half of what they told him about their work: job titles had become more arcane and the descriptions were even more bewildering, but he could recognise the euphemisms for closures and redundancies amongst their talk.

It didn't matter, though. After the cold months since Jane Conway had died, their welcome was like the sun's return. Even the digressions into gossip and their news for each other washed over him with the same warmth.

Yes, friendship is good, he reminded himself. All that happens in the world is bearable unless you are alone. Father Holloway was a mentor, but never a friend. You might feel wisdom, and certainly learning, ooze from him; you would feel experience and strength of viewpoint, albeit forbidding and all too ready to condemn. But he never managed to radiate this warmth of friendship, least of all when Gerard most needed it. For anything approaching that, he relied on Mrs Cormac, the housekeeper, whose cooking, baking and sympathy helped to soften many of Father Holloway's passionate denunciations of various aspects of Gerard's ministry, and some of his parishioners. His bishop, too, had offered him compassion and understanding, but as if dispensed from several levels above, so that Gerard felt a rather detached benevolence rain down on him. But then, that was all he had been able to offer Jane, when she had needed so much more.

Oh no, not again.

However much he tried to keep her memory in the backmost cupboard in his mind, she kept leaping to the front, accompanied by the image of her angry, grieving husband, shouting at Gerard when the funeral was complete, jabbing his finger as he accused. He felt his face flush yet again at the memory, and of Father Holloway, so clumsily and inappropriately trying to defend him by cursing and blaming the man, with no thought for the pain that he was expressing.

'Sorry, Gerard,' Nick's voice broke his thoughts. 'We've been jabbering away here like we always do and haven't given you a look in! So, tell us, what's happening with you?'

'Can't you ask a simpler question?' Gerard laughed, self-consciously. 'After fifteen years there's too much to say.'

'Cardinal, yet?' asked Jenny.

'Cardinal? Well, that's an idea, isn't it? No, up to now just a parish priest. A comfortable little parish, as well, for the most part, up near the Peaks. I share the presbytery with an older, more senior priest, and that's about it. No, I haven't scaled the same sort of heights that you both have – no management positions or jet-setting around the country.'

'So what is it?' asked Nick, and this time he was serious. 'You're not just on holiday, are you?'

Gerard shook his head, but found it too hard to speak. Jenny leaned across the table and put her hand on his.

'Look, we get you're in trouble. We're pleased that you thought of us to help. Can't you tell us what it is?'

'No, not yet. Trouble isn't the right word, although I don't know – I'm troubled, yes, but not *in* trouble, if you see what I mean. I've been granted a, well, a sabbatical if you like. Maybe indefinitely. Actually, I tried to hand in my notice as it were, quit the priesthood altogether, but the bishop persuaded me to take time off on pay, and not decide till later. They've been kinder than I think I deserve, so I'll take advantage of it. Basically, I did something terrible and don't know how to make it good. No,' looking at their faces, 'no, I didn't steal the candlesticks, or molest the choirboys or anything like that, I just made a terrible mistake that … sorry, please don't ask me for details yet. I'll tell you when I can, but at the moment it's too raw.'

'What do you want from us, then?'

'Does sanctuary sound too pompous, or ridiculous?'

'It sounds bloody ridiculous, a couple of atheists like us giving sanctuary to a priest! Tell us what you want, and we'll tell you if we can do it.'

'All right.' Gerard took a deep breath. 'I need time away from the ministry, away from my parish and far away from Father Holloway and the bishop. I don't know yet what I want to do, or how long I need to do it, but I'm fighting demons, and I need to be with friends who don't believe in demons. Does that make any kind of sense to you? It did to me on the train when I rehearsed it, but now I've said it out loud it just sounds stupid.'

He didn't miss the exchange of looks between Nick and Jenny.

'Look, I'm not ill, I don't need nursing and attention. You've got your jobs, and there's no need for me to interfere with how you live. If I can sleep here, and share company with you in the evenings, I can amuse myself during the days. If I can't find things to do and see in London, then I'm in a worse state than I thought!'

'Of course,' said Jenny. 'What do you think we are? But you mustn't mind that we're often not here till late. This is the earliest I've been home on a Friday for I don't know how long, and next week it'll be even worse.'

'I'll be around for a couple of weeks,' broke in Nick. 'No worry, there, Gerard, I can show you the sights, go on a few lads' nights out. There are times though, when one or both of us might have to stay away from home for a day or so. Both our companies are spread out across the country.'

'Are you all right for money?' Jenny asked, straight to the point.

'I'm fine there. The Church may not pay that well, but my parents left me their houses. I sold our old home just before the slump when prices were sky high, and I'm getting rent from the other two, so yes, I'm fine. All unearned, and I don't feel so proud of that, but at least I can survive well. Talking of which, er … I should give you something for my stay?'

'Don't you dare! I only asked in case you needed help while you're here. Have you got anyone else to see? Friends, fellow vicars, anyone like that?'

'Not really. I know one or two priests from conferences and the like, but no one I particularly want to catch up with.'

'Knowing you, you'll probably have a huge coterie of friends before you're done. At uni you were one of the few who seemed to have friends in every little group and clique on the campus. I don't know how you did it, but every time I looked up, you were with someone from yet another group.'

He shrugged. 'I just like meeting people, nothing special. And if someone seems interesting, a coffee always seems to turn them into a friend.'

He squeezed her hand, then shifted the subject quickly to one that had caught his interest on his discreet survey of the room.

'Your photos, I see that old uni one of our crowd in the garden at Crosby Road. Good memories there. Do you still see any of them?'

'Not really,' said Jenny. 'You know, the usual Christmas card, some with round robins in them keeping me up to date with spouses and sprogs we've never met.'

'And that picture on the end? Can that be my godson who never was?'

'Our James? Yes, that's him. And over there, and there,' and Jenny pointed to different shelves, where their son grew from toddler to proud young teenager in new school uniform. 'Yes, he's away at boarding school now, so you'll have his room. Don't take any notice of the posters and stuff he's got in there.'

'Did you ever get him baptised?'

'Of course not! You would have been godfather if we had, you know that.'

'I know I put first dibs on it, but over the years, who knows?'

'No, if we ever wanted to go down that road, it was always your role, that. But we'd have felt real hypocrites, a pair of atheists like us. I know it's your life, but we were never a church family so apart from the party afterwards, what's the point?'

'And I so looked forward to doing that as well,' said Gerard ruefully. 'So I've never got to know him. Not since he was a baby.'

'Well,' said Nick, 'he's got an exeat next weekend, and we're off to take him out for the day. Do you want to come with us and meet him?'

That took Gerard by surprise, and he stuttered while he thought about an answer.

'It's all right, you don't have to. Just a thought, as you brought it up.'

'It would be great to meet him, but I think it would make his day out a bit self-conscious instead of relaxed. No, if he comes here for a visit while I'm still here I'd love to get to know him I expect, but you should enjoy your time with him without bothering about me. How old is he?'

'Fifteen in February and doing well at school. It's down in Sussex, not one of the big ones. I think he's like you at the moment – more into the arts and literature than anything resembling business. I'm pretty sure he's not into God, though.'

As they lingered over the tiramisu dessert she had made, their conversation broadened out into ordinary topics – holidays (European travel and would they use the new channel tunnel when that opened?) and politics (was John Major managing to live up to Margaret Thatcher's legacy and why on earth did they sack her? Were they ready for the pensions time bomb that surely awaited their generation in a few years' time? What was the impact on them of Black Wednesday back in the autumn? Why had the unemployment and homeless figures suddenly become so bad?).

Positions between Gerard and his friends proved strongly divided over these topics. Before the disagreements became too heated they moved onto safer ground with discussions about recent films they had seen and admired or hated: *Jurassic Park* (3 enjoyed), *Sleepless in Seattle* (1 enjoyed, 2 bored) and *Mrs Doubtfire* (2 enjoyed, 1 missed altogether).

As the wine bottles flowed from full to empty, discussion shifted to the more philosophical – what would the new century and millennium bring? It was only a handful of years away now, yet no one seemed to be preparing or even aware of it.

'Swords into ploughshares, swords into ploughshares,' asserted Gerard. 'The Cold War is over, looks as though Israel and the PLO are on the point of declaring peace – put the defence budget into providing homes, jobs and food.'

'New business opportunities in the old Soviet territory,' responded both Nick and Jenny. 'Plenty of growth, plenty of new trade. We survived and the twenty-first century will be the Golden Age.'

'Except,' Gerard couldn't resist, 'they thought the same a hundred years back, probably. Right up till 1914 no one foresaw the possibility of world war. There may be another Franz Ferdinand in the wings right now who'll take a bullet that turns the whole thing upside down without warning.'

'You just said swords into ploughshares – now you're turning them back! Well, we've got another twenty-odd years to sort that, if it takes a century between these game-changers,' blurred Nick. 'Cheers.'

'You didn't used to be the pessimist, Gerard,' said Jenny. 'Only the best in everyone, that was you. "All is for the best in the best of all possible worlds." Remember?'

They didn't ask him any more about his troubles, and when he went to bed soon after, he was surprised at how disappointed he was not to have been pressed to unburden himself. It was an ordeal he had been dreading. But he was expecting, after decent prevarication, to be able to tell them Jane Conway's story and the crisis it had precipitated. They had not pressed him, though, and he wondered if he would be given an opportunity to explain what he was doing there.

He expected to dream again, but whether it was the wine or the feeling of at last being in safe harbour, he slept the most undisturbed sleep he could remember for at least a year.

CHAPTER 2

On Saturday Arnold finished rewriting the second verse of his poem for the second time. He read it again. It was good now. The frenzy of inspiration had left him, and he enjoyed the teasing out of the thoughts and words. In two days, he thought, it would be ready. Possibly, he might even be able to read it at the Troubadour's session this week.

He couldn't understand those other poets he knew, who scribbled down the first thoughts and claimed it was complete, their muse had spoken. What was the point of it if you didn't work, make every syllable count, measure every word? Free verse didn't mean don't-care verse. Lazy tossers most of 'em.

He walked into King's Road to celebrate, and down to Sloane Square. He enjoyed a good sneer at the decadence of moneyed trendiness, safe in the knowledge that none here were his audience. From Sloane Square he caught a tube to the Embankment and walked to the National Gallery. He recognised the attendant by the door and grunted a 'Cheers!' as he went past. It always surprised him that the attendants never seemed to recognise him back, even though he granted them his 'Cheers!' equally, every time he went in. Were his six feet four and fifteen stone really so hard to remember?

As soon as he was in the museum, he trod the familiar way to *A Wheatfield with Cypresses* and stood in his familiar spot before it. Even after all these times, the magic worked on him, but he still couldn't see why. He recognised every stroke of the brush, every bold field of colour. He knew the swirl and shades of the clouds, and every tree and every swathe of corn, intimately. He reverenced the painting as the work of a fellow craftsman and artist, but, and this was what was so unfair, he could not understand why it moved him so much; why every time he looked at it, something seemed to move in his stomach, and a broad smile of contentment broke across his face.

Once, must be about fifteen months ago, he thought he might have found the answer when he joined a party listening attentively to the lecturer who was explaining the history and composition of the painting. Arnold listened eagerly, swallowing the lecturer's words and gazing hard at the painting, trying to recognise everything he said about the balance of the composition, the almost frenetic brushwork and the desperate sky.

Listening with such eagerness to another admirer's words, he very nearly saw beyond the veil that hid the secret from him. He felt such excitement that he stared again at the painting, and missed the last sentences of the lecturer's exposition. Before he realised what was happening, the party had moved to the opposite side of the room, leaving him alone with the picture and the mystery again.

He had tried to recreate that lecture and fill in the missing revelation several times since then, but never came close to it. No matter, though; it was still as magical as ever. Now, with his new poem in progress, he felt even closer to the painting, and from the warmth he derived, drew confidence in his own composition. He became aware of another admirer beside him and turned.

'Bloody marvellous, innit?' he said. The words could have been a complaint or an insult, but the smile that went with the tone showed he meant only what he said.

The newcomer nodded. Arnold looked at him for a moment. ''Ow can anyone do that? Know what I mean? 'Ow can a man take what we all see, and make such fantastic emotion from it? Tell me that.'

His new companion seemed uncertain how to respond to these overtures. He looked younger than Arnold, and under stress. Arnold always noticed if people looked as though they were under stress. He was quite smartly presented, but Arnold could see that he was unsure of himself.

'Arnold,' he said, putting out his huge hand, 'Arnold Gill.'

'How do you do? Gerard Tisserant,' the other responded, taking Arnold's hand.

'Gerald, eh?'

'No, Gerard. It's a French name.'

'Really? You'd never tell, to hear you.'

'I hope not, I've lived in England since I was three months.' Arnold nodded and then turned back to the painting.

'Like I was saying, Gerald, 'ow does a man paint like that? Eh?'

'Maybe if he was a happy man, he wouldn't have painted like that. Perhaps he would have settled for bland, comfortable landscapes and still lifes.'

'Yeah, I know what you mean. That's just the question, innit? Is it, like, fair for us to enjoy the work that comes from torment? Shouldn't we enjoy someone's comfort, instead? Yeah, I know. But then their sufferin's even more pointless, isn't it? At least what it's produced teaches us somethin', don't it?'

'What? What have you learned from his suffering? You looked in raptures at the painting, not sorrow. What sort of learning is that?'

Arnold looked at him.

'Alchemy! That's what it is, that's what we experience, innit? Well, that's right, ain't it? He took his base metal, right, of insanity, injustice, poverty, see, and look at the gold he's produced. If he was happy, what could he have transformed that into?'

'Yes, that's fair, that makes sense. Does it go the other way? Are happiness and security transmogrified into dinginess and dullness?'

'You bet it does, Gerald; I was in King's Road before I came in here. You should see the dullness and dinginess in that place.'

'You surprise me. I thought it was full of rather lovely things down there.'

'No, nothing of the kind,' Arnold reflected. 'Well, some of the things, yeah. In fact, most of it, now I think of it.' And Arnold burst into a loud laugh against himself.

Gerard noticed the attendant frowning at them from his chair. Loud laughter was obviously not the required response to Art.

'Tell you what,' he said to Arnold. 'I'm going downstairs for a coffee. Can I get you one? Probably easier to talk about it all than in here.'

'Yeah, ok, cheers. Nice one.' And they went downstairs to the National's cafeteria.

At this time of year and this time of day there was not much of a queue and plenty of space for them.

For five minutes they danced the usual sarabande of new acquaintances. Where do you live? Big bedsit, well, flat really, in Brompton, quite a nice place, suits me, but rent keeps going up. You? Staying with friends in Kensington, but home is in Derbyshire, small town up there. Not sure how long I'll be staying here, but a few weeks I reckon. Work? Printers' shop in Fulham, but real work is a poet, just don't pay well, know what I mean? You? Ah, not anything at the moment, sort of taking a bit of a leave, as it were.

No more clues as to what sort of work Gerard was taking leave from – so far away from his parish and so soon after his disillusionment, he was reluctant to own up to his ministry. He bounced the question back.

'Tell me more about your poetry?'

Arnold sat up and beamed. Most people he met for the first time changed the subject pronto as soon as he mentioned poetry. Not this Gerald bloke though; he seems interested, must be ok.

'Have you published?'

'Yeah, got two books out, only a small press, but you know, it's out there, some of my babies have launched into the world, yeah? I'll give you a copy if you like sometime. Yeah, I run a couple of reading sessions, and sometimes a small poetry fest around Earl's Court area. All small stuff, 'cos not that many people bother, but it works for me. Tell you what then, Gerald, I'm running a reading in a couple of days' time. Do you know the Troubadour, in Brompton Road? Just near the cemetery? Come along if you like, there's some good stuff usually. Yeah, quite a bit of crap as well, but people 'ave got to start somewhere, 'aven't they? Come along? Starts at eight. Troubadour, just near the cemetery. Good place, you'll like it there.'

Arnold didn't need more than a question or comment to ignite his monologue motor. Gerard found that after the initial glancing introductions he could just sit back and let Arnold talk through his philosophies, anecdotes of friends and fellow writers, the magic of London in the small hours of the night, why Van Gogh was such a magnetic, but elusive, genius and he could never tire of visiting *A Wheatfield*, more than any other painting in this whole damn building.

Gerard had come to the Gallery in search of another painting that he thought might help him throw some sort of light on his own struggles, but had found Arnold and *A Wheatfield* first. These intrigued him as much as the more conventionally religious pictures he had sought.

He quite liked the artist but was not especially excited by him; certainly he had never experienced anything like Arnold's reverence for *A Wheatfield with Cypresses*. What a religious devotion that was, and if Father Holloway accused him of heresy for thinking in those terms well, stuff Father Holloway then!

Gerard found a smile opening his face – only been in London three days and it looked like he had found a friend.

CHAPTER 3

When Jez woke, late Saturday morning, the first thing he saw from his window, as always, was the tall blue building. He liked it, strangely. It was such a curious shape, he enjoyed simply studying its curves and spurs, each side reaching out to embrace whole districts – or perhaps open-mouthed to eat them. Jez preferred the embrace. There was a comfort in it, and the colour, too, such a restful shade of blue. Yes, he liked the building, it was his friend, however distant. Today was a special day, a golden day. He had pulled off a brilliant deal at Piccadilly last night and was well set up for several days. He had found six wallets, all packed with sterling, euros and dollars, and knew both rent and supply were well taken care of for the next three weeks. As for food, he knew of four McDonald's within walking distance that were looking for staff, so food and drink were no problem for a while, either.

It was time; he found his gear, then his vein, and several minutes later went out, happy, to meet the day.

Unlike last night, he had no trouble walking in a straight line, so only his broad smile made opposing walkers look sideways, and then step a little sideways too. It only took him twenty minutes to find the first restaurant. Good: the recruiting sign was still on the door.

He knew the procedures well and in two minutes was talking to the manager. In another minute he was walking back towards Fulham, yelling abuse at the whole establishment.

That was a bad mistake; he had forgotten that he'd been thrown out of that restaurant just six months before, because he had not had time to shoot up before the shift started. He had panicked halfway through taking the order for a half-pounder Mac, fries and coffee, had a screaming fit, and thrown a cup of hot coffee into the queue. This did not match McDonald's corporate image or code of practice, and he had not dared go back in there again until this morning's euphoric forgetfulness.

This time, though, he could control himself, he could, he could, he would. With last night's windfall he could plan further than the next six hours at least, and with that he could build his life properly and control it. It didn't take long for his good mood to return, and as optimistically as before, he set out for the next branch.

This time, he remembered to make up a false name for himself. It would be easy to slip into a casual job, cash in hand, with the right name. In fact, on his third restaurant, he did just that and celebrated by getting drunk and missing his starting time. Never mind, he still had four of the wallets in his room; he wasn't stuck yet.

He turned back towards Earl's Court and Fulham. Later, later, he could sort out the job. He wanted another lie down first. It was all right; he still had money to spare, and tomorrow he would get a job sorted out. He needed a job before he could reform himself, he understood that. Discipline, that was always his weak point.

Jez was under no illusion about his frailties and never had been. In fact, that was probably his saving grace he reckoned – he never kidded himself that he was strong, or clever, or worth much. He knew he always gave up and looked for an easy way out of any challenge or imposed routine. That was why he needed a framework like a job, to help him. That and a couple of friends, of course, who would help him, take him in hand and look after him, until he could hold his head up again and stand on his own feet. But who would be friends with him? He didn't deserve it; he couldn't offer them anything back, could he? When he was in prison a few years ago, he sort of had a friend, at least someone who kept him safe from the really bad men.

He was on his own now, though, and that wasn't so good. The old feeling of panic began to hit his stomach again, and he paused in mid-step.

'Cheers, Jez, all right, then?' a loud voice boomed in his ear.

'Eh? Oh, Arnold, cheers.'

'Hey, Jez, going to be around on Wednesday? I've got a new poem, I'm going to read it at the Troubadour. Come along if you can, mate, it's a good'un.'

'Right, yeah, yeah I'll be there,' drawled Jez. Life had picked up again. Good old Arnold was a friend, he'd forgotten that. 'Hey, Arnold, before you go, can you spare me a tenner? I'll pay you back on Wednesday, honest.'

Arnold looked at him closely.

'What you up to, Jez? You not still on that junk, are you?'

'Well, only a bit. I've nearly kicked it this time, honest, but I need some bread.'

Arnold sighed heavily and took out a handful of change.

'All right, then, have some of this. I want it back, mind.'

'Course, course. Wednesday, God's honour.'

It was only after Arnold had gone on, muttering, that Jez remembered that he had four wallets full of dollars and euros back at home in Fulham. He tried to call after him to give the money back, but Arnold had already stopped to talk to someone else, a young girl. One of his tarts probably, thought Jez enviously. No, that's not fair, Arnold's ok, he's a friend. Why shouldn't he be friends with the tarts as well, eh?

He didn't get home too early. As soon as he was through the door, he headed for his syringe and the tourniquet. Panic faded with the rush, and ecstatic relief washed through his whole system.

CHAPTER 4

Wednesday morning was a cold one. Autumn was getting impatient, pushing the Indian summer aside in its hurry. In Nick and Jenny's house, Gerard couldn't feel that. There was a luxurious comfort in their heating and deep carpets that belied the wet chilliness that now suddenly pervaded the outdoors.

For the first time that week, he was dressed and downstairs before they had left to join the crawl along the roads to work.

'Gerard,' said Nick in greeting, 'what have you got planned for tonight? Fancy a curry and a club?'

'Sorry?' said Gerard, just behind in the conversation.

'He's asking you to join him in another lad's night out,' laughed Jenny. 'As I'm going to be in Manchester for the next three days, he wants you to help him recapture his carefree bachelor days. While the cat's away and all that.'

'As if I'd call you a cat,' protested Nick, 'in your hearing, anyway. You'll be out on the northern tiles yourself in the evenings, knowing you.'

He'd already been on one of Nick's nights out and found little pleasure in it. Actually, he felt that Nick had taken as much pleasure in his discomfiture as in the paid entertainment. That was unfair, perhaps, but then surely Nick had been unfair to inflict that on him. Unless, yes unless Nick really thought that Gerard had shaken off his religion with his pastoral duties and so had entered the world of fleshly men again.

By Nick's standards it was pretty harmless, of course, but after the meal in the Indian restaurant (and fair's fair, Nick had chosen really well there), they went to a nightclub with dancers and then a stripper, and Nick was drunk while Gerard wondered what on earth he was doing there. He enjoyed the meal and the wine afterwards, but the cabaret was utterly beyond him. His boyhood had been filled with warnings against sin in all its manifestations, not least sexual. In his life he had experienced many of the deadly ones and worked hard to eliminate them from himself. Lust was the one sin that alarmed and intrigued him most. Also, it was one he found most elusive in his own make-up.

It alarmed him because his parents – Catholic in faith, fiercely puritan in morality – and then the family priest and his teachers at the seminary, had imprinted him with nightmare stories of what happened to the promiscuous, both on Earth with disease, and subsequently in Hell. As he grew older, Gerard marvelled at the contrast between the images in advertising, popular books, films and television, and what had been so deeply instilled in him in his most vulnerable years. Sex was undoubtedly sinful, the most sinful act imaginable; when he tried to imagine it, which was frequently during his adolescence, shame and fear swallowed all pleasure and excitement.

Gerard was not so naive as he grew, not to realise that this instinctive recoil was a warped reaction; that sex was a function, both necessary and delightful. His early imprinting was too strong, though, and had erected an impervious barrier that common sense could never penetrate.

Most of the confessions he took were to do with sex, and his confusion about it grew each time he pronounced penance for its degrees of sinfulness. Even when congratulating new or expecting parents or conducting baptisms, Gerard couldn't forget that this joy came about through what was a sin. If it was a sin so deadly outside marriage, its intimacy and shameless exposure must still contain sin even when legalised through the marriage service. Poor Gerard could see his own illogicality perfectly well. But just as for an arachnophobe who recognises that most spiders are utterly harmless and actually tiny, when one crawls across the pillow, horror and revulsion will always trump knowledge and logic.

So when Nick, his host, his good old friend from youth, took him to see the strippers, his sense of sin collided with his guestpitality and left him an unhappy man. He couldn't enjoy the night, but neither could he tell his friend of his abhorrence. Thank God for Arnold tonight!

'When are you off?' he asked Jenny.

'After lunch. Couple of meetings this morning about the redundancies, then on my way to break the news and hold some counselling sessions. You know, help with relocations, retraining or payoffs. That usually takes a long time to go through, and that's only after they've faced the first shock of knowing we don't need them.'

Gerard looked at her with sympathy.

'Is that most of your job now? Sacking people?'

'At the moment, yes. We've kept them going for as long as we can, but we're at the point where we either let some go now or lay off a whole lot more in six months.'

Gerard noted how her voice changed from laughing, friendly, good old Jenny, to a cooler, more professionally detached tone. For the first time, he saw her as colleagues and subordinates must see her. It reminded him of the bishop's sympathy which spilled easily from his lips, completely bypassed his heart and left his sleep untroubled.

'So?' asked Jenny, seeing his look. 'It has to be done. I try to make it easier for them where possible.'

'In my ministry, I met a lot of people made redundant. I saw the effects on their pride and self-respect, their belief in their ability to provide and their fear of never working again. I offered counselling if they came to me. I think your job is harder, being the executioner as well as the counsellor.'

'Yes, we probably mean slightly different things by the word. You apply a plaster, I try to offer practical help in the situation. No, sorry Ger that's very unfair. I remember those times you spent hours talking with other students. Father Confessor they called you. And that was long before any question of you being a priest. That time with Ann McGoldrick when she was at rock bottom, you sat up with her all night. You saved her life then, I think. She certainly thought so.'

'No no, that's an exaggeration,' he protested.

'She didn't think so. She told me afterwards that she was on the brink of taking an overdose, just ending it all.'

'All I did was sit up, let her talk, hold her hand and stay. That's not special.'

'Dear Gerard, of course it was.' Jenny smiled fondly, remembering. 'Her mother had just died, she was panicking about the course, money had run out, her court appearance after the demo arrest was looming, and she was getting into the heavy stuff, not just the dope we were all smoking. You were the only one of us who could do more than say "Tut-tut, there, there, it'll be all right." What you did for her that night saved her from the OD. So – sorry, I shouldn't have dissed your counselling just then. But my guys, I do need to give them practical guidance to get them on their feet after redundancy. A lot won't take it, most will be swearing at me and blaming me, even though the decision came from a few levels higher up.'

'They're not all of them hapless victims of the evil system though, are they, Jen?' Nick butted in. 'Remember that guy you told me about in Fleet? What was it his manager said in his appraisal report? "You seem to set low personal standards and then consistently fail to achieve them."'

'Ouch,' said Gerard.

'Yeah, a bit brutal I thought, but I liked it. He'll be one of your victims, Jen?'

'Come on, it's getting unprofessional now, change the subject. We have to leave in five minutes if we're to get in by eight thirty.'

'All right, on my way. Gerard, mate, are you on for tonight?'

'Sorry, I've arranged to meet someone tonight, down in Brompton.'

'Brompton? I didn't know you knew anyone there.'

'It's someone I met, a poet actually.' Gerard felt himself reddening and became even more self-conscious. 'He's giving a reading tonight, and I promised him I'd go along. I'm sorry, I didn't know you were planning anything.'

'No problem, you go to – Brompton, you say? – and enjoy yourself. If you're back before me, you know how to use the video? I'll see you when I get back, later. Hey, before you go, is he clever or dim, your poet?'

'What do you mean?'

'Well, a backwards poet writes inverse – get it?' and he laughed loudly.

'And on that note, darling, we're going to have to go now, or I'll miss the connection this afternoon. Sorry about him, Gerard. Bye, see you on Friday. Take care of yourself.' Jenny leaned forward to kiss him on the cheek, and they left. Gerard shrugged, uncertain whether he felt guilty or amused at seeming to have snubbed Nick.

CHAPTER 5

The evening had turned cold, letting autumn show its daunting side. Kate, getting ready to find her position, coughed and grimaced as her chest felt scraped by the trapped mucus. This was not good weather to be out in, but she had no choice.

Mahmoud had called to collect earlier, and she felt strongly how unpleased he was at the week's meagre earnings. Not her face, though. At least he left that unbruised this time, but he was skilled in pain.

She took up a position near the Waterstones bookshop, the better pitches taken already by the other girls. A few people passed, but no men seemed inclined to take up her invitations.

Gerard took the tube from Bloomsbury, where he had been exploring museums and bookshops, to Earl's Court. Although twilight was officially a little way off, the heavy cloud and drizzle made the afternoon cold, depressing and prematurely dark. No bare arms on display tonight, although swarms of people still moved in and out of the region. Arnold's directions were clear, and in plenty of time he found himself staring at the huge carved black door that led into the Troubadour.

It was his first visit, although he had seen it from the outside before as he passed by. The atmosphere hit him with a warm smile as the damp cold fell off him and fled back into the street. Bach played loudly on the hi-fi, welcoming him as he peered around the cafe and looked for an empty table before getting his coffee. Beside the front door, shelves by the window held up row after row of painted coffee pots. Against a far wall he was surprised to see what looked like an ancient portcullis with a large yellow lantern hanging from it. At a table beneath this false gate, two teenage girls sat with books, reading aloud to each other. Their bench looked as though it had been looted from the same castle as the portcullis, Gerard thought, with the same heavy black varnished wood, and two high pointed sides like pew ends. Between them and the counter, at a longer table, two chess players sat absorbed in their game, the clock at their elbows rapidly switching from one to the other as they moved. They didn't seem to take more than a dozen seconds each to reflect and decide on their next moves. Another man sat at their table, awaiting his turn to play the victor.

Most of the other tables were taken as well. Gerard raised his brows at the number of people sitting with notebooks or papers on the table, writing away; were they all the poets for tonight's reading? Perhaps – although some looked more like students working on assignments or essays. There seemed to be only one couple there simply to enjoy drinking a coffee and talking with each other.

There was one empty small round two-seater table, right in the middle of the cafe, so he put his coat down on a chair to reserve it and then queued to buy a coffee, looking around him and wondering where the poetry reading would be. He was startled to see that he was being overlooked by an ancient painted wooden Indian Chief, standing above the counter. Following his eyes upwards, Gerard saw that poised above him were scores of old instruments hanging precariously from the ceiling: stringless banjos, violins, mandolins, a big bass drum, tubas, a whole orchestra in suspension.

There was no sign or notice to enlighten him as to where and when the reading would be held, but he couldn't believe it would be in this room against the Bach, (no, that had just given way to Vivaldi). The warmth inside the cafe, and the strange furnishings excited him, and he felt eager to listen to the reading. There was a quirky welcome to all in this place, but with a combination of humour and respect that did make him feel truly welcome, however anonymous. Thank God, again, for Arnold, he thought, for leading him somewhere he could feel at home at last.

That notion took him by surprise, for he'd thought he was at home with Nick and Jenny, and a place like this was outside his normal experience. Yet it already felt like home in a way that Kensington had never quite managed. For the first time in months, he felt a spontaneous smile bubbling over his face.

'Cheers, Gerald,' a huge hand thumped Gerard's shoulder. 'You came, then? Great. Nice and early too? Great, great. Come on then, let's get downstairs.'

An even greater warmth bathed Gerard at the greeting, and he gladly followed Arnold into the kitchen and down the stairs which opened into a long room. Several people had already arrived, but it was not yet time for the reading. Before people suddenly took to their seats and proceedings began, apparently of their own accord, Gerard was introduced to half a dozen of the poets and audience. He didn't have the chance to speak to any of them, however, for no sooner had they exchanged 'Hi's, or 'Cheers', or 'How do you do?'s than they turned back to their earlier conversations, leaving him with an acknowledgement of his existence, and no more.

Tonight was a guest night, and the audience was full of spectators who had come to see an American poetess. Gerard didn't recognise her name, but looked forward to a new discovery. It was a long time since he had taken notice of what was happening in the contemporary arts world, and what he remembered as being new and exciting in his own day was probably now passé or, more likely, forgotten.

There were a number of readers from the audience before the guest, and he listened to them with slowly reducing interest; most were on the familiar ground of alienation, urban nihilism and iconoclasm. It was the same when he was young and wrote and attended such readings. One or two poems were more hopeful, but naively so.

Each poet clearly felt deeply what they wrote, but deep feeling alone did not equal intellect or poetry. Gerard remembered as he listened why he had stopped going to such readings years before: he wanted a gourmet meal and was given only rich tea biscuits instead.

The last reader before the guest was Arnold. Gerard suddenly wished not to be there; instead of anticipation he dreaded embarrassment on his new friend's behalf and didn't want to see mediocrity when he had expected merit. But the prospect of both mediocrity and merit was dwarfed by farce when, as Arnold was about to begin, the door from the kitchen stairs burst open, and a body hurtled out onto the floor. There were squeals from the audience, and the two or three nearest the door jumped to the body's aid. It was a living body, at least, for as the first hands touched it, it groaned and turned over.

'Hey, sorry about that,' it drawled. 'Arnold, mate? Sorry, didn't mean to interrupt you, like.'

The squeals turned to laughter and Arnold strode forward with exasperation. Gerard stood to get a better view. He saw a tall and very thin man with a white face and greasy hair straggling down to his shoulders, being lugged upright by Arnold's huge ham-like hand.

'Jez, you bloody menace! Sit down there and shut up, can't you? Christ, you ruined my opening.'

His return to the front brought the strongest round of applause of the night, which he acknowledged with a mock bow and hand on heart.

'Dearly beloved,' he began, 'we are gathered together to witness Jez making a wazzock of himself yet again.'

'Hey, I owe you a tenner,' remembered Jez.

'Shut up, or I'll take more than a tenner off you!'

The laughter in the audience turned to shushing, in sympathy with Arnold. He looked sternly at Jez and then winked at the audience, who laughed. Gerard smiled with appreciation at the way he had handled the situation. Jez was sitting quietly with a sheepish grin on his face, but obviously meant no trouble. The sight of him sitting there, only half present, eyes flickering side to side and then to nowhere discernible, disturbed Gerard as much as his abrupt entry. He must ask Arnold about the incident later and find out the story.

'I want to start with a poem I wrote a few years ago,' began Arnold. 'It's about this picture, right, that I really love, I do. It's by Van Gogh, and called *A Wheatfield*. The picture's called that, I mean; the poem's called something else, the poem's called, "Swirling Skies".' He cleared his throat and looked at the audience for reassurance. They were still on his side, and Gerard noticed that some were smiling gently, as though knowing they were about to hear a known and loved work.

The poem was quite short, and Gerard relaxed with relief; praising Arnold was not going to be an insincerity, after all. It was strong and economical, and the imagery seemed to have caught Arnold's fascination with the picture without the pretentious or forced similes he'd heard from earlier readers. Gerard wondered for a moment if the poem had been selected for his benefit, remembering their first encounter.

'And now,' Arnold continued, 'here's a new poem that I only finished the other day. It's still wet behind the ears, but I like it. It's called, "Late Autumn". Yeah, the title's crap, I know, but I can sort that later.'

'Well, Gerald, what do you reckon?' asked Arnold anxiously as soon as they had left the cafe. The night was keeping its cold promise and compounding it with a thickening mist that softened the yellow streetlights and the sounds around them. Each breath let a damp taint of car fumes into their lungs. It was not easy to see shapes clearly more than about twenty yards ahead.

'Good, very good, I thought,' Gerard reassured him. 'You didn't need to worry.'

'I don't know,' said Arnold, thoughtfully. 'That opening was the first bit that came to me and sparked it all off, but I don't know, I think it could do with a bit more work. That fourth verse, I don't know.'

'I thought it was fine, honestly. I don't think you need to work on it anymore. It was a hundred yards ahead of those others we heard.'

'Really? I liked those two of Paul's, you know, the war poem and the love poem about this girl, right? The one he fell in love with when he was a nipper?'

Gerard remembered the man. He'd not been impressed; perhaps he had done Paul an injustice, perhaps his attention had lapsed at that point, and he had not listened properly. Gerard hoped that a time would come soon when he could make up for it and give Paul a proper hearing. His own recollection was of a couple of rather simplistic complaints about the pain of war and how love hurt, even after many years. There must have been more to them than that, if Arnold had been impressed.

'He's a lot better now he's dropped all that rhyming crap,' Arnold declared. 'His stuff used to be so loose, you know, every word there to make up the rhyme, and sod what it does to the poem. I told him to drop that and just write. He's a hell of a lot better now he's doing just that. Don't you agree? All that shite about metre and rhyme, it just gets in the way of the poem.'

Gerard had heard these arguments years before and was not any more swayed now. Before he could pick up the discussion, though, Arnold suddenly shifted direction.

'One good thing about nights like this, eh?' said Arnold, as they walked down Warwick Road. 'You can't see that bloody tower, and they can't see us. That's right, isn't it?'

The mist was thickening even as they walked.

'What tower?'

'You know, that blue monstrosity there.' Arnold nodded in the direction of the block, but it was too well wrapped up in the mist to be visible that far down the road. Even the red aircraft warning light on the top was hidden from them.

'I don't know it. I mean, I've seen it, of course, but what is it?'

'Spies, Ministry of Defence spies. Spent the last forty years spying on Russia from there, but they don't need to do that any more, do they?'

'So what do they do now?'

'Spy on us, of course. That's what they're up to, they're spying on us. Anyone they think doesn't conform, that's what. Cold War? Not any more, it's the Cold Peace they're working on now. You keep your nose clean, Gerald, or they'll be onto you.'

Gerard looked with interest in the direction of the tower, but the thickening fog refused to let his gaze through. He had never really looked at the building or taken in the unexpected curves of its concave wings and really didn't have much idea what Arnold was talking about.

'Too early after all that for bed. Fancy a coffee then, Gerald? Before the walk home?'

Gerard looked doubtfully at his watch, and at the fog. Then he remembered that if Nick was out on the razzle tonight, it might be another two or three hours before he had company at home. He agreed with pleasure and followed Arnold to his flat in Philbeach Gardens.

He felt a frisson at a new chapter beginning in his life with a new friend to introduce him to it.

Before he reached the Kensington house that night he was also to start another, far more sinister, chapter.

CHAPTER 6

The house was one of the newer ones in the crescent, on the inside of the curve so that it backed onto the actual Gardens. At this time of night, this time of year, the gardens hid coyly and might as well not have been there, but in the spring and summer they would be the reason and magnet for that whole crescent.

Tonight Gerard saw only the front of the house, the entrance hall with mirror and communal telephone, stairs with carved spindles and newel post holding the banister rail and then Arnold's flat off a first floor landing, the stairs curling up to at least one more level.

The flat itself was larger than he expected, with a good sized living room, galley kitchen and a bedroom whose walls were covered with laminated verses – all his, Arnold assured him, one of his approaches to marketing his poetry. He clearly enjoyed showing them off and then led Gerard back to the living room for coffee.

As he put the kettle on, Arnold set out four mugs and went out to bang on two other doors along the landing.

'Couple of mates 'ere, see if they're still up,' he explained.

In short order, two more people appeared in the doorway and came in.

'What's up, then?' said the first, a man in his thirties with long fair hair and a deep baritone Yorkshire voice. 'You on fire or summat?'

'Fancy a coffee? Gerald, this is Ashley, Ash, this is Gerald, he was at the reading.'

'Cheers, I will, thanks. Hallo Gerald – not seen you before, do you live round here?'

'And,' Arnold continued, before Gerard could reply, 'this is Shelagh. Sheil, this is Gerald, come back for a coffee. Want one?'

'Hot chocolate for me, please, can't take coffee this time of night, as you know.' Shelagh was tall with dark hair refusing to be tied down to any particular style or shape and large pink-framed glasses. 'Hello Gerald. Not seen you before …'

'I've just said that,' said Ashley. 'Give him a chance to tell us all.'

'Hello, Shelagh, hello Ashley. Yes, I'm Gerard, and I've only recently been in this area. I'm staying with friends in Kensington, and I live in Derbyshire, and that's probably it for now.'

'Cool,' said Ashley. 'Do you want us to tell you our life stories?' He said it with a smile that took away any possible sarcastic sting.

'No, no,' Shelagh chipped in. 'Life stories, boring – unless you're a therapist of course. Are you?' suddenly looking straight at Gerard.

'No, that's not me,' he started, then thought, 'not precisely, anyway.'

'So, what do you do?' she persisted.

'I'm … on a sabbatical, leave, whatever you want to call it, and trying to keep it at a distance for now.'

'Oh, sorry, I didn't mean to embarrass you,' she gabbled, blushing.

'No, no, that's all right,' he said. 'I had a rough time and need a break, that's all.'

'You mean you're on sick leave? That's cool,' said Ashley.

'Oh, talking of sick leave,' Shelagh interrupted. 'Dawn, girl I used to work with in social, I heard today she died. Believe it? She was only about forty, forty-five maybe.'

'Ow, that's heavy,' said Ashley. 'Did you know her well?'

'Fairly, but not friends as such. I liked her, but we never went for a drink together or anything. Too late now.'

'I always wonder what it's like, dying,' Ashley mused. 'I mean, you got family around the bed and that, maybe a nurse checking on you, but when the moment comes, you're on your own. What's it like? I'll find out one day, I know, but you can't help wondering.'

Gerard took a breath, and said, 'There's all sorts of different ways. For some people it's easy and gentle, others fight till the last second and are terrified. I've sometimes had to help people across that moment. Sometimes had to be there right at the end.'

'Wow. Are you an assassin then? A hit man?' Ashley's eyes lit up.

'No! Certainly not!'

'Yeah, but a hit man on sick leave, suffering from burnout, what a great film that'd make! "Can He Manage One Last Job?" like.'

Before he could riff further on that idea, a phone started ringing somewhere to interrupt him. To Gerard's surprise, it turned out to be in Ashley's pocket, not from downstairs.

He took the phone out into the hallway to answer it, and they just heard quiet murmurings, no words.

'Always happens,' Shelagh said.

'What's that, then?' said Arnold, coming in with the four mugs.

'Ash got a call again, just in time to miss coffee.'

'Problem?' Arnold asked as Ashley came back, replacing his phone.

'Yeah, goin' to have to go into work soon, system's going slow.' He looked at Gerard. 'I'm support for the company DP department.'

'DP?'

'Sorry, Data Processing, you know, computers and that. IT some of them call it nowadays. When they play up it's me who's got to get it all running again.'

'That's why you've got that phone thing?'

'Me mobile, yeah. Useful, but it weighs a ton in me pocket. Handy for calling Darren, an' all when either of us is away, too.'

'Darren's a window dresser for one of the big chains,' Shelagh told Gerard helpfully.

'That's right, and like me 'e gets sent out to all the branches to set stuff up. Christmas coming up, 'e's going to be busy, so shan't see much of him for a month or so. Ah, one day they'll make it so's I can stay home and fix problems from me own room instead of 'avin' to rush off hither and yon all the bloody time. Not for a few years yet, though, methinks.'

He sat back down and started drinking his coffee. Then looked at the three of them, grinning.

'Hey, you know our latest panic? You know it's the big zero in a few years?'

'Eh?' Shelagh muttered.

'You know, 2000, the new century, new millennium, all that stuff? Well, they reckon all our systems are goin' to crash then because of the dates. All the companies, especially the banks and that, are getting their knickers in a right twist in case everything goes Cinderella on the stroke of midnight!'

All three looked back at him blankly.

'None of us know computers, mate,' said Arnold. 'Why should that make a difference? It's just another day, isn't it?'

'Ok, keep it simple – every date in all the systems is in a format, day-day, month-month, year-year, ok? In other words, the war ended in '45, not 1945. It saves space in the machine, that's why. Up till now that's been ok, but what happens when the date is 20 something, not 19 something? Never happened before, and no one knows if they'll just roll the date over at midnight, or it'll set back to 1900, in which case every new bit of data on all DP systems will be wrong. All sorts of stuff could happen, they think – all the banks run out of money, your credit cards won't work, planes will fall out o' sky, nuclear plants will blow, everything that runs on computers, that's basically the whole world, will stop working. That's one view, anyway. Other one is it'll make no difference and we'll not even notice. But no one knows, that's the fantastic thing, it's all new and guesswork. Tell you all what, train up quick in computer programming instead and you'll make shedloads of cash by 2000, you'll need huge wheelbarrers to get your pay home. I'm thinking of going out as a consultant and charging thousands a day to fix people's systems. Join me? No? oh well, your loss.

'Anyway, love you and leave you, ta for the coffee, Arnold. Need to get our system back up and running before payroll day or I'll not be able to give Dave his rent this month. Cheers, Gerald, good to meet you.' And Ashley was up and out of the door.

Out of the corner of his eye Gerard could see Shelagh tense up to ask him something, which, he guessed, was about his helping people across the threshold. He quickly changed subject.

'I don't think I understood any of what Ashley said then. Are computers that important? I've never had to use one.'

'If you've got a few days to spare, Ash will tell you exactly why you use them now without realising and why you should have your own computer and how the world will change when we all have these portable computers at home,' said Shelagh.

'Strange world 'e lives in, not much to do with real life. Nah, pen and paper is all I need.'

'We use them at the library,' Shelagh said, 'but I don't see what I'd do with one of my own. Just a really expensive toy, that's all.'

'If Ray's anythin' to go by, waste o' money the whole thing.'

'Lives upstairs,' said Shelagh, 'spends all day playing noisy computer games on a portable thing. Drives us mad. You'll probably hear him sometime.' Gerard felt a pleasant surprise at the assumption that he was going to spend more time in this house. New friends again.

'I know Nick and Jenny, the friends I'm staying with, have got their own, but that's for their work. They never use them otherwise. Like those heavy phones. I know they both have car phones, but why lug one of those house bricks around in your pocket? I can't see it.'

'They're getting smaller now, a bit easier, but you're right, I don't see why I'd ever want one.'

Gerard shifted the conversation again, remembering what happened at the Troubador.

'Tell me, Arnold, when you got up to read, who was that fell through the door?'

'Oh, that was Jez. He's a junkie, waste of space really, but he's harmless. Lives in Fulham, just round the corner where I work. 'E's always round our way here, though. Always about to go clean, but always next week, never now. If you're staying round this way for a bit you'll get to know 'im. Just don't give 'im any money, right? 'E's always scrounging, can't hold a job down, so 'e 'as to scrounge off mates. Don't, that's all. Underneath all that, well, who knows, 'e could be all right. Means well an' that, but you know junkies, eh.'

'Poor Jez,' said Shelagh. 'I always feel sorry for him but there's something really creepy about him. Poor bloke, but my heart always sinks when he comes round the corner.'

'Is he dangerous?'

'Only to himself. Not a malicious bone in him, utterly non-violent, and always on the point of giving it up, but he never will.'

'Echo in 'ere is there? Din't I just say all that?'

'All right, all right, boss man, I can talk too, if you let us get a word in.'

'She can talk, too!' said Arnold, winking at Gerard. 'If you don't get a word in when she takes a breath, you never will.'

'Said the pot to the kettle,' retorted Shelagh.

All three talked on, Arnold and Gerard taking up increasingly familiar sparring positions, on people like Jez, the drug problems, poets, homeless folk and whatever else appeared mid-flow, while Shelagh tried to probe more into Gerard's life, and especially his helping people at the point of death.

Politely, friendlily, he turned every approach from her aside and left her more and more intrigued, less and less satisfied. He kicked himself for having said that; what was it, vanity? A desire to confess, that he was now quickly backing away from? Need to make an impression? Whatever the reason, he'd blurted out something that should have remained utterly private, and he could see that it would always be hanging between him and Shelagh, unless he never happened to see her again.

It was late, very late, and the weather outside was so unwelcoming with this early deep mist that he was ready to take a taxi back to Kensington and bed, whether or not Nick was back from his lads' night out on the razzle.

He put his coat back on and bade Arnold and Shelagh goodbye.

He thought that the evening's adventures, pleasant and friendly as they were, were over, and only welcome sleep awaited. How wrong he was!

CHAPTER 7

Kate had wandered down to the front of the station and was chatting with a couple of the other girls about Christmas, about the fog, about their childhood, about almost anything that might while away a quiet hour. They knew that it was one of those nights, that even though the pubs were emptying, and drunken punters were returning in good spirits or sullen, the girls would not be working hard. Perhaps it was the fog, perhaps the time of year, they didn't know precisely, but they recognised that for some reason, the customers would not approach them. Soon, the three would split up and try again to hustle some more business, but they were not hopeful.

She'd had little success this evening – just two punters, both reluctant to pay the full price and both of whom rushed from her room as soon as they could.

They didn't dare to give it up as a bad job yet, though. Mahmoud had done his rounds already today, but he might still come back again for a spot check. The eldest of them still remembered the day three years before when he had done that and found a girl not working when she was supposed to be on the streets. His anger was famous, and the girl took three weeks to recover.

They all knew of this, but none of them ever mentioned it, just as none of them ever suggested that on a night like this they should call it a day and go into the private warmth of home.

With an unspoken accord, they moved apart to different pitches along the kerb. Kate returned to the corner of Penywern Road opposite Waterstones and waited. Groups of people, lads from the pubs, hotel stayers, the leather boys from the Coleherne, passed her. One or two threw her a look as they passed, but she could tell that the looks were idle interest only, not speculation. She shivered and coughed in the fog and waited; and waited.

She hoped for a customer now, looked forward to the company and the comfort. She knew better than to think in terms of human warmth or affection. This line of work brought you all sorts of things, but never that. At least though, it would take her out of this clamminess that was chilling her through to the bone. Perhaps it was time to take the initiative now, rather than wait for the homegoers' appetites to take her away. As soon as she made that choice, there was a drought of punters. Naturally. She was cold, tired, not rich and it was foggy, so of course there were no punters tonight.

'Business?' she asked routinely of the next single man who passed. He looked at her, startled, and shook his head apologetically, muttering, 'No, no, sorry!' and vanished into the fog, faster than he had appeared.

'Getting too old for it already, am I?' she thought wryly. 'Only just sixteen and already frightening them away?'

She remembered childhood tales of Jack the Ripper operating in the famous London fog, a hundred years earlier, and shivered, looking for her friends along the kerb. They were too far off, though. Bored and shivering, she ambled back towards the station again hoping for a punter, then back to her chosen stand. Through the thickening clouds, she made out a dim silhouette coming down Penywern Road towards her.

Ten yards away, she was sure it was a man's figure. Customer after all? At this time of night, she wondered, he might be from one of those rooms in the tall blue building that always seemed lit up, whatever time or day it was.

He got closer, and she moved to meet him with her standard, 'Business?' greeting on her lips.

CHAPTER 8

The next morning Nick was nearly late for work. He'd come home late from his night out and had had no chance to talk with Gerard before falling into bed. Two consecutive nights out on the tiles had left him exhausted. He was just able to grab a cup of coffee from Gerard, hoping to restore a small measure of humanity before the new day's challenge.

'I can't do this anymore, it's terrible,' he muttered. 'I feel dead, I really do. Just leave a coffin outside the door tonight, and I'll climb in – then I'll wake up in time in the morning.'

'Wrong tradition and wrong timetable, I think,' laughed Gerard, with a marked lack of sympathy. 'You vampires are meant to climb in at dawn, not be out working in the day.'

'Whatever! I don't think I can face the office, and I certainly don't think I'll get much work done. I'll find some quiet storeroom and have a kip in there, that should do it.'

'How are the mighty fallen! In the old days you'd have stayed to dance the sun up – now see what work has done for you!'

'All very well for you, Father G! I don't know how you manage it, you stay-out. I was asleep when you got back. There I was, tiptoeing in at half past twelve, thinking you were tucked up with a cup of cocoa for the last two hours, and then you lurch in, God knows when, but it was well after two thirty. I don't know, you poets! What a life!'

'Well, we were talking late.'

'We?'

'Arnold, my friend, has a flat near there, Philbeach Gardens. I went back and met a couple of his neighbours. That's all.' Gerard wondered how much to tell him. All night he'd felt full of the evening and his new acquaintances and the awful story he'd learned. Looking at Nick's face now, though, he felt reluctant to share it. Suddenly he doubted that the laddish executive would be impressed with the strange woman – Shelagh was it? – and the gay man, Ashley. Both seemed so far removed from everything Gerard had known and completely at odds with Nick and Jenny's world.

And he needed to think over the other, much more upsetting, encounter before telling anyone.

'What about your night?' He turned the focus away from himself again.

'Abso-bloody-lutely great! You should have come, honest. Hey, have you heard this one?

'This man goes into the pub, lurches over to the only other guy there, and asks if he could buy him a drink. "Sure," comes the reply. The first man then asks, "Where are you from?" "I'm from Ireland," replies the second man. The first man says, "You don't say. I'm from Ireland too! Let's have another round. To Ireland!" "Sure. To Ireland!" replies the second man, and they both knock back their drinks. Then the first man asks, "Where in Ireland are you from?" "Dublin," he replies. "Never! I'm from Dublin too! Let's have another drink – to Dublin!" "To Dublin!" they both go, and knock it back in one. Then the first man asks, "What school did you go to?" "St. Mary's," replies the second man, "I graduated in '65." "You're kidding," says the first man, "I went to St. Mary's and I graduated in '65, too! Let's drink to St Mary's." They both buy another drink and "To St Mary's!" and down it goes. About that time, in comes one of the regulars and sits down at the bar. "What's going on?" he asks the barman. "Nothing much," he says. "The Dooley twins are drunk again."'

At which Nick laughed loudly, punching Gerard on the shoulder. Over the hurried breakfast, he delighted in telling Gerard the details of the club, the cabaret and the girls writhing around a tall pole with £10 notes tucked into their G-strings by drooling punters. He didn't actually own up to planting a tenner himself, but a rather coy smirk invited Gerard to draw conclusions.

Gerard couldn't tell whether Nick gave him the juicy details with a malicious relish, or quite simply did not yet understand how uncomfortable and alien this talk was to him. Gerard marvelled at how his friend revelled boastfully in the sorts of details that used to be whispered to him in shame through the confessional curtain. Even in that dark anonymity he would blush for his penitents; he tried not to blush for Nick now but was still uncomfortable.

'Look, Ger, I'm going to be late back tonight, really late, I'm afraid. Work, this time. I've got a meeting in Birmingham; doesn't start till three and promises to go on for three or four hours. The manager there, God knows how he got the job, seems to have delusions of adequacy, and I need to help steer him to safety for a while. You'll be ok?'

'I'm a big boy now, Nick. I've got used to looking after myself. It's all right, I'm hoping to get a ticket for the National tonight – a new play by some American, I don't know him, but …'

'Nah, no good asking me, I never did get into the theatre bit. Jen's the one to talk with about that. Give me a good film any day. Still, you're all fixed up for tonight, that's good. I felt guilty about leaving you on your own, but …'

'No problem, Nick, you told me when I came that you'd both have late work sometimes, so I've been fine looking out for things I've missed, not being in London. Good luck with your errant manager.'

'Cheers. When I'm back to normal hours, we'll have another razzle out, ok? You could do with letting your hair down a bit I reckon.'

And Nick left, charged and ready for the day in Birmingham, a super-efficient, super-effective businessman now, the lecherous hedonist submerged until the next free night. Gerard made himself another coffee and sat back, wondering what to do. The story he'd heard on his way home from Arnold's had made it even harder to listen to Nick's adolescent drooling this morning over the strippers of last night.

He sat back and remembered again walking down Earl's Court in that thick fog. As a child he had read stories of London by Dickens, Conan Doyle, Stevenson and others, where the London fog was almost a character in its own right, but he'd never experienced such a thick one himself until last night. Maybe not an old-fashioned pea-souper, but autumn was making itself unambiguously felt, even as early as this.

He recalled the momentary shock of fear when a silhouetted figure had suddenly appeared by the lamp-post, obviously preparing to accost him. The sodium yellow light, refracted by the fog, magnified the shadowy outline, and his start of fear magnified it yet again. When the apparition spoke, it startled him almost as much as the first materialisation.

'Business?' It was a small voice, young and sad, and with it the figure shrank back to reveal a girl, fair hair dampened by the weather and sticking to her forehead, and such weary eyes. Gerard recoiled as he realised what she was asking him, and muttered,

'No, no, sorry,' in shocked embarrassment, and scurried onwards. After about a hundred yards towards Brompton Street, he suddenly stopped. His embarrassment was superseded by another appalled thought: what was a girl like that doing anyway, on a night like this, and so late? Images of Sin returned, like the pressing of a switch; they all had Father Holloway's damning scowl stamped on the front of them, but this child, like Jane Conway, was surely nothing to do with Sin?

It was late, wet, cold and still a long walk home. So far he had not found a passing taxi and was resigning himself to the walk. He wanted to push on and pretend the encounter had never happened; after all, she'd probably even forgotten he had passed. Like a hitch-hiker, he thought, who never knew the drivers who passed without stopping, she would never know the men who passed without stopping. That was only an excuse, though, because against his will, against his longing to be free of his pastoral burden, against his desire for the comfort of his bed, that small face, weary, sad and scared, forbade him to move on.

He made a bargain with himself that he hoped would let him go straight home. Turn right at Brompton Road, again at Warwick Road, carry on to Penywern, then back down to Earl's Court. If she were still there, he'd talk to her. If, as he hoped, she'd moved away, he would walk back to Kensington, hailing the first free taxi he saw on the way.

There was no escape. She still stood there, small, miserable and vulnerable.

She looked up in panic as his purposeful footsteps approached her. How could he ever have been the frightened one of the two, he wondered?

'Business?' Her voice was sullen and certainly not encouraging. No seeker of eroticism would catch fire at that tone. He paused and looked at her, perplexed.

'Well, yes and no …'

He saw how she flinched from him as he said that. 'Yes, yes please,' he said, blushing hard. 'Er, do you have a room near here?' She relaxed a little on hearing his voice; he didn't sound menacing. What was she so frightened of, he wondered? But at least two self-evident answers occurred to him simultaneously.

She tucked her arm through his and led the way. He felt oddly touched by that little gesture. Heaven knew what she meant by it, but it gave him a feeling of being trusted. Her youth and size hurt him, and he wanted to be trusted again.

Her room was only three or four streets away in a flat above a shop, part of an old, tired terrace off the Earl's Court Road itself. He wanted to speak to her during that interminable walk, but she felt as tense as he was embarrassed as she clung to his arm, so that he couldn't find anything to say. The roads were almost empty. Occasionally a taxi did indeed pass by, and three times he heard police sirens racing towards some routine emergency. Twice they encountered drunken groups of youths – mostly transients and visitors, judging from the accents – but otherwise the fog seemed to have blotted out the rest of the world and insulated them from others.

For the whole way home she was quiet; she was leading him, yes, but there was no other communication. The evening felt as unreal as any moment in his life had ever been. Momentous events, such as the first time he had been permitted to take Mass and felt the miracle of transubstantiation, had seemed vastly more solid than this extraordinary situation, standing with a teenage prostitute who was about to tell him her fee.

'Look,' he began, when they entered her room, 'it's not what you think. I just want to talk to you.'

'That's all right,' she answered, warily. 'It's fifteen pounds for counselling. That gives you half an hour. Sit down, and I'll make some tea if you don't want to screw.'

Gerard gasped. He didn't want counselling – he was here to counsel her! But then she was giving him her time, and that was what the fifteen pounds was for, presumably. He took the money from his wallet and laid it on the grubby table. It took her five minutes to make the tea; did that come off the half hour, or had they not started yet?

'What do you want to talk about, then?' she asked him. She was still sullen. Looking around him, he understood why she was not cheerful. She couldn't be making many fifteen pounds in a week if she could not somehow brighten up this dingy room.

'You, really,' he answered, gently. Despite his tone, she flinched again and looked at him with real fear in her eyes. He saw exhaustion as well as fear there, and his heart melted with compassion for her. In all his life, that was the one emotion he had never associated with the idea of prostitutes or sex. Moral condemnation was easy, Father Holloway was a past master there; remote pity, as a form of piety, too. His own revulsion at the idea of sex had caused him to consider prostitutes, but with distaste and sometimes disgust. Now he was with one, face to face, he knew none of these.

'Who are you? Police?'

'No, nothing like that.' He felt himself stumbling here; he did not want to acknowledge his priesthood now, not until he had resolved Jane Conway, and Sin, and his own emotions. On the other hand, what else could he say to give him the right to talk to her? Then he remembered the fifteen pounds: that was the justification she had given him for talking.

'No,' he repeated, 'I'm nothing to do with the police or anything like that. Can I ask you questions? About you, your life? I promise that nobody else will know what you say to me.'

'Who do you work for?' she asked, still suspicious.

'Myself. It's my own curiosity. Haven't I bought that right?' He blushed in shame at using that tactic. Even if he didn't touch her body, to say that was using her as a prostitute, and he felt soiled. He couldn't think of any other approach to reach her, though. From the way she shrank, he saw that she felt that brutality and was diminished still more. She was deathly scared, there could be no denying, and Gerard felt completely at sea. He didn't know if it were him that she feared, or if she suspected his motives in quizzing her. Maybe it was just that the night was cold, dank and advanced, and her only desire was to sleep. He silently offered an apology for telling an untruth and tried again.

'Let me put my cards on the table,' he began, crossing his fingers under the said table. 'I'm a writer, a novelist, and I'm trying to create a scene with, with women in your position, but I don't know what your position really is.'

'So why are you writing it?' she demanded. 'I thought you was only supposed to write what you know about.'

'Yes. That's why I'm asking, so I can know.'

She recognised the possible stalemate here, in the same instant as he did, and shrugged. It was nothing to her, after all she had her money. The time would pass more quickly if they actually said something.

'What do you want to know, then?'

'Tell me about yourself,' he said. 'If your story is typical, that'll tell me a lot of what I need to know. I want to know about the life, how you came to live here, doing … well, this.'

Gerard felt himself blushing again. His earlier pastoral ministry had given him all sorts of embarrassing situations, but he had always dealt with them easily. This evening he felt out of his depth, the more so because it was only his interfering that had brought him here to begin with.

'Got a smoke?' asked the girl, after rummaging through her bag in vain.

'No, sorry.' Yet another black mark, he felt.

'Don't worry, I'll wait.' Time was passing quickly, and he felt that their conversation wouldn't even start until his fifteen pounds had expired. 'All right then, I'll talk, but no recorders, right? No notes. Ask questions and I'll answer, but only in 'ere. Don't ever stop me again, 'cos I won't know you, and I never said nothing to you, right? And if I ever see your book and you've written about me, you're dead. So am I!'

She muttered that last phrase under her breath, but Gerard just caught it. As he heard it, it was as if he were walking through the fog outside and found his feet had led him, unseeing, to the edge of a drop whose bottom he couldn't see. All he could do was grope his way through the alien territory and pray he could reach the other side safely. His first instinct that this child needed rescuing grew to certainty as he watched her and listened to the sullen, wary voice.

Gerard was not so intrusive or naive as to believe that every prostitute or thief or murderer or whatever other sinner he could think of was waiting for him to gallop up on a charger and bring rescue, conversion and a wholesome, holy life. He had met pastors like that in his training and early work; they appalled him with their smug assumption that virtue was their monopoly. No, Gerard had no missionary vocation; that was never what service had meant for him. So his stopping for this girl and exposing himself to ridicule, rejection or even temptation, was an exceptional act. It was unprecedented, unpremeditated and provided him with no map of where to go from here or how to find his way past the unknown dragons.

'What's your name, then?' he began.

'Kate.'

'Kate what?'

'Just Kate.'

'OK. How old are you, Kate?'

'What's that got to do with it?' She was more defensive now, and he was able to answer his own question: definitely under eighteen, probably even younger.

'OK, no problem,' he tried to soothe her, but she didn't look very soothed. 'How long have you lived here?'

She shrugged. 'Year.'

At thirty pounds an hour, this was starting to look like an expensive night. She was still suspicious of him, and not especially interested in his writing career. He crossed his fingers that she would not ask him for his own name and titles of books, but she accepted what he said without curiosity. He wished he had some cigarettes to offer her, to give her a contact that wasn't ruled by fee and tariff but simple human kindness.

'Kate, tell me, why do you live like this?' He abandoned the roundabout way, half coaxing and half-sparring; he had little time or money tonight.

'How else!' It worked! She had given him a way forward.

'Work? What are you trained for? What can you do?'

'Fuck; blow; bend over. That's it.'

'Come on, is that what you want to do? Always? Live here like that?'

'It's all right for you, you've got a home, you can pay. I ain't got nothing apart from here. If I give this up, where do I live then? How do I live?'

'I don't know, that's what I'm asking. Waitressing? Shop work? Secretary?'

She laughed shortly, a bitter laugh rich with irony, and with no grain of amusement.

'Oh yeah, me and hundreds of other tarts looking. Where would I live? You think flats like this fall into my hands? Them jobs don't pay rent.'

'Then how does everyone who works like that live? How do they pay their rent, if you couldn't?'

She looked at him, and for the first time he felt her actually registering him as an individual, not a punter. It wasn't flattering, though. She showed no sign of kinship, or friendliness. At least her guard of wariness had fallen slightly; he had penetrated that far.

'You haven't got a clue, have you? You think I can go to McDonald's tomorrow, put on a red and white pinny and live happy ever after? You think he'd let me go like that? You think I could live here and take shorthand somewhere in an office? If I leave here I'll never get another flat; I'd never have the bread to put down first, and never earn enough to pay the rent after. Anyway, he'd never let me. I'd be dead first.'

'Can't you go back to your parents? Are they alive?'

'Oh yes,' she said, with a sneer. 'They're alive all right. Living nicely thank you, down in Southampton.'

'Why don't you go back there then? Get a job there and live with them until you've built up enough for a flat again?'

'You've got to be joking! I ain't going nowhere near him again. Perv! He ain't getting me again!' She shouted this at him, and with a jolt of shock Gerard understood.

'You mean, your father – abused you?'

'In one.'

'His own daughter?'

'All of us.'

Again, Gerard felt the pit opening in front of him. He'd heard this in the confessional many times, only ever from victims and never from the abusers. He was naturally aware of the recent scandals associated with the Church and felt doubly uncomfortable with the new direction of her story.

'Can you talk about that?' he asked. And suddenly the initiative had firmly passed to him. His tone was authoritative, and gentle at the same time. With an unexpected sense of relief he felt his ministry slip back onto his shoulders and his identity return. This was nothing to do with his church, or Father Holloway or anything but Gerard Tisserant. Now he knew how to proceed, and his questioning became more assured, without intrusion. 'Father Confessor' they had called him at university, a name without malice or jeering, and now here he was again.

Once she began to open up, all Gerard needed to do now was nudge her gently as she talked and talked. None of her customers had wanted to listen to her life, or shown more than a passing interest in her as an individual. Really, it didn't take that much to break her reserve, and his quiet sympathy drew out her history like ink onto blotting paper.

He heard about how her father had persuaded her to pose for him when she was just coming into puberty, and had then started to touch her, and finally raped her, threatening her with death, with injury, with being put into care if she ever whispered to anyone what he did. Kate had two sisters, one and two years younger than her, and in horror she saw how, as they too began to bud, he would take one or the other into his bedroom when their mother was settled in front of the telly for the night or out at the pictures, her regular weekly ritual. She watched her sisters change from laughing children to moody, timid creatures, just as she had done. And none of them dared to talk to each other about it. None of the three dared share the terrible secret, though they all knew what he was doing to each of them.

Did their mother ever suspect? Perhaps. Kate could not be sure, but she didn't dare to tell her. In some perverse way the girls, as well as being frightened of what he would do if they told, also felt the need to protect him. This was perhaps the worst of the perversion that he visited on them – that hating his touch and fearing him as they did, they were nonetheless complicit in their own corruption. The more they shielded him, the greater grew his power. They could truly believe that they would be punished, because they covered for him when he had done with them. They lay awake at night, crying silently, remembering his awful gropings, his rough attempts at tenderness and the apology afterwards. They all knew his smell, knew his eyes staring through them, seeing anything but his own daughters, knew his brutality if they demurred or cried out in pain or retched.

Sick at herself, Kate saw that she could not help her sisters anymore. Terrified to tell their mother, or any adult, she took the only course that promised relief. One night, when she knew he was asleep, she slid fully clothed from bed, pulled her secretly packed bag from the cupboard and left home.

London was easy to reach and frightening when she arrived. She had no plan apart from getting there, drawn irresistibly to its vast anonymity and its promise. It didn't take long for her to find kindred spirits living on the streets. Kate would not descend to that though. No, she would get work and live in her own flat. London was huge, there were thousands of places that might give her a job so she could pay the rent and buy food. She could live safely here, no sweat.

By the following Saturday she had found her preferred doorway and had been shown where to get hold of the cardboard at lunchtime to make a decent mattress. There were many old hands to help a newcomer, including her new best friend, a veteran of fifteen who knew which hotels were good for bin diving after mealtimes, and where were the good pitches for begging people's loose change. Before too long, she recognised which sorts of men would offer her money, but not charity.

Money came, but not enough for a room. Her new friends on the street offered her all manner of drugs to make life easier, but that was something she resisted. She was afraid of losing money, but more afraid of losing herself. She'd seen the acidheads and the cokeheads and the junkies and swore that she'd never lose herself in the way they had. She may have sunk, but there was still a long way down yet, and she had no intention of going there, thank you very much.

Then one day a man spoke to her. She was begging, as her friends had taught her, and the man stopped and spoke. He put money into her hat, but instead of walking off without speaking, as most of the professional looking men did, he stopped, smiled and spoke to her. Immediately she thought she knew his game, oh yes, she had his number all right, like most of the pervs who stopped. Not this time, though. She admitted it, he was different; he only wanted to help her. Not like the missionaries who stopped her and her friends every day and tried to interfere, to pressure and preach; this was a man who seemed to know her, and what her life was like. His smile was like the sun breaking through cloud. He offered to help her and lend her money, no – give her money, as a deposit on a small room somewhere. With an address she might get a job. She could always pay him back when she had found work, if she really wanted, but he didn't want or expect repayment. He only wanted to help a poor child on the streets, that was his sole wish. He took her hand and smiled his beautiful smile.

'My name is Mahmoud,' he said.

Gerard noticed how the time had gone. As Kate spoke, he quietly pulled another fifteen pounds from his wallet and rested them on the table under the tea mug. Kate glanced at it, shrugged and carried on talking. She'd stopped looking at him as she spoke, staring down at her own mental pictures deep in the heart of the table. He was thirsty, but rather than stop her, he got up himself, put the kettle on, washed their mugs and refilled them. She talked through all his movements and drank from the hot mug as he put it down.

'I thought he was magic. Really good, really kind. He found the room, paid all the deposit, helped me get some clothes, was really sweet, you know. I felt really safe. This was what I come to London for, know what I mean? This was it, I thought I'd really made it. I let him sleep here, of course. With me I mean. It didn't seem like just screwing at first, he was so kind. Then it started. I'd seen the other girls in the house, of course, seen them on the stairs and outside. I didn't know he owned the whole building. I thought he just rented the room for me.'

'What happened? How did you get pulled in?'

'Dope, of course. Now I was safe, I didn't mind having a snort, or a spliff. He give it me, see. It was only when I was in the gutter that I wasn't going to chance it. I was all right now, though, wasn't

I? So I had a joint or two. Then some coke. A few uppers, not all at once, mind, but gradual like, over the weeks. Then he stopped giving them to me, said I ought to start paying. He couldn't afford to keep supplying me out of his own pocket. Said it was about time I looked for that job. Talk about a mug! He knew I'd never get a job. I tried, though. I would have worked, but he knew I'd never find anything. Started to get stroppy, said the landlord was after the rent. I couldn't keep living off him, sponging, he said. So there I was, getting hooked on the coke, getting hassled for the rent and Mahmoud turning against me. He knew what he was up to, of course. Me? I was still green. Make a good salad you could have, out of me. Christ! Talk about just come off the boat! Really guilty I felt, you know, letting down the only bloke who'd been decent to me. How was I going to get money again?'

'Who suggested you go on the streets?'

'I did it first, secret like; the other girls helped, but he knew. Course, he was waiting for that. First day, he came in, shouted at me, swore at me, called me all names. Then he hit me. Not on the face, not to mark me, like, just to hurt. Then he told me. Every man I brought back, charge them thirty. He'd know how many I'd had. He'd come every day for the money, and he'd give me a bit to spend for the week. Just enough for a bit of food and a bit of dope. That was it. That's what it's been since then. He takes it all, and if I don't make enough he beats me up. Doesn't usually mark the face, but you know when he's hit you.'

Gerard looked at her, trying to see the marks Mahmoud was careful not to leave. They were there all right, in her fearful eyes, the way her shoulders hunched protectively around her neck, in the constant fidgeting of her fingers, the defiant way she glared back at Gerard, the dim light, the dirty windows, the dust on the table and walls, and the finger smudges around the door. Oh yes, Mahmoud left plenty of marks, however carefully he hit her.

'What about the other girls here?' Gerard asked after a pause.

'What about them? They knew what was happening. Where do you think they come from? It's no different, he runs all of us here, and his other places. He collects from us every day, and any of us who don't hand over, he does us. Simple.'

'What about the police?'

Her laugh was all the answer he got, and needed. He persisted. 'If you all spoke, they'd have to do something. You could clear him off the streets by tomorrow. Why don't you?'

'Then what? He's got mates, you know, minders. First time any sniff of the Old Bill around here, we know what would happen. He's probably got mates in there with them as well, so who do we talk to? They'd never prove a thing. And at least we're all still alive. Wouldn't be if they come round, if Mahmoud found out any of us talked.'

'Come on,' Gerard protested, 'he's not going to kill anyone. That'd make it worse for him, for one thing.'

'That's all you know. Listen, Mahmoud don't think like that. We're his property, right? Because he fixed us up here, and we earn his money. We got no rights, we got nothin' except what Mahmoud gives us. He don't even reckon we can think, or nothin'. If he don't like what we do, he can beat us, that's how he sees it. If he thinks we've fingered him, he'll kill us, 'cause that's his right. He's got rights, we got none. He might have killed a couple of girls already, we don't know. He could have, easy. Last year, two of the girls went missing. They jumped on the tube and ran away. We never knew what happened to them, but Mahmoud went as well, couple o' days later. He come back, they didn't, but none of us believe they got away. There was something about him the rest of that month, none of us would have risked crossing him, or even talkin' to him. They didn't get away, that's all we know. We never did find out, but Mahmoud got to them, we know that. And we ain't giving him the chance to get us, neither. Forget it, no one 'ere's going to point at him. No one's going to do a runner, neither. He's got us, and we're fucked – every way.'

'Can't I do anything to help you? Would money get you out?' He was horrified at her response. She jumped from the chair, and backed against the wall. From nowhere, a knife was in her hand, and it was pointing towards him.

'What did I say?' he pleaded, stepping backwards from her, his hands open in front of him. 'I want to help you, not hurt you. You should be out of this.'

'Christ, I thought Mahmoud was smooth, but you're worse. Look you, I got protection, there's nothing here for you. You wait till Mahmoud knows you been poaching on his patch, he'll string your guts out on the line, he will.'

Gerard listened again to what he'd said to her, and this time heard again Mahmoud's first promises of help and salvation. After what he'd done to her, it wasn't surprising that the next time she heard a man offering her money to help her out she should think of Mahmoud all over again. How many like him were there in London?

'Kate, I'm not Mahmoud. I promise you, it's a genuine offer, but if you don't want it, all right. I haven't got any houses to offer you shelter, I haven't got a job to put your way; all I can do is give you enough money to get away from London. I can only do that once, the rest is up to you. If you don't want it all right, I'll not push. Ok?'

The knife wavered, but didn't drop; she wondered but was not convinced.

'Shall I go now? I'm staying quite near here, Kensington, but I often come this way. If you change your mind, you can stop me, the usual way, and I'll know. Nobody else watching would understand, but I'll know, and the money will be yours. You wouldn't have to see me again, but you'd be out of this trap.'

She let the knife fall now and sat at the table again, sullen.

'I don't know if you're straight or not. If you are then you're mad. Mahmoud would kill me. No he wouldn't, he'd just cut me so I couldn't work again anywhere. He'd kill you, though, no trouble.'

Dear God, thought Gerard, what sort of man is this Mahmoud, to create and live off such despair?

Suddenly the late hour swept in on him, and he knew that he was finished for the night.

'Look, Kate, I've got to go now. I'll leave it up to you. I don't know how much I owe you for tonight, but take this towards it. I mean it, when you're ready, stop me and I'll help you.' She barely glanced at the notes he left. He didn't know if he was under or overpaying her, but she needed something.

The night was still dark, still foggy when he left. And he too felt dark and foggy as he thought over Kate's story: her abject fear, the cruelty and abuse from Mahmoud, the two missing girls, Kate's complete helplessness, her unwillingness to try to escape, and how painfully young and frail she seemed.

He had half expected to see dawn breaking over the rooftops, but there was no light yet. The district was not asleep, though, not completely. A few ghostly figures still wandered along the fogged roads; drunken voices still shouted a long way off, muffled, through the dark; sirens still blared almost routinely as blue flashing lights sped by him or across nearby roads.

As he saw the ambulances, he wondered just how many had been sent because of Mahmoud and his like.

And how had he ever managed to get himself involved in such a world – and why?

CHAPTER 9

After Nick had left him to his own devices the next morning, Gerard could sit back and think again about Kate's story and what to do about it. He was a man of principle, a man of meditation, certainly not a holy man – he couldn't stomach that thought – but a man of various virtues and qualities which emphatically did not include physical courage or muscular strength. He knew without need for soul-searching that he couldn't take on the London underworld himself. He didn't actually know if Mahmoud was a key part of the whole London underworld or just a small self-contained outpost of it. Whichever it was, he knew that it was beyond him. But, and this was the frighteningly tantalising part, now that he had heard Kate's story he knew that he was bound to be a part of it, and whatever that part was to be, he desperately wanted to live as long as the subsequent chapter and beyond.

He wondered how sympathetic Nick and Jenny would be, both to Kate and to his need to help. And who else could he ask? Might Father Holloway agree to come galloping to a rescue? Hmm, not very probable, and anyway, his anathematising of Kate afterwards, and probably of Gerard himself, would be nearly as bad as Mahmoud's treatment. There was only the one person he sort of knew down here, but he wasn't convinced that poetry was that effective a weapon against drug-dealing pimps. He would certainly get a book's worth of material out of it, but that was no good to Kate. On the other hand, who else? And Arnold did seem to know a lot of folk in the area. Even if he didn't get involved, he could perhaps point Gerard towards someone who could help.

He walked straight back to Brompton, to Arnold's flat. Empty; he'd forgotten that Arnold too would be at work. He contemplated visiting the printers in Fulham to speak to him, but was unsure how that would be received. Maybe he would, or maybe he'd be discreet and wait until the evening and see how it panned out.

The weather had well and truly caught up with autumn. Still misty and cold, it left the plane trees with shiny black trunks, scarred where the papery bark had peeled, their dull leaves growing more and more like lace as they withered before giving up the ghost and falling to the street. To stay outside in this end of year dampness was a dismal prospect, but this unexpected insight into the other London world pushed Gerard to explore further.

Yes, he would seek out Arnold again and ask his view of what Kate had told him. Lunchtime, perhaps, and that would give him a little time to look for himself.

All over the city there were stories to learn. He knew this well, but his own confusion over Jane Conway had stopped him asking about them. He'd given his pounds to the beggars in their blankets, aware of Nick's disapproval when he did that on their evenings out. Nick looked with dismay at the addicts and drunks and always passed on without thinking about them any further. Each one of them now suddenly seemed to Gerard like another Kate, manipulated by a Mahmoud; how many could he talk to? How many could he try to rescue? The idea of his ever helping anybody again after his failure with Jane was laughable.

And Kate, for God's sake (was that really him, Gerard, blaspheming like that? What was happening to him?), what about all that money he'd given her last night? He'd lost count of how much he had put on the table for her. It was more than his week's allowance, just for her. If she really wanted to get away, why couldn't she catch a train with that and head somewhere safe? Was he being taken for a mug and falling prey to one of the oldest cons? Perhaps, but he was in it now. There was no excuse for turning his back on the girl unless he had proof that she was stinging him. While there was a chance that her story was true (and he couldn't forget how scared she was last night) he couldn't back down on his word. Would his money last? It would have to!

As Arnold was leaving his flat on his way to work in the print shop, the door below opened.

'Hi Arnold,' called a woman's voice.

'Wotcha, Sheil,' he answered cheerfully. Her appearance always brightened his day. ''Ow you doin' then?'

'Not bad. Off to work?'

'Yeah, you?'

'Not yet. I'll have a coffee first. Thanks for last night, it was good.'

'Just a coffee with mates, that's all.'

'Who was that guy?'

'Gerald? Just a bloke I met. He come to the Troubadour to hear me, so he can't be all bad, eh?'

'I liked him. Are you seeing him again?'

Arnold shrugged. 'Dunno. He's staying over Ken' way, so he might come over, might not, up to 'im. Why, interested?'

'Yes. Not like that – well, I don't think so, but there's something – I'd like to know him better, that's all.'

'Goin' to get 'im dancing up on the Common with you? Call up the full moon, or whatever it is you do there?'

'I think he might. Like I said, there's something.'

'If I see 'im I'll tell him you've got the hots, shall I? Get you in there?' and he laughed his way downstairs.

Shelagh went back into her flat and made coffee. She wasn't needed at the library for another hour, so was in no rush. It was such a change from her social work days, it was hard to believe her luck that the job had fallen into her lap so easily. Although she'd focused enough of her rituals helping people find their way out of their own miseries that she damn well ought to have had the good fortune – she'd worked for it. Still, Gerald's arrival prompted her to think that another of her intentions might be bearing fruit. 'Gerald?' She was sure his name was slightly different, but no matter, she hoped to find out in time.

As she thought about him she tidied her little shrine, preparing it to received autumn's offerings as they became available – seeds, acorns, cob nuts, shiny conkers. It was early for most of those yet, but no harm in preparing the way. She still had some ears of barley that she had taken from a field in Middlesex last week, with her friends. It was certainly time to celebrate Harvest at least. She put a clean new candle in the holder, ready.

The room held a blended smell of burnt incense, essential oils of different kinds, burnt sage and, underneath all that, old marijuana. Naturally the smell, in the way of smells, leaked from her room to pervade the house and, mingling further with the other particular smells emanating from the other flats, provided a pungent welcome to all visitors.

She looked round her walls at the pictures of an eclectic set of deities and figures from various traditions: Celtic, Norse, Indian, Japanese, Native American, although she blocked out the thought that a number of them were purely speculation from nineteenth and early twentieth-century folklorists and anthropologists. While she'd been initiated into a particular pagan group and called herself a white witch, she liked to connect with as many gods and goddesses as possible, though she couldn't say whether it was to hedge her bets, or avoid upsetting any one in particular, or just that she took aesthetic pleasure in them.

Her favourite poster, just inside her front door, was of the Great God Pan, his broad laugh showing off his long goat's teeth, his goat's horns sweeping smoothly back over his head. He was sitting cross-legged on the grass in a wooded glade, his pipes in his hand with eight or nine children sitting before him, enjoying his stories and teachings. When she looked at it she felt such an innocent joy and a sorrow that the world couldn't be like that for everyone. It reminded her of her favourite chapter from *The Wind in the Willows* – 'The Piper at the Gates of Dawn' – and the dreams that particular part had given her as a child when she first read it.

Dream catchers and rainbow-casting crystals dangled from two paper lampshades either side of the room, adding an extra hazard for tall and unwary guests.

The only religions she had no time for were those three monotheistic ones from the eastern edges of the Mediterranean that had shaped so much of European history and culture. No, in her view Abraham had a hell of a lot to answer for. And Moses, with those commandments. Interesting, she always thought, how evangelicals and avowedly Christian public personalities harped on about scrupulously following the Old Testament Commandments given to Moses, while paying little attention to the New Testament Beatitudes which were a lot closer to her own codes of behaviour.

Each full moon, new moon and on each of the eight Celtic Sabbats, she met up with others in her coven to perform rituals that somebody or other had formulated to celebrate the passing seasons. They usually met on Wimbledon Common or Putney Heath and sometimes even Hampstead Heath, but as long as they weren't disturbed by passers-by they felt they had successfully honoured their gods. Once a month they would meet up with other pagan groups for a 'moot' in one of the small group of pubs that felt comfortable with their presence. Maybe Gerald would be interested in coming to one of those. She must ask him next time.

As she did eight or nine times a day, she took a wide tooth comb from her shoulder bag and pulled it through her thick hair, hoping to bully it into some kind of obedient shape.

By mid-morning Arnold was on top of his day's tasks. All the urgent work so far was completed and waiting for the customers' pleasure to come and collect. The jobs with a more protracted deadline were well in hand, so he could amuse himself for half an hour without his boss creating.

He slipped the A4 sheet he had prepared from its plastic cover and looked at it again, appraising its worth. It had taken him a good hour's work this morning to finish. Those three tantalising lines from his new poem were written in exquisite copperplate and bordered with illuminated motifs of autumn in stark black and white – no greys – ready to be mounted on blockboard and hung with all the others on the crowded wall of his bedroom. He tried to look at it dispassionately, viewing it through the eyes of his most damning critic, and still found it good. He sighed with pleasure, wondering secretly if he were really cut out to be devil's advocate.

It didn't take long to fix his handiwork onto the board and laminate it as protection against damp and time. After that, it was all clear for a coffee break.

It was while he was sitting with his coffee, trying to capture a thought to fix in a new poem, that Gerard appeared.

'Arnold?'

''Ello, Gerald. How d'you find me here?'

'You said Fulham. That narrowed it down a bit.'

'Fair enough!' laughed Arnold. Before Gerard had a chance to give the reason for his visit, Arnold had produced the blockboard poem for approval.

''Ere, Gerald, what d'you think of this, then?'

Gerard looked at the board quickly. He vaguely recognised the opening and assumed it to be Arnold's own.

'Yes, that's good, really good. Now …' It was too late. Arnold had his encouragement.

'Glad you like it. Took me ages to write that. Not the poem, I done that already, but getting the lettering right. Does it work, is it all right, d'you think?'

'I envy you, Arnold, I really do. I wish I could do half as well. Yes, I think that's really good, I do. Look, I want to ask you …'

'What about the illumination?' asked Arnold anxiously. 'Is it a bit overdone? It's no good losin' the message in the wrappin', you see what I mean? Tell me straight, 'cos I don't want to hang it if it's crap.'

'Don't worry, Arnold, the message is loud and clear. How many are you going to do?'

'I'm puttin' this up on my wall first, you see, and if it's still all right next month, well, I'll print out and mount a whole lot more – maybe a couple of hundred.'

'Really? Where will you sell them?'

'Festivals, next summer. You'd be surprised 'ow many go at places like that. It's got to look just right though, or I'm going to lose loads. Some of 'em I can give to some shops to sell, not round 'ere, but out in the tourist spots and villages, 'Ampstead, Greenwich, Camden Lock, you know?'

'Good thought, I hope it works. Anyway, Arnold, I came to ask you out for a drink if you're free. I need to talk with you about something.'

'Yeah, why not. Hang on a mo'.' He shouted to the back of the shop, a garbled voice replied from behind the door, and then Arnold was free.

'Got to let the boss know, right?' he laughed. 'Come on, then, where is it?'

Gerard led the way to a bar on the high street. He found them an empty corner where, if he spoke quietly, he was sure no one would overhear and maybe report it back to Mahmoud.

Without naming her, he précised what Kate had told him. He described Mahmoud's hold over the girls, the fear and beatings they endured, how he lured them in through kindness – a veritable Samaritan until they were safely in his power – and then closed his trap. How, he wanted to know, could they get the girls away from Mahmoud? How could they find the man and persuade him to relinquish his hold? How could they defeat him and free the streets of his shadow?

Arnold listened and scratched his beard briskly as Gerard talked.

'Well now, Gerald, that's a bit of a problem. I don't know this guy myself and if I did, well, I don't think I'd fancy tackling him.'

'No,' said Gerard grimly, 'I don't fancy it myself. It's got to be done though.'

'Why? What's the point? It ain't nothing to do with you or with me. It's 'ow the world goes, innit? This Mahmoud is the guy there at the moment, right? I'm not saying he's a good guy or that I like what he's doing, but he's the one who's there now. What's going to happen to the tarts if you put him away? Unless you're the bleedin' Lone Ranger you're never going to clean up this city, or even this patch. And I tell you one thing, I sure as hell ain't Tonto.'

'You can't turn your back like that.'

'You watch me, Gerald, you just watch. SEP.'

'SEP?'

'Someone Else's Problem. Not mine, not yours.'

'If I hadn't gone back to her that night I might even try to agree, Arnold, but I did. I didn't mean to, but I've made it my problem. And I don't know where to begin.'

'Bullshit, Gerald. Who knows apart from you, and this tart?'

'You.'

'And that's it? So who knows if you don't do sod all about it? She ain't expecting anything to happen, I'll tell you that. No one else is. No, mate, take my tip, leave well alone. You want to end up in the infirmary? Or mortuary? That's what'll happen. No, forget it, no one'll know.'

'But I'll know I turned my back.'

'What on? An army, mate, a whole bleedin' army of tarts, pimps, ponces, minders, heavies, gangsters, mafiosi, the lot. What else can you do but turn your back on them? Then run like buggery before they notice you. That's all you can do. So, what's your tart's name?'

'Kate, but please don't keep calling her my tart, she's nothing of the kind.'

'Fair do's, no offence. Kate, Kate. Can't place her. What does she look like?'

'Very young, too young, shortish fair hair. She's painfully thin, face almost pinched. Not the sort you'd expect to find in that game honestly.'

'Why not?'

'Well, I don't know that much about it, but to be honest, I'd expect a bit more, I don't know, what would you say, a bit more, obvious appeal?'

'Oomph?'

'If you like.'

'Pizazz?'

'Maybe.'

'Sex?'

'That's it, yes.' Gerard was blushing by now, as Arnold saw very well, of course.

'I think I know who you mean. She's short, ain't she? Very young.'

'Yes.'

'Yeah. Nice girl, but don't say much. Straight in, hand over the cash, straight out again. Don't laugh much.'

Gerard looked at him, shocked. It had never occurred to him that Arnold might know the girls in that way.

'What? That's what they're there for, innit?'

'But they're people.'

'Right on, Gerald, me and all. And people need things. That's one of them.'

'What about a girlfriend or even a wife? Wouldn't that be better than using a girl like that?'

'What's this "using" business, then? I pay. They get their rent, I get my end away and we both go off happy. No hassles, no clinging, no jealousies, no nothing bad. Know what I mean? Like getting me groceries at Sainsbury's.'

'How can you say that? They're not groceries, they're people, with feelings, with histories and lives.'

'Sure, Gerald. Like a copper, when he's out of uniform he worries about his kids' school reports and parents' evenings, his dentist's bills, getting his wife flowers for the anniversary, all that bollocks. Put his uniform back on him, he's a copper, pure and simple and that's how we all treat 'im. These girls, at home, they worry about the same sort of things, sure, but when they stand on the streets, they're tarts, selling a service. I prefer to use that service than tie myself down to one woman who won't let me write my poems or read them, or do other things I like to do. Trust me, I tried it once.'

'What? You were married?'

'Sure.'

'What happened? Do you mind my asking?'

'Why d'you think I brought it up? Disaster, sheer bloody disaster. Liked the idea of a poet at first, thought it was romantic, like? You know? Women! Once we was married, different story. Wanted me to spend me time putting up shelves, or turning the garden over, or watching bleedin' telly with 'er. What she didn't like was me sitting in me room writing poems. Or going out at nights to readings. I tried to be fair, but when you've got to write it, you've got to write it, there's no option, know what I mean? Well, one night I got back from a gig, Golders Green, I was reading something there. Fair do's, I was pissed by the time I got back. I'm not saying it was all her fault or nothing like that, but she hit the roof. Go spare? I tell you, mate, you could 'ave launched a space shuttle off 'er mouth that night. Told me, it was poetry or her, she wasn't being ignored anymore.'

'So you chose poetry.'

'No way. I loved her. I did, honest. I promised her, I'd look after her, spend time with her. No more gigs, no more poems. I'd married her, I'd be fair. Near broke my heart to say it, Gerald, I don't mind telling you, but she'd put it on the line fair and square. Least I could do, wasn't it? Took her upstairs, and pissed as I was, shagged 'er.' Gerard blushed. 'Bloody fantastic it was, straight up. Best we'd done it for years. Then we rolled over and went to sleep. Next morning, woke up, remembered what I'd promised. Well, got to be fair. But when I got downstairs, she'd made sure I kept my part of the bargain. She'd torn up every notebook I had, every magazine I had, every copy of my own books, every carbon copy, every bloody thing to do with my poetry, years' and years' worth, most of it from long before she knew me. She'd trashed the lot and threw it out. I didn't 'ave nothin' left. Nothin'.'

Gerard thought of the enormity of that sacrifice. And thought of that woman's loneliness as her husband vanished night after night into the realms of his mind and soul that she could never enter, would never be allowed to enter. He understood why she had done it, but his heart went out to the image of Arnold, discovering the loss in the morning of all that had given his thoughts and feelings expression.

'Then what?' he asked at last.

'That was it,' Arnold replied. 'If she'd trusted me, I'd have tried. Honest, she'd 'ave 'ad my best shot. I didn't want to lose her, but she didn't let me. She didn't give me the chance. That was the breaking point. I ended up losing the poetry and 'er, all in one go. I packed a case and left, that same day. Took pens and paper as well, to get started again, but some of the best things I ever done were in that black bag she filled. They hadn't all been published, neither, so they've all gone, for good. Haven't made it all back yet, but I'm working on it. But that's why when I gets hungry, I eats out. See what I mean? Home cooking costs too damn much.'

CHAPTER 10

Over the next few days Gerard kept watch along Earl's Court, trying to spot Mahmoud. He saw Kate several times, but she never approached him. She glanced towards him several times but made no other acknowledgement.

Often after those visits, he would meet Arnold for a drink and a good-natured argument about art, poetry, the current state and future of the world, what the coming millennium would bring them, all the opportunities and blessings that the world would experience, or conversely all the apocalyptic scenarios that could end human life. They soon found a pattern where each would deliberately choose and exaggerate a position they knew was contrary to the other's, and often in fact to their own, just for the fun of the disputation.

During those same days, Jez used the last of the money in his wallets and panicked again. He had some smack left, but it wouldn't last much longer. The trouble was, the year was in that slack time between summer tourists and Christmas punters. There were still ways of getting himself money, but he didn't like doing that as much. It was getting dangerous these days. He'd known several lads on that game now dead from the plague. Some of them had been glad to pass it back into the community once they knew they'd contracted it. Taking the Johns' money was one thing, but it wasn't as satisfying as taking real revenge. Giving them the plague, now that was satisfying revenge for what they did. Jez never thought that way, though. He was buying his supply, that was all. Anyway, he seemed lucky as it had passed him by, so far.

He took a trip up West, on spec, but this time fortune had had enough of him and turned her back. He couldn't dip any wallets at all and had to rely on half a dozen back alleyways to raise enough money. He must have another shot at getting some work, he really must. When he got back, that would be the time. Once he worked he could chuck the habit, he knew. Just needed some support like a decent job, regular pay and some mates.

He wondered about this new guy hanging around, what was his name? Gerald, Arnold had said. Yes, Gerald. Maybe he could help him; give him some money, perhaps. It was worth a try. He'd often seen him hanging around lately, and now Arnold had actually introduced them, he could approach him. In the meantime, though, a trip up to the Circus might be in order. If only it wasn't so cold and wet now; that didn't help anything at all.

The night of the fog had truly let in the autumn weather. There were days of weak sunshine and nights when the moon could just about be seen peering myopically through the London light haze, but it seemed now that every day was cold.

The shop doorways were occupied earlier, with the sleepers choosing their pitch before the dark set in. Long, empty evenings faced them, filled with well-heeled shoes stepping across them for hours to come, and nothing to do except prepare for a long sleep until morning. The longer-term sleepers knew a few tricks to keep themselves almost dry and warm, but they had to be bedded down early. Before the confluences of commuters and travellers at the opposing end of day tides had finished their journeys, these resident nomads were as snug as they could be. Colonies in the larger doorways kept a form of society, providing solidarity and what little humour their situation could offer. For some groups, their morale was higher for just a little while, than that of the housed workers who scuttled past them in resentful, well-fed warmth.

Gerard passed them every day, but now he couldn't help watching them; he looked at the men who stopped to talk to the girls, perhaps to offer them money. None of them looked like his idea of Mahmoud, but many of the girls resembled Kate. Yes, he saw many Kates and possibly Mahmouds too, but Gerard's eyes were less accustomed to the corrupters than to the products of their schemes.

'Tragic, of course,' said Jenny over dinner the next evening. 'Nobody enjoys seeing so many people unable to cope, but there will always be casualties, by the nature of things.'

That morning Gerard had got up after Jenny had made another very early start, to find Nick had been on another lads' binge. Nearly late for work already, he inched slowly downstairs, clutching his head.

'Another good night?' grinned Gerard.

'Don't,' Nick moaned, wincing at the sound of his own voice. 'I used to be able to handle it but it's getting its own back these days. I tell you, it's the wrath of grapes. Point me at the Alka Seltzer and I'll be better by lunchtime.'

'What time is Jen due back? I'll cook for you both tonight,' said Gerard. 'Anything you can't eat?'

'Everything at the moment. No, whatever you like, Ger, that's good of you. Say about seven, seven thirty? Make it eight, in case she's held up. You know where everything in the kitchen is? Great. See you later then, be good, and if you can't be good …'

'… practise harder,' Gerard joined in their old joke, and Nick managed a small grin as he reached for his coat.

Gerard did cook for them, having spent an enjoyable morning at the food hall. Jenny had already cooked Italian and Chinese as well as English dishes during his stay, so he chose French as his theme. He selected food he'd enjoyed on a holiday in the Languedoc some years earlier, minus the pate de foie gras, having been sternly lectured once on the evils of its cultivation.

He'd offered to cook partly through guestpitality, to thank them for all they were doing for him, but also because he knew he must be close to overstaying his welcome. And he wanted to open up to them about his dilemma over Kate. He had told them very little about what was happening to him, and hardly anything about the friendships that were forming around Brompton. He felt this was unfair to them and a poor reward for the unconditional friendship they had shown him.

Nick pushed his plate, now empty, away from him and sighed with contentment. He produced another bottle and filled new glasses for each of them.

'Thanks, Ger, that was really something. You didn't cook much at Crosby Road, did you? Certainly not like that.'

'That's not fair – my beans on toast were without parallel! No, Mrs Cormac, our housekeeper at the presbytery, used to give me a few tips. Never had a chance to cook there myself, of course; she was absolute boss, but she never minded me trespassing in her kitchen and watching, even making notes. And I tried my hand out on self-catering holidays or visiting during those years.'

'Well, here's to Mrs C, then, she did a good job with you.' Nick raised his glass and studied the candle through the crimson filter of old port.

'Trouble is, Gerard,' he murmured, returning to the discussion, 'since there's been universal education, the opportunities are there for everyone. Jenny and I have been able to take them; that's why we're here. We're not unique, there's no end of folk like us who have climbed. At university we all had ideas of what we wanted. You wanted to give service, and lo and behold, you're a priest, giving what most of us couldn't even begin to. Good, you took your opportunity. We wanted careers in business and look what opportunities we've had. That's what this world is all about.

'Sadly though, there are some characters who just can't cut the mustard. Let's face it, there are large parts of the gene pool that could do with a good splash of chlorine. Yeah, yeah, I know, only a joke. Like Jenny says, it's tragic, and we should all do what we can to help them, but basically, they can't cope. Isn't it a bit patronising to try and raise them up again where they'll still be unable to manage? Don't they have a right to fail, just as we've got the right to succeed?'

Gerard looked at him in astonishment.

'A *right* to fail? The *right* to sleep in cardboard when the pavement's covered with frost? The *right* to lose all dignity, to beg what spare tenpences you rich can grandly bestow on them on your way home? The *right* to be raped and abused? To be attacked by thugs in the small hours? What are you talking about, Nick? You're in a totally different world! Most of them are not like us, given golden opportunities, but who decided to go rough instead. They're out there for all sorts of reasons, most of which are things that happened to them, not choices they made for themselves. Abused at home, at school, put into care because their parents didn't know how to be parents, lost their job through no fault of their own, illness, mental illness, addiction, I mean ... so many reasons people fall through a net that was never needed for us when we were kids. And nothing to do with being feckless or lazy.'

'What, all of them unlucky saints? Come on Ger, you don't believe that all of those on the street just drew the unlucky card.

Or were "born under a bad sign"…' Nick sang the last phrase with a smirk and slightly off key.

'No, I agree with Gerard, Nick, you're pitching it too strong,' said Jenny. 'I said there'll always be casualties, but not that we've got to ignore them or blame them. But, having said that, Gerard, what you're proposing is another thing altogether. You're about to declare war on the underworld without knowing a thing about the rules of the game and who stands to be damaged, or what the enemy might do to you, or to the girls. Give money, by all means. If you can afford it you're right to …'

'I'd question even that,' Nick butted in. 'Are they going to use it well? Will they get themselves a flat, or decent clothes, even a pair of shoes? Unlikely. They'll spend it on booze or drugs. Now don't look like that – you know it's true. I think it's probably more immoral helping them do that than ignoring them.'

'Different subject, darling.' Jenny returned the discussion to Gerard's plans for Kate and Mahmoud before he could leap back at Nick's assertion. 'Ger, I'm sure that despite whatever troubles bring you here, you're a fantastic priest. We knew you all those years ago, remember. You've always had this highly developed sense of right and wrong. Add to that, you've probably got a hotline to the angelic troubleshooters – sorry if that sounds blasphemous, it wasn't meant to be – and I can see you're determined to sort out this Mahmoud character. All very laudable, and noble. With deepest respect, though, you're not Randolph Scott or Shane …'

'… or the Magnificent Seven, I know! Why does everybody start comparing me to old Westerns because I want to try and help one poor girl out of a life that's going to be cut very short if she isn't given a hand? I'm out of my depth, I know, but I also know about her. I've met her, so what else can I do?'

'Is this what you intended when you came to London? Father Confessor again?' Nick asked with interest.

'No way, just the opposite. I need a complete rest from moral decisions and advice giving. I just wanted space to coast through a few months of life without anyone calling on me.'

'So why aren't you? I mean, you used to do exactly this at uni – no end of people in trouble. You'd sit down with them or sometimes drag them off to Student Aid, and even down to Citizens Advice a couple of times, I remember. A saint, a bloody saint, and I mean that. Now you're doing it again, but this time you're about to play with the real baddies. What is it that makes you gallop at windmills like this?'

'Oh please, don't keep pinning me down with metaphors from fiction! I'm a real man faced with a real person in real despair. Randolph Scott and Don Quixote are nothing to do with this. Homelessness and heroin had no place in my last parish. I knew from the confessional that there was such a phenomenon as prostitution there, and abuse, but I saw precious little of it myself. The more I've seen since I've come here, the more hopeless I feel about being able to do anything at all. But I still can't pretend that I shouldn't even try.'

Yet again, Gerard caught the glance between Nick and Jenny that was often there when they all discussed issues together. It irritated him, because it left him out. More than that, he felt there was a judgment implicit in their glance.

'Poor old Gerard, he's off again,' he seemed to hear. 'Hasn't got a bloody clue, has he? Always was a bit odd, but it's only harmless Gerard!' he read in their exchange. So frustrating that even their shared history didn't afford him a bridge to cross the chasm between their diverging views. It had nothing to do with Nick and Jenny's atheism, either. Friendship spanned that particular abyss well, but it couldn't reconcile their material differences.

Later that night, he heard voices from inside their bedroom.

'It's a bloody nerve,' said Jenny. Her voice was quiet, but the words darted straight through Gerard as he lay in his bed next door. 'I mean, he's staying here, but how often do we even see him now? I'm sorry for him, and I love him dearly, don't get me wrong. But who the hell does he think he is, moralising at us because he's got himself tangled up in something he doesn't begin to understand?'

'Fair do's, Jen, he's got no choice by his lights. Anyway, we told him when he came that we're busy and can't play nursemaid. As I remember, we were relieved he said he'd entertain himself. Can't turn on him because he's doing just that. Anyway, it was his idea to cook for us tonight. He didn't need to but that's him, he's trying to pay us for putting him up. Bloody good it was too.'

'I know, I know all that, but apart from tonight, how often does he come in before we're asleep these days? Christ, he's worse than you were when you were a student!'

'Good for him, then, he's not wasting his time. Would you rather he hung around moping all evening?'

'I still think he's got a bloody cheek. I've a good mind to start giving him a bill every week.'

'Don't even think of it. Come on, this is Gerard, remember? He's here because he's in trouble.'

'What trouble? He's never even told us that much. I don't like what he's mixing himself up in. I don't care about his so-called friends; that's his business, and after all, his gaffer was supposed to have mixed with all sorts of undesirables, so it's not up to me to fault him there. If he's going after heavies, though, that's different. This guy murdered the girls, he said. Do you think Gerard's got the bottle to nail someone like him? And when he doesn't succeed, where is this clown going to come looking for him? Where he's staying, maybe?'

'Here?'

'Why not?'

'For Christ's sake, Jen …'

'Never mind Christ, I'm worried for our sake. I don't fancy us being targets in some squalid little war of the pimps because our old chum, dear old Gerard, has let his conscience bid farewell to common sense. Do you fancy being slashed or stabbed or whatever? Because I don't.'

Gerard slept badly that night.

CHAPTER 11

Shamefaced about its recent ill-treatment of everyone, next day the sky brought bright sunshine back to South Kensington. The remaining leaves on the plane trees along the roadsides shone like gold lace, and the sky between the roofs was clear blue, broken only by the airliners that appeared above the narrow streets like gondolas as they seemed to coast slowly to or from the airport. The air was mild, and raincoats were a mistrustful precaution only. The smell of the morning hinted deceitfully that autumn and winter were already done, and spring was waiting its turn. After the dismal week of fog and all-pervading moistness, the brightness spread from climate to spirits as if through blotting paper, and Gerard felt his own new bonhomie mirrored on faces normally dour in the morning. He turned away from the station as he decided to walk to the river instead, perhaps to take a boat to Greenwich and enjoy the sunshine in the park.

As he strode along Lillie Road to work, Arnold felt a new poem bubble up from deep inside. He stopped in a panic, scrabbling in his pockets for the constant pencil and notebook, while he mouthed the opening lines over and over, just as they had risen unbidden into his head as he walked. The thought captured safely for now, he continued trying out the sounds and theme as he walked. Another good day in front of him, perhaps.

Jez lurched in a chemical daze from his room into the unaccustomed brightness. He had to do something drastic today to get some money – his supply was just about out again. The West End it was, then. He turned his feet towards Knightsbridge, then Piccadilly. Even though the season was wrong for the big lucky money, there was still enough there for a careful man like him. Beaming with a vacuous contentment, he started weaving uncertainly again between the press of workers heading for the tube and buses.

Kate lay in bed, no reason to get up yet. Last night had been quite profitable, more so than usual these days, and she didn't expect Mahmoud just yet. She could afford to sleep a bit longer. She didn't feel so well lately, not so much energy. She coughed harshly and fell back on the pillow with a sigh. It would be better if the damp weather didn't smear everything in her room, making the torn wallpaper so clammy, the sheets and furnishings so cold and sticky. There was the slightest hint of mustiness with each breath. The aerosol covered as much as possible with synthetic rose odours, but it really wasn't an improvement.

That guy the other week, offering her all that money to get away – was he for real, or was he just poaching her? Kate couldn't tell. She wondered if even if he was another ponce, might it be better for her? He seemed to have enough money to be one, like Mahmoud, but there was definitely something about him, though she couldn't put her finger on it. Against all her experience, she was almost inclined to trust him. Certainly, she'd never intended to tell him as much as she had. It wasn't only the pile of notes he quietly topped up as she spoke, either. Mahmoud had already had that money of course. Well, he would have known about it, and she wasn't going to risk keeping it and taking another beating; not worth it.

He'd been hanging around like he said he would. She hadn't approached him and he'd kept his distance, but he was definitely interested in her. He might be strange, but he wasn't weird, not one of those types. He didn't look strong enough or streetwise enough to take on Mahmoud, but if he really had money to throw at her, there was hope of a sort.

In the morning Gerard had enjoyed his trip to Greenwich, relaxing in the park and exploring the two sailing vessels, the *Cutty Sark* and the *Gipsy Moth*, followed by lunch in the market. After that he returned to the West End. Since his arrival he'd sated his thirst for art, music and elevation of the spirit and now found a new restlessness. He sat at a cafe window table by St Martin-in-the- Fields, stirring his coffee over and over, even though there was no sugar in it. Kate's face kept coming back to him, and here was his restlessness. He wanted to help, but how? In his old parish he had resources, contacts and authority. Here in London he had himself only, and that really wasn't enough.

He also felt more strongly that it was getting time for him to move on somewhere else; he couldn't keep sponging off Nick and Jenny. Fish and guests go off after three days, and his eavesdropping last night confirmed that. He had passed his best-before date a long time since. How to do it without seeming to snub them? And where to go?

His ministry steadfastly refused to call him back. The idea of returning to his parish and Father Holloway's austere rule depressed him; his views had hardened over the Church and the extent to which it should govern his thoughts and actions. Unfortunately, it had not yet been replaced by anything else, and Gerard had no new thoughts or directions. Technically he was still a member of the Church, a priest even, but his heart had turned away from it, almost in the instant that the news had reached him that Jane Conway had followed his commands and was dead.

He valued most his growing friendship with Arnold and the brief introduction to some of Arnold's circle. That made him feel guilty about Jane, and about Kate, but at the moment he saw no way out of that. As to his search for a new path, no, he was lost. At the moment, there was nowhere else for him to seek, so he passed his time with momentary enjoyment, and longer dissatisfactions.

It was on one of these days of unexpected Indian summer that events suddenly moved.

After breakfast one morning, he suddenly thought of the reading at the Troubadour and decided he felt like a coffee and treat. Yes, the warmth of the cafe and the sound of Chopin on the loudspeakers welcomed him home. There were still three chess players in the corner. He queued for a cappuccino and a florentine and looked with affection at the ancient advert for a boon and a blessing to men: 'The Pickwick, the Owl and the Waverley Pen.'

There was no trouble finding a seat in the older front half of the cafe, just managing to avoid a chess player's arm as he suddenly clicked the timer at the same instant he made his move. As Gerard drank, he watched the passers-by kicking up the fallen plane leaves along the street. Many seemed as aimless as he, but less troubled, playful even. A voice broke his thoughts.

'Hello, it is Gerald, isn't it? Gerald, or …?'

He looked up, startled, at the tall smiling woman with the waves of thick, dark hair framing her face, and her pink-rimmed glasses. He recognised her but couldn't place her. His uncertainty must have showed.

'Gerard, yes. I'm so sorry, I've forgotten your name?'

'Shelagh, Shelagh Newman. We met, a while ago now? In Arnold's flat?'

'Of course, yes, I remember.' He stood up and proffered a chair. 'Yes, that was a while back now, wasn't it? How did you remember me?'

'Why shouldn't I? Just a minute, I'll get myself a coffee and I'll be back.' Leaving a scarf and woolly hat on the table, she swept off to the counter. He was flattered that she recognised him and embarrassed to have forgotten her.

'Have you seen Arnold lately? When are you coming round to visit us again? I should be at work now, but they can miss me for an afternoon – time to do a spot of early Christmas shopping, eh? I hate Christmas but haven't got the guts to boycott it. Not even as if it's my religion, eh?'

Like Jenny and Arnold, Shelagh didn't seem to need contributions to her conversations but was quite happy to deliver monologues as long as need be. Gerard didn't even try to interrupt, but just relaxed and let her talk.

'I love the library, I really do, but it's good to play hooky sometimes, isn't it? I did feel guilty about leaving social work, you know? But in the end I couldn't cope with it. I just felt everyone's problems too much to really help them. I never enjoyed the court work either.'

'And the library?'

'It's great. Helping people, but completely differently. Sometimes helping people complete their forms for benefits, or applications for council housing, as well as showing them where the book they want is. And the schoolkids who want to look up something for a class project – I love that. You can see them learning and hear the cogs whirring sometimes when they're getting excited. Yeah, it's great.'

'But not today, eh?'

'Well, sometimes you need time out. What about you, Gerard, what do you do? You never told us the other night.'

'Not much at the moment – like I said, I'm on a sabbatical. But I know what you mean about taking on others' troubles. I've got form there and not been particularly successful at it.'

'Do you want to tell me? I'm a good listener.' He thought and quickly decided.

'Thanks, Shelagh, but not yet. I've got a bit of work to do on myself first, and I'm not ready to come clean. Someday maybe, but not yet.'

'That's cool. You know where I live, in Arnold's house. I also make good brownies and flapjacks, so you're welcome any time.'

After Gerard had gone on his way, feeling lifted by such an uncomplicated exchange, Shelagh headed back towards her flat, but now less pleased with herself at missing her day's work.

Perhaps she ought to clock in to work after all. It wasn't fair on the others in the library to vanish for a day, even though she'd been looking forward to going to the West End for some shopping and calling into Atlantis in Bloomsbury to get the new editions of her pagan mags. She'd tried to order them for the library, but the chief librarian, a church warden among his other responsibilities, vetoed them immediately. He knew of her affiliations, and they sparred and bantered good-naturedly. But stocking a public library with such material was a step too far for him. Atlantis it was, then.

She decided: off to the shops, a quick lunch and then into the library with her headache (the alibi she'd phoned in that morning) mercifully cleared. But she hoped to see Gerard again before long. There was definitely something about him, and not just his deflection of any talk about himself. Some sort of mystery there, and he couldn't be that far from her world view either. She could feel that sense of otherness in his aura. Yep, Mr Gerard might find himself being one of Shelagh's special projects. She enjoyed a good challenge, and his reticence offered her just that.

While she was wondering about that mystery, Gerard learned the truth about his adversary.

CHAPTER 12

After leaving Shelagh in the Troubadour, he was walking past the tube station when a voice called his attention:

'Got a light, mate?'

He looked down, startled, to see Kate, unlit cigarette in her hand. She looked frightened.

'Don't look. He's on the other side of the road. Guy in the light jacket not looking at us yet, but he will.'

'I'll see him in a moment. No, I haven't got a match. What do you want?'

'Keep it casual, try your pockets a moment.'

Gerard went through a pantomime of checking his pockets while he avoided looking towards Mahmoud. He asked her,

'Do you want the money? To get away?'

'Yes, but I'm frightened of him. He's going away from us now, down Hogarth Road.'

'Did he see us talking?'

'No, he wasn't looking our way.'

'All right. Thanks. I'll see you in a day or two, and we'll arrange it. He won't harm you, don't be frightened.'

He walked back to the pelican crossing and reached the other side of the street. He had Mahmoud in his sights now, and immediately felt wary. The man who he thought was Mahmoud looked wrong. He was quite young, close to Gerard's age, perhaps in his thirties, and was dressed smartly but casually. Somehow he looked far too straight, too respectable to Gerard to be a pimp. However, as long as Mahmoud hadn't seen that it was Kate talking to him, he felt committed now. Time to move in. Mahmoud seemed to be alone; so much the better. He was moving away from the shops and restaurants of Hogarth Road towards Knaresborough Place.

Gerard walked a little bit faster and gained on the other man. Before long he was walking close behind him. Once near enough, he slackened his pace to keep close without overtaking. They'd not walked more than a few yards in tandem like this when Mahmoud stopped abruptly, swinging round to face Gerard. His hands were folded into fists, his legs poised to sway instantly in any direction, and there was a look of such ferocity in his face that Gerard backed away in reflexive alarm. The apparent respectability he saw in Mahmoud from behind had vanished, and he believed anything of this man, in particular that he was capable and ready to kill Gerard this very instant. Too involved now to back away, he tried to hide his fear behind a steady voice and manner.

'What do you want?' Mahmoud demanded, his whole concentration on Gerard. 'Why are you following me?'

'Are you Mr Mahmoud?'

'Who are you? You're not cops, are you?' The question was not for information – Mahmoud knew that Gerard was no policeman, but his tone was no less hostile for that.

'Can we talk?' he asked.

'Who are you?'

'My name's Gerard Tisserant.'

'So what? Who are you?'

'I want to talk about a friend.'

'What friend?'

'I can't give you her name. She works for you.'

'What do you mean?'

'She's one of your girls. I know. Can I talk to you about her?'

Mahmoud unclenched one hand and slipped it into his jacket pocket as he moved quickly and quietly towards Gerard who felt a wave of fear down his back at the movement, knowing that the hand in the jacket was not empty. For the first time in his life, he felt he was face to face with the enemy, whatever the enemy might be. At this moment it bore the face and menace of Mahmoud.

'Can I talk to you?' he repeated, marvelling how steady his voice sounded to him.

'Who are you? What do you mean she's one of my girls? What do you want?'

'Shall we keep walking as we talk?' Anything to break that threat in Mahmoud's stance, anything to keep his own body moving and active lest it freeze into paralysis with fear.

'There's a girl who's working for you.'

'Who? What's her name? How do you know anyone works for me? You don't know nothing, you're guessing, aren't you? Who are you?'

'I know she works for you, and I know she doesn't want to anymore. I know what work she does as well.'

They walked rapidly on, Mahmoud in thought. Gerard wondered if the other were testing his stamina, they walked so fast towards Knaresborough Place.

'I'm not doing anything wrong, Mister. There's nothing you can accuse me of.'

'That's not what the police think,' Gerard hazarded. He was taken aback at Mahmoud's reaction to that – a scornful laugh.

'Them? Why do they care? They got bigger things to worry about than a few girls. They don't know nothing about all this, most of 'em, anyways. And those who do, I make sure they're not bothered. You don't know nothing neither, do you?'

'I know, and they know.'

'Liar. What you after?'

'I want to buy her off you.'

'Don't know what you're talking about, Mister. You can't buy no one. You won't even tell me her name; how can you buy?

Listen, you want a shag, you go to your woman with your money. Why you talking to me about all this shit? It's nothing to do with me, I'm a respectable man. You think a good Muslim like me will get mixed up in this?' He raised his voice louder as passers-by came within earshot.

'I say, you want woman, why you come to me? What you after, I'm a respectable man. If you want sex so much, leave me alone, there's women on the street give you what you want for money. You're a pervert, you know that? Leave me alone, find one of the tarts, they're what you want, isn't it?'

Out of the corner of his eye Gerard saw a middle-aged woman look hard at him as Mahmoud shouted his abuse. A younger girl across the road seemed to be laughing at the scene. He flinched harder at these reactions from others than he did at Mahmoud's jibes. He walked on, this time drawing Mahmoud after him, protesting loudly all the while. But he still followed. That fact alone made Gerard think he could still win against this humiliation. He tried a new tack.

'All right, Mahmoud, I don't want a … a woman, not like that. You know that's not what I'm saying. Will you let this girl go? I'll pay you, that's all I'm saying.'

'What's her name? Which tart is it?'

'No name, not yet.'

'No name, no bloody deal, Mister. What slag's been talking to you? Tell me or I'll break your bloody jaw.'

Gerard recoiled against this threat, convinced that Mahmoud would do it.

'You think I'll tell you so you can break hers? No, Mahmoud. You say yes and name a price. I'll give you the money, and when one of your girls is missing, you'll know. Let it go then.'

'What about the others? You want to buy them too? Discount on a dozen, eh? What'll you give me for a dozen?'

Gerard recoiled from the sneer. What about the others? They must be like Kate, trapped, but how many could he help?

'Well, Mister? What's your price?'

'What do you ask?'

Mahmoud didn't even stop to ponder.

'Two hundred thousand, cash.'

'You know that's too much.'

'Why? You taking away one of my assets. I could make that much from her before long. I already spent money on that girl. Given her a home, given her all sorts of good stuff. I take care of my bitches, they can't complain. Easy cost me two hundred grand. You just paying back my overheads, man, I still lose money.'

'You don't even know who she is.'

'I treat all my girls the same.'

'Supposing she just vanishes without telling you?'

'Oh no, they only vanish when I want them to vanish. Them tarts don't vanish for long when I'm looking for them. I tell you, you take that girl away, you're both dead. Don't matter where you go, I got friends, I got contacts. In less than two weeks, you're both dead.'

Gerard believed the threat. Why hadn't he just given the girl the money?

Because he guessed she would give it straight to Mahmoud. He knew her fear of the man now and how completely trapped she felt.

'Mahmoud, why don't you just let me take her? You've got enough girls on the street to choose from, why can't you let this one girl try a new life? How would it harm you?'

'Listen, Mister, no one takes nothing from me. I don't want to let her go. Now fuck off. If I see you talk to any of my girls, she's dead, see? You stop and talk to any, then you've killed her, right? Your fault.'

'You've got a whole racket going that would put you away for a lifetime, Mahmoud. You listen to me. If you don't let her go, and I'll pay you for her, then I'll take you to the police station, and they'll all go, all the girls, everything. You'll lose it all and spend the next twenty years in prison.'

Mahmoud stared at him.

'You'd do that to me?' he asked.

'Yes, I would.'

'Just a minute, let me think.' Mahmoud stepped away from Gerard and pulled a chunky mobile phone from his pocket. He punched in a number and muttered two words into it. He came back to Gerard.

'I've got to talk to a mate about this. Wait, he'll be here in a minute.'

Gerard wanted to run. He didn't trust Mahmoud or his new conciliatory tone.

'Well? There's enough witnesses. There's nothing to think about.'

'So why don't you do that, then? Why you trying to buy one girl when you can free the lot of them? Eh, Mister? Why? 'Cos you can't. You ain't got no witnesses, the pigs couldn't touch me. I know they wouldn't, I make damn sure. So don't try and threaten me again.'

As he spoke, a dirty white van pulled to a stop beside them, ignoring angry hoots from other drivers. Two men, obviously the friends summoned on the phone, climbed out and stood by him. One was white, and bigger, much bigger than Mahmoud. His blond hair was cropped very short and underscored by a blue tattoo on his forehead with another one over the rope-like backs of his hands. By the size of his chest and wrists, the only muscular development his heavy leather jacket displayed, Gerard guessed that he spent some hours a day in a gym and was in as near peak condition as he could be.

The other was also large, another part of Mahmoud's muscle. He was dark and bearded, and, Gerard guessed from the subcontinent, but he wasn't able to say which part. He too looked full of menace and studied Gerard as closely as if cramming for a test next morning.

Gerard noted with relief that they were still in sight of passers-by and not in a secluded alley. What was most frightening about the newcomers was not their size, but their expressions. They were concentrated on Gerard and suggested that of all the most disagreeable things in the world that needed eradicating, his case was the most urgent.

Without taking his eyes off him, Mahmoud passed on the salient parts of their conversation.

'Dave, Farid, look at this man. He thinks I ought to go to prison. He's trying to take one of the girls away. Will you remember his face?'

Dave nodded, his eyes never leaving Gerard's face.

'I don't want to go to prison. If you see him anywhere on my patch, or talking to any of my girls, see that he never does it again. And make sure whoever he talks to never speaks to him again, or anyone else she's not meant to.'

Dave nodded slowly, his cruel gaze still focused on Gerard.

'Right,' he said slowly, his only answer. Farid just grunted

'You got any more to say to me, then?' Mahmoud asked Gerard. The menace issuing from the two henchmen was almost strong enough that he could cut it with a knife. Except that it would be he, Gerard, who would feel the blade. His heart thumping faster, the sweat broke out on his forehead, and again the sense of evil washed over him, more tangible and more real than any of the evil his tutors and mentor had described. This was not any metaphysical abstraction of evil, but a powerful presence of deliberate human corruption. However had Kate felt irresistible charm emanating from this man? Whatever threats Mahmoud made, Gerard knew that he had the ability to honour them without compunction; his men would unhesitatingly commit murder if Mahmoud ordered it.

He felt his insides turn to water as the full, malign attention of all three was focused on him.

They made no move towards him, but just stared, learning every line of his face and body. He dared not run and knew that he mustn't show fear, despite what every part of him was feeling. He forced himself to calmly look back at each of those faces and then with slow deliberation turn his back and walk, not run, towards the station.

CHAPTER 13

Gerard didn't go back to Earl's Court that afternoon. He made straight for the South Bank instead, to wash off the taste of fear and corruption. By the time he reached there, Indian summer had given way once more to autumn dreariness, and heavy cloud looked as though dusk was already touching the skyline. It was too late for afternoon audiences, too early for the evening visitors, and too cold for browsers at the bookstalls.

The visit completely failed to relieve his memory of Mahmoud, Dave and Farid. The tide was low, and smelly mud lined the concrete at the river's edge below the railings. By the steps of Hungerford Bridge a girl huddled in a blanket, a sign propped up by her feet:

'HOMELESS AND BROKE. PLEASE HELP.'

He'd seen so many such notices since moving in with Jenny and Nick and had responded variously with anger, sympathy, hope and despair. This time he compounded despair and anger. Despair, because he could see how easy it was for Mahmoud, all the Mahmouds, to prey on such hopeless misery. Anger, because these children should be at home with a loving family behind them and hope in their lives.

Kate and others had shown him how hollow such visions of the domestic ideal were in reality. Even so, he never got used to seeing children like this. Why were the Mahmouds triumphant, as the world headed towards the third millennium? Why did the young have so little support and cause for hope?

As his depression grew with these thoughts, he found himself accosted by a thin, whining voice behind him, instantly recognisable.

'Hey, Gerald! It is Gerald, isn't it?'

He turned and sure enough, there was Jez's haggard face grinning at him, framed by the black straggly hair that he'd again forgotten to brush.

'Hello, Jez,' he replied. 'What are you doing here?'

'What?' Gerard was coming to expect that anxious look whenever Jez was asked a question. 'Just, you know, seeing what's on. Pictures. You know. See what's showing.' He gestured with his head at the National Theatre.

Whatever he was on, Gerard thought wryly, it was taking him somewhere a lot nicer than this afternoon.

'Hey, Gerald, you couldn't lend me a fiver, could you? Tell you what, make it a tenner, and I'll pay you back next week. Promise, I'll have some bread by then. Can you?'

'What do you want it for, Jez?' Unnecessary question; he only wanted to buy more dope. Gerard may be green, but he'd worked that out on his first night at the reading in the Troubadour even before Jez had managed to stagger to his feet.

'Hey,' Jez began, 'I just want to get a coffee, you know?'

'For ten pounds?'

'Well, you know …'

'Come on, I'll buy you a coffee now.' Jez would not have been his choice of company at the moment, but even that evergreen confusion was better than his own solitary gloom. He steered them into the National's dry shelter and led the way to the buffet. Jez was visibly overawed by the building. His voice dropped as if he were in a church.

Jez's eyes were wide as he looked upwards at the height of the ground floor, the notices and giant photographs on the walls and the little bookshop by the coffee area. Even though they were not there for a performance, Gerard felt his own endorphin rush that theatres and concert halls always gave him. Perhaps that was why the Catholic Church had appealed to him, he mused – the theatricality of its services and rituals. The thought vanished from him as instantly as it had arrived, and he didn't even have time to be troubled by residual fears of heresy.

He bought a coffee for Jez and himself, and they sat at one of the tables.

'Hey, Gerald, you know, this is, like, really good of you.'

Gerard nodded, aware of the temptation to patronise Jez in this place.

'That's ok. It's too cold now to hang about outside.'

'Yeah, yeah, right. About that tenner, could you make it fifteen?'

'Why, Jez? Why do you need that stuff so much?'

'I don't need it. I'm not, you know, hooked, or anything like that. No way. No, I'm nearly off the stuff now. I just need a little bit to get me started. Once I get a job, you know, start earning my own, I won't need it then. I'll never use it again. See? It's only a bit I need to get me started again. I'll be fine then.'

His voice trailed off slowly as he looked around at the vast foyer. As he watched, Gerard felt the strain and fear of Mahmoud recede. He didn't know Jez that well, and had less in common with him, but felt safer, more at home with him.

'Jez, why not now? I'll let you have the fifteen quid, sure, but use it on something else. Leave that stuff alone, Jez, before it kills you.'

'You're right, Gerald, you're absolutely, completely, totally right. Ok. I've quit. I'll never take the stuff again.'

Gerard looked suspiciously at him, but there was no trace of irony or satire in Jez's face.

The turnaround was too abrupt to be believable, yet Jez seemed to mean it.

'Hey, Gerald,' he drawled in the closest to excitement that his voice could reach, 'don't give me the bread, I don't need it, honest.'

'All right. Tell you what, why don't we stay here and get tickets for one of the theatres?'

Jez looked blankly at him. Nobody at home, thought Gerard.

'What theatres?'

'Here. This is a theatre. It's got three auditoria. I can see if they've got any spare tickets for one of them.' He heard himself speaking slowly and loudly as if to a simple child. Jez didn't seem to notice. He just looked bewildered, like a simple child.

'This? It's a cafe. It's not a theatre, it's a cafe. Isn't it?'

'Yes, but it's in a theatre.' Jez's look of confusion, bordering on panic, dissuaded him from trying any harder. 'All right. Not now. Another day, maybe. Shall we go back now, then?'

'Yeah, right. Er, Gerald, you couldn't let me have that twenty quid now, could you? I've got to see this guy, right? I need twenty for him.'

Already he had forgotten his renunciation. Gerard looked at him in despair.

'Oh Jez, can't you just try? Is life so bad you've got to kill yourself like this?'

'What? No, it's great, Gerald, really great. You're a mate, you know? Like Arnold, he's a mate. I just, you know, need to get some stuff. It's cool, I've nearly stopped, straight up.'

His tone had almost descended to that of a mantra where he was not listening to anyone including himself. Somewhere, hidden in his grubbiness and confusion and vanished self-esteem, was a spark of optimism. Gerard could sense it and saw that the litanies of both self-pity and determination were Jez's way of keeping that spark alight, however faintly.

Today, though, he was a lost cause, just as Gerard felt himself to be. His confrontation with Mahmoud returned to taunt him, and he flushed with the memory while his hands suddenly shook with the fear.

For the whole tube journey back towards Kensington he re-enacted the meeting, berating himself for ever speaking to Kate and to Mahmoud. And for making unkeepable promises, for making unkeepable threats, for exposing all the girls to danger and himself to humiliation. Despite the sense of evil and threat, he didn't really believe there was any physical danger to himself, but the awareness of putting himself in Mahmoud's power was too much. He forced himself to quit the train at Earl's Court and walk the rest. If he did not return there now, he feared he would leave it altogether – leave it to the likes of Mahmoud to run as they wanted and leave Kate to despair, decline and, finally, death. No, he couldn't just leave it. Dullness had already returned with the night to Earl's Court, and as he left the station his heart sank deeper when he saw the lights and the bustle of people with absent faces. No sign of Kate or the other girls yet, and no sign of Mahmoud.

Heavy hearted, Gerard set off home, up to Brompton Road and then towards Jenny and Nick's Kensington comfort.

Mahmoud saw to it that it was another four days before he got there.

CHAPTER 14

Close on midnight Jenny ran through to the reception desk only to find a line of patients already waiting. She tapped her foot impatiently, itching for the queue to lessen while the rubbery, disinfectant smell of hospital only heightened her impatience and anxiety.

'Excuse me,' she grabbed the arm of a passing orderly, 'I'm looking for …'

'Try Reception!' came the reply before she had a chance to finish.

At the front of the queue, a drunken older man had become bogged down in an argument with the receptionist, and Jenny's impatience turned to anger. She called out loudly to the front.

'Can't you speed it up? We're all in a hurry here!'

The receptionist, weary and flustered, snapped back at her.

'Please! I'm doing my best; there's only one of me – I'm trying to help all of you. I'll be with you just as soon as I can.'

'I've got a friend dying in here, I want to know where he is.'

The rest of the queue turned on her, saving the receptionist the trouble of answering, and Jenny drew back under their hostility.

Her evening had turned into a nightmare with the visit from the police. Gerard was at the hospital, unconscious. He seemed to have been mugged, although his wallet was still intact. This address was in his wallet and could they help? Did he live there? Well, in a way, he was staying with them for a few weeks. Well, could they help out? Yes, of course, Constable, which hospital? University College. How bad was he? Couldn't say just yet. Would he take them there? No, they'd have to drive themselves, but he'd tell the hospital to expect them.

Then there was the drive with roads blocked by red lights at every junction and worry about Gerard making each delay feel protracted forever. Nick parked the car as she ran in to find his ward. Now she felt that nightmare give way to a Kafkaesque confusion that might prevent them ever finding Gerard's bed. Contrary to the policeman's promise, no one seemed to expect them or to know what they wanted.

As Nick joined her, the situation suddenly shrank to its true proportions.

'All right, Jen? Found anything out yet?'

'No, just a minute. Don't lose our place.' Calmer now, Jenny crossed to a doctor on the other side of the room. Nick watched her ask him something and saw him reply with a gesture down a corridor leading off from the room. He saw her smile thanks and beckon him over. Nightmare and confusion had withdrawn; Jenny was back. Two lifts and a long corridor later they found the ward and the duty nurse.

Yes, he had been brought in that evening – were they family? No. They couldn't see him yet. He was out of surgery but too ill for visitors and heavily sedated with painkillers. And besides, visiting hours were long since over. Sorry for a wasted journey, but no, they couldn't even see him from the door, they must come back tomorrow. But he would be all right. Broken ribs, bad bruising and maybe a hairline skull fracture. They would know by morning, but she thought they should be able to see him tomorrow.

They both took the morning off work to visit him, bringing grapes, flowers and books.

'I expect it looks worse than it really is,' Gerard smiled weakly up at them.

'I bloody well hope so,' said Jenny. 'It certainly looks bad enough.' This was true. Gerard's head was heavily bandaged. His eyes were bruised and swollen, his mouth gashed. Three ribs were cracked, he had been told, and he had further bruising the length of his body, from two pairs of Doc Martens with steel toe caps, and two pick handles. His skull was not fractured after all, but the doctors were worried about possible bruising and swelling to the brain. Tubes and wires connected him to monitors and an IV stand.

'How long will they keep you here?'

'I don't know. They're worried about concussion, so they're going to keep an eye on me at least for another three or four days.'

'Why are you in a public ward like this?' asked Nick, keeping his voice low and looking around at the other occupied beds.

'Shouldn't you be in intensive care?'

'They don't think so. It's all right.'

'Let me arrange a private room for you. It will be a nightmare in here later.'

'No, no, honestly, Nick. But thank you for the thought. Bless you.'

His voice was weary. He was glad to see them, but that couldn't begin to ease the dreadful shock of his first taste of physical violence. He thought he had understood violence at school, but the rough play, even bullying, of adolescence was far removed from the systematic beating that had just been administered – like an injection, he thought irrelevantly.

Glad as he was for Nick and Jenny's support, he had a more urgent need. Although he trusted them, there were some things he couldn't ask them to do. An orderly had already promised to phone Arnold and ask him to visit. Arnold would know who to see.

After their first reassurance that Gerard was not, after all, dying, Nick and Jenny found small talk hard. Gerard told them what little he could remember about the attack, but after the first kick to the head he had only blurred impressions and no focused images. A grubby white van reared onto the pavement just in front of him; two men, both large and both carrying sticks, were suddenly in front of him, behind him, flanking him and, in a welter of shocking blows, on top of him. His arms flailed out in a vain attempt to defend himself, but he did not know how. He registered each of the many blows that landed on him, even though he was not aware of them hurting. The pain came only after the two had left, and then all the damaged nerves shrieked loudly as the bruising started, and the fractures screamed even louder when he tried to move himself.

After the van had gone, people were suddenly there who were invisible before. A gentle hand held his, and a voice talked soothingly to him. Someone else put a folded jacket under his head, and the comfort stayed with him until the ambulance arrived to bring him, with brisk, professional compassion to the hospital.

He was distressed as he recalled these events, that he didn't know who owned the comforting hands and voice. He wanted to see them and thank them when he was discharged, but he had no clue as to who they were.

Jenny and Nick were reduced to platitudes. They were true to their resolve not to hint at any suggestions of I-told-you-so, though they all knew that this was Mahmoud's handiwork. He was in all of their minds, but his central role in the attack was taboo, so the only important topic was barred.

When Arnold burst shaggily among them, he had no such qualms. But then he was used to finding friends in Gerard's condition, or worse.

'What you doin' 'ere then, mate? I told you to run like buggery, didn't I? Bloody 'ell, they've done you good and proper 'aven't they? 'Ow you doin' then?'

Nick and Jenny faded back in the face of this eruption into the whispered wards. Other patients and visitors looked up, startled at the noise.

Gerard smiled painfully at him and introduced him to Jenny and Nick.

'Cheers!' Arnold greeted them, sticking out a fist for them to shake. 'You're his mates, aren't you? Putting him up? Great.'

They were suddenly in the background and knew it. Jenny leaned over and kissed a small, undamaged part of Gerard's face.

'We'll leave you now. We'll call the hospital first thing – if they're letting you out, one of us will come and get you. If they keep you in, we'll visit again tomorrow. Look after yourself.'

When they had gone, Gerard lay back with guilty relief.

'Good to see you, Arnold. Thanks for coming.'

'I didn't bring no grapes nor nothing. Didn't know if you had a mouth left, know what I mean?'

'I know. Look, can you do me a favour?'

'Sure. What?'

'Pull those curtains round the bed first, this is private. Thanks. Now, can you find Kate and tell her what's happened?'

'Why? What good's that gonna do?'

'I don't know, it just feels the right thing to do.'

'Does this Mahmoud character know it's her?'

'No. I didn't tell him anything about who it is.'

'So she won't 'ave 'ad the treatment like you yet. Why tell 'er? All it'll do is frighten her even more.'

'Give her some of the money as well. Prove that I'm on the level.'

'Bloody 'ell, Gerald, what are you playing at? Why not send a letter to Mahmoud telling him when you'll be on his patch again? Make a return fixture, like. I told you once: leave it alone. See what happens when you interfere? You don't know what you're taking on, do you? Even after this.'

'I've got a better idea, but I've got to keep faith with Kate. And she's got to know it. Look, please go and see her. Give her some money for the usual so she can give that to Mahmoud, and then give her the extra so she can keep it safe. She can't give that to him, because he'll know she's the one I'm trying to help. Otherwise, she'll hand it all over to him, and never get away, I know. Like this, she won't dare not keep it safe.'

'Where's this money, then? I can't sub you for this one.'

Gerard winced when his ribs yelled at him as he leaned for his wallet in the bedside locker. There wasn't enough cash for what he needed. He gave Arnold his cashpoint card and offered him the pin number.

'Steady on, mate,' protested Arnold. 'You're giving me everything you've got. 'Ow d'you know I'm not going to take the lot and bugger off out of here? You can't go trusting everyone like this. I mean, you've only just met me, 'aven't yer?'

'Arnold, the only other people I'd trust with this are the two who have just gone. But I don't trust them to find Kate. You, I trust to do both. Please, I still feel lousy, don't argue, just do it, all right?'

'Course I'll do it, mate, but I don't like it. You're not helping 'er, and you're not proving nothing to nobody.'

'Maybe, but I can't choose now. Now Mahmoud's done this to me, I've got to hit back. This is the only way I can until the ribs are mended and all the bruises are gone. It might not be much, but what else can I do? Eh?'

The doctors wanted to keep Gerard in for at least two more days, perhaps three or maybe even four, but the x-rays and scans allayed their worries about his head injuries. His broken ribs were excruciating when he tried to move or turn, and he relied heavily on the nurses and their painkillers to keep him comfortable. Neither Jenny nor Nick could visit him early in the day, so he prepared himself for a day of rest and idleness. It didn't turn out like that, though.

He sat propped up against the pillows, eyes closed, only vaguely aware of the background sounds of the ward. He winced once more as he tried to shift his position and felt the newspaper resting on his bed slide to the floor. He tried to lean over, but gasped as the rib stabbed him again, and he slumped back in resignation. Now he was properly awake he heard sounds more clearly, footsteps at the end, trolley wheels clattering, muffled voices in the corridor outside, two patients further along talking to each other, and his nose took in afresh the smells of the ward.

There was a further sound he couldn't identify at first, but it came from inside the ward, one of his fellow patients. He strained his ears. What was that sound? Another patient had heard it and quickly identified it as Gerard heard him shout,

'Oy, stop blubbing, mate, we're all hurting in here!' Then yes, he could hear that it was a quiet sobbing. Not wailing, nor screaming nor moaning, none of the usual sounds of human pain, but a quiet, constant sob.

He managed to raise his head and look to find the source. It was an older man, his darkish face looking straight up, unseeing, at the ceiling, a white cap affair on his head, his arms resting on the bedcover, and tears running down from the corners of his eyes onto the bedding. Apart from the man who had shouted at him to shut up, no one seemed to be taking any notice, not even the nurse at the end of the ward.

Gerard looked helplessly along the row to the man; he couldn't lie back and pretend he didn't know there was a soul in pain and probably a body as well. This was going to be difficult; how to move and not hurt himself more. He gasped as, trying to sit upright and turn himself round on the edge of the bed, the bruises along his ribs stabbed him again.

'Nurse,' he called out, but his voice was too quiet. He rang the bell by his bedhead, and in a few seconds a nurse appeared at the end of the ward and came briskly to him.

'Can you help me stand, please? I want to visit someone down there.' She frowned, puzzling as to whether he was attempting a delicate euphemism, or he actually wanted to visit another patient.

She helped him turn, taking his weight if it threatened his bruises again and then gently easing him onto his feet and leading him to the crying man's bed.

'Thank you,' he smiled gratefully at her. 'I'll be fine from here.'

Gingerly, he sat down on the bedside chair and took hold of the man's hand.

'I'm Gerard,' he said quietly. 'Can I help?'

The man looked blankly at him, shook his head and continued sobbing.

Gerard said nothing more but sat there, held his hand and let him cry. He watched the man's chest heaving with the sobs, the tears running down to the already dampened pillow, and he wondered at the cause of this tumult. Without thinking, Gerard picked up a tissue from a box on the man's locker and wiped the tears from his face. Neither said anything, but they stayed there with hands joined.

Gradually the sobbing slowed. As the grief quietened, Gerard became aware again of the ambient sounds of the ward. He looked around; the other patients had lost interest long ago and only the nurse was still watching them.

He felt a squeeze from the man's hand.

'Thank you,' he whispered. 'It is all right now, thank you, thank you.' And he detached his hand from Gerard's, turned on his side and closed his eyes. The nurse was beside them immediately and helped Gerard stand up while protecting him from the worst of the pain from his injuries. She guided him back to his own bed where he too, slept.

While Nick and Jenny were there the previous evening, he had known there were others in his ward. The whispered buzz of visitors with home news and gossip provided a backdrop to his own conversations and later, his solitary thoughts. Occasionally a loud voice broke through to his awareness. Sometimes it was the same voice.

He became aware that its position was changing and that it seemed to move from bed to bed. The next day, during visiting time, that same voice at last broke through his drowsy semiconsciousness:

'And how are you feeling now? Hello? Hello?'

Suddenly Gerard realised the voice was talking to him. He raised his head to see who owned it. Standing at the foot of his bed was an Arabic-looking man in a clean white smock-type shirt with a beige sleeveless long jacket over the top. He wore matching white cotton trousers, and on his head was a white skullcap that Gerard later learned was called the taqiyah.

In shock, Gerard gasped and sank back again onto the pillow. The man looked nothing like Mahmoud, but he feared that this was an employee, come to ensure his withdrawal from the conflict. The stranger looked offended.

'What's the matter? Are you all right?' Not the most penetrating question to ask of a bandaged and bruised hospital patient, perhaps, but strangely it reassured Gerard a little, who looked up from just above the sheet.

The Arab looked to be in his forties or maybe young fifties, quite tall with a thin, smiling face that was framed with a tightly trimmed beard and moustache. Like Mahmoud, he was well dressed and smart; unlike Mahmoud, he radiated friendliness and trust.

'My name is Yasser, Yasser Ibrahim. Not Yasser Arafat,' he laughed. It sounded like a well-rehearsed and well-repeated line. Gerard, wincing painfully, pulled himself up in bed and extended a hand.

'Gerard, Gerard Tisserant,' he replied.

'Ah, Mr Tisserant, that does not sound very English, no?'

'No, I was born in France.'

'Quite so, but grew up in England, I think? Your accent and the way you say you were born there, rather than admit to being French. Am I right?'

Gerard agreed, and gestured for Yasser to sit down.

'Oh, thank you, thank you, yes, I will. I understand I must thank you. I am visiting a member of my mosque. He is over there in the corner, recovering from an operation, poor man. He is new to this country, and since he landed everything has gone wrong for him. He came with his wife, but she died soon after. He is a civil engineer, well qualified and experienced, but he is not allowed to work. He's been told that the best he can hope for is to be a cleaner or caretaker when finally he is allowed a job, and he has so little money now, and his home is small and not what he is used to. Poor man, it was all too much for him, and he fell ill. He tells me that yesterday he despaired so much he wanted to die and then, like an angel, you sat with him and took much of his pain from him.'

'Not an angel, no, but he was so sad, and no one was taking notice of him. I didn't do anything, really I didn't.'

'That is not what he told me, no? He felt you take his fear and depression off him, and today he is happier than I have seen him. So on his behalf and on behalf of my mosque, I say, "thank you", yes?'

'Your mosque? Are you a priest, then? I'm sorry, that must be the wrong word, I mean no offence.' Yasser beamed at him.

'Of course, no offence, no. I suppose "priest" is not wrong but different. I am imam of the mosque near here. Khatib – another word for my duties. "Preacher" is closer than "priest", yes?'

'Imam? I'm sorry for my ignorance, but I have no knowledge of the structure of Islam and a mosque.'

'Why, certainly! In front of a true Christian in his own country, out of courtesy I would hesitate to say that ours is the one true Faith, but in my country and the mosque it is, so with no insult meant, I say to you "Salaam Alaikum".' He put his hands together and made a small bow towards Gerard, smiling with his little laugh all the while.

'Then let me reply,' said Gerard, wincing again as he tried to smile. 'Pax Vobiscum.'

'Oh, a Latin greeting? Excellent.' Yasser laughed warmly and looked with new interest at Gerard.

'Are you khatib too, then?'

'In a way. I was a priest of the Roman Catholic Church.'

'Was? Are you allowed to slip away from it so easily that you can say you were, not are, a priest?' There was no accusation in Yasser's voice as he said this; rather genuine intellectual enquiry. Despite his different faith and the programming from Father Holloway regarding Islam, Judaism, Hinduism, Buddhism, non-conformism and all the other heretical, damned, non-Catholic beliefs, Gerard felt himself opening up to Yasser. Before he could enter into debate, Yasser recalled where they were.

'And what has brought you here, if I may ask? You look as though you have been involved in an accident, yes?'

'Not an accident, no. I was supposed to end up like this. I was beaten as I walked home.'

'Mugged?'

'No, it was personal.' Once he started, Gerard found it hard to stop talking about Mahmoud and Kate, his challenge to the pimp and his helplessness against the scale of corruption and despair. Unlike Arnold and unlike Nick and Jenny, Yasser listened to him in a silence that was loud with serious attention and respect. The seriousness on his face turned to anger as he heard about Mahmoud.

'And he had you beaten? You, a priest? He ordered the beating of a man of God?'

'I never actually told him I was a priest.'

'That has nothing to do with it. You are a man of God and he is a Muslim. He brings shame to my faith and to the world of Islam. What can I say to you, my friend, to atone to you?'

'Yasser, it wasn't you. Why should you atone? It was one man, one evil man. He might have been an atheist, Christian, or any religion. His belief had nothing to do with it. Come on, people like him have always been around.'

'That may be, I know, but you have not always been around, and he has not always been around, and I have not always been around. His evil action has brought us together; Allah always has a purpose in what he does. There must be an atonement I can make to you on behalf of Islam. Let us talk.'

Yasser was not shooed out for another hour, and during that time he rocked yet more of Gerard's understanding of the world. They took turns to describe the underpinnings of their respective faiths, each listening with respect to the other and neither demanding agreement with either view. They each described a leading historical figure instrumental in the establishment of the religion. They were both learning, and each recognised the common holy writings and teachings that were shared by their beliefs.

Yasser spoke with concern of an increase in fundamentalist Islam in London and other parts of the country, fuelled by the Rushdie *fatwa* controversy. He preferred a more interfaith (ecumenical, in Gerard's terms) ethos with those in the community around him. The predictable white backlash against Muslims from some sections of the home community both distressed and frightened him; if both sides could not reach out to each other and talk, he foresaw and dreaded a new ghettoisation in just a few years, maybe even before the new century.

Gerard had always been uncomfortable with Father Holloway's pitying denunciation of Islam and its adherents' errors, while not feeling able to refute him. Listening now to Yasser and questioning these new perspectives, he marvelled at his mentor's bigotry and great ignorance. He was feeling unsteady and not just because of his concussion: another prop of certainty was sliding away from under him, and his life's previously firm base was yet again wobbling.

In his parish, and the surrounding villages, there was only a very small Muslim presence and none of the extreme preachings that made London headlines. On the contrary, the few Muslims he encountered, he had met despite Father Holloway's stern warnings, through the community work they were doing, which inevitably overlapped with his own mission. But the headlines in the national press and clips he had seen on TV showed a new, threatening energy arising that provoked an opposite and equal reaction from the home community. Now Yasser reminded him of the other side, the one he had seen in his own community – charity, hospitality and devotion. It was clear that Mahmoud's activities had nothing to do with any facet of Islam but were simply corrupt and criminal.

Before Yasser left, he asked,

'I did not see a visitor with you yesterday, or today. Have you no family here?'

'No family, no.'

'Of course, you cannot marry, can you, no?'

'No. But I have had visitors – friends I am staying with have been in every day, and another friend I have made locally, he has been in, so I am not lonely.'

'Good, good. Loneliness is hard, very hard sometimes.'

'Have you family here?'

'Not here, no. I have a son in Egypt, but otherwise no. My wife – and only one of her, whatever you may have read somewhere – died five years ago.'

'I'm sorry, Yasser, that is awful.'

'It is hard, yes. Allah trusts and helps me, though. I might feel lonely in the world sometimes, but I never forget he guides me and knows me. It helps me. And the members of my mosque are kind.'

When the imam left at last, they clasped hands, and Gerard promised to call him when he was discharged, looking forward to sharing a coffee and more conversation. Alone again, he noted with interest how he had spoken for the Church that he was rejecting. Well, there was the hierarchy, bureaucracy and rigid dogma, all of which he hoped to leave behind him, and then there were the overarching principles, summed up for Gerard in the Beatitudes. These he hoped to carry with him always.

It was a further two days before he was discharged, during which time Arnold visited him again, confirming job done. Yasser also stopped by his bed again on his next visit, saying,

'And while I am here, I like to visit the other poor souls who share his ward. I know not everyone receives visitors, no?'

When Nick finally drove Gerard back to the Kensington House, Jenny told him of a 'wonderful coincidence'.

CHAPTER 15

'Do you remember Ann McGoldrick from university?'

'Yes, of course I do. Not that I've seen or heard of her since then, but yes, I remember her well.'

'What do you think? I bumped into her yesterday! She and her husband were in town for the day. They live in Oxfordshire now. Well, I was in Knightsbridge, turned a corner, and there we were, face to face. She's invited us, all of us, to see her on Saturday. Can you come? I told her you were staying with us, of course, but I didn't tell her what you've been doing and what's happened to you – that's not for me to say. She was so thrilled at the thought of seeing you again. Can you come?'

Gerard remembered Ann well, a Northern Irish girl he had been close to when they were both students. As Jenny had reminded him, Ann had experienced a very dark night of the soul shortly before Finals, and he had sat with her, helping her through the crisis.

After they graduated, she had gone into journalism back in Ireland, and he had entered the seminary and then taken Holy Orders. They exchanged about three letters each, eight Christmas cards and then nothing; each had moved conclusively out of the other's orbit. Strange, he had barely thought of her since then. Even during their recent reminiscences, neither Jenny nor Nick had mentioned her more than the once. He would have expected other figures from their student days to reappear now, rather than Ann. Yet here was radical, atheist, scathing, warm, laughing Ann.

His ribs still sore, his bruised face still aching, he welcomed the thought of retreating with dignity out of London, even if only for a day.

'Will she expect to see me just out of the wars, like this?'

'Of course not. I told you, she knows nothing of what you've been up to down here.'

'She'll have to know some of it, of course. I don't see Ann accepting a face like this without a lot of questions!'

'Hmm, I'd not go into too much detail if I were you. She might agree this wasn't your finest hour.'

'Ooh, that's a bit near the mark isn't it?'

'I'm sorry, Gerard darling, and I'm not rubbing it in, but you didn't play this one as cleverly as you could have, even you must admit that. I'm not talking about the rightness, or morality or anything else, just that your strategy was complete cobblers. Do you really think Ann won't pass a comment or two to that effect, unless age and domesticity have mellowed her beyond recognition?'

He worried about that on Saturday morning, all the way to Ann's home near Witney. She and her husband lived in a refurbished old farmhouse still quaintly called The Farm, with a half-acre of land attached. His cracked ribs still pained him as the car turned a corner sharply, or changed speed suddenly, but he had enough painkillers inside him still to be able to manage without complaining.

As it happened, while age and domesticity had marked Ann, they'd not mellowed her too much. After their slightly self-conscious greeting, both searching for strange or familiar features in each other, he saw her eyes light up with a once-loved and well-remembered fire.

'Well, Ger? What's happened to you? You were always the pacifist bugger, so why is it you with the bruises, then?'

'Tell the nice lady, Gerard,' said Nick, grinning.

'Nothing much,' said Gerard. 'I said the wrong thing to the wrong guy, that's all.'

'It really was a beating? You didn't fall downstairs?' said Ann.

'It was a vicious beating from a vicious pimp,' broke in Jenny. 'Don't let his modesty fool you, he's been a bloody hero, and those are his scars of honour.'

From under her greying hair, Ann looked appraisingly at him.

'You've been a naughty boy, haven't you? Crossing a pimp, and you a nice Catholic boy, too! Tut-tut, Gerard, you've been out of my influence too long. But fair play to you, having the guts to put your fists up.'

And that was it. No more interrogations or justifications, just a reunion that healed another part of him and made him wonder yet again about all the might-have-beens. It was obvious that Ann's husband, Joe, never thought about any of those might-have-beens. He and Ann seemed to fit together so perfectly that there was no room between them for doubts about either's past choices or mistakes. More even than Nick and Jenny, they seemed at one. And Joe welcomed Gerard as Ann did, for Ann's sake.

Gerard had never even heard of Joe, but quickly felt as though he knew him. Joe was like an animated background, a chameleon, but a large, amiable one. Completely unthreatening, he was also unthreatened by this bruised apparition of Ann's past. Gerard found that he would listen with more than polite interest to all that people said. He obviously remembered it, but had little of his own to offer. He was strong; his massive paws showed that. And every look showed his devotion to Ann. Gerard learned that most of the house had been shaped by him under Ann's dictation, and he took a gentle smiling pride in it. But he didn't seem inclined to take a more active part in conversation. He answered questions in his Devon accent, slowly with a smile, and he knew what to ask to draw other people out. Beyond that, he listened with interest and patience and smiled – easy to overlook because he retired so completely, but present the whole time, watching and smiling in approval.

Joe was an engineer and after graduating had worked across the world on civil projects, mostly bridges and dams. He was now employed by a local engineering firm and still worked away from home from time to time, but hardly travelled overseas anymore.

It was later in the afternoon that Jenny raised the subject. Gerard took it at face value at first. Only later did he see that it had all been rehearsed between the four of them.

'Gerard, darling, you know Nick and I are both away for the next few days? I'm sorting out the Glasgow branch.'

'And I'm in Hamburg for a conference from Tuesday.'

'Well, are you going to be all right by yourself? All things considered, you know.'

A few days earlier Gerard would have reassured them that he could cope just as well alone, and why shouldn't he? But since the Mahmoud incident he was afraid. He hesitated a moment too long, and it was Joe who took it forward.

'Are you busy in London, then? Stay here for a while if you haven't got to get back yet. Plenty of room.'

'Yes,' came in Ann, 'do. Give us a chance to catch up properly, won't it?'

'That's a good idea,' Jenny added on cue. 'Yes, until we're back, why don't you, Gerard?'

Nick was the only one not saying anything. He didn't need to add his voice, though, as Gerard needed no urging to accept the offer. Objections about a lack of spare clothes, toothbrush and so on were brushed off by Ann, who seemed always prepared for such contingencies.

So later that evening Nick and Jenny drove back to London, leaving Gerard in convalescence with Ann and Joe. Before supper

Chapter 15

Ann took Gerard out to the back to help round up the dozen hens that she kept and showed him where they expected to find eggs.

'Got to make sure they're all locked up tight. Foxes and badgers do try and get in if we're not careful. In the early days here we lost a lot of hens like that, but Joe's got the run sorted. They've got space and the fox doesn't get in.'

They ate a peaceful and simple supper and chatted easily about their last few years. Ann did most of the talking while Joe sat and nodded, smiling. Occasionally he added something, but mostly he smiled, and poured more wine. Gerard reflected that there were far worse ways of being a host. He was surprised to hear that they had been married for eleven years. They must have met before she and Gerard had exchanged their last Christmas cards, yet she had never hinted at Joe's arrival in her life and had never told him that she was, after all, going to get married.

'It all happened so quickly,' she explained the next morning when Joe was at work. 'That's strange, too. Joe's the last man in the world to do something hasty, you know? He's solid, steady, two hundred percent reliable, the best man in the world; you know every wife thinks that of her man, but he really is. Did you think I'd settle for less?

'We'd only been going out for a week when he got an offer to work abroad in Saudi. He'd be out there for about two years. We talked about it – he's always wanted to work in the Middle East. He's built dams and bridges in South America, Indonesia, Southern Africa, but never the Arab countries. Dream come true for him, it was. Trouble is, so was I – another dream. I could have waited for him, but I didn't think a week was enough to justify it. He did, though. Turned the job down there and then and lost the chance forever. I still don't know why. I mean, I quite like myself, nothing wrong with my self-esteem, know what I mean? But even so, I couldn't see why he would choose me over Saudi. He did, though! Couple of other blokes I went out with earlier got jobs elsewhere and went straight off without me. Without even asking if I wanted to go with them, would you believe? It hurt, course it did, but I didn't hold it against them. That's what I expected Joe to do. But he didn't: he chose me. And how could I say no to that? Best choice either of us ever made, too.

'You've noticed, he's a bloody sight quieter than me, but he listens, one of the best listeners I know. When we had our trouble that time, he was so kind, so patient and so strong.'

Gerard had not heard of this trouble, but he let it pass. If Ann wanted him to know, he would in due time.

'Well, he's not usually a hasty man, so when he chose that quickly, it was inevitable, like. No time to hesitate, and why should we? So we stayed together and moved down here for the job he took instead. Married later in the year, though we didn't really need to.' She paused momentarily, and Gerard saw a shadow cross her face, to be immediately banished.

'We've been here ever since, part of the furniture in the village. You'd never have thought it of me, I know, back in the old days: Firebrand Annie, Annie the Fenian Trot, quietly married to a civil engineer and playing my part in the smallness of English village life. Not what our plans were, eh? He's not our old sort either. No intellectual pretensions or philosophies and no concerns with literature or high Art, nothing like that. Just an utterly decent, utterly loveable man. Tell you what, though, I never did a better thing in my life. So there!'

He gave her a hug.

'If only you knew how good it is to hear a wife say that, Ann. The number of leisurely repentances I've listened to after the hasty wedding! I think the one thing I've missed in a long time is a friend with a happy story to tell me. Thank you, and bless you.'

'Aah, don't go blessing me, Gerard. I've cut with your church forever, don't think I haven't. And I'm damn thankful I have, too. Joe never had a faith, well, not what you would call a faith, anyway, so don't go blessing him, either.'

'Don't worry. I'm not so happy with my church at the moment, myself. That's why I'm here, after all.'

Although the evenings were now dark and cool, they took Gerard for a late walk through the lanes around the small town. This was a ritual they carried out whenever they could: before putting the day to bed they walked arm in arm around their territory, re-establishing, day by day, a connection with their land rather than with just their living room. The excuse was Gwen, a golden retriever who needed the exercise, but Gerard felt that it was just as much their need as hers. He was touched that they walked carefully so as not to hurt his ribs or aggravate his other injuries. He guessed they would usually move faster, but this evening all three were content to match his slower pace.

They walked and chatted together on safe ground. It was always Joe who called the dog and kept an eye on where she was running off to, once free of the lead; but Joe was also right there with them. Gerard stayed for a week before it was time to return to London.

In that week he learned more and changed more. The first change came two nights later.

CHAPTER 16

'You doing anything tonight, Gerard?'

It was Joe who asked him that at supper on his third evening there. It was a polite question, as Gerard had not done anything on his own while at the farmhouse. He didn't know the area, so walked with them, or watched television with them and once played boardgames with them. Evenings were shared, and it suited him here.

'No. Anything in mind?'

'Yeah. Going to see an old mate. Like to come?'

Gerard agreed with pleasure. He didn't know if this meant a meeting in the pub or somewhere else. Whichever, he was glad of a chance to learn a bit more about Joe; talking with him wasn't easy, and he still felt a little uncertain as to how Joe might view him, a single male stranger from Ann's past.

The meeting turned out to be somewhere else, not a pub at all. Ann was busy working in a studio Joe had built her at the back of the house, so she didn't come with them but gave Joe a heavy carrier bag to take. They walked together with Gwen trotting in front and then waiting anxiously for them to catch up; Joe was affable but didn't say much. Occasionally he pointed out some feature to Gerard, a particular tree maybe or an owl flying across the road ahead like a silent gliding ghost. Most of the time they walked in a brisk companionable silence.

At last they came to their destination: an old stone cottage at the end of a small terrace. Joe knocked loudly on the door and then opened it using a key of his own. He gestured Gerard inside.

''Lo, George?' He shouted. There was a muffled answer from the end of the dark hallway where Gerard could just make out a light wooden door. The house smelled old and musty, and his breath still showed in the cold air of the hall. It was not a healthy house. Joe led the way into a room which contrasted so strongly with the hall that Gerard recoiled. A close, dry heat leapt at his eyeballs and throat, along with a blend of stale urine and drying laundry. Gwen bounded in, licked a wrinkled hand on the other side of the room as her tail wagged violently and then lay down, head resting on sleek paws.

George was sitting in a wheelchair on the other side of the room. A few wisps of white hair stuck out from the sides of his head, and his red cardigan was stained with several weeks' accumulations of dribble and spillage. A couch with sheets, blankets and pillows rested against the side wall.

'Now then, George, keeping well?'

''Lo then, young Joe. You're late tonight.'

'Ann's sent you these things, I'll put 'em in the fridge for you, all right?'

Before George could say whether or not it was all right, Joe had stepped down into a cramped kitchen where another wheelchair waited by the step. George looked at Gerard.

'You Joe's friend? Pleased to meet you.'

He held out an arthritic hand to Gerard, who took it gently, trying not to hurt it. He introduced himself and was told to sit himself down. By moving aside old papers and some old clothes, he was able to.

'Joe,' in a loud whisper, 'empty the doin's, will you? It needs it.'

'Right you are, George.' And Joe took the pan out of a commode in the kitchen and through a back door into the garden.

George picked up a used plate from the floor beside his chair and held it out. Gerard moved to take it but was waved back.

'No, no, you sit there. Joe'll wash it for me.'

Joe did wash it, then he made the bed, and then he put the kettle on and made them all tea. And then he sat down, all at George's command.

'What's she sent, then?'

'Made you a pie, steak and kidney, some pasties, fruit cake, and sent a few tins. Sixty fags, too.'

'That's good. Thank 'er for me, won't you?'

A round wooden clock, nearly hidden on the mantlepiece, chimed eight o'clock in a sad minor key. A fan heater near the wheelchair whirred noisily. Neither of the two friends spoke, and Gerard shifted uneasily, sipping his tea. George remembered him.

'Not seen you round here. Known Joe long?'

'About two days.'

'Old friend of Ann's, had a bit of an accident,' Joe put in. 'Gerard's come down for a few days to convalesce and get to know the area. Brought him along with me,' completing the explanation for Gerard's appearance.

'He's a good boy, Joe is. Annie too. Good boys to me, both of 'em. Eh, Joe? Good boys to me?' And he laughed wheezily at his joke. Joe laughed back, but seemed to recognise the joke of old.

'Every week he comes round, don't you, Joe? Every week, ever since my Edith died. True, ain't it? Do you know, the night she went, about two at morning it were, the doctor asked me if I had family could come round. "Not a soul," I said to him. "None of 'em lives here anymore." "Alright," he says, "'ave you got any friends?" Annie and Joe was the only ones I could think of, because I know Annie and Edith got on well.'

'That's all right, George,' said Joe, trying to stop him talking.

'Well,' George carried on, 'Joe 'ere, he got straight out of bed when the doctor called and came straight out here and sat up with me all night. Been out 'ere every week since, too. Nine year ago, and he ain't missed a week yet, least, when 'e's not workin' away.

And then Annie comes and sits with me. Mostly it's Joe, though. Twice he come out, don't you? Every week. Never miss, 'cept when you're away, 'cept then. You're a good boy, Joe.'

'Well,' Joe shrugged, 'as long as someone'll do the same for Ann when it's my turn.' And he leaned back comfortably with a swig of lukewarm tea.

George asked querulously for news. Joe thought for a few moments and then relayed the bulletin in a desultory fashion: this farm's TB scare was ill-founded; that village's bypass was about to start work; Mrs X had been seen red-handed by some neighbours letting a man – a stranger at that – out of her house at five in the morning; Mr Y, a respected pillar of the next community along, hadn't got home until nearly six that same morning; Old Z thought he'd won several thousands on the pools last weekend, but it worked out at sixty quid only. It was all small beer, parochial stuff, but George took it in with delight and comments. He had no snippets or gossip to give back, so instead he got Joe to make them another tea.

'Joe,' he said eagerly, after the local news was complete, 'I've been given this form to fill, by the council, you know. I can't rightly foller it all, can you 'elp me?'

'Let's see it then, what is it?'

'I think it's about money, but I can't remember everything they want to know.' He turned to Gerard. 'I don't know. I forget things now, and don't always make sense of what's in these things. Think I'll sell my head and buy a cabbage, eh? Buy a cabbage, Joe.' And he wheezed with laughter.

'Ah, you're doing ok, George, don't you worry. Give us the letter, I'll sort it.'

While Joe worked on the form, often interrupting George with questions about this account, those savings, these benefits and pensions, Gerard was treated to a long life history.

He was shown two albums full of photographs that went back to between the world wars, in which George and Edith were younger than Gerard was now and looked a great deal more cheery and blithe. He saw pictures of George's wartime comrades and was shown the only other two who lived until peacetime. He heard a passionate, if dribbly, denunciation of all right-wing and Tory politicians, most of the named ones from the sixties and seventies having dropped out of the news before 1982. George was a radical, even if out of date. He told Gerard angrily why he and so many of his comrades-in-arms determined in 1945 that the servicemen would not be ignored this time, and how they came to vote Churchill out of Downing Street as soon as they had the chance. England would be a land fit for heroes, and for everyone this time – not like when his father was discharged after being wounded on the Somme in 1916. Gerard thought briefly again of Kate, and the children he had passed in doorways and under bridges, only a week or so ago.

He also saw many photographs of Edith, young and old, and held in his hand a chunk of metal cut from George's father's leg after his first injury at Mons. Gerard was not called on to contribute or speak, just to receive the relicts of these memories.

After forty minutes or so, Joe had finished the forms and promised to send them off to the council first thing. He signalled to Gerard, and they both rose. Gwen seemed to have expected the move, because she was on her feet with tail wagging before Gerard was upright.

The gibbous moon was out as they walked back, lighting the road and the land in an eerie monochrome, with blocks of silhouetted trees and hedges across the fields. Gerard shivered in the sudden autumn night cold, a shock after George's overheated house. Too early for frost, but temperatures were low.

'Don't take everything 'e says too literal, Gerard. We do go on holiday most years, but I make sure either neighbours or social services keep an eye on him while we're off. I don't know how long he's going to hang on there, but he's set on not leaving. It was their home, their whole life together, and he's afraid of leaving her behind if he gets shipped out. It'll happen sometime, though, it has to. I just hope I can keep visiting and keep an eye on him when that happens.'

'You're a good man, Joe. Not many would do that for so long for a neighbour, both of you. I'm sorry it's taken so long to find you both, I feel like I've missed out.'

'Well, none of it's anything new to you, is it? Ann told me all about you back in your uni days. Father Confessor, they called you, didn't they? She told me how you got her through her bad patch and sat up with her all night that time.'

He wasn't sure how to respond, so kept silent as they walked.

'Reckon it were you that gave me Ann,' Joe carried on after a few steps. 'If you hadn't pulled her through that night, she'd not have made it through the course. Might 'ave been even worse than that, she was so low. But as it was she did get through, and so one fine day we met. I'm glad you came down; I'd never have had the chance to thank you otherwise. She told me all about you – I knows you were close friends, comrades, and I knows it meant so much to her.'

Somewhere in his mind, Gerard saw a pair of scales quiver slightly. Jane Conway was in one pan, heavy and pulling it down. But now Ann, from all those years ago, was on the other side adding a tiny piece, just a touch, of weight. Though still a long way short of a full balance.

They stopped off for a couple of drinks and spoke far more than on the journey out. Joe wouldn't stay till closing time, though, because that wouldn't be fair on Ann at home.

There was another, less comfortable, surprise two nights later when he stood in the kitchen, watching and helping Ann prepare the evening meal for when Joe came in from work.

'I don't know,' he said, 'I would never expect to see you up in Knightsbridge. You seem much too much at home here to be interested in that sort of place.'

'Quite right, I am. I've not been there for, oh I don't know, years.'

'So lucky, then, wasn't it?'

'You've lost me, Ger. What are you talking about? Pass me that veg knife, will you? Ta.'

'When you met Jenny I mean, last week.'

'Last week?'

'In Knightsbridge.'

There was a pause during which they both realised that something wasn't adding up. He walked to the sink, picked up a tea towel and started drying the pans in the drainer.

'So when actually did you invite us down?'

'Last week. Well, first time was about three weeks ago. We were talking on the phone and, well, it seemed like a good idea, all things considered.'

'Three weeks ago? She told me she'd met you only last week. By chance, the first time in years.'

'Not that many years. They've been here before, you know. Spring, that was the last time. She told me, oh, last month that you were going to visit them and stay over. I invited you all here then, but she said no, not yet, they'd see how you were first. Then last week she called and said could they bring you after all.'

'I see. Did she also ask could they leave me with you?'

Ann's silence answered the question. Gerard looked around the kitchen for something else he could do to help, but it was all finished; there was nothing left to hide behind.

'What do you think of it all then?'

'What can I think? None of us know anything. You never told Jenny what's going on and you haven't told me.'

'Didn't she tell you about my stupidity?'

'No. What am I supposed to say, Gerard? You're hiding from us all the time, and we only get glimpses of you. I can see from your face you're in trouble, and it's not just your bruises I'm talking about. Do you want me to know?'

He was about to give way and tell her everything, but a saucepan boiled over at that moment. By the time she'd mopped up the mess and thrown the cloth in the sink, she saw that the confessional moment had gone, and his barrier was up again.

Gerard wanted to talk. Ann and he had always talked all those years ago, every time either was troubled or frightened about work or exams, or needed their eyes drying after another relationship had crashed, or even filled with the angst of growing old at twenty-two. Now, though, his problems and his guilt felt too large and too much his own.

He longed for the barrier of the years to crumble, but despite their surface closeness, he and Ann had a lot of ground to make up. He was surprised how fond of her he still was and how easy some things were between them, but there was still some distance to cover.

CHAPTER 17

Far away from the Oxfordshire dusk, the eternal lights shone from the blue tower in Lillie Road. An officer standing at one of the windows on the twenty-fifth floor looked down at the dusky street. Not knowing who it was, he watched Arnold stride home from his day at the print shop. He spat as he passed the block. It was lit up on all floors, the machine as busy as ever. In truth, Arnold had no clue what they actually did there, but he had ideas aplenty about its role. He would never know, of course, if he was right, but that never mattered. His own ideas were enough to make him shudder and spit. Within a few seconds he was out of sight of the watcher up high.

He felt like having a social night tonight. Life was good – his latest poem was completed, and he'd earned a night out. He headed towards the Blackbird on Earl's Court, a grin breaking up his beard for no other reason than an overall sense of wellbeing. Somehow even at this frantic time of evening, he had no trouble walking between the crowds. Commuters and drifters, whether facing him or with their backs towards him, seemed to part in time for him to pass through them without his having to think or try. He was just at the doors of the pub when a tiny, diffident voice greeted him.

'Arnold?'

He recognised the tone: before he looked down he knew what he would see.

''Allo, Kate?' he replied. 'Got time for a bevvy, then? I'll buy.'

She was shivering, but whether from fear, illness or the cold night, he couldn't tell. He knew it was cold, because he liked watching the patterns of his breath condensing in the air, but he didn't feel the cold himself very much. Kate had got so thin lately that she could probably never feel warm. She would probably never feel relaxed or happy again, either, he thought. Still, not his problem.

She followed him through to the bar and found a table while he bought her a vodka.

The barman, an Australian, nodded at Arnold.

'Right, Arnie? What's goin' on?' gesturing towards Kate. 'She can't do her business in here, mate, you know that?'

'No, Kev, don't worry. Poor kid's frozen, I'm just gettin' 'er a drink, nothin' else.'

'It ain't right, she's much too young to be on the game. Why aren't the police or social services or someone lookin' after them? Catch a girl like that in Melbourne or Sydney? No way.'

'Do you want to give 'er a job here? Be safer for 'er.'

'Nah, bad news, mate, bad news gettin' mixed up there.'

'Just what I thought, yeah. But a mate's got the bit between 'is teeth and wants to 'elp 'er get away.'

'Good luck to him if he manages that, but keep me out of it.' He took the drinks across to where she was sitting.

''Ow you doin', then? Still 'ere?'

She started when he said that and glanced around, her eyes wide, looking for Mahmoud.

'What's happening?' she asked. Her voice whined pathetically; he wished she would grow some hard edges, and sound a bit gutsier. That whinge reminded him too much of his wife complaining about his obsession with poetry before she cured him of herself.

Kate coughed and leaned forward to whisper. 'What's happened to him? Is he out yet?'

'Gerald? Yeah, he's gone away.'

Kate shrivelled in front of him.

'What do you mean? He can't have gone. He was helping me, he can't have gone.'

'Nah,' Arnold reassured her, his fist enclosing his pint glass with comfort, 'he'll be back soon. Just gone visiting, that's all. 'E won't forget you, don't worry. He's a daft bloody pillock, ole Gerald, 'e won't back down on you. So, what's up with you these days?'

He noticed that she wasn't carrying any obvious bruises, so hopefully Mahmoud had not identified her yet. That was good, anyway.

'I want to get out. He said he'd get me out. When's he coming back?'

'You really goin' to scarper?' he asked. 'Where you going, then?'

'Shh!' she hissed, below the general noise. 'Don't say that, he'll hear. He'll kill me, he will. I'll never get out of here. He was going to help me. When's he back? Where's he gone?'

''E'll be back, don't worry. Give him a chance, he got a hell of a beating from your mate, when all's said and done.'

Somehow, he noticed, that didn't seem to reassure her. After another two vodkas, she left him and returned to the street, ready to prepare for the evening.

It was too early to expect customers, but she couldn't stay in her room any longer. Since Arnold brought her the money and message from Gerard when he was in hospital, her room had shrunk and grown darker. She didn't doubt him anymore – Arnold had soon talked her out of those suspicions, but she feared Mahmoud's anger even more.

Just a few days ago the entrance to the tube station had suddenly looked too tempting, and maybe like a possible escape route after all? She hesitated and lingered, looking through at the steps and the dribble of people coming and going. For just a moment she thought she could, but then came his voice just behind her left shoulder:

'Kate, you got money for me?'

She knew he meant something more than the usual, and it was obvious why he was asking.

'Money? No, Mahmoud, I give you all I got last week.'

'You got no extra? Don't hold out on me, you cow, or you're dead. Got my money?'

Somehow she kept her pretence.

'Honest, I haven't got nothing. I give it all to you.'

'What business you doing, then?'

'All right. Nothing much, but it's all right.'

'Who's been talking to you, then?'

'When? There's hundreds of people here, some of 'em talk. Who do you mean?'

'You know who I mean, you bitch. Don't you talk to no one, or I'll mark you. You know what I mean.'

He was only fishing. He knew one of his girls was ready to talk and then do a runner, but not which one. He must be having this same conversation fifty times, or a hundred times or … Kate had no idea how many girls he ran; sometimes he seemed to own the whole world, but maybe it was just her whole small world. She knew how frightened she sounded and wondered that he didn't see straight through her. But then, these days she was always frightened.

As he turned abruptly and walked off she breathed again, in relief. She headed towards the Brompton Road and the cemetery, a spot she always saw as her sanctuary. Mahmoud, Dave and Farid were never likely to be seen in here, and she could sit on one of the benches along the paths and truly relax. There was no sense of morbidness in the attraction, just peace and beauty, neither of which found a way into her life anymore.

Now, some days later, she dreaded staying in her damp room. She didn't sleep well at the best of times, but now she woke at three every morning, her heart racing in alarm at … what? There was nothing different, yet she felt shock every time consciousness returned. Her heart pounded too much at night for her to sleep with any comfort before about two. Small wonder she wasn't seeing many punters these days – there was less and less for them to spend their money on. She tried, oh yes, she tried to give them all manner of pleasure and excitement, but her natural appeal was fading almost beyond recognition.

If only he'd come back with the money. She wouldn't hesitate this time but be on a train up north in minutes. As soon as Mahmoud's back was turned, she'd be up to Manchester, or Glasgow, or Edinburgh, or somewhere far off where he'd never track her down again. If only that guy would come back soon. She had no idea what to do when she got to wherever it was, but if only she could get away, that would sort itself out later.

CHAPTER 18

Arnold left the Blackbird to head back to Philbeach Gardens. The early crowds were thinner, and he strode through them without noticing. The four pints he'd already drunk confirmed his mellowness, and he beamed at the world as he passed it by. Yes, poor old Kate was a worry, but not his worry. If Gerald wanted to interfere, well that was Gerald's business. Arnold had too many other things on his plate to take everyone else's troubles on board.

Once inside the house, he ran up the stairs to his flat. Before he could close the door behind him, another greeting reached him.

'Arnold?'

This voice didn't whine, and he was always glad to hear it.

'Wotcha, Shelagh. Comin' in for a quickie then?' And he laughed loudly. She laughed with him and followed him in. Contrary to his implied promise, he put on a kettle while she spread herself out on his worn sofa.

'Where have you been, Arnold? You're late tonight.'

'Just stopped off at the Blackbird. You know how it is. What you been up to yourself? You don't look like it's a full moon or nothing.' Shelagh glanced down at her baggy navy blue jumper and agreed.

'Not tonight, no, you won't get weird, disturbed dreams. Well, not from me, anyway.'

'Don't you bet,' he leered. 'You always give me weird dreams.'

'Pervert,' she said, contentedly. She took off her pink-rimmed glasses and rubbed her eyes. 'I'm too knackered anyway to concentrate on rituals tonight. Must be getting old now I've passed the big three-oh.'

'Don't look a day over forty,' Arnold reassured her as he passed her a cup of coffee. Decaffeinated, she always insisted, and he sat on the floor by the small gas fire with his own mug full of strong black.

'I don't get it,' he said, 'if you're meant to be this witch, like, what're you doing raising your spirits or whatever you do, here? Why aren't you out in the country like, back to your real nature, or at least out on Hampstead 'eath?'

'Hampstead Heath's getting that busy on full moon nights, you need a ticket like at the supermarket deli counters. Doesn't matter where I am, I can still make contacts.'

'Who with?'

'The Goddess,' she said simply. Arnold just raised his eyebrows sceptically and buried his nose back in his steaming mug.

'Come on, you know you're never going to believe me unless you try it yourself, and I'm not letting you in on my rituals until you really try to believe me.'

'So 'ow long have you been doin' all this stuff, then?'

'Hmm, about three years.'

'And you're still living in a bedsit like this? Don't seem to be doing you that much good. Why ain't you won millions on the lottery, and have your own temple, like?'

'Magic doesn't work like that. You should know, I've told you that before often enough. You're starting to sound like my parents. They always get at me for my beliefs. "Not how we brought you up," they say. "What's wrong with Church of England if you have to be religious?" I don't know. Do parents ever understand things?'

She changed the subject quickly to one that interested her more these days.

'Hey, what's happened to that friend of yours? Gerard?'

'Everyone's asking after him tonight. 'E's gone off with some friends down the country, that's all I know. He'll be back sometime. Why?'

'I don't know. I just had the feeling we'd see more of him, and then when you told me about his mugging, I just wondered. Bumped into him at the Troubadour a little while back and just thought he'd be around more, that's all …'

'Oh, he's all right. Ok bloke, he'll be back. Do you fancy him then?'

'Not really. He looks nice and vulnerable, I always like that in a man. Means they'll let me get on with what I like rather than risk being kicked out. I like to be shown a bit of respect.'

'Like to be boss, you mean.'

She considered for a moment then, 'Yes,' and they both laughed.

'Pity,' he said, 'I could really fancy you myself if it wasn't for that.'

'No chance. I'd rather just come and bum some coffee off you. No, I don't fancy him exactly, but there's something about him. He's got power. I could feel it in him that night. I think he might be one of us.'

'Us?'

'You know, a witch or something like that.'

'Gerald? Nah, shouldn't think he's the type.'

'Do you think he'll let me give him a tarot reading when he's back? I want to know more about him. Hey, have you written me any poems yet?'

'Not yet. Don't worry, one day I'll write you a great poem, all about you, and how sexy you are, and what I'd do if you'd let me.'

'Careful, or I'll turn you into a toad after all. No, when you write my poem I want some respect. And no taking the piss out of my being a pagan. Whatever you think, that's sacred.'

'OK, but if you're going to take that line, you've got to pay.'

'Pay what?'

'Come and 'ave a drink out with me tonight. I feel like a night out, and I want a bit o' company. Coming?'

'Now?'

'Yeah, why not? Come on, we'll get a meal, pizza or Chinese or something. You on?'

'You bet, I'm starving, and it's not payday for a few days yet.'

'That's no good, you're paying, didn't I say?' Shelagh threw a cushion at him.

As they walked to the tube to head up to the West End, they passed another familiar figure.

'Hey, Arnold, mate?' it whined. 'How you doin'?'

'Oh not now, Jez,' Arnold growled. He was looking forward to a good evening with Shelagh, and he knew how easily if he was allowed, Jez could leech onto them and spoil the mood.

'Come on, man, don't be like that!'

'Not tonight, Jez,' broke in Shelagh. 'Piss off, there's a good boy. Tell you what, call tomorrow, I'll talk to you then.'

'I might not want to tomorrow, you know?' protested Jez, slurring hurt dignity. 'Hey, can you lend me some bread? Just to get into town. A couple of quid will do, honest. Make it ten, just to be sure, Ok?'

Arnold was about to protest again, but Shelagh dived into her handbag and produced a £5 note.

'Here, Jez, take that and do what you've got to do, right?'

'Great, Sheil, great. You're a mate, you know that? I'll pay you back tomorrow, straight up.'

With the cash, Jez moved off and left the two of them. He'd not expected to need to travel back to Piccadilly yet, but he was losing control over the money. It should have lasted him at least another week, or until he got a job. Somehow though, it seemed to have trickled away before he was ready, and he had to try for some more.

The tube was busy, still, but that was good. If there were crowds around now, there was money around too; megabucks, probably. Some of it must come his way tonight, one way or another. Why shouldn't it? He was just as entitled as the bastards who had got it.

He clung onto the rail by the door area of the train, crushed by swaying bodies. He felt eyes on him and looked blankly at the ceiling until the eyes released him. As he swayed with each bump and roll of the train, he could feel the jacket of the man next to him through his own coat. Years of practice had taught him to detect the shape of wallets, cheque books, notebooks, diaries and all sorts of clutter that people carried in their pockets. Wherever the bulk of his mind was, at least a part of it rummaged through strangers' pockets and their bags. Most bystanders missed this part of his activity and just registered the empty eyes rolling around in their sockets independently of each other.

As the rumbling train pushed him up against the man, his hand, hidden by both their bodies, moved more adroitly than seemed possible and put the fat pigskin wallet into his own coat pocket. His eyes didn't flicker, his colour didn't change, his swaying, hanging body never lost its rhythm for a beat. His victim, in his twenties and out on the pull with fifteen new, crispy £10 notes, recoiled from the stale reek that accompanied Jez wherever he went. He glanced with distaste at the thin, grubby face, framed by the ratty black hair, but said nothing. Jez looked like he was miles away in his own world – and so he was. Soon he would find he was £150 richer in there, too.

At Victoria they both left the train. The half of his mind which still lived in his body wondered, as it had done for years, why that platform always smelled of stale cooking. His victim walked briskly through the crowds in front of him, eager to escape the degenerate. Jez carefully avoided watching him out of the corner of his eye and instead let him vanish towards the Victoria Line platform, eager to reach the wild West End clubs.

It looked like being another good night, if he was only careful. He didn't usually strike so lucky so early. If he was canny, he could get another half dozen or so before it was time to come home. He wouldn't need to give up the smack yet, he had a reprieve.

Shelagh pushed her plate away contentedly.

'Why am I here, Arnold?'

'Do you mean, like, "In the Beginning ..."?'

'No. Why have we just had this meal? I was going to have a quiet night in, sprawled in front of the telly and kidding myself I was about to go and do something productive. Instead, I've lost a fiver to Jez, let myself in for at least a morning of listening to him promising to reform and lost all chance of going and doing something productive. How did you do that? And why?'

Arnold shrugged. 'I suppose me natural charm is just too strong, innit? No, just time for a good night out. Pizza place, what better razzle than that, eh?'

'Where are we off to now, then? Too late for a show, isn't it? Movie? Gig? Night club? Moonlit walk along the Embankment? Where are you going to carry me off?'

''Ow about the 'Ilton, or Savoy? Usual place at the Ritz? Nice comfy beds there.'

'Forget it. Treat me like a lady, not a lay.'

'All right, then, what do you fancy? Music? Who's on at the Town and Country, then?'

'Let's have a look. Come on, we'll split the meal. Here's my cut.'

'Cheers, ok then. Let's hit the town then, Sheil!'

Time Out magazine gave them a view of who was playing where that night. Shelagh spotted a listing for a pagan group she'd seen at Glastonbury earlier in the year, and Arnold cheerfully went along with the idea.

He sniffed as they went into the hall at the bottom of the stairs – the smell of burning grass tugged at his nostrils, and he grinned broadly. As his eyes got used to the gloom, he switched off from the loud thud of the band's rhythm and looked around for whoever was smoking. Then he changed focus and just looked around for someone who wasn't sharing a joint and actually saw one or two.

He tugged on Shelagh's arm and pulled her to beside a group busy skinning up. She followed obediently, but her attention was on the stage where the two singers had broken into a loud monotone chant in invocation of the woodland deities.

The melamine tabletops vibrated in sympathy with the underlying drum and bass beats, and the smoke-clouded air shimmered with the insistent force of the cry for nature's liberation. She closed her eyes, swaying in time to the voices, and felt herself back in the huge throng in the fields outside Glastonbury where this same band had led ten thousand into the same chant. The sweetness of the dope in her nose reinforced her memory. It grew suddenly stronger, and Arnold's voice broke into her reverie:

''Ere, Sheil, have a blow.'

Shelagh opened her eyes to see a large joint waving in front of her. It was hot and strong and took her throat unawares. After the coughing subsided, she enjoyed two or three more deep drags before handing it back to its creator.

She clung onto Arnold's arm and, eyes closed again, swayed to the music which had moved back to the verse. She knew having a smoke might be a bit risky, seeing that she had to be fit for her library work next morning. But what the hell, it was a night off for both of them. She listened to the words, tracing the path through the woodland, and set herself to follow it, through wilderness and growth, through barren winter and spring's renewal. She was skilful enough at visualisation for the imagery to be as vivid behind her eyelids as the clubroom was in front of them. The hallucinogen in her blood heightened the scene, so that soon it took life independently of the song.

A small part of her registered that the band had finished and were acknowledging the applause. The rest of her journeyed through the dark forest, deeper and deeper, away from the airy world, to find a guardian. She smelled wet moss and felt the softness under her feet. Streams of sunlight burst through the treetop canopy and dappled the undergrowth. From time to time the sunbursts landed on her face, and she broke into perspiration. She felt a towering presence in front of her, still hidden in the shadows of the massive trees. It was the guardian she had sought on this journey; she had been seeking it for several months, but it had always eluded her. Now it was calling her, but she had just enough sense left to know that a crowded club and a bloodstream full of hashish were entirely the wrong circumstances in which to follow the call.

She tried to come back to the music with Arnold holding tightly onto her, and the band now loudly playing a different song, but the woodland had become more real to her than the rest. She again heard the voice calling to her from the dark of the wood, luring her on, and she tried to stop herself moving towards it. Her feet started to walk further away from the light and from the world. A tug at her arm and shoulder pulled her back, and she felt herself trip, then fall down and down, until Arnold's voice broke through the forest clamour.

'Sheil? This way up, come on girl!' She opened her eyes, then closed them again as the room lurched. As soon as she shut her eyes, the forest reasserted itself; as soon as she opened them she saw the carpet spin around in all directions, and nausea gripped her.

'Outside,' she managed to croak.

'Bloody 'ell, and 'appy birthday to you an' all,' Arnold muttered as he grasped her under the armpits and tugged her towards the door. It wasn't an easy journey as she was mostly dead weight, and the floor was full of bodies dancing to the rhythms of the band who knew how to play an audience as well as they played their instruments.

He got her to the outside at last, and she leaned against the wall, sweating and gulping air.

'They wasn't that bad,' Arnold told her. 'Some of their songs were ok, I thought.' She smiled, weakly.

'They're good, yeah. It's not them that made me sick.'

'Can't have been the shit, that was all right.'

'No, it wasn't the dope, it was me. What am I, Arnold? A stupid cow, that's me. Uh-oh, get back!'

He jumped away from her just in time, as the nausea resolved itself.

'Come on, let's find some clean pavement at least,' she offered. 'Sorry, Arnold, I've ruined the night, haven't I?'

'Nah, no worries. Let's face it, we'll remember tonight better for you puking up, won't we? Was it the nosh? I don't hold with all this healthy veggie stuff, it ain't good for you, I've always said it. If God had meant people to be vegetarian, he wouldn't have made butchers so healthy looking and ruddy now, would he? 'Ow you doing?'

'Bit better. I just feel stupid now, not sick, but I don't know it's an improvement. Can we go for a coffee somewhere?'

'No sweat. Come with me, then we'll take you home and tuck you up, like. Ok?'

They walked in the cold night air for a while, looking for somewhere quiet and clean-smelling for a coffee. Her vision had cleared with her stomach, and she cursed her stupidity. All the lessons she'd been told so strongly – and told others herself – about mixing drugs with magic, and what did she go and do?

'Is that Jez?' Arnold asked suddenly. She looked up and sure enough, on the other side of the road, oblivious to them, Jez was walking along with another man. Arnold didn't recognise the companion, but he guessed what Jez was at.

'I wondered if that's 'ow he did it,' he said.

'Did what?'

'Earned 'is junk. 'Ere, watch this.'

'No, don't!' Shelagh protested, but she was still too weak to be assertive. She was too late, anyway.

'Oy, Jez. What you doin' then?' Arnold's voice roared across the road. She watched Jez leap in panic and stare wildly around him. His alarm was mirrored by his companion, who twitched nearly three hundred and sixty degrees, on the qui vive for any assault or arrest. Arnold laughed loudly and pulled Shelagh along the pavement with him. There was nowhere for coffee that she could face, and soon they were closer to Earl's Court than town.

Back home, he sat Shelagh down while he made them both some tea. His own head had stopped floating as he'd helped her out of the club. It was a letdown but what the hell, it was only a night out after all. He'd have another one after his next poem.

Shelagh listened to the clatter in the kitchen and thought again of her stupidity. Sickness had given way to headache, and tomorrow she would be good for less than nothing. She wondered whether to ask Arnold now to ring in for her in the morning, or wait and see if she was better then. She doubted it – in her younger fitter days, tricks like tonight's could knock her out for twenty-four hours. Gods knew what she would go through now. She hadn't smoked for a long time, but she should have known perfectly well that if she were going to enjoy a joint, she should leave the psychic work alone. What was happening to her? She wished she had someone to talk to about it all. A face rose before her mind's eye – Gerard, the 'man of power'.

Why him? What did he have to do with her straying senses? She found him attractive yes, but that wasn't it. That sense of power, whatever it was, and he seemed sensitive with it. And yet he kept his secret and wouldn't give anything away about himself. She wished he was still around. He could help her. Maybe she could help him, too.

CHAPTER 19

Less than a mile away Jez stumbled back into his own room, disappointed and frightened. Arnold's startling appearance had frightened both him and his John, with the result that Jez found himself suddenly alone and made no more money that night.

He switched on his single bar fire and waited, shivering, until the cold of the near-winter night lifted, and he could take off his overcoat. Bloody Arnold and Shelagh. They were doing all right, why did they have to stop him? He wasn't harming them. A few more days, that's all he needed, a few days and a bit more bread, and he could give up the stuff. He didn't need it, no way, but he couldn't cut it out just yet. Give him a few days, but he needed the bread first. He nearly had it, as well, until bloody Arnold and Shelagh had got in the way.

He was hungry but didn't think there was anything in the kitchen and couldn't be bothered to look. He huddled up in front of the fire and wondered if he should take some more yet. He was running low and thought he might need it more in the morning. In his old familiar way, he gradually sank into apathy and then sleep, curled up foetally in front of the one glowing bar, wondering what to do about money and smack for the next day. A couple of feet away on the floor was his stained greatcoat and in the pocket, forgotten, a fat pigskin wallet.

He dreamed fitfully. In one dream, he was back at that strange cafe place with Gerald, the one with the grey concrete walls and all the posters. This time, when Gerald asked him to quit taking the smack, he did. The two of them walked to the river, and Jez stood proudly, shaking packet after packet into the water. In his dream he watched trout and salmon leap from the Thames and flit, shimmering silver, back and forth above the cerulean waters, stoned out of their gills on his stuff and refusing to return to the river. How he and Gerald laughed at the sight! Already in his dream, his greatcoat was clean and fitted him. His luxuriant hair blew in the river breeze, and Gerald tucked his arm through Jez's to lead him across Hungerford Bridge into a London that smiled and welcomed them both. Somewhere in his unconscious head, he was aware that Gerald wasn't really around now and hadn't been for several days. Before relapsing into the comfortable dream where he hoped he'd be back again soon, he had the thought that there was no other way he could quit the junk. Only Gerald could help him.

Along Earl's Court some of the girls on their vigil noticed a new man looking at them from a distance. A catalogue shopper, one of the girls called his sort. Look, think about it, and maybe even make a choice. Usually they chickened out and left after a quarter of an hour of agonising. Viv, the girl who came out with the phrase, had a theory that catalogue watchers were all virgins, otherwise why couldn't they come straight up to you?

This time, though, it was not a catalogue watcher who studied them. Yasser had always been aware of the prostitutes in the different areas of London, but had never taken notice of them before, except as sinners. Maybe they were to be pitied – in the abstract, of course – but they were still sinners. But that was changing. Gerard's story had forced him to look again at them. Unlike Gerard, he was firm and content in his faith. The Quran was a rock for him, unambiguous in its strength and truth. But he still lived in the 1990s and appreciated that its interpretation must reflect their world, as well as the Prophet's (Peace be upon him).

A new viewpoint had come to him now, through meeting Gerard and learning a little more about this sinful world of men. He'd never studied a prostitute before. Which one was Kate? Yasser couldn't tell, but he looked at them as a connoisseur would study a painting. There was no eroticism in his study, and no fantasy; just a keen interest in another subspecies of the genus humanity that delighted and frightened him. He hoped Gerard would return soon. This priest had interested him, and he looked forward to talking more to him and showing him that Mahmoud and his type were nothing to do with Islam. He would be a truer representative, and Gerard could see that Islam was nothing to fear.

Nothing much seemed to be happening. The girls waited, passers-by passed by, traffic was less jammed and so became faster and more frightening. From time to time Yasser was unintentionally jostled by groups cramming the pavements as they wove their way through the evening's adventures while the leather boys walked along two by two on their way to the Coleherne.

London suddenly became an alien place to Yasser. He wasn't born there but had lived in the city for so long that he felt like a native. He knew its ways, and he knew his own people. Despite all the evidence, he believed in people's goodness and knew that the world was improving. Gerard's plight forced him to look at his home and discover that it was indeed a strange and frightening land. These girls, these sinners – even the ones who intimidated him with their brassy laugh and confidence – they were young girls, they were daughters and sisters. They were people. And they were frightened.

A strange emotion washed over Yasser. He felt anger, disgust and hatred, all for one man he had never met and, until last week, had never even known of. His fists and jaw tightened as he watched a young girl approach yet another hurrying man.

Come home, Gerard, come back. Show me Mahmoud. I'll help you, my friend.

CHAPTER 20

Safe with his friends in the Oxfordshire early-winter darkness, Gerard had no sense of being missed. He certainly didn't believe that Nick and Jenny missed him. Before his week was up he must talk with Ann about that. It hadn't occurred to him before how ungrateful he'd been to them for their hospitality; it shamed him and made him embarrassed to return.

He had to go back to Earl's Court, though. Kate still needed his help, and he didn't want to leave Arnold without at least a goodbye. And Yasser might be a good friend, if Yasser didn't think he was imposing. No, he couldn't vanish without a word. But what of Jenny and Nick who had offered him shelter and sanctuary without question and without stinting? Gerard flushed again as he remembered the eavesdropped conversation through the bedroom walls.

There was little enough he could offer them, apart from money; at least that wasn't a problem for him, not for a long time yet. But his life had diverged so much from theirs that he was at a loss how to return their generosity and kindness, and he felt more and more uncomfortable about it.

'They want to be closer to you, too,' Ann told him. She had just poured the two of them a flute of wine, and they were seated by candlelight. Joe would be home from work soon, but they had time for quiet talk now. 'You aren't making things easy for them, you know. Why can't you say what's going on?'

'Because I don't know how, Ann. That's the simple truth. There are a lot of things happening inside me, and they haven't finished yet. Added to that are the things outside me, like this beating up. I don't know what to say that doesn't sound like self-indulgence or a bad soap. After all, when I tried to talk to them about Mahmoud and the girls …'

'Your pimp?'

'Yeah, anyway, it turned into an argument, and I felt Jenny turning against me, so I stopped talking. They've helped bring me to harbour, but I'm not home and dry yet. They're lovely people, always were.'

'As well as heartless capitalist bastards …'

'That as well,' he grinned at her, 'but somehow I can't talk to them in my own vocab or on my own terms. Whenever I try to talk about my own work's concerns, there's just this polite incredulity or sense of being indulged. "Dear old Gerard, he's off on his thing again. Bring him back to the real world in a minute." I can hear them, Ann, even though they don't say it out loud, and I don't know how to talk to them anymore. And that's not to put them down, no.'

'Except for Nick and his pervy ways!'

'Well, maybe that. But that aside, I can't find much common ground apart from the old days. And at the outset, they did provide that harbour I needed without question, without delay and as the true friends we'd always been. It's just that I still find myself on rocky seas and can't tell them why. Sorry, the metaphor lost me there!'

'Can you tell me? Why do you need a harbour?'

'I'm afraid I'm losing my faith. I mean afraid, too. I can't talk to my mentor about it, because he'll try to excommunicate me and damn me all in one go. And I can't talk to Nick and Jenny, because they have no faith, except in money and their work, so they'll not understand the enormity. Ironic – Father Holloway would understand the enormity and not understand me, so I'm damned, and they'll understand me and not the enormity so I'm trivialised.'

'Try me, Ger. After all, I was brought up a good Catholic girl till I discovered sex. I might be able to understand both horns, as it were.'

Gerard sat and thought; his heart beat faster and he noticed himself tense up. For a moment he was yet again poised between confession and retreat. Ann reached across and took his hand. Hers was cool, and he trusted it. He returned the clasp and looked briefly at her.

'All right. I don't feel clever about it, and you won't admire me for it. But here goes. Let's start with Father Holloway. He's been my mentor for seven years now. I think he must have taken orders back in the time of the Inquisition – sometimes he looks that old. And his pronouncements, especially when I've done something he disapproves of which is most weeks, are purely medieval. He's barely cottoned on to the twentieth century yet, while the twenty-first is only just around the corner.

'He's a good man according to the book. Absolutely honest, full of integrity, knows his theology perfectly, and has an unerring sense of morality according to the truest Roman traditions. He would have made a good Inquisitor. Every word of the Mass and every movement absolutely choreographed; no variation, lest he displease the Lord and we all be damned. Variety and variation are the work of the Evil One.

'Any problems, I can always ask him, and he always makes time for me. Honestly, there's no way I can fault him. As a mentor he's perfect. But he terrifies me. I don't ask his advice if I can help it and nor do most of the parishioners; his theology is good, but he won't ever bend it to help a human problem. That's the Devil's temptation, he calls it. What God has laid down is right, however much it may hurt. Mere men, even priests, may not compromise it. That's his line. So when a parishioner called with a dilemma, it was me she spoke to, not Father Holloway.'

Gerard held out his glass for Ann to refill. His other hand still held hers tightly, and she made no effort to disengage.

'Interesting academic problem she brought me. Would the Church countenance contraception to prevent a life-threatening pregnancy? I would have consulted Father Holloway, but what's the point? We both knew what his answer would be. I'd just baptised this woman's baby daughter, so I asked her what she meant. Well, the woman had had a difficult labour which the doctors bodged. Poor devils had been working a nineteen-hour shift by the time it was her turn, and something went wrong. They saved the child, a beautiful little girl who is blooming. The whole thing damaged the woman's own system, though, and they told her that on no account should she become pregnant again. The trouble is, she's a good Catholic, and knows that that might be sinful. Hysterectomy is out, I don't know why but it seems to be; contraception is all that's left, but only if the Church will give her dispensation.

'I suggested a third, godly, option: abstinence. That would be the safest bet of all …'

'Oh great, a celibate man is in a fine position to preach that to the ordinary woman!'

'Turned out she'd tried that, but her husband didn't appreciate it. She was his wife, after all, and if he wanted to … you know, then he had every right. So he did.'

'Raped her?'

'Uh-huh. As you say, I could pontificate from my lofty position, but what sort of ice would that cut in that set-up? This was a special case, surely. Even Father Holloway must accept that this was out of the ordinary. How could God demand that Jane Conway must risk death, especially with such a lovely baby girl to look after?'

'You asked him?'

'I put the case in my most eloquent way. I didn't mention Jane by name for a long time, but posed the question and her circumstances as a hypothetical after-dinner discussion topic. I could have been a lawyer, I was so thorough and passionate in my pleading. No good. Poor Jane was dismissed as an unreconstructed whore of Babylon in a couple of sentences. I was a dupe and tool of the Devil, and must serve penances to keep my soul intact. I should go on a retreat to pray for understanding of God's moral Law, and also study about a dozen thick volumes from the seventeenth century onwards as well as a bundle of papal encyclicals. After all that, I may just be in with a chance of saving my soul from error.'

'That was what he said? What did you tell Jane?'

'Nothing doing. I kept the party line and told her not to even think about committing such gross sin. Father Holloway approved, and I felt my own salvation was that bit more secure. Some months later, Jane called me again, distraught and terrified. She'd followed my injunctions and was pregnant. This was urgent now – could she have a dispensation for an abortion? Surely that would be possible in order to save her life?'

'But why didn't she just go and get an abortion? She didn't need your say so, for goodness' sake.'

'Like I said, she was a good Catholic. It really meant everything to her, and she couldn't consider acting without the Church's sanction. She feared for her soul more than her life, yet she was terrified for her life.'

'Did you ask Father Holloway again?'

'Yes, but I knew what he would say. Sure enough, he was angry with me for even thinking it, and I should tell Jane "no" in no uncertain terms. Hating myself, I told her that it was too great a sin. She should put her trust in God, and he would protect her. Some sins were too gross to be forgiven, and the killing of a child in the womb was one of the grossest. She must pray and the Lord would protect her if she put her trust in Him. He wouldn't let her down. She was a good Catholic. She obeyed me, her infallible priest, the voice of God's justice and mercy.

'She obeyed me and died in labour. The baby died too. God forgive me, she obeyed me, and they both died. Father Holloway told me I was right and that she was right. He told me she was with God and Christ, because she stayed true to her faith and the Law.'

'I don't think God will forgive him,' put in Ann.

'But it was me she came to, Ann, and I failed her. I couldn't see what was wrong with what she asked. She wanted to live, to raise and care for her daughter, and I killed her. I killed her, because I was afraid of Father Holloway. I never thought she was a sinner – she wasn't, Ann, she was never a sinner, but I was too cowardly to save her. And how can I ever follow a Church that made me condemn a woman and mother like that? And how can God or anyone forgive me such cowardice?'

'Gerard, oh Gerard, come here!' Ann, tears on her cheeks, pulled him to his feet and put her arms round his neck. He held tightly onto her as the grief and guilt of that time poured from him. He sobbed loudly, uncontrollably, at the fresh realisation that Jane had trusted him, had trusted him to death. Against him, he was aware of Ann crying too, in sympathy with him and with Jane, whom she had never met. Her own belief had long since faded, but she knew what racked him, and she grieved with him.

They stood like that for a long time, until the noise of their grief subsided and was succeeded by a calmer, more peaceful, feeling. He didn't want to let go. Jenny had kissed him chastely on the cheek, and hugged him briefly, but no one held him like this, as though they meant it, as though he mattered. And he didn't trust himself to let go. So they stood there in the dim light, as the candle grew shorter and shorter, arms tightly round each other.

At about the same time, they became aware that they were not alone. They had no idea how long Joe had stood watching them.

When Ann realised he was there, she stretched an arm out to him. As he came closer, he saw the tear tracks on their faces in the candle's glow. Gerard also held out an arm, and he slipped between them, a brawny arm around each. He gripped Gerard extra tightly for a moment in reassurance, and at this, Gerard felt something inside him click as if a lock had opened. The three of them stayed there, holding onto each other tightly as the candle guttered to the end of its life.

CHAPTER 21

On Sunday morning Gerard gazed out at the mist-sodden fields rocking past the train window. Joe and Ann had promised to see him again soon, but it was time now to return to Kensington and the crusade. He knew that he had a retreat there whenever he needed it, and he felt refreshed and, for the moment at least, ready for action.

He was less sure of his welcome in Kensington. He didn't know that Ann had already spoken to Jenny and given her some idea of what had tormented Gerard. Instead, angry whispers through the bedroom wall, and apologetic absences in order to lay off more employees across the country populated his thoughts of Nick and Jenny's house.

The train journey to Victoria was swift, and the dank weather didn't hold up their progress. Once at Victoria, Gerard took a tube to Kensington. This time he needed his heavy coat to keep himself warm, and his luggage was much lighter than a month previously. Even the platform with the kitchen smell was cold, and he huddled by the wall with a handful of other travellers.

The tube carriage was only half full. For the most part, his fellow passengers were absorbed in newspapers or their tinny clanking headphones. Two men, possibly in their forties, and sitting side by side near the door, were playing some game together: they seemed to take it in turns to look furtively at the other's face and quickly look forward when the other turned. Gerard watched, wondering if it were some form of pickup. The men looked very similar, down to the colour of their clothes and their stubbly cheeks, and he couldn't believe they were strangers.

And then one of them tried to suppress a smile, which triggered the other. Both laughed, and one leaned forward to mutter in the other's ear. They got off together at Sloane Square, and Gerard watched in a strange fascination.

The other passengers paid no attention to the private play he'd spied. Most of them paid no attention to anything in the train outside of a book or the free magazine. Three, like him, had luggage with them. None had any aliveness or anticipation in their eyes, only a travelling emptiness. As he scanned his fellow passengers, he saw with a jolt that a pair of eyes returned his look, steadily and with a trace of amusement, or was it mockery?

He made himself hold the look rather than scoot his eyes down. It was a woman, but how old, or young, he couldn't say. Maybe in her thirties, he thought. What made him look at her so closely? They breached all the usual etiquette of avoidance on the tube, but something about her caught at Gerard; he wanted her to look away again for a few minutes so he could study her discreetly, but she kept looking back at him.

She didn't lose her half-smile; his returned gaze hadn't shaken her composure. She could be a poker player, he thought wryly. He smiled back openly at her in acknowledgement and then let his own eyes move on, feeling he'd somehow scored a point in a game he hadn't even entered. What on earth was he coming to?

There was something different about this woman, though. Her coolness, for one thing. Gerard had grown used to the various tribal appearances in London. He may not have known the names and rules of the tribes, but at least he now recognised the shaven heads, the coloured dreadlocks, the black-and-silver goths, the black-and-painted pagans, the respectably suited, the leathers, denims, Armani, casual smart and casual scruffy, the plain and the gaudy, the anonymous and the beckoning. He was always exhilarated by the richness of the tribes. As to where he stood, he always felt that he was anonymous and casual, the least interesting and satisfying of them all. Which, perhaps, was partly why he responded so strongly to the woman's notice of him – the simple novelty of another person, female at that, noticing him on a tube train!

That was not all. Almost like an anthropologist or a spectator at the bars of a monkey cage, she looked from one traveller to another – looking, taking in, then unhurriedly and utterly unselfconsciously, moving on to the next. Pause, look and evaluate? Then on to the next and the next.

Where did she fit into his tribal categories? Certainly not anonymous and certainly not scruffy. She wore a short black leather coat with very tight black denims. They looked new and unmarked, and he suspected that for however long she wore them they would never look faded or scruffy. Her fingers, wrists, ears and throat were rich with jewellery, mostly chunky silver, but also cloisonné set in broad findings. And yet, her own frame was slim. Such heavy jewellery ought to have looked excessive on her, but somehow it didn't. Her face, pierced at her nose and the edge of her lip, was winter pale, making the shock of her auburn hair even more startling.

Gerard looked sideways, waiting for her scrutiny to return to him, but it didn't. He watched her through Earl's Court and South Kensington until Notting Hill Gate, when she stood and waited for the doors to open.

On impulse, he followed, and left the train by the next door down. Appalled at his behaviour and excited by new sensations, he followed many yards behind, but made sure that she was still in his sight.

Another thing pleased him – she was a fast and smooth walker. Her body moved efficiently, so that with little apparent effort she quickly covered a great deal of ground. He didn't know why he was following her, just that he didn't want to lose sight of her. What was her voice like? How and where did she live and with whom?

He found himself making up a biography for her and stopped in alarm. What was he, Father Gerard Tisserant, doing thinking like this about any woman, let alone a complete stranger whose morality was as yet, decidedly ambiguous?

As he stopped, so did she, and then she climbed four steps up to the front door of a large block and pressed on the intercom. As she waited for a response, she looked along the road and saw Gerard staring at her. She stared back at him, still impassive, until the door opened, and she went in, out of his sight.

He didn't tell Jenny and Nick about this escapade. All the way to their house he cursed himself for stupidity and weakness and – here it was again – sin.

Jenny welcomed him so enthusiastically that he forgot he'd been nervous of returning. Very quickly though, guilt at his poor guestpitality swept over him, and he resolved to be more grateful and attentive to them.

She sat him down with a large scotch and told him all about Glasgow, the theatre and the galleries she'd visited, and how much more vital a place it was since her first visit, years before. She asked him about his time with Ann, telling him how wonderful Ann was looking, how sweet Joe was, and what an extraordinary coincidence it had been bumping into Ann like that in Knightsbridge, almost like fate. Gerard remained discreet.

Nick poured him another whisky, and said,

'Hey, Gerard, listen, you'll like this: A guy goes into a bar, orders twelve scotches and starts knocking them back as fast as he can. The barman says, "Hey, why are you drinking so fast?" The bloke says, "You'd drink this fast if you had what I've got." The barman says, "Why, what have you got?" The guy says, "50 pence!"' and he laughed loudly, inviting Gerard to join him.

He poured a large one for himself and then found it hard to say very much at all.

Bit by bit, Gerard grew less and less comfortable as the afternoon wore on in a fine malt haze.

'She's coped so wonderfully, don't you think? And Joe too, of course,' Jenny said later, in the evening, as they relaxed after another of her triumphant meals.

'Coped?'

'Well, I know it was all a long time ago of course, but they have coped well, you must admit it.'

'With what? I don't know what happened.'

'Didn't she tell you?'

'Of course she didn't,' broke in Nick, with a whisky truculence, 'he'd know what you meant if she had.'

'Oh shit. I should have kept quiet, shouldn't I? Sorry, Gerard, I thought she'd have told you.'

'Well, are you going to leave me in the dark? What happened to them?'

'Go on, Jen. You've started this, you carry on.'

Jenny prepared herself for a dramatic tale. Through his worry, Gerard could see the theatricality in her deep breath, her glances around the room, her upright pose and wide-eyed sympathetic gaze. Of course, her heart most probably did go out to Ann for the distress she'd suffered, but another part of her clearly relished telling the story.

'She met Joe when, eleven years ago?'

'Something like that. Married sometime after.'

'Yes. And of course, already pregnant.'

Gerard sat up in surprise. This part was news to him.

'Poor Ann wasn't too sure about that. She had her career, and motherhood was never that hot a priority with her, was it?'

He nodded, remembering student Ann's denunciations of women who lost their lives and prospects through breeding too early. Breeding at all in some cases, he remembered.

'Well, she wasn't the most pleased of expectant women, but Joe, ah, Joe was in very heaven. Sorry, Gerard, I'm on your pitch here, aren't I? Well, he wanted nothing more than a happy, healthy, bouncing baby boy, unless it was a happy, healthy, bouncing baby girl. He didn't really care which. He and Ann were producing issue – that was the big part of it all, they were having a baby! I don't think I've ever seen a man so smug and pleased with himself. In some ways it was quite sickening.'

'Come on, Jen, you were doing some frantic knitting yourself, as I remember. You frightened me, you were getting so broody.'

'Balls! We were already quite busy enough then with James. Sorry Gerard. Well, maybe just a touch broody, but that was just solidarity with Ann, nothing to do with Joe. Anyhow, Gerard, you get the picture don't you? Rustic idyll, wife up the spout and giving up her career, husband as chuffed as you can imagine, and both of them earning next to zilch, Joe having passed up on the chance of working for the oil millions. So far so good. And now we move on to Act Two. Ann miscarries.'

'No!'

'True. And very nasty it was too. There was something wrong with the pregnancy itself. I never learned all the gruesome, squelchy gynaecology of it, but it made a hell of a mess of her, and she was very ill for a long time. They told her never, ever to have another child as it would probably kill her.'

'So did they give her a hysterectomy?'

'They suggested it, in fact strongly recommended it, but she really didn't want to go down that route. Afraid of more surgery, and I don't blame her.'

'So what happened?'

'Dear Joe saved the day. Had the snip, the unkindest cut of all.'

'Made a vas deferens to him, as well!'

'Yes, Nick darling, thank you for that contribution. Anyway, Gerard, rather than risk Ann's health, and rather than gamble on her never forgetting the pill, he rubbished forever his chances of conceiving again. Ever. And considering that's why he married her, and he was so excited at the thought of being daddy, I thought that was rather remarkable.'

Gerard could see the three of them standing together in the soft candlelight of the farmhouse – the tear tracks on Ann's face as she held him for comfort and the feeling of Joe's massive presence as he came forward to join in their embrace, in mourning for Jane Conway. And also, he'd just discovered, for their only child.

CHAPTER 22

Gerard was surprised how much he enjoyed coming back to London. His week in the country had lifted much of his tension and unhappiness; London's light and bustle exhilarated him again and brought another part of him back to life. The jostle of crowds moving past him as they forced their way to the tubes and buses gave him an extra awareness and edge.

He started to wonder, too, where he would spend this Christmas. For the first time in years he wouldn't officiate or assist at any Mass or service. That hurt him. It was a surprise, but it pained him to realise how he'd separated himself even from that. No way would Father Holloway let him back in just for Christmas to do the business and then go away again. No, he must reconcile himself to being an outcast this year. Was that so bad? Wasn't Christ an outcast himself during his few years? Especially that first Christmas?

That may have been true, but it didn't cheer Gerard at all.

He wondered, too, about his life in London. To return felt like coming home, but Kensington wasn't his home – and neither were Nick and Jenny home. He must speak with them soon and make a decision.

The place he felt most at home was around Arnold and his circle. But that took him close to Mahmoud and danger. He hadn't dared go back to the area since his return from the country, but perhaps it would be time soon.

And then again, to his alarm, he remembered the woman from the tube train. The Notting Hill Woman, he dubbed her. What was

Gerard, Father Gerard, sinless Father Gerard, doing thinking about such a woman all the time? What was he doing looking along the carriage of each train he was on, in case she was there? Her world and his were too far apart for him to even remember her!

It took Gerard several attempts to reach Earl's Court. Each time he walked towards it, he would veer away towards Cromwell Road or Fulham, or double back to Kensington. Each time his tube train pulled up at the station, he froze and looked down in shame until the doors closed and he was carried away from Mahmoud and danger.

At last he nerved himself for a coffee at the Troubadour. It seemed a positive compromise, or at the least, like dipping a big toe into the water. It was close enough to feel like Earl's Court, but removed enough to feel a tiny bit safer. He could look out through the window at the fading afternoon light. Soon it would be gloomy enough for the street lights to shine yellow, but at the moment the day was still just young enough to cope with its own illumination.

He was enjoying the coffee, watching the chess players slap the timers on their clock, would-be writers scribbling in their notebooks and people walking by the shedding trees outside, when a voice brought him back to the room.

'Hello again, Gerard. Is this always our meeting place, then?'

He looked up, startled, at the tall smiling woman with unruly dark hair and pink-rimmed glasses.

'Shelagh! Hello, hello.'

He stood to greet her and insisted on buying her a coffee. When they were both seated again, she started her eager interrogation.

'So how long have you been around? Arnold didn't say you were back.'

He gave her a brief account of his time in Oxfordshire, omitting his confession.

'But Arnold told me you'd been beaten up, mugged was it?' She looked earnestly concerned, and he felt drawn to tell her something of the story of Kate and Mahmoud. He kept his voice low, not wanting to be overheard, and she had to lean forward across the table to hear him so that her hair almost brushed his face.

'That's incredible,' she said, 'I mean, you actually challenged him? That is so brave, so cool.'

'So stupid,' he said, 'as Arnold and others have told me.'

'But I never even knew someone like him was running things here. I suppose I never thought about it really, it's all around so you never notice, you know?'

'Are you free tonight?' she suddenly asked. 'Come and eat, and you can tell me more easily than here. I'm not a great cook, but I do a mean beans on toast.'

'That's kind of you,' he exclaimed in surprise. Then he remembered himself and his promises about Jenny and Nick. 'Look, I can't do tonight, but does the offer stand for tomorrow? I'd love to.' So the next night, honour and courtesy satisfied with Jenny and Nick, he returned to the house in Philbeach Gardens. This time it was to see Shelagh, but he had hopes of seeing Arnold as well.

As she let him in with a welcoming smile and a kiss on the cheek (another surprise to him), he felt a stab of alarm as over her shoulder, he saw strange posters and a calendar. There was nothing remotely Christian in the images facing him. He could take the Earth Goddess style figures on the calendar, but the horned demon, cloven footed with bared teeth and surrounded by laughing children made his blood chill. A smell of incense, not one he recognised, hit his nose as soon as he came in.

No one else was there: it was to be a quiet meal for two. Surrounded by these images, he wondered whether Shelagh could be a devil-worshipper. And if she was, how could she be so open?

'What's up?' She had felt him recoil as she kissed him, and in her turn felt uncertain. She looked at his face and saw him gazing at her pictures.

'Don't you like them?' A naive question with a self-evident answer. 'I normally cover them up if I'm expecting someone who'll be fazed by them.' Flushed with embarrassment, and anger at her own embarrassment, she covered them with an Indian bedspread which fitted so well over the offending patch of wall that this was obviously its sole purpose.

They both tried to cover the awkward moment, but he couldn't forget the grinning demon face, and she couldn't forget his shocked face. It wasn't a good start, but they tried to mend the evening.

'Are you better now?' she asked. 'I mean, your face, after …'

'Yes, yes it's fine now, thanks.'

Another long pause.

'Did you have a good break?'

'Oh yes, I spent time with old friends. Haven't seen them for years.'

'Good.'

And another conversation bumped its nose on a wall at the end of a cul-de-sac. In his turn, Gerard tried to keep some light small talk going, but with the same lack of success.

It was a shame, because Shelagh had cooked a good meal for them, and Gerard recognised how he would have enjoyed it. As it was, they were polite, smiled a lot, forced laughs at nothing, and shrank separately in their chairs.

Predictably perhaps, it was Arnold who rescued the night. He knew Gerard was back, and Shelagh had told him of the meal. Incorrectly but luckily, he took that as an invitation to gatecrash at about the coffee-and-mints stage. Accordingly, as Gerard was wondering how to escape without offence, there was a hammering at the door, and Arnold's voice came through.

'Sheil? You there?' As if he didn't know.

'Gerald! Good to see you mate, 'ow you doin' now? 'Ow'd you get your feet under the table this soon? I've been tryin' bleedin' years.'

As on other occasions, Gerard felt a delighted relief with Arnold's appearance. Shelagh, who should have been angry with him if the night had gone to plan, grinned too with welcome reprieve. Suddenly, the posters and images went, and the room became just a room again, not a devil's den.

As always, without trying or thinking Arnold pushed the other two into the background as he enthused about his new poem and two new readers he'd heard at the Troubadour the week before.

'Class, that's what they've got. Real class. Not just a nice idea with no more thought, like a lot of the crap we get, but real crafted stuff. Fantastic lines, some of them!'

'So what did you come for, Arnold?' interrupted Shelagh. 'Was it me you wanted?'

'Sorry, mate, just got a bit of news. Old Ash, right? Well, he's going. Moving in with Darren at last, over in Fulham.'

'Really? That's a shame, I like Ash. Couldn't get Ray to move out instead, could you?'

'Ray?' asked Gerard.

'Him upstairs. You haven't met him have you? Not many people do.'

'Well, 'e ain't got much time for anyone else, 'as 'e? Bleedin' computer burpin' and fartin' all day and all night. Can't he get a life or somethin'?'

Shelagh shrugged.

'I'd sooner lose him than Ashley. Be a bit more peaceful at night. Who's moving in?'

'Dunno. Don't think he's told Dave yet.'

'Dave?' Gerard interrupted, remembering the muscled, tattooed giant standing beside Mahmoud.

'Landlord,' Shelagh said. 'You know – wicked, heartless type, out into the cold, cold snow sort of job.'

'Not really, he's a sight better than lots of 'em round 'ere.'

'I know,' she protested, 'I was joking! Actually he's a bit of a sweetie: retired teacher, and we're topping up his pension for him.'

'How much is the flat?' Gerard asked. There was a pause while they both looked at him.

'You serious? It ain't anything like Kensington, you know.'

'Would you rather I didn't? No, I know it's not a bit like Kensington. Let's face it, since I came to London I've spent more time this end than I have with Jenny and Nick. It's not fair to keep freeloading off them the way I have. I'd rather be settled before Christmas.'

'Come up and 'ave a look now, eh? Ash's in, I know.'

And that was it. Ashley invited them in, showed them the single room and kitchen, gave them coffee, and Gerard was welcomed as the new resident. Ashley just had one warning.

'This place, Philbeach Gardens, right? Is a hotbed of violence, you know.'

'What?'

'True – seven or eight years ago there was an armed siege here. Straight up, a guy from Edinburgh, escaped prisoner he was, got into a flat here and held them hostage. The siege lasted nearly two days. He was shot dead in the van after they caught him. So be warned, it's not always as lovely and peaceful as it looks. On the other hand, it's gorgeous in the gardens out back in summer. Do you play tennis? Plenty of chance for that when you're a resident.'

Jenny and Nick accepted his decision with congratulations and no obvious protest.

'You'll be more settled if you've got your own place,' Jenny assured him. 'We've loved having you here, and you know you're always welcome to come and see us. But if you're not going back to your parish, well, you're probably doing the right thing.'

'Go for it,' Nick urged him. 'You like that part, and there's masses of talent there.'

'Oh Nick!' Jenny turned away wearily.

He took them out for a huge meal the day before he moved. The talk was less constrained than it had been for some time, and Gerard recognised that all three felt a sense of release. Again, he remembered Jenny's angry voice muttering through the wall about his selfishness and lack of consideration. He'd wanted to make up for that, but it felt too late now.

Jenny gave him a hug and kiss the next morning before she set off to work, and he passed out of their life again with no clearer idea of his direction than when he'd reappeared all those weeks ago.

CHAPTER 23

Shelagh had taken the day off work to help him move in. Gerard was touched.

'Travel light, don't you?' she commented on his one suitcase.

'Oh, I've got more back home. I'll fetch some of it down in time. If I stay in London, that is.'

'Planning on leaving us already? That's mean.'

'No, no, I don't mean that. Well, I've got a lot of thinking to do about where I'm going in life. That's why I'm here – it was always temporary, but who knows?'

After most of his belongings were unpacked, hung up or displayed, she gave him a small package.

'Just a little welcome,' she said. 'I would have given you something else, but after the other night, I guess it would have been wrong.'

He took off the tidy wrapping to reveal a statuette, a Buddha. It was less threatening than the horned figure in her room, and he recognised that she wanted to give him something special and of spiritual significance. He grinned at the thought of Father Holloway's face.

'Thank you, Shelagh. This is really very kind of you. I didn't expect you to give me anything.'

'Well, you're our new member, we can't let that go unmarked, now, can we? I know you didn't like my posters, but, well, I hope he's more suited to you.'

'He may be. I must confess, I know very little about him. This is my background, you see.'

And he unpacked the last package from his case – his wooden crucifix, which he hung from the wall above his bed. Shelagh gasped in embarrassment.

'Oh no. Oh my God, I didn't even think of that.'

'Well, I'm in plain clothes these days, and in disgrace as well, truth be told.'

'Plain clothes? Are you a priest or something?'

'Something is probably closer. A priest on leave of absence.'

'A Catholic priest?'

'That's right.'

'Oh, good God! No wonder you didn't like the posters. I thought …'

'Yes?'

'I knew there was something about you, but it didn't occur to me you were Catholic.'

'What were the options then?'

'I thought you were probably a pagan, like me. Then after the dinner, I thought it must be a different religion – that's why him,' indicating the Buddha. 'I never even thought of Catholic!'

'Obvious choice I'd have thought.'

'For you, obviously. I hardly know any Christians in my normal life. Most are into Paganism, or Buddhism, or Krishna, or Sai Baba, or something like that. Or there's Arnold who's not into anything except his poetry.'

'Oh dear, Shelagh. Are we going to get on, or are we going to be enemies?'

'Why should we be? I wouldn't have got you this if I thought we were enemies, would I now? As long as you don't damn me or burn me. I want to be friends – I felt that ever since that night Arnold brought you here.'

'Deal, then, I won't damn you or burn you, as long as you don't put a curse on me.'

'I'm strictly white. I can recommend a good black witch who'll do some hexing if you want, but I'm into healing work and bringing good luck. Is that so evil?'

'I don't think I'm qualified to talk about what's evil anymore. A couple of months ago, yes, I could have anathematised you with my mentor, but I've rather lost my way since then.'

'Perhaps I can help you find it?'

'My way, whatever it is, isn't your way, Shelagh. I can tell you that much.'

'Doesn't matter. You can talk to me, and maybe find something for yourself; I don't believe in converting people to my beliefs. Deal?'

'OK, deal.'

'Hug, then, to prove it.' Before he was aware of her moving, she'd wrapped her arms around him and then held him close. He put his arms around her in reply, not wanting to seem churlish, but not feeling comfortable. As she pulled away, she saw his wary look and laughed.

'And I promise not to seduce you either. I know you priests aren't supposed to go in for that, though from what I hear that doesn't stop most of you!'

He blushed and avoided her eye, wishing he wasn't so transparent.

'Are you allowed to drink?'

'Certainly; Mass wouldn't be the same without the wine!'

'Of course, silly me. Sorry, I feel like I'm walking in quicksand now, always about to make a gaffe that'll upset you forever. Come and have a drink at the Blackbird – arrive properly in the neighbourhood, eh?'

'The Blackbird? Right on Earl's Court, isn't it?'

'That's right, just a couple of minutes.'

The thought of Mahmoud or Dave or Farid seeing him panicked him for a moment. But if this was to be truly home, he had to face going out sometime. It wasn't easy, but the first time never would be. He drew a deep breath and,

'OK, I'm with you.'

As they walked in through the pub door, they heard some shouting, and two drinkers rushed past them into the street with one turning back to shout an insult into the dark bar. The young Australian behind the bar shouted back,

'Yeah, and you too! Moron! Hi Sheil, what'll you have?'

'Here,' said Gerard, 'this is my thank you for helping me.'

'My usual, please, Kev. Thanks Gerard, I didn't bring you here to pay for me.'

'That's all right. And I'll have a bitter, please, a pint.'

'Coming up.'

'What was that all about? Those guys who just left?' she asked.

'Ah, that was nothing. I tell you though, God must really love idiots, he makes so many of them. Every day brings more.'

'Gerard's just moved in, he's taken Ashley's flat.'

'Really? I didn't know Ash was off, that's a shame. Well done, mate, welcome to The Court. I didn't mean you were one of the new idiots every day, I don't know you yet. I'm Kev.'

'Hello, Kev. You live round here?'

'Yeah, couple of years now I been here. It was only meant to be a couple o' months, but money has this strange habit of slipping away, you know?'

'Don't worry, Kev,' said Shelagh. 'These things work out; your boat will come in soon.'

'Yeah well, knowing my luck when it does, I'll be at the airport! Right, here's your drinks.'

And as simply as that, Gerard found himself at home again and with friends.

'Right,' said Shelagh, 'tell me more about this girl and the pimp. I only picked up some of the story the other day.'

He glanced round the bar to be sure he was safe and not overheard, and then reiterated and filled out the story of Kate, Mahmoud, and now Yasser.

She'd heard some of it from Arnold, but Gerard's own account was different. She agreed with Arnold that he was stupid to have got involved in the first place. But once he knew what he knew, Gerard was right, he couldn't abandon her.

She was always vaguely aware of the girls hanging around, but they were just wallpaper to her, not anything to notice particularly. Having learned what was going on, though, it was easy to get angry and fired up with crusader spirit.

'How can I help?' she asked.

CHAPTER 24

The next morning, Gerard rang Yasser. The two met at the Troubadour before lunch.

'Well, my friend,' said Yasser after a cappuccino and an exchange of stories from recent weeks. 'Now you live closer, that is a good thing. What about your young friend, Kate? What to do about her?'

'I'm ashamed, Yasser. I'm truly ashamed, but ever since that beating I've been afraid to go nearer Earl's Court than this. I tell myself it's to protect Kate from him, but it isn't. I'm afraid of being beaten up again, or even killed. When I remember the blood of the holy martyrs I'm ashamed that a simple beating is enough to frighten me off. I used to think that if God demanded my life, I would happily lay it down. Not anymore.'

'I understand that. So what about Kate?'

'If I talk to her in the street he'll probably kill her as well. I should have given her the money to get out without talking to him.'

'So why didn't you?'

'Naivety. I really believed I ought to confront him rather than steal her from him. Pitiful, aren't I?'

'Of course you're not! Naive, yes, and brave. But are we going to leave her fate in Mahmoud's hands now? While you were away I watched the girls. I may have seen Mahmoud, but I don't know which one he is. I never knew before what an international language vice is, just like music or love, eh? But without the joy.

'And I tell you what else I find, yes? Mahmoud is not the only one here, and he is not a boss. No, I learn that he answers to an old gang family in East London. What is he called again? I think it was a name like Knight? I think that was it, Hugh Knight? Something like that. Your Mahmoud runs a small section here, but he is not a kingpin. How is that then?' And he sat back looking smugly at Gerard.

'How did you find that out?'

'I mention the scandal of a Muslim behaving as he does to some members of my mosque, and gradually I learn more things. You should convert, my friend, and join this little information exchange. No, no, I am joking, I do not really suggest you turn your back on your own church, or your own God.'

'If Mahmoud is only a pawn, not a king, does that make it easier or more dangerous to rescue her? Will we have the Knight family after us, or just Mahmoud?'

'Ah, I like how you say, "us"! I am part of this, aren't I? But she's still in trouble, and she still wants to get out, yes, whoever is top of the tree? How can we do this? Who else knows her?'

'Only Arnold, and he's not involved. Who can blame him, either?'

'We are all involved. We know what's happening and that involves us all. Even if we do nothing, that's still involvement – we're supporting Mahmoud's side.'

'You're the only other person who seems to understand that, Yasser.'

'Well, and our God, Allah, and ...?'

'Just God.'

'Just God? Poor Divinity, how is He reduced?! He tells us we are involved. I don't think we can fight all the Mahmouds, and free all the Kates of this world, or even this town, but just one is a start, eh?'

'Stop rubbing your hands like that, Yasser, you're enjoying this!'

'Of course! Yes, it may be a holy and moral fight, but I feel an unholy anticipation. And, let me say, I am a very pacific Muslim, too. I have never ever bruised my knuckles on another's chin. Now, what is our aim? Rescue Kate or stop Mahmoud too? Tell me.'

Gerard sat and thought, as Yasser looked at him eagerly. They both knew the answer of course.

'How can we stop him? And must Kate wait there until we've got him?'

That question was also on Kate's mind. She often saw Arnold and badgered him, but more and more feebly. She was giving up the sliver of hope that Gerard had given her. It was over a fortnight now since she'd seen him, and the money he had passed to her from his hospital bed, through Arnold, was long since gone. She'd kept it safe to begin with – the first contribution to Gerard's miraculous hoard that would free her. As time passed, though, so too did the money, so slowly that Mahmoud didn't notice. With little pleasure to show for it, bit by bit she let it go, and the hoard barely even existed now in her imagination.

Arnold didn't bother to mention her pleas to Gerard anymore; he knew his friend wouldn't listen to his bluff common sense, but why encourage him by reminding him of Kate? He still kept an eye on her, though. He believed that he was taking advantage of the girls' services purely for his own comfort, or just that it was easier and pleasanter to walk through the middle of Earl's Court and down to Cromwell Road on his way to Warwick Road and the Gardens. Perhaps he was right, but whatever his true intent, he knew that Kate was still alive and unbruised. And even he felt a pang of uneasiness now at her thinness and obvious frailty.

Kate herself was finding work ever harder. Her prices dropped to ridiculous levels.

'Business?' she offered dully.

'You're joking,' or 'What with?' or 'Fuck off!' were the commonest replies.

'How much?' they sometimes asked.

'Eight quid?'

'What's that for? To keep your clothes on?'

Mahmoud was not sympathetic.

'You know how much you owe me? When 'm I goin' to get it, slag, eh? How much you think I pay for this place? You owe me money. Give it to me quick or you're dead!'

So she went back out onto the street, her price dropping even lower. And still she could barely make enough for the H and the rent.

The day after his talk with Yasser, Gerard took the train into town. He was worried about Kate and ashamed of his fear, but still unable to approach her and carry through his plan. He coped with this by trying not to think of her. Although, several times a day as he was talking with someone or daydreaming as he walked, he would suddenly stop, and his vision would relocate to several miles from where he was standing.

He stepped onto the train, and as the seats nearest him were full, he stood near the door, clinging to the rail overhead. As they rattled and rolled through the tunnels towards South Kensington, he thought again of Kate and how he and Yasser could help her. If he were seen anywhere near the girls, Mahmoud would come to know of it, and he might be beaten once more, while the girl would probably be killed. He couldn't put Yasser in danger, even though Yasser wanted to help. Arnold clearly wouldn't help. He wondered about Shelagh's proud offer, but no, he couldn't put any other friends at risk. So what to do?

The train pulled into Sloane Square station, and he leaned back to let some passengers edge past him to the door. As it drew away again a minute later, he saw a familiar head at the other end of the carriage. The face was turned away, but he was sure he recognised the short auburn hair. After all, he had followed it closely enough once before. As the tube swayed, pulling him forward and back, he strained to keep the head in his sight. His heart had doubled its beat as he recognised the girl, and he dreaded lest she turn and see him. Kate, Mahmoud and Yasser completely vanished from his thoughts.

CHAPTER 25

She stayed on past Victoria, St James's Park and Westminster, but quickly slipped from her seat at Embankment. He barely got to the door quickly enough, but he was on the platform in time to see her halfway up the stairs. The press was too much for him to run through, and by the time he reached the concourse she'd vanished. In dismay, he stared along Villiers Street and towards the gardens; no sign. Then he walked quickly back to the other end of the concourse and out to Hungerford Bridge.

The girl was already halfway across. He followed, keeping enough distance not to look as though he were obviously tracking her, but close enough not to lose her if he could help it.

At the end of the bridge she stopped by a beggar and handed him a coin. Rather than the common embarrassed scurrying past, she stopped, bent down to stroke the head of the beggar's dog and glanced back along the bridge to meet Gerard's look. He squinted to try and see her expression in the darkening afternoon; he couldn't make it out, but whatever it was, he recoiled and tried to look away. A mother and teenage daughter walked between them then, and he lost sight of her. For a suspended minute he stood on the bridge, face hot with shame, heart thumping and a numb sense of impending loss. Or was it another disaster?

He wanted to run away, across the bridge and back to the station, or into Charing Cross to leap on a train down to the coast where he couldn't see her or anyone he knew ever again. And he wanted to run after her and explain – what? He couldn't even begin to rehearse a mitigation. He was afraid he had lost her, and hoped she wouldn't see him again.

A heavy push from others crossing towards the South Bank started him moving in her direction, but he saw the beggar was alone once more.

At the bottom of the steps he looked around, but couldn't see which way she had gone.

Humiliated at his behaviour and not recognising his own impulse, Gerard slouched to the Festival Hall to lose himself in the bookshop and cafeteria. The books held no attraction for once; he was too embarrassed at his recent actions to take pleasure in literature or escapism. Instead he sat down at a table by himself with a cappuccino and wondered miserably what he thought he was doing. A voice from behind his shoulder echoed his thoughts.

'I've got an alarm and a knife in my pocket. I'll use them both if you're not careful. What are you after?'

He felt his face burn even redder, and he wanted to weep. He kept his head turned down towards the table. The chair opposite him pulled across the carpeted floor, and she sat down. Every part of him registered her, but he couldn't look up.

'Are you police?' He shook his head, still looking down. Her voice had an odd timbre. Gerard couldn't recognise her accent, and in the middle of his humiliation found that this extra mystery made her even more fascinating than when she was just a challenging face.

'Private detective? No? You've followed me before. Is someone paying you? Still no? Pervert, then?'

Gerard recoiled and began to shake his head indignantly. He paused and then shrugged his shoulders very slightly.

'So? I'm holding the alarm, so be careful. Look at me, I can't talk to your crown.'

Dying in his seat, he raised his head slowly and forced himself to meet her gaze.

'What do you want of me? Were you waiting to rape me?'

'No!'

'Ah, so you can talk then. Not rape. What then?'

Gerard shrugged his shoulders again and whispered,

'I honestly don't know. I never meant to alarm or menace you.'

'But you followed me, several times.'

'This is the second.'

'When was the first?'

'Some weeks ago, I don't remember when. Notting Hill. That was the only time.'

'Do you often follow girls on the tube?'

He shook his head again.

'Never.'

There was a long pause, then,

'Aren't you even going to offer me a drink after all that following, then, pervert?'

He flinched, but kept her eye as he had done before. Then he stood and faced her, uncertainly. He didn't even know how to ask her what she wanted. She saw his paralysis and waited a long minute, staring coolly at him before breaking his misery.

'You can get me a large brandy.' He'd expected a coffee, but accepted her order and went to the bar around the corner from their table. He half supposed her to have left when he came back with her brandy, but she had stayed. Beneath his shame and fear, he was glad to see her still sitting at the table.

'Well, what now?' she asked. He blinked in surprise and looked at her.

'What happens here in your fantasy? You've got me at your table, you've bought me a drink. Now what?'

Gerard shrugged again.

'I didn't really have a fantasy. I saw you on the train and couldn't help myself, but I never expected … this. I haven't rehearsed this part, or even dreamed it. I didn't expect to talk to you.'

'You're a liar. If you followed me, you fantasised about me, yes?'

'I don't know. All this is new to me. I don't think I fantasised, but after last time, I looked out for you. Then I forgot, until this afternoon.'

'Why? Why did you look out for me?'

'I don't know. I'm sorry. I sound feeble and gauche, I know, but I really haven't ever behaved like this before. I don't know what happens now, and I don't even know what I want to happen now. Yes I do, I want an earthquake to swallow me, or a gunman to come in and shoot me or something stupid like that. Anything except really to have behaved like this.'

'And been caught, mm?'

'Caught or not, I've never behaved like this.'

'So why with me?'

Gerard blushed again and played with the handle of his cold coffee cup. She waited a long while, then sighed, drank the brandy in one large swallow and stood up.

'I've still got my alarm and my knife. If you follow me again like that I'll use one of them. Understand?' He nodded, staring down at the table again.

She strode off to the door, leaving him flicking the glaze of his cup with his fingernail. Two minutes later, her voice, coming from standing over him, brought him back to full awareness.

'Fuck you. Why don't you say something? Anything?'

'I'm sorry.'

'Not that! Say something. What do you want?'

He couldn't answer and just felt disgust at himself. What would Father Holloway think? Or Arnold, Ann and Joe? What did he himself think?

She sighed heavily.

'Are you married?' He looked up, startled.

'No.'

'Divorced?'

'No.'

'Girlfriend?'

'No.'

'Why don't you get yourself a girlfriend then, so you don't have to play these fucking stupid games with me? Or are you homo? Gay?'

He shook his head more vehemently.

'So what is the matter with you? Why don't you have a girlfriend?' He thought his behaviour answered that question, but at last he could speak.

'I can't. Not allowed, you see.'

'Not allowed? Who says you're not allowed, your mummy for Christ's sake?' The strange timbre in her voice still tantalised Gerard, while the exasperated contempt humiliated him further.

Some reactions tend to turn any anger aside: meekness and feebleness are two. Anger will give way to other, perhaps more destructive or more emollient, emotions, but pure anger can't last long against feebleness, and the girl's anger had reached that stage. Though she was no friendlier to Gerard.

'Who says you mustn't have girlfriends? Or are you HIV?'

'No, nothing like that. My vows.'

There was silence for a moment, and then she sat opposite him again. There was a change.

'Tell me these vows.'

'All right. I've not told many people in London this, but you're entitled to know.'

'No I'm not, but I want you to tell me.'

He did. She sat and listened to his priesthood in Derbyshire with Father Holloway and, like the ancient mariner unable to stop, he went on to Jane Conway's death and his leave of absence. Still possessed by the need for confession, he then spoke of Kate and Mahmoud, his beating and now his fear of trying to help Kate further.

By the time he'd finished, concertgoers were arriving for the evening's performance, but he didn't notice the extra press and rush of bodies past their table.

He let out a long sigh and looked at her.

'None of that explains why I terrorise strange women in London, does it?'

'Have you really been celibate all your life?'

'Yes. That's one vow I never broke.'

'Never even kissed a woman?'

'On the cheek, as a friend. No more than that.'

'I thought all you priests were two-faced, you know? Screwing your housekeepers and altar boys, and spawning bastards everywhere until the papers found out. Not you?'

'Some might, but none that I personally knew. Certainly not Father Holloway.'

'No. Baptised in vinegar, that one. I think that explains why you started chasing beautiful women over the river. You shocked I called myself beautiful? You must think I am, or you wouldn't keep following me.'

'Where are you from?'

'Germany. Berlin. What used to be East Berlin, but is now just Berlin. My name is Silke.'

'Thank you, Silky?'

'Silke. Just like that. Why do you thank me?'

'For offering your name. And for listening to me. I think I'm not in as a good a way as I thought.'

'I think you're in a bloody awful way. I think I forgive you, too. I don't think much of you behaving like that, but I think maybe I forgive you after all.'

'Thank you.' At last, he could smile. A rueful smile, but nonetheless, a smile. 'And now what?'

'And now I go to work. You like music?'

'I love music. What kind?'

'Jazz, cabaret music, Brel, Weill, Tom Waites, Nick Cave, that sort.'

'I don't know that much. Why?'

She handed him a card advertising a night club – drinking, music, entertainment. It was in Soho, and there was a small picture of a black cat in the top corner.

'Come to this club one night. Not now, I don't think I want to see you tonight, but come sometime soon. You can look at me without having to track me across town. I sing there. Jazz, Kurt Weill, you know. Have a drink while you're watching me.'

'Thank you. I don't think it's my kind of place though.'

'Don't knock it, you don't know it yet. What's your name, priest?'

'Gerard, Gerard Tisserant.'

'Gerard, that's good. I was afraid you would say George or Jack, or something too ordinary for a sad priest. Gerard Tisserant? You're not the painter, right? No, he's much older than you. Come to the club one night, bring one of your friends if you want. You will need lots of money though.'

And this time she really did leave. Gerard sat alone for a little longer, recalling her voice with the mid-European lilt and wondering again what he thought he was doing. He could hear Father Holloway's endless warnings about the Devil's traps for simple and well-meaning folk. Was he at the gate of one such, he asked himself? And was he going to walk through, or do the right thing and turn his back?

CHAPTER 26

As Gerard walked along the road towards his front door, he thought of Silke singing at that moment to strangers. He frowned slightly as he thought of the men staring eagerly at her. She might stare back at them and then smile at one. He shook his head impatiently to clear himself of the thought and mentally uttered a penance, though for what, he couldn't say.

'Hey Gerald, hey man, good to see you!' His heart sank at the reedy voice behind him, but he couldn't pretend he hadn't heard.

'Hello, Jez,' he said as he turned. 'What's up with you?'

'Great, really great. Hey, you know, I kicked the stuff?'

'Really, when?' Gerard was interested now and gave Jez his full attention. Jez still looked ill and pale, whatever he had managed.

'Look, do you want a coffee? Come on up.' He kicked himself as he heard the words come out of his mouth, but this sounded too important.

Jez sat in the comfortable chair and lolled back. Mozart was playing on the tape deck, the Piano Concerto no. 20. This was something new to Jez, but he was trying, really trying.

'Tell me then,' invited Gerard. 'When did you kick the stuff?'

'Oh, ages now, straight up.'

'Last week?'

'Nearly, nearly, straight up, Gerald. It's great isn't it? Hey, what's this, you know? Music, like?'

'It's Mozart, Jez.'

'Right, right. Hey, got some water? I'm thirsty.'

'Coffee no good?'

'What? No, it's good, but I need some water, you know?'

Gerard, disillusioned but unsurprised, fetched him a glass.

'When did you say you kicked it then, Jez?'

There was a long pause as Jez tried to play the question back and find an answer. At last he closed his eyes and shook his head instead.

A moment later, he looked at Gerard again.

'Arnold lives here, doesn't he? And Sheil?'

'Yes, that's right.'

'Great. I owe Sheil some money. Don't tell her I'm here, I can't pay her yet. Tomorrow, honest, I'll get money tomorrow, you know? It's really good you're living here now, you know? Good people here, good friends. Yeah, one day I'll live in a place like this. Good to have friends round you, isn't it?'

'Where are your friends, Jez?'

'Here of course. You, Arnold, Sheil, everyone. No, got lots of friends where I am now, you know, everywhere. Life's good, isn't it? Bloody good. Now I'm off the stuff, I can do anything I want, that's right, isn't it Gerald? Anything I fucking want, I can do it.'

Gerard looked closely at him, but Jez wasn't being sarcastic or ironic.

'So you're really off it, Jez?'

'Eh? What's that?'

'OK. When are you giving it up?'

'Soon, man, real soon. Will you help me? I can't do it by myself.'

'I don't know.' Gerard drew his arms across his chest and relaxed further back into his chair. 'What do you mean, help you? What would I have to do?'

'You know, help me. That's all, help me.'

'How?'

'Help. You know.'

'When?'

'Soon, real soon. I'm nearly there, honest. Look, I got to go now. Have you got any bread I can borrow? Just for a couple of days. No, tell you what, I'll ask Sheil. She lives here doesn't she? Don't worry, man, I'll ask Sheil.'

As he spoke, Jez was vaguely aware of his hand in his greatcoat pocket fumbling with something. Then he remembered – another wallet from earlier in the evening. He beamed at Gerard.

'No, its ok, I've just remembered I'm ok after all. Don't worry about the bread.'

As he heard Jez lurch downstairs and out of the front door, Gerard wondered how he had become his friend. He'd not made any overtures to Jez that he could remember. If only he could actually like him, it would be more understandable. But no, he wearied Gerard so greatly that he just wanted to run away and shout at Jez to leave him alone.

How was he supposed to help him kick his addiction? He wasn't a doctor, and he had no idea how to help someone undertake that. Then he thought of Jane, and of Kate, how they had turned to him. Not much help for them here, either. And who could he turn to for himself? He'd tried Nick and Jenny, but that hadn't worked. Arnold? Shelagh? Ann and Joe? They would all try to do something for him, but …

Silke.

The shame of this afternoon swept back; Gerard couldn't believe what was happening to him. He was not usually slow-witted with people, but awareness of covert sin had paralysed him. Hot and blushing, he found the memory of his gauche silence at least as shameful as his stalking of her. He remembered the club where she was singing right at this moment. He would probably never go there, but even so, he tried to picture it and hear Silke's voice.

Gerard sat in his armchair and turned off the light. Traffic noise and sirens forced themselves into his room, and he didn't know a moment's silence. But the sounds were all outside his room and outside of him.

Across the landing Arnold was lost in a new poem that had come to him yesterday. He was writing frantically now, preparing for his third volume. The first two sold badly and were soon remaindered, but Gerard had seen a copy of each in the Poetry Society library. The third was in preparation, and for now Arnold was seeing less and less of his friends.

It was a full moon tonight, and Shelagh was visiting three other witches in Wimbledon to perform a celebratory ritual on the Common.

About now, Ann and Joe would be walking Gwen around their territory, holding hands and looking in companionable silence at the slow decay of autumn.

Nick and Jenny would probably be at opposite ends of the country, saving their companies and laying off their staff. In the Kensington house, their glass-and-clipped posters would be alone and unlooked at, the reproduction furniture polish slowly overlaid by dust until their return.

Above him he heard the beep … beep … blurt of the unknown Ray's solitary computer games.

In growing darkness, Gerard sat alone in his room and realised how far he was travelling away from his friends.

Jez's worry when he left Gerard was more immediate. He needed money, and lots of it, because his supply was almost exhausted. The wallet he found in his pocket had proved a disappointment: twenty pounds only. There were the usual bank cards, credit cards, charge cards, phone cards and cashpoint cards, but only twenty pounds in actual money. He had to have more than that.

It was still quite early, so he if he took a trip uptown, he'd probably strike lucky. As he walked down Epirus Road, he saw a woman let herself into the front door of one of the converted houses. The block of apartment buzzers by the door gave him an idea, and he tailgated the woman as she was about to close the front door behind her.

Once inside, he took the stairs away from where she walked in order to reassure her and help her forget his face. On the third floor he found his lucky break – a door was open and the room behind it obviously empty. Who knew how little time before its owner returned? Checking he was still alone, Jez took a deep breath, held it and walked into the open flat. It didn't take more than a minute to find loose cash in a drawer, slip it into his pocket and run. As he reached the top of the stairs he heard another door open and voices sounding along the hall; they were relaxed, chatty voices, parting. It was his victim coming home! Quickly, Jez scuttled downstairs and out of the building, making no sound as he closed the door behind him.

Simple! Easy! His first burglary, and it was a piece of piss, so easy! He wanted to celebrate and tell everyone how good he was, because Jez was definitely progressing and graduating now. Could anything stop this man? He'd actually burgled, yes BURGLED, a flat, and he had the money to prove it! He was cool, oh yes. He was clever, he had the brains, Jez. Yeah, he was the man all right! He didn't need his friends to keep lending him money now. He could cut out his visits to town and just go up when he wanted to buy, that's all he needed. He didn't even need that anymore, not if this buzz stayed – God, it was better than a rush.

CHAPTER 27

No one had seen Arnold for several days, but the whole house knew he was at home. Late at night they would hear an eruption of boots clumping down the stairs and the slam of the front door behind him. Typical Arnold, they told Gerard, always the same when he was caught up in a project.

None of his current friends had known him when he wrote his earlier books, but they all knew him when he was organising a gig, say, or producing an occasional newsletter for his street poetry group. If everything was going well, he became so exultant he would rush off and pound the streets to work off his energy, laughing as he walked. If he was blocked, he would rush off and pound the streets to work off his frustration, swearing as he walked. No one had seen his face this week, and there was no bulletin on his progress.

In fact, this week he was happy. He had enough new poems to fill at least half the new volume, and his notebooks promised him another twenty. All things being equal, he'd make the deadline. But, and this was what drove him out, he couldn't find a central image or theme to bind the contents together. The poems were all good, he knew that, but he needed something special at the heart, or at the head. Just one thing to make the collection stand out.

He liked the night-time streets. He liked the yellow of the sodium lamps, especially when they reflected off wet roadways. Empty roads suddenly filled by late revellers breaking all speed limits with the roar of an engine, itself drowned out by the selfish bass of the in-flight entertainment, the constant sound of humanity somewhere nearby, planes crossing the country, sirens racing to nearby emergencies, burglar alarms, drunken shouts or his own rapid footsteps on the pavement – all of these delighted Arnold on his nightly excursions. One night's walk could furnish him with images for poems that mightn't surface for another two or three months. No matter, they were there, caught in a notebook as soon as he could reach a pen.

'Hi, Arnie, horny tonight?'

A girl's voice called him as he pounded along Cromwell Road. He stopped in surprise.

''Lo, Jude. This ain't your patch?'

'Bored with hanging around. There must be a few Johns round the hotels here. Fancy a wrestle?'

'You bet, but I'm broke at the moment. Give credit?'

'No chance. Come back when you're rolling in it, then we'll have a roll.'

'Cheers. 'Ow you doin', anyway?'

The girl shrugged. 'So-so. Wrong time of year.'

Round the corner, waiting until she was out of sight, Arnold jotted the exchange down in his notebook just in case. Sad, he thought. Jude was definitely fit, a good kid. Not that much of a kid these days, but, well, deserved better than an empty night. What was wrong with everyone, leaving her touting for nothing like that?

Now he was working on the last poems, he must avoid the clubs and bars. Time for them when he'd finished. The streets were enough for him when the inspiration had him by the throat. He loved walking past the terraces that were all flats and bedsits, like his. The best was when most were in darkness with just one window lit, preferably uncurtained, so he could glance in as he strode by. He didn't want to stop and stare in, to learn the layout, the wallpaper, the plants, the bookshelves and the ceiling rose. No, what Arnold needed was the fleetest of passing glances, perhaps with a person in view as he passed, so that he gathered no more than a hint of another's life, just the seed of a poem.

His notebooks were full of such seeds, and like nature's patterns, the seeds sown far outnumbered by an order of thousands, the mature plants that grew. Even so, Arnold collected all the seeds he possibly could and never ended up writing a poem from one of them that didn't satisfy him in the end.

Not too far away, he knew of an all-night store; it didn't take him long to reach it. He squinted as the harsh strip light punched his eyes after the softer streetlights. His nostrils inhaled the unexpected pungency of the spices that hovered inside the front door. An old Indian man wearing a dusty woolly hat stood behind the cash desk and stared suspiciously at him as he walked towards the first aisle. Arnold muttered his usual,

'Cheers,' but for once his heart wasn't really in it.

As usual the store wasn't full at this time of night. An Asian woman with a pink head scarf was filling a basket, fully aware of the sniggers from two students at the end of the aisle behind her. Each time she looked, it was hard to catch their eyes, but she was sure they were sniggering at her. She was right.

Her basket filled more quickly because she was out of sight of the old man by the front window, and she feared to leave the safety of the shop which now felt dangerous.

Arnold coughed loudly behind the students. They jumped and looked up at him. The sneer that began on their lips died before reaching full expression. According to the store's private etiquette, no voices spoke, but the students found themselves at the door and paying for their cheese, lager, cigarettes and Rizlas before the woman had finished her nervous shopping.

She looked at Arnold, still discomforted, and continued to stuff groceries hastily into her bulging basket. He wondered if he should reassure her, but decided not to bother. He walked around the shelving stacks again until he was out of sight of anyone and then stopped still and looked up and down. There was no movement and no sound, just Arnold and empty aisles, with shelves fully loaded in case another lonely insomniac found the fridge empty.

Although it was behind him, he felt the movement of the little wall-mounted camera swivelling to scan unoccupied space He turned to face it and nodded back at the little red light on top that winked so promiscuously at him and every shopper.

'Not a bad job that, shop telly 24 hours,' he said cheerily to the old man at the till, cocking his head back at the camera. Unlistening and unresponding, the old man glared indignantly at Arnold's empty hands. What was this large man doing breaking his nocturnal privacy and not even buying anything to pay for the privilege?

'Ok then, Mars bar.' Arnold wasn't hungry, but fair do's, this was the old guy's livelihood, after all, and not that lively either, this time of night. 'Mars bar and twenty Embassy for rent, eh? Cheers.' On his way back, he took a different turning from his usual, because he caught sight of a small fire behind the darkened office buildings – a reflected flicker of flame. Something new to investigate, and maybe something dangerous. He'd crossed midnight's line and was in the small hours now, so what was going on there?

He knew he could look after himself, and maybe there was an interesting encounter waiting.

He found a small patch of wasteland, a brazier made from what looked like an old dustbin, and a motley crew sitting around it. In a tattered armchair with high back sat a figure Arnold had never met. He was old with lanky grey hair, a tatty beard and a grubby Crombie coat, its grease stains catching the light from the fire. He sported an old brocade curtain draped around his shoulders and wore a glittering hat. The glitter came from the brazier's firelight reflecting off at least twenty cellophane toffee wrappers stuck to the crown. He twisted his head round as he became aware of Arnold's presence.

'Who are you, coming into my realm?' a sonorous voice boomed. He might look old and decrepit, but the voice suggested a previous life on the stage. 'I'm King of this land, and no one passes without a tribute. Eh?'

'What tribute do you want?' Arnold joined in the game, interested to see what would come.

'Got a toffee? See this crown? See it? Eh? Solid gold, all of it. Gold toffee wrappers, hundreds of 'em. See the jewels? See them? Eh? See the colours shine in the streetlight? Eh? Cellophane, that, off the toffees. How many people give me that, eh? Everyone. What you got?'

'Sorry, King,' said Arnold. 'Got a Mars bar, but no toffees. Paper don't shine the same way, though, do it?'

'Eh? What you goin' to give me, then? Price of a tea? Price of a cider? Eh?'

He gestured towards an old-looking woman sitting by his feet, her face lost somewhere far away, with lines from years and disappointments scored around her eyes and mouth.

'See my queen there? See her? Eh? Beautiful, my queen. Royal she is – it's true. Do you want her? How much? Shut up, I'm working. How much then? Box of toffees? My robe's worn out. Eh?'

'Sorry, King. No offence, love,' to the unnoticing woman, 'but time's getting' on a bit, now, ain't it? I'll pass. Ta, though.'

'What do you mean, it's too late? It's not three yet, not even daylight. You're in my land now, in my time. It's never too late when I'm working, so do you want her? No? You refuse a queen? Treason! Off with his head!' None of the group around him responded, and no one pulled an axe or knife from under a coat. They just sat vacantly, gazing at the scene but not really present.

'Always a king, me, even asleep. Always a queen, her, whatever you pay. Come on, give me a tea. Give me a beer. Give me a toffee. Give me … Give me … Eh?' At which, his head fell forward, and a loud snore filled the air.

Arnold looked around at the scene, drinking in the detail. Then a great grin opened up across his face, and he sat by the fire, notebook out, writing down all that was there and all that had been said. Now he had his central poem and image for the new collection. 'Cheers, Sheil,' he muttered. Her invocations on his behalf seemed to have worked after all.

CHAPTER 28

'Pardon?' Gerard shouted, flustered, to the barely covered girl leaning over him. She mouthed the question again, but he still couldn't hear over the music. She repeated it patiently for a third time.

'Sorry. A whiskey, please,' he replied.

So far, his evening at the club was less shocking and sinful than he'd feared. His hearing was in greater jeopardy than his soul. So was his wallet, at the prices charged.

He didn't have much company; at this time customers were few and far between, but perhaps half past eight was too early.

On the stage area at the end of the room he could see microphones, two keyboards, a double bass and a drum kit already in place.

No sign yet of Silke's band. What time would they start? Would he wait for her – them? How long? Did she really sing here? Or was that just a story to rid herself of this sad stalker? He blushed, humiliated again at the thought, but he would wait it out for at least another hour before conceding that she'd made as big a fool of him as he had done of himself.

He was not a fool, though. Long before his self-imposed deadline, he saw Silke at the bar with the other three members of the band. She didn't notice him at first, and he had the chance again to watch her unseen.

Her make up was startling on her pale face. She wore no pallid or pastel colours – lips of deep garnet, starkly black eyelashes and black cropped hair closely framing just her upper face. He wondered if it was dyed or a wig – striking as the look was, he preferred her auburn hair. Her costume too was designed to swallow up light. She was the only woman in the band.

Silke spotted him from the bar and returned his scrutiny before waving and crossing over to him.

'You braved it, then, priest?'

He smiled awkwardly and gestured to her to sit down, his self-conscious smirk opening out into a true grin of pleasure.

'Yes, I've braved it. Didn't you think I would? What will you drink?'

'No, no. keep your money safe. I've got my own. You've noticed the price, of course; don't even think about buying the staff a drink or you'll not manage the tube fare home.'

His heart lifted as he watched her, while inside another voice whispered, 'Sinner!'

'Quiet, it's not true, I know it,' he whispered back silently. The voice laughed sardonically.

She told him of how she and the bassist had moved to England after the wall fell. They already played together, had been lovers, but not still. Now there was only the music.

Gerard looked jealously at the bassist, quiet at the bar. Nothing special there.

'We will play soon. Can you see us all right here? Good. Enjoy the show, priest.'

He did. He didn't know many of the songs, even those sung in English, and yet again his education took a leap. Little of the music was modern. Even he, could tell many of these songs must be fifty or sixty years old, though anyway, he hardly ever listened to music of this century and certainly not to jazz of any description since his student days. An aficionado would have told him that as jazz, this was too adulterated, overly clever stuff. But, new to this, he neither knew nor cared. Silke's band were doing strange things to him.

Songs of a desperate night-time search for a new whiskey bar; a fantasy of a hotel cleaning girl inviting a pirate ship to capture and kill all those male guests who had degraded and dismissed her over the years; songs of lost souls groping in a cold world for comfort or validation.

He must have heard such rhythms and words before, but, no, no. This music was touching parts of him that his beloved Bach and Monteverdi had never dreamed of approaching. He wasn't sure that it was even his soul that the music stirred. Some part of him that he had kept hidden in dark rooms, stood up at the sound of her voice and the songs' decadence. This was surely not the soul of Gerard?

Her voice was harsh, not mellifluous, and talked to areas of life that he'd only seen as shadows in Father Holloway's preaching and warnings. For a moment, behind Silke's head, he seemed to see the giant form of his mentor make the sign of the cross and cast her to flames. But Father Gerard felt alive – the flames warmed his soul to life instead of incinerating it to ash.

Songs about the drunks and whores in an Amsterdam bar, and all with such strong rhythms and triumphant passion, that they found a way into him that he would never have recognised before. For the whole performance Silke flirted coldly with the audience and with the band members, but she never once looked at Gerard.

They played for forty minutes and then took a break. The audience was enthusiastic while staying on the polite side of rapturous, and the band was soon at the bar, untroubled. He waited for her to come back to him, but she did not. He noticed how it was the drummer she hovered next to, hanging onto his arm while he joked with the bassist. Gerard watched, but spent the break alone except for forays by various hostesses who each invited him to spend his money to gain her company. Each time, he declined;

partly because he was aware of sin and partly because he didn't relish being robbed, but mostly because he feared Silke's disapproval if she saw.

In the living room at the house in Kensington, Nick poured Jenny another Bacardi and himself a malt. She took it with a nod, her eyes still on the film; he sat back down in his own chair.

Neither would say it, but they both felt comfortable once more in their home, not waiting to see if Gerard would come home before their bedtime and talk with them, or if he would creep in silently during the dark hours again.

Neither would say it, but they also both felt that they'd missed an opportunity to talk privately with him, to get to know the real Gerard again and ask his advice about how to feel alive in each other's company once more.

'I hope he's all right, now,' muttered Nick without warning. Jenny glanced up in surprise, then half smiled.

'I'm sure he is.' They both turned back to the film.

Shelagh tapped on Gerard's door, but the flat felt empty. She scribbled a note and slid it under the door. Back in her own place, she made the coffee she'd started, but put the second mug back on the tree. It was a dull night now.

'Well, priest? What do you think?' Silke intercepted him before he could leave at the end of their second set.

He smiled with relief and pleasure and sat down again. Now the band had finished for the night, she relaxed enough to spend time with him. The other members of the band seemed unsurprised and unbothered when Silke announced that Gerard was coming back with them for a nightcap. Ian, the keyboard player, lived closest to the club and they all returned there.

The flat triggered more memories of his younger days for Gerard, than Nick and Jenny, or even Ann or his own space in Philbeach Gardens, had done. Yet Ian was not a young student. Younger than Gerard, certainly, but he was mature, worked during the day, and was paying for his children who lived with their mother and step-father in Wales.

Like Arnold, he didn't seem to care about anything else, and even though he had responsibilities, he lived entirely in his own orbit. He no longer saw his children and had almost stopped regretting it. His life now was all about the music, whether it was Silke's band or the other band that he sometimes toured with around Eastern Europe.

As to the rest of what happened in London, or the country, or the world, he was not quite oblivious, but if it didn't have an effect on the bands, or the music, or his rent, he chose to remain untouched by it. Or to not look at it.

Karl, the bassist, and the drummer, Russ, spent the time talking to each other and barely registered that Gerard was with them. He formed no opinion of them, except for an instinctive mistrust based on their closeness to Silke. Tonight, though, Silke talked to him.

'What have you done about your girl?' she asked him. 'Is she safe yet?'

'No, she isn't safe at all. I don't know what to do about her. Mahmoud's on the lookout, and if he sees me talking to any of the girls, I really think he'll kill her. I don't feel very clever about it, but I don't know what to do.'

'What about your other friend? What was his name?'

'Arnold?'

'No no, not the poet, the other one, the Muslim.'

'Yasser. I know. When we talk we're the two heroes going in to clean up the whole town. But I've found out what being beaten means, and I don't ever want that to happen again. I wouldn't forgive myself if I let Yasser in for something like that.'

'*Das ist Blödsinn* – that's nonsense! He's a grown man; he knows the risks. What right have you got to choose to protect him and keep this girl in danger?'

'What should I do? What would you do?'

'I wouldn't have got involved. But now you're involved, you can't let her stay there. You have to get her out. Take your friend along. Try again.'

'I want to, but don't know how anymore.'

'You should think quickly, then.' She looked coldly at him. 'You rescue her soon or you bury her soon. Which do you choose, priest?'

CHAPTER 29

Next afternoon Yasser visited Gerard for yet another battle plan. It was his first visit to the flat, and he looked around, approving the restrained, tasteful austerity of the décor and furnishings. As soon as Gerard had sat him down with a coffee, the conference began its usual inconclusive circularity.

'We have to get her away soon, Yasser. How shall we do it?'

'Take me there now. Show me the girl. I've looked, and I think I know them all by sight, but I'm not sure which one is ours. Can't we rescue them all?'

'In our dreams, maybe.'

'I know. Yes, I know. All right, just the one, for now. Let us go. I like this, Gerard, a crusade made up of a lapsed Catholic and a good Muslim. If both sides are fighting together we have to win, eh?'

He clapped Gerard on the back and almost trotted down the stairs from the flat. They passed Shelagh on the stairs.

'Oh, Gerard, are you in tonight? Can you come in for a coffee later?'

'Er, I think so …' He glanced hesitantly at Yasser who delicately looked away.

'Yes, all things being equal, I'll be along. Eight?'

Shelagh gave him a wide smile and a nod and carried on up the stairs. Yasser looked sideways at him.

'No, Yasser, stop thinking that.'

'I wish you joy, my friend. Is she Catholic too?'

'No. She's just a friend.'

'Fine, fine. Enjoy your friendship.'

It wasn't dark yet, but most cars and buses had switched to sidelights. When they reached Earl's Court some of the girls were already starting their shift. Kate wasn't there yet. Maybe she had a customer already, but Gerard didn't think so. He clutched Yasser's sleeve, though, when he saw Mahmoud on the other side.

'Ah, is that him? How banal he seems. I expected someone who looks evil. Wait here, Gerard, I have to speak to him.'

'No! That's what I did, and you know what happened.'

'Indeed. You and I met, that is what happened. This is different – you spoke to him as a favour, to help Kate. I will speak to him as imam. He must hear that. He will not harm me, he is a Muslim.'

'Careful, Yasser, he's not alone. That's his thug there, just along the street. I can't remember his name – Farid? Tariq? Something like that.'

'So? Another Muslim, and a better one than Mahmoud maybe. All right, thank you for warning me. I'll try not to provoke him. Here goes!'

Gerard watched their argument from across the road, standing deep in the recess of a shop doorway so that if Mahmoud should look over, he would be invisible. In the event, though, Mahmoud didn't look round. Whatever Yasser said to him had touched the right chord. Mahmoud hung his head before Yasser, and at one point he tried to pick up Yasser's hand to kiss it. Gerard saw his head nodding rapidly in agreement as Yasser showed him his iniquity and his own mortal risk. The body language showed no indignation, no denial, no aggrieved innocence and no threat. The interview was as different from Gerard's attempt as was possible.

After fifteen minutes they parted and Yasser returned.

'Is that it?' asked Gerard, incredulous.

'Yes, it is done. I was imam, you see, my friend. I reminded him of the Quran's injunctions and warned him of his peril. He resisted, but I wouldn't let go. At the end he asked to see me again tomorrow. Will you come with me?'

'Did you tell him about Kate?'

'Not by name.'

'Why not?'

'Let him prove his good faith first. Tomorrow perhaps, we can give him a name, but for now I want him to think of his sins and truly repent. Ah, Gerard, this is so good. What were we afraid of all this time, to keep that poor girl in such a state?'

'I'm still afraid, Yasser. I'm still afraid of him. Two weeks ago that man was evil. Have you really turned him round in fifteen minutes? I hope you're right.'

'I'm sure I am. Allah was with me, and we have saved her, and Mahmoud as well. I understand your fear, especially after what he did to you, but I think tomorrow he will apologise. Yes, I do believe he will go as far as that.'

'But you didn't give him Kate's name.'

'Not yet.'

That evening Shelagh cooked him another meal to help celebrate. He was beginning to get used to vegetarian food, to his rather pleasant surprise. The pictures stayed uncovered, and they were easy with each other. He had brought along a bottle of wine, which was potluck as he had no idea what wine suited vegetarian food, but it seemed to work.

She wanted to know what he planned for Kate, and who was that interesting man with him this morning?

He told her of Yasser's visit in hospital and how their first talk on their respective religions led to a growing friendship.

'And Kate, if she is let go? What will you do with her?'

'Me? I don't have any plan for her. That's hardly my place. If she can really get away, I'll give her money to start, but I won't own her, or run her after that. She's had too many people doing that already. If Yasser has really done with it, then maybe the other girls can get out as well.'

'So let her back on the streets homeless and jobless but with a bit of cash in her back pocket? Really, Gerard?'

'What else?'

'She's got to detox under supervision and get all those nasty drugs out of her system. And that takes time. Then go into rehab, and after that she needs to be somewhere away from this whole environment so she doesn't get sucked back into it. And none of that is exactly cheap. How are you arranging all that?'

Gerard closed his eyes and thought. As he realised how little he'd considered the what-happens-next, and tried to put himself in the newly-liberated Kate's shoes, he felt himself get hotter and hotter.

'I don't know, Shelagh,' he shrugged, 'I really hadn't thought beyond getting her away from him so she can make her own fresh start.'

'If – and I think it is only if – your Yasser has done what you think, then tomorrow you had better start thinking about all of this. Here, I'll give you the local social services details. I don't know – well-meaning do-gooders who don't think of the consequences! I see what Arnold meant when he talked about your Lone Ranger attitude.'

'Oh please, not another Western figure. Why does everyone compare me to them?'

'Good question. Maybe think on it. But to be honest, you've probably got a bit more time to work it all out, even though Yasser expects this big apology and about-turn tomorrow.'

'He believes he's persuaded Mahmoud, because of his position as imam and Mahmoud's background being Muslim.'

'And do you believe it?'

'I want to, more than anything at the moment. Perhaps he has, but why would Mahmoud listen to him if he wouldn't listen to me?'

'Aha.'

'What?'

'How will you feel if he doesn't let Kate go?'

'Sorry, I'm not with you.'

'Not a little bit relieved? The tiniest bit smug?'

He looked at her, hurt.

'How can you say that?'

'Yasser won't have succeeded where you failed, will he?'

'Is that what you think of me? Shelagh, I thought we were friends. Do you think I'd be smug at seeing Kate trapped there any longer?'

She reached across the table and held his hand.

'I'm sorry, Gerard, that's not what I meant. I know you're trying to rescue her, but you want to do the rescue yourself, and why not?'

He stopped his retort and played back the conversation to himself. Then he blushed.

'I want Yasser to succeed. He's one of the best men, the finest men, I've met in a long time, along with Joe. And I could never have said that before … before, when I was with Father Holloway. No, he wouldn't allow a Muslim to be anything better or nobler than bitterly misguided.'

'Is that your church's position, then? So patronising and arrogant?'

'Much of it, yes. I was uncomfortable with it but could never have acknowledged it before. Yet a part of me still thinks that it should be only Christian charity and mercy that fights and frees Kate. God, how awful. That's how crusades start, isn't it? I keep thinking I'm doing ok, and I have all the right understanding and all the right insights, and then I'm made to listen to myself.'

'You do have the right instincts, of course you do. But like the rest of us, you've got a whole lot of other baggage on your back. I've got my parents' hang ups colouring my reactions, sabotaging all my instincts and patronising my beliefs, and you've got Father Holloway sitting on your shoulder, whispering in your ear. I don't know what Arnold's got.'

'His wife, I think.'

'Arnold? He's married?'

'Used to be. Ah, perhaps it's not meant to be public knowledge – forget I said that. But going back, we're all grown-ups now. I thought everything in my ministry was God's voice, God's wish, but actually much of it was my parents and my priest from where I grew up.'

'Your parents were really religious?'

'Oh, ardent! Both staunch Catholics, and all through my childhood, I was urged – forced? – I don't know, but it was assumed that I was a good little Catholic boy and would have some role in the Church. First Communion at age eight, encouraged to help out at the services, altar boy, choir boy, acolyte, and absolutely no thought of questioning the beliefs or history of the Church. They always wanted me to become a priest or a missionary, so after a short diversion to uni I was led willingly back to the fold.'

'No, that's horrid, brainwashing you like that from the start! Didn't you ever rebel?'

'No way, I wouldn't dare, not against my dad. Very severe, with an advanced sense of sin and guilt that Father Holloway would applaud. Say the wrong thing at home, or worse, to friends and neighbours, and I'd be banished to my room for days with hardly any food. Yet he loved, as well. A good stick and carrot job, needing his approval and love and dreading his punishment. You don't grow out of that sort of training easily.

'It was only when I was dealing with real parishioners and their problems that I started to see how much of the theology was irrelevant. Father Holloway would talk for hours about sin, the awful sin of refusing to baptise a child, and then segue on to the Trinity, and so much that had nothing to do with the devotion and trust, or the fears, that people brought to the confessional. Sometimes I just felt a fraud teaching little ones the catechism.

'And when … something happened … that was my fault because I had to follow the teachings, I just wanted to break away from it all. No, I can't tell you yet what happened, but it ended any loyalty I felt to the Church. So I lost all faith in the structure and its strictures, though not what lies behind it, the divine presence. I believe in that and love that as strongly as ever, but the whole structure became ossified and a barrier.

'And yet, when I conduct a Mass, oh, you wouldn't believe how powerful, how wonderful, how healing that is. And part of that huge kick of power is fifteen hundred years of refinement, practice and, more powerful yet, sheer belief.'

They sat silently for a few minutes, Gerard remembering, Shelagh pondering.

'Have you ever said this all before?'

'Hmm? No, I don't think so. Some of it, but no, not a full confessional like that.'

'Thank you. I really am honoured.'

'And you? What demons are on your shoulder?'

'Not now. Mine are all trivial in comparison. Another time I'll tell you more about me and my folks and my beliefs. What about Yasser? Does anything hold him back?'

'He has his demons, too. He lost his wife a couple of years ago. It's taken him a long time to move on from that, but he has. But now he's anxious about what's happening with Islam's place in the country. Now, he hears more and more of his people becoming radicalised and resentful and has already lost one or two of his congregation to more extreme, very anti-British imams in other parts of London.

'He suddenly finds himself fighting a rearguard action against a militant movement of his own people, while the host population react by firebombing mosques, or daubing graffiti, or attacking Muslims in the street. Whose side is he on? He must defend his people without fanning the flames. And with all that, he's resolved only to do good. And his good is a good I recognise, based not on high theology and scriptures, but simple humanity. And what has he done? He's freed Kate. I'm ashamed I don't feel better about his success.'

The next morning, however, Gerard felt even worse about it. So did Yasser. So did the three girls who walked up to them in Warwick Road with bruised and cut faces. Gerard recognised them all, but Kate wasn't there.

'Why don't you stop interfering? Fuck off. Leave Mahmoud alone,' one of the girls said. The words were unclear, because of the gaps in her teeth and the blue swelling around her cheek bones. Gerard remembered that she was one of the prettier of the night patrol. She wouldn't be able to claim that for several weeks.

'Who the fuck are you two? What you doing here, anyway?' cried another, through a face as badly beaten. Before either could even think of an answer, they saw Mahmoud on the other side of the road. He laughed across.

'Is that your girl? What'll you pay me for these? Going cheap for you two, eh? Interested? What'll you give me for them then, eh?'

Gerard didn't know the Egyptian words that Yasser shouted across the pavement, but the anger and despair didn't need language. As he cursed Mahmoud, Yasser began to cry and broke off. He turned back to the girls.

'I am so sorry, my dears. I didn't believe even he was as evil as this. What can I do?'

'Leave us alone. Just fuck off, both of you, and leave us alone. It's nothing to do with you.'

'Hear them, khatib? Listen to them, priest. You don't belong here, they do.'

‘Come along, Yasser.’ Gerard tugged his arm and pulled him away, still weeping and still cursing Mahmoud.

‘I told you, mate, I bleedin’ told you, didn’t I? You can’t beat Mahmoud, you just ain’t in his league.’ Alone of their friends, Arnold was unsurprised and unsympathetic. ‘You two, you’re meant to be the good guys, but you’re not. You’re just the nice guys. Good ain’t the same as nice.

‘Now, I want you to ’ave a look at these – my poems for the new collection. You wouldn’t believe what I saw the other night, it was really surreal, but just what I needed. It’s the centre poem, and honest, it took no time to write, it just poured. I’ve not done one as quickly and simply for I don’t know how long. But “The Toffee King”? Perfect. It’s the image, the symbol I was looking for all this time. ’Ave a look and tell me. And you don’t ’ave to be nice about it, neither; get your gun out, Randolph, and shoot down what don’t work.’

CHAPTER 30

The communal phone woke everyone in the house when it rang loudly in the hallway. It was Shelagh who eventually left her bed to answer it and then climbed the stairs again to bang on Gerard's door.

'Gerard! We're in big trouble. Can you come round?' He had never heard Jenny so agitated.

'What's happened? Is it Mahmoud?' he said, his own fear dominating.

'Who? No, Nick's been arrested. For assault. I know it's gone midnight, but please, Gerard darling, get here if you can. Now, please.'

The taxi got him to the house fifteen minutes later: ten minutes wait, five minutes drive and a quarter of an hour full of whirling disbelieving thoughts. He thought of Nick possibly hitting out at someone, remembering the bruises on Mahmoud's girls. He flinched in disbelief. Not Nick, surely? Gerard remembered lying on the ground in Cromwell Road, feeling heavy boots stomping on his bruised face. Was this the sort of thing Nick could do? His own attackers had never been found, so what had Nick done so foul that he was under arrest?

By the time he reached Jenny, he was as agitated as her voice on the phone. They hugged tightly as soon as he was through the door, both seeking support. It didn't take him long to slip back into the role of comforter as he saw and felt her distress. Jenny, normally so assured and controlled, was in pieces and now calling on him.

The story began in sobs, ended in disbelieving anger, and was punctuated by glances at the phone as she waited for it to bring her more news.

Jenny had been at home in the house all evening after a relatively early end to her day. Nick was due home at about eight, but was obviously delayed, perhaps by business in the West Country branch near Bristol where he was working that day, or perhaps by a bar. Whatever the reason, she didn't begin to worry until ten o'clock, when she'd not even had a phone call to let her know how long he would be. She watched the news in case there had been a train smash, but it gave her no clue as to why she was still waiting.

She finally got a phone call at eleven thirty, when Nick, as distraught as her, told her where he was.

'They won't let me go, Jen, they want to keep me here.'

'What have you done?'

'Nothing, I swear, but they keep saying I attacked this kid with my briefcase.'

'Why?'

'But I didn't. I was trying to fend him and his mates off. I've been here since seven, Jen, and they've only just let me phone.'

'Have you got a solicitor?'

'No, I don't know one here. Jen, they hit me …'

She heard voices at the other end, arguing, and Nick's voice calling something to her, but she didn't hear what, and then the connection was cut. She stood there trembling with disbelief. This didn't happen to people like them.

The police were on their side, and they always helped. Yes, of course.

She and Nick and all their old friends always mistrusted the police in the abstract, and during their university protest days always called them 'brutal pigs'. But really, they knew that police were there to help people like them. A misunderstanding is one thing, but all she'd heard was the argument on the phone and a hand from a blue uniformed arm slamming the phone down before she could find out what was happening.

Dialling 1471 gave her no clue, so she had to go through directory enquiries before finding the number of the police station. At first the policeman on the other end denied all knowledge of Nick.

'I can assure you there's no one here of that name, madam. Why do you think we've got him?'

'Because he's just bloody well called me from your police station, that's why! Find out for me, now.'

There was a pause, and then in a different tone,

'Bear with me a moment, madam, and I'll see what I can find out.'

She was kept on hold, with the tinny sound of a Brandenburg Concerto to soothe her until a new voice cut in.

Yes, her husband was indeed helping them at the moment, following an incident outside the railway station. No, no one had been seriously hurt, but there was an assault. Yes, of course he could come home after he had signed a statement.

'You mean a confession?'

'I mean a statement. He's reading it through now. When he signs it we can release him on bail.'

'You're charging him?'

That depended, but a charge was not out of the question. He was not at liberty to tell her, of course.

So why was the phone call cut off earlier? And who hit Nick?

A misunderstanding, he thought. They were certainly not in the habit of harming people being questioned. She must have misheard, understandable with the surprise, perhaps.

'Don't bloody lie to me, I'll have our doctor look at him as soon as he's back home. God help you if there's a single unexplained mark on him.'

He understood she was distraught, but that tone really was not well advised or justified. He would phone her himself when Nick was ready to return home. Just as soon as he signed the statement and the paperwork was complete.

'If you mean you're waiting for him to sign a confession, you'd better order his breakfast first – make that two – I'll be down there myself by morning.'

But, she told Gerard in disbelief, breakfast was off. Ten minutes later the same policeman rang her, smug with the news that Nick was even then being put on a train home, having signed a full statement that, yes, was a confession of an assault on a teenager who lived by the station. He had been charged and released on bail. He would be home soon.

Gerard took control while they waited. He called their solicitor and explained what had happened, telling him what time Nick was expected home. Then he fed Jenny coffees, keeping her away from the whisky bottle she wanted, and sat holding her hand.

There was a lot to talk about, most of it in the past when they were students together and one or other of them needed the other's help. He admired her anger and guts in the way she spoke to the West Country policeman just now and reminded her of how she spoke to the hospital receptionist when he was recovering from his own beating. They spoke of Ann and Joe, and he told her of Joe's long-kept faith with old widowed George. All the time they were talking, both looked at the clock, willing its faster turn, and listening to the street, waiting for the sound of the key in the front door.

When Nick arrived at last, tired and close to tears, Jenny renewed his interrogation. It took all of Gerard's diplomacy to let Nick have a period of recovery along with a calm reception and a sense of being home again. After food and a drink, and at last a real kiss and loving welcome from Jenny, he was able to tell them what happened.

Before he started, he rolled up one trouser leg.

'Look at that. D'you see it? The bastards did that as soon as I was in the station.'

A raw graze ran down the back of his leg to the top of the heel. 'Bloody copper's boot did that. Two of them held me against the wall, and the one behind trod on me.'

'Wait till your solicitor gets here,' advised Gerard. 'Tell him everything then, don't waste it now. Sit with Jenny, I'll wait next door.'

'No,' Jenny put her hand out to him. 'Don't leave us – you've saved me from going mad tonight, don't go now.'

The bell suddenly rang. Nick paled and went still, but it was the solicitor, a Mr Taylor, not the police, and he breathed again. Jenny and Gerard both stayed with him and heard his story.

As he was walking towards the station, two young teenagers on mountain bikes circled round and round him, causing him to stop. He felt irritated at first, not threatened, but as they began to jeer at him he felt more and more uneasy. One of them came close enough to brush against his briefcase, which he hastily lifted out of harm's way. As it happened, it was into harm's way, because in moving it he collided with the biker on the other side of him, who fell.

Nick didn't even have time to check whether or not the boy was hurt, because a policeman appeared beside them, and arrested him. As well as Nick, the two boys were taken to the police station where their parents were summoned. Nick didn't hear what they said in their interrogation, but he did see the families leave, the boy with whom he had collided giving him a smirk and a finger as they went out.

He thought that he would just have to make a statement and could then come home. Of course he was in the clear, he'd done nothing. It was a drag though, that he'd have to come back later to give evidence against the kid.

It turned out not to be as simple as that – as he stood by the main desk he asked to be allowed to call Jenny to tell her he was catching a later train. Trying to be funny? Of course not. Didn't he realise he was in serious trouble? What were they talking about? He hadn't done anything. Before he had finished the sentence he found his face pressed against the wall and a searing pain in his leg.

'You've not been asked to talk yet. Didn't you hear? You're in trouble!'

This was impossible – things like this just didn't happen to Nick and people like him. What was to be done? He sat in the interview room and listened to what he was supposed to have done – attacked two youths, unprovoked, hitting them with an offensive weapon, to wit, a hard-edged briefcase. Better sign a confession now, and he might get off with a probation order. If not, there might be a more serious charge waiting – his choice.

But he hadn't done anything. Perhaps he'd benefit from some time to think it over, and remember better what happened? They emptied his pockets, removed his belt and shoes, gave him a receipt and left him in a cell with the light off.

He sat, disbelieving, in the dark, barefoot, his leg bleeding, and for the first time in his life understood real fear. Hours passed, he didn't know how many, during which his fear grew and grew. The waiting ended suddenly when the door was noisily unlocked and flung back with a crash against the wall. Two policemen stood in the doorway for five seconds before converging on him.

'Time to talk to us now,' said the larger one. Neither of them looked friendly – they were both hard men. He tried to explain, but the larger one – he didn't think to look at the numbers on their epaulettes – pushed him hard, and he staggered back, collapsing heavily on the bed.

'That was the wrong answer,' said a scowling voice, 'we'll tell you what you're going to say. We've got it written down for you to sign.' Nick demanded a solicitor, but when they asked him who, he had no name or number to offer. He demanded his one phone call, but they told him the lines were all busy until he signed.

Putting his name to such a damaging lie was impossible, and he held out at that. He resisted for another hour, during which the larger policeman, the one with the foul smelling breath and fists that could have been cut from the ham bone, leaned over him closely and whispered the things that might happen to him if he caused trouble on the shift, or led to their being late home through not co-operating.

After the fifth time of asking, they let him ring Jenny. He tried to tell her what was happening but they cut him off almost as soon as he'd made contact. That was it, those few exchanges with her were the sole sympathetic human attention he'd had all night, and it had taken him at least three hours to get even those few seconds. There was nothing to look forward to now in this ordeal.

'But why did you sign it?' demanded Jenny, tears on her cheeks. 'You didn't do anything, so how could you sign a confession?'

'You don't know what it's like – you don't know. The other one was going out, and I was alone in the cell with this … this Neanderthal. It was awful. He knew nothing, he was thick and brutal, and I couldn't bear being in his power anymore. I signed it to get away from him. Much longer and I'd have confessed to murder, too.'

Gerard watched Jenny's face take on horror, sympathy and a small measure of disdain for this little cowardice. He saw with dismay how her disdain might slowly grow into contempt. Nick had already suffered enough, without facing this sentence.

'I'm not sure you could have done anything else, Nick,' he said quickly. 'You didn't do anything wrong, but I don't think many people could hold out against that intimidation. A statement taken like that can't be valid, surely?' he asked the solicitor, who was busy taking notes.

'Common humanity and justice says of course it isn't valid,' Mr Taylor replied. 'Trouble is, got to prove it all. Their word against yours, and let's face it, local bobbies are going to be believed sooner than a rich outsider businessman accused of beating up a local kid. Let's get some proof – go to the doctor tomorrow, get him to say what he thinks that injury on your leg is. If he says size twelve shoe, police issue, we're in with a chance. If not, we'll have to dig elsewhere.'

'Can't you send someone down there to find witnesses?' asked Gerard.

'Like to, like to, but sadly I don't have Perry Mason's budget. If you'll pay for the train fare and hotel bill, I can try some on the spot enquiries myself. I will be talking to the arresting officer anyway, and see what the boys say.'

Jenny nodded at once.

'Of course, whatever it takes. We can't let the pigs get away with that.'

'Good, good, but a word of advice. "Pigs" as a descriptive term for policemen doesn't go down well in court. Please try to drop the habit.'

'You heard what they did to Nick, and you think they're not pigs?' she shouted.

'You've never been in anyone's power like that,' Nick mumbled. 'I never thought I could be so scared.'

CHAPTER 31

'Does that surprise you?' asked Silke.

'Of course it does,' said Gerard. 'The police, they don't do things like that. They're there to help and protect us. They help us keep the law, not make it up for themselves.'

'Come on, priest, do you really think that? What sort of a healthy person likes to dress up all day in a uniform with handcuffs and baton? Police everywhere are like that.'

Gerard remembered his few encounters with police forces, and stories of his former parishioners. Then he remembered the big miners' strike, less than ten years ago, and the behaviour of the Metropolitan Police who had been sent to the North to break the strike. His parish was not quite in the mining areas of Derbyshire, but the stories of the battles with the flying pickets and the brutality against the local striking communities had easily reached their ears, and he and Father Holloway had watched the local news bulletins with despair and disbelief.

Credit to Father Holloway, he had joined in with the relief efforts to provide food and money to the striking families in nearby parishes, and his sermons during that period were full of encouragement and support.

But apart from that episode, all of Gerard's own experience with the police had been either neutral or positive.

'No, that's not true,' he concluded. 'Police are not all like that. Some individuals maybe, but all the police I've ever known myself have been different.'

'Over here, you belong to the establishment so of course they're different. If you were Polish, or East German, thirty years ago you'd have found the police treated priests like they did your friend. What about your girl then, the prostitute? Why didn't you tell your marvellous police about her? They'd have locked up your Mr Mahmoud, wouldn't they?'

'She was too afraid to talk. We have to have proof.'

'Haven't you got your proof now? You and your friend can tell them about his beatings. Why haven't you done that?'

He shrugged.

'We were scared to, partly for ourselves, and partly because of what else Mahmoud might do to the girls if we failed.'

'So you didn't trust your wonderful policemen to do their job then?'

'It's not the same, that's not fair.' Gerard found his irritation building up at Silke's antagonistic sophistry. It was bad enough losing yet another of his pillars of certainty, that the British police were wonderful and reliable. Confusing an argument about their newly discovered brutality with the lack of evidence in another case only drove him deeper into upset.

'So what's your problem?' she asked him. Was she mocking him? Sympathising? He couldn't tell from her voice or face.

'Everything,' he shrugged back.

'Oh no, no, *nein*, don't say that. Next thing, you'll start chasing women over the river, and they might not be like me – they might not talk before they use the knife. I know what's wrong with you, and I know what to do about it, too.'

'Tell me then.'

She looked at him for a moment.

'No, not yet. This is boring, let's do something else. I've got another two hours before I work, take me somewhere.'

'You want to go somewhere with me? Really?'

'Oh Gerard, relax! Chill out, as the children say now. We are grown-ups, it's allowed to go out somewhere together. You chased me, after all, so now let's enjoy the catch, eh?'

Gerard felt his mouth broaden in a smile such as it hadn't known in a long time. She winked at him, took his arm and led him out into London.

CHAPTER 32

Shelagh was late coming home, but that wasn't unusual. She had been on the Common with her group to greet the new moon. Their big festival of Samhain had passed – the night that marked the passing of summer, the New Year of the Celts, and the time when the veil between the worlds was at its thinnest. They had celebrated that night in a cemetery, trying to commune with long-dead ancestors, who, frustratingly, had stayed stolidly uncommunicative. The moon, though, still demanded homage when new and at its full.

There were only six in her group, and despite all the demands for commitment to prioritise ritual evenings over any other call on time or emotion that came from parents, partners, work, night classes or holidays, she could always bet that at least two of the group would be missing at any of the festivals.

Nevertheless, the ritual had felt complete and rewarding and left her refreshed and still slightly spaced out. The group had long since learned to ignore the curious dog walkers and indeed, the dogs, who had no qualms about crossing into the circle of protection that their leader had so thoroughly cast at the beginning.

Now, energised by the ritual, Shelagh was home and restless.

Just as the kettle for hot chocolate was boiling she heard Gerard's footsteps on the stairs – his attempts to walk silently without disturbing anyone were always unmistakeable – and she opened the door to call him in.

'Gerard? Come and have a drink of something. Don't worry, I'll cover his lordship up;' 'his lordship' being the poster that had so upset him on his first visit.

'Don't worry about him,' Gerard replied as he came in, nodding at the Indian bedspread covering the poster on the wall. 'I'm used to him now, and he doesn't look such a bad chap after all once you get to know him.'

'Oh well done, that's progress. I'll get you joining our circle up on the Common yet.'

'No, I won't go that far, but, well, things change, don't they? Is that where you've been tonight?'

'Yep. Tonight's the night. Welcoming the New Moon and its energies. But what's this about things changing? Has something happened? Not been a naughty priest, have you?'

He felt himself blush slightly.

'Not exactly, though I'm sure Father Holloway wouldn't agree.'

'Oh? You can't leave it there. Let me get the drinks first, and then you've got to tell me all. Who's keeping you out on the tiles so late? What do you want, alcohol or tea?'

'I've had a few drinks already, so I'll go with a tea, please. Anything except Earl Grey.'

'You don't like Earl Grey?'

He grimaced. 'Like drinking joss sticks. No thanks, I'll have real.'

Gerard settled down in the armchair, the electric lights replaced by three candles, and Shelagh curled over both seats of the sofa opposite, nursing her hot chocolate. He told her a little of his afternoon with Silke, the trek across Hyde Park, finding late conkers, the short river trip and then coffee before she met the band for the evening's performance. He was recognised in the club now as a follower, and apart from mutterings from the other band members, was left alone to enjoy her singing.

'All very light and trivial, but life just seems rather brighter now than most of the last year.'

'So who is this Silky, then? I've not heard of her before.' Gerard thought he heard a slight edge to Shelagh's voice and wondered, with a strange mixture of alarm and smugness, what this could mean. He clearly had some thinking to do later.

It was true, some of his darkness had indeed lifted under Silke's influence, and innocuous as their afternoon had been, it felt like a glimpse through an open door that he might someday enter. Like Shelagh, he felt alert and charged after the day's events.

He gave her a heavily edited version of his friendship with the singer, omitting the train ride and his following her and her challenge to him with the threat of a knife. Instead, their meeting was a chance encounter in the South Bank Centre (not exactly false) and some impromptu counselling from her (not exactly false) when he was at his lowest point.

After he had finished, she looked at him silently for a while, their faces flickering in the candlelight.

'I wonder.'

Pause.

'What?'

Longer pause. Again,

'What?'

'I wonder … are you finding your soul again?'

'Sorry, Shelagh, I really don't understand what you're saying. My soul is my soul and is part of me. I can't find it or lose it, it is me.'

'I think you lost it, and that's what's brought you here. Bear with me,' as he was about to interrupt again. 'I'm only thinking this now, and I don't know if I can explain properly, but please let me try without interrupting, or I'll never be able to think it through.'

'Ok,' he said, though reluctantly. 'I'll try not to interrupt, but I want a right of reply afterwards. Fair?'

'Course. Ok then, here goes: when I first met you, I picked up a sense of power, which is why I thought you might be a pagan like me, initiated, maybe even a priest or some position like that. Yeah, yeah, you are a priest of course, I know, but I thought in a tradition like mine. But at the same time I felt a sort of, I don't know, emptiness? A lack? A … I can't think of the right word, but there was a hole where *you* should have been. Whatever, the part of you I can only think of as your soul, your essence, was absent. You were adrift and lovely, as you are, there wasn't enough of you there. I don't think any of this makes sense, I'm sorry.

'I don't mean depression, 'cos I've met a lot of depressed people in my time, and most of them still have their soul, even Jez, though he gets emptier by the day. Is it your anchor I mean? That would have been your faith, but that's taken a knock, hasn't it? You've lost that, or at least the flavour of it that came with that Holloway monster, and nothing's filled it. But that power I felt, it's still there. That's why you've found yourself with Arnold, me, Yasser (I'd love to meet him properly sometime, do bring him round), even Jez and now this – Silky?'

'Silke,' he corrected.

'Silke, ok. When you came in just now, it was the first time I've seen you alive. Did you have sex with her?'

'No! Good God, no, we just had a good time in company together.'

'But she's given you something that's started you growing again. Maybe even this Mahmoud character has, but not so obviously. He started you on your crusade after all, though that seems to have stalled. Anyway, there's something in you that's attracted these strangers (me included) to you, and I bet you never expected that when you came down here, did you? Not your usual social crowd, are we?'

He shook his head, in agreement. His urge to talk over her and refute her had faded, and he wanted to hear more of what she was thinking.

'There's something in you we all responded to, despite the, what's the word – void? But there must be something in us that you needed, need still perhaps, even though none of us are aware of it. And you do feel different tonight. Whatever happened with Silke, or didn't happen, you're not quite so empty. That's what I mean when I said, you're finding your soul. And even as I say all this, I can hear how rubbish I'm explaining it, it's all too vague. I said I'd only just thought it and haven't worked out yet just what I mean. Sorry, forget it all. More tea?'

'No, no thanks, Shelagh. I was gearing myself up for a good argument then, getting all defensive and angry, but that's gone. I need to think about what you've just said. If you're right, then thank you for helping me find my soul again. Odd, that it still feels a hideously blasphemous thing to say, despite all my doubts and questionings of the last few months.'

The next morning Gerard had no answers to Shelagh's questions, but he did have an urgency about Kate. He rang Yasser, and they arranged to meet for a coffee in Knightsbridge at ten. Gerard had suggested the Troubadour, but Yasser pointed out that they were more likely to be overheard by a contact of Mahmoud's there than at Harrods, and they'd already caused the girls enough grief.

At nine forty-five they found themselves in the queue at the counter, both eager to talk and plan.

'But can we ever do more than talk and plan?' asked Gerard. 'We've both tried talking to Mahmoud, and that's only led to beatings and bruises. Thanks to Arnold I did manage to pass more than enough money to Kate for her to get a train far away, but I think she just hands it straight on to him. I'm stuck.'

'What about the obvious? Tell the police.'

'What do we tell them? They'll only take action if we can prove it, and what evidence have we got apart from hearsay? And what would happen to the girls when the police let him go?'

'His word against a priest and an imam khatib? What doubt can there be? Of course they'll believe us and clear him from the streets.'

'I have another worry about going to the police. Can we trust them?' Gerard saw Yasser's shocked response and told him Nick's story.

'That upsets me. I hear many stories from the mosques lately about police stopping and searching Muslims. They assume that we are all jihadists. Thanks be to Allah, I have not experienced it yet myself, but more and more of my people mistrust the police. I didn't ever think it happened to white Christians like your friend. Do you mean that as well as being racist you believe they are corrupt?'

'I don't know, Yasser, and I'm worried. Not all police, obviously, but if only a few are in the pay of Mahmoud, or whoever's pulling Mahmoud's strings, we daren't tell them about what he's doing without enough strong proof that even corrupt officers can't ignore it or tip him off. And as well as marking us out to him again, we might be giving Kate away too.'

'So she is already in the gravest danger, yes? We can't make it any worse for her, so it's you and me isn't it? I don't want to believe the police here are corrupt and in his pay, no? But even the idea of that makes it complicated. What is happening with your friend?'

'We're waiting to hear from his solicitor, who's gone down there. He sounds optimistic, but he would, after all that's why he's paid. I can't believe Nick will come to trial or be found guilty, except that he did sign that confession.'

'Under duress, though, that must count, eh?'

'His word against the local coppers? A rich outsider businessman? I imagine local magistrates will take it at face value.'

'I pray for justice for him. As you do as well, of course.'

'Of course, and I also hope the solicitor will do his part well. But this doesn't help us with Kate.'

'That Mahmoud knows us both, so we can't be seen near her. I could recruit one of my jamaat perhaps, but to ask a worshipper to help a prostitute wouldn't go down well. Wrong questions might be asked of the wrong people, and I don't want the new extreme Islamists to start visiting and preaching at my mosque.'

'Jama …?'

'Jamaat – what would you say, parishioner? Member? Congregation? Anyway, one of the regular worshippers at my mosque.'

'What do we actually want to do, hmm? Save this one girl or close down Mahmoud and bring him to justice? I want to do both, but Kate is my priority. After she's safe, we can see about taking down Mahmoud. Or rather, find someone else who can.'

'No, we are men of peace. There are others who will work any violence that needs doing to him. Actually,' and Yasser leaned forward with a satisfied smirk and dropped his voice, 'I think we may have an ally.'

'Who?'

'Not yet, I need to be sure of him first. But if I am not being led astray yet again, I think we may be able to get Mahmoud in our sights and bang – pull the trigger! And let me tell you, I am a peaceful Muslim who doesn't like pulling triggers. But in this case …?'

'What can he do?'

'He might soon be ready to give evidence against Mahmoud, and he has knowledge that would stand up in court.'

'Soon?'

'There are things he wants that I'm not able to promise. But he has knowledge, he has knowledge my friend. A little longer and I think I can persuade him to do the right thing.'

'Whoever he is, please don't tell him Kate's name under any circumstances. Not till we find a way of rescuing her.'

'Well, if we can indeed put Mahmoud out of the way, then all the girls can be freed, including your Kate. Don't lose faith, my friend. Our ally may deliver the goods, yes?'

'It must be soon, Yasser. It must be very soon.'

Chapter 32

And so they found themselves back in the same position again, agonising over their own impotence, aware of the need and yet unable to produce any plan to fulfil it. This time there seemed to be a faint glimmer of light at the tunnel's end, though neither could yet tell if it was daylight or a flamethrower.

CHAPTER 33

That evening at the club Silke was surprised and a little disappointed not to see Gerard come to hear her sing again. He'd been there three nights now, and somehow she expected him tonight as well. He had seemed brighter, more human, since their afternoon, and she had begun to hope that she could cure him. Vanity of vanities! It hadn't escaped her that the band were less sympathetic to his presence and his association with her, but what did that matter?

He was a sad man and not at all the threatening figure her mind had painted when she first caught him watching and then following her. She hadn't been bluffing when she first threatened him with a knife and alarm, but hearing his story brought instead a great sense of confusion. Physically he was not unattractive, but there was something too *lasch*. What do the English say? Wishy-washy? But he had had a shock that had undermined all his beliefs, and she understood that suffering. Underneath, with the way he tackled Mahmoud and despite his beating still wanted to help the hooker, she could see that he had a strong core, and she'd hoped that befriending him might restore it.

Silke knew the effects of such shock only too well. After the fall of the Wall and news about the workings of the German Democratic Republic came out, she learned that her grandmother, her lovely *oma*, had been passing information and gossip about her family and neighbours to the *Stasi*. All the times that Silke had talked about the West, its freedoms, its music that she longed to be able to play, the harshness of Honecker's regime, the inevitability of Soviet collapse and her fear of nuclear holocaust, all of these her granny had fed to the secret police. It was a miracle that they hadn't come knocking on her door to take her away, as had happened to three or four of her friends over previous years. Oh yes, she understood the aftershocks of such betrayal. It took a move to England, away from Germany forever, and a new start as a singer before she could stop shaking and crying whenever she thought of it, which was most days. That a neighbour was feeding information she could live with – most families had to – but not her *oma* who had loved her so much.

Her sad priest had some way to go yet, but she knew he could find his core again.

'Silke,' shouted Russ across the room. 'Come here, we've got news!' They had finished the set for the evening and while the band were packing up the equipment and instruments, a stranger had come across and started talking animatedly with Ian and Karl.

'We've got a tour, girl, we've got a frigging tour!' laughed Ian. 'Here, Andrzej, tell her!'

'Hi, Silke, I'm Andrzej. Hey, your singing is amazing, I'm knocked out. Listen, I've got contacts in Poland. They run venues and they want bands. Not rock bands, they can get those any day of the week, but what you're doing. Yeah, they'll eat you! I can get you twenty bookings in February around Poland. End up in Warsaw and then, well, maybe on to Czechoslovakia or Hungary or both. What do you say?'

She looked at the others first. 'Is this straight? For real?'

'Course it's real,' said Karl. 'Stop being so suspicious, we're on the way. This shitty club's done it for us after all. Come on, girl, cheer!'

'What are the dates? Where exactly? How much do we get paid? You've got to tell us all this first. We've got a regular gig here, and we're not giving it up unless it's rock solid, right?'

'For fuck's sake,' groaned Karl, 'here we go again. We're heading for Poland in the New Year, are you coming or not?'

'Give me a chance – you only told me this twenty seconds ago. I never heard of you before,' to Andrzej. 'I want to know more before we give our notice here and maybe end up with zilch – *Schluss mit nichts*. Ok?'

'Yeah, yeah, ok. Ok, Let me call my contacts, it'll have to be tomorrow now, and I'll see you here with dates and itinerary, when, Monday?'

'You can do it that soon? Really?'

'Listen, I'm a fixer, I'm great at it. When I see a good deal coming up, I'll move a mountain to get it done. It's what I do, and it's why I'm here. Yes, I can do it that soon, really, you'll see. What do they say, "A pigeon on the roof's better than a sparrow in your hand"? No, it's the other way round, but you know what I mean. Grab the chance while it's there, man, grab it.'

Andrzej and the others hogged the bar, talking excitedly about this new chance, but Silke couldn't join in. For one thing, she didn't believe this was anything more than a scam that would leave them broke with no bookings.

For another thing, she couldn't get Gerard out of her mind. Why, she wasn't sure. She certainly wasn't in love with him, that wasn't it. There was something about him, though, that wouldn't let go. That sadness; that was part of it. And the fact that he embraced the music that was so obviously new, alien even, to him. But there was something missing from him that she understood from her own history, and she wanted to help him get to land, as she herself had managed.

'Hey, Silke, wakey-wakey, what's up? Come and join in for God's sake,' Russ called to her.

'In a minute. I'm just thinking what to do about the priest.'

'Oh, fuck the priest, come and have a drink.'

'Fuck the priest? Yes, I will. Not yet, he isn't ready, but I will. Ok, tell me about this tour then.'

CHAPTER 34

What a week it had been! Jez didn't need to look for punters or bread anymore. This new business, that was the stuff! He was a burglar now, a successful burglar. Big-time Jez, yeah! One of the big boys. Not only that, he'd pulled off the trick twice more now. Three-times Jez, that's him. Both times he was able to take enough to see him through for weeks. Wallets, some jewellery and loose cash, though that never amounted to much more than bus fare. But he was on the way. They seek him here, they seek him … somewhere, whatever, he was on his way. His old cellmate, Matt, would be proud of him.

Tomorrow, Friday, he was going to try it again, but this was to be the big one with his apprenticeship over. He'd walked a huge radius around the Fulham, Brompton, Earl's Court area, and gone as far as Kensington on one side and Holland Park on the other. He'd made a point of working out which streets and buildings had the rich flats and which were the cheap student or transient rooms, even though many had an almost identical plush stuccoed Georgian exterior.

Tailgating, that was his secret, and preparing to tailgate, that was the key. Checking that no one spotted him waiting, not spending too long by one set of doors, being casual, not wasting time once inside, heading along a different corridor or up the stairs instead of the lift and being careful not to alarm the person you followed into the building.

Three successes showed the world that Jez was the king of burglars, the stuff of future legend, the Master thief. He was invincible immortal, brilliant – he was high. Although, of course, he mustn't actually let the world know all that.

Time to celebrate with another high, a top up. It was time, anyway.

When he surfaced it was time to take a walk outside, tread the streets again and feel some air instead of the fetid atmosphere of his room. Autumn was moving fast into winter, the sunshine luring outdoors any who were unwary and lightly-dressed, and then laughing aloud at them as they realised after five seconds that yes, it really was cold, and t-shirts gave no protection against the new winds from the north. Trees in small gardens and along street edges speeded up their striptease, exposing more and more bare twigs and then larger branches, as they shrugged off their red, yellow and brown skimpy clothing, letting it flutter down into heaps on pavements and in gutters. The lights in the tall blue building came on earlier and earlier, displaying more clearly whether any watcher was by the window, coffee mug in hand, looking down over their domain.

Maybe now, rather than tomorrow. His head was clear now, after all. Why wait? They wouldn‘t be back from work, and it wasn't yet that transition time between the streams who left work for homes far away, and those coming into town for a night's entertainment. Yes, time to prove himself again. Perhaps just a little top-up to make himself invincible once more, and then tools in his pocket and off on the treasure hunt.

Muttering the directions along with loud warnings to himself not to draw the attention of passers-by, he walked in the growing darkness towards South Kensington and the road where his target apartment block stood. The street was almost purely residential with one or two office premises at the end, but no shops. Why he chose this target, he couldn't remember, but it was now firmly fixed in his head that it was the right choice, and no doubts, arguments or reality checks were going to shake that conviction. This was the one that would make him rich forever.

All of a sudden, while still in the High Street, he caught sight of himself in the lit shopfront of a store that was preparing for

Christmas, and thought he saw two figures in the window busily dismantling him. He didn't stop to realise that they were, in fact, window-dressers removing a mannequin whose display time had ended. With unfortunate timing, as he looked in, his own reflection overlapped with the dismembered dummy, and he just saw his own rude disintegration. He screamed, turned and ran back towards Fulham, ducking in and out of alleyways to shake off these demon assassins who, in truth, had never even registered his existence. In and out of stores and shops, down cul-de-sacs, and through mews, he forged his escape from these nightmares.

He ran on, pushing through the shoppers and walkers, nearly overturning two pushchairs in his panic, dodging and whimpering until he found himself two streets away from his bedsit. For the first time, he dared to look behind him. It was clear. No one was taking any notice of him. Just another crazy junkie, nothing to look at here, folks, just carry on home.

His nightmares lasted through until Sunday – dreams of spotlights on him as masked figures cut away his limbs one by one, and, worst of all, waved his gear tantalisingly in front of him, laughing because he had no hands to reach it and give himself that quick rush of blissful oblivion.

By Sunday lunchtime he returned to exhausted normal and forgot he had ever seen that store window. His nightmares stayed fresh, but the memory of the trigger had gone.

He did, however, reject the idea of South Kensington. Too close and not that great an area. No, there were better pickings elsewhere. Luckily, there was still enough money from his earlier triumphs, as well as three untouched wallets, to feed himself while he rethought his plans.

CHAPTER 35

Tuesday morning, a cold sun was shining, and the streets felt welcoming as Jez walked towards his new target. He was unlikely to be recognised in Holland Park. Unusually, he'd thought enough to improve his looks a little and had bought some cleaner trousers and a button-up shirt from a charity shop. They were in quite good condition and did actually fit him. To complete an air of possible respectability he even visited a barber for the first time in seven years. It was important that if any residents should spot him once he was inside the block, he shouldn't look out of place – not like an addict trying to steal, but like someone who seemed to belong. Just to give himself some more cover, he also bought a cheap paperback from the charity shop and carried it in a cardboard envelope. Admiring his strange new appearance in the mirror he thought that, yes, he could pass for a courier delivering an urgent package. Just to complete the illusion, he even carried a clipboard for a pretend signature.

In his rare lucid states, he remembered pieces of advice from his prison days, and simple cover during burglary was something he remembered his cellmate bragging about. He'd also learned how to pick several different types of lock. While he had never before thought it a skill to practise, he now saw its value and had fashioned a clumsy set of picks, although he hadn't yet been able to try them out in earnest. It didn't occur to him that even though Matt boasted so much about his skill as a burglar, he was still in prison.

He had also noticed, again in his few clearheaded days, that people along the streets and around formal office buildings, seemed to have started wearing a badge on a lanyard to prove they belonged there. Jez had no idea what it meant to belong somewhere, as the concept had been outside his experience for many years, but it did have an appeal. Maybe a badge on a lanyard would give him a real status, as well as a pretend one. He was a professional burglar now, learning the tricks (could he get a BTEC, he wondered?), and he should look professional. As he walked, he looked at himself sideways in shop windows and held himself a little straighter, pleased and surprised at what he saw. Maybe he could even go straight, kick the H and live as a respectable thief. Stranger things have happened.

On his way, holding the package with the book, he passed Gerard.

'Hey, Gerald,' he called. 'How are you, man?'

'Jez? Is that you in there? What happened? What are you doing?'

'Good, ain't it? I'm off for a job.'

'Really? That's great news, what doing?'

Jez suddenly panicked again. He couldn't say, 'I'm off to burgle someone,' but also, he couldn't think what else he might be doing. He stalled.

'Oh, you know, things.'

'Are you getting clean, Jez?'

'Yeah, yeah that's right. Nearly there. Next week, definite.'

'When's your interview? Have you got time for a coffee?'

Gerard didn't know what prompted him to ask. Of all his preferred coffee companions, Jez didn't even make it onto the longlist, but he hadn't seen him around for a while and still wanted to encourage and help him quit his addictions. He was saved, however, as Jez looked as startled at receiving the invitation as he was to have offered it.

'Oh, oh, cheers, Gerald, and that, but, you know …' he stuttered, trying to understand how this could happen to him now, of all moments.

'It's all right, Jez, I don't want to make you late for your job. Good luck, and I'll see you another time, ok?' and Gerard turned away with a nod and a smile.

As he walked off, he wondered why he always felt he needed to befriend and help Jez. His heart would sink when he heard that whistling, whiny voice building up to ask for money, but he couldn't turn his back. Worse than that, Jez always seemed to be glad to see him, even just now when he obviously didn't want to have a coffee with him. But Jez's new smart appearance and the mention of a job intrigued him. And why was he carrying a clipboard to an interview? Perhaps he'd misunderstood, and Jez already had the job and was carrying it out. No, he was going to have to see him later and find out the story. If Jez really was changing, then Gerard wanted to be able to offer some kind of support to keep him straight.

In the meantime, Jez walked on towards Holland Park and his next job. Later, he'd try Knightsbridge or maybe go south to Chelsea. These were where the rich people lived, and sometimes rich people got careless. Usually of course, they didn't, which was how come they stayed rich, but Jez hadn't yet got that far in his calculations.

He clutched his parcel a bit too tightly and marked the cardboard. He must be careful, be cool, be the Man, not tense and scared. Today was going to be the big one! He'd looked at the streets and apartment blocks, and he had chosen well. There wasn't a concierge, porter, receptionist or whatever they called themselves, in the way, stopping honest thieves like himself going about their business.

'He's not in today,' he could imagine the stupid voice.

'Leave the package with me, and I'll see Mr Whoever-you-want gets it. Please sign here. Who sent you?'

All these bloody questions between him and the empty apartment he needed to get to. This one though, he just needed to get into the building again.

Last week he'd tried three separate blocks in Kensington, successfully tailgating his way in, but without actually entering an apartment. He was just getting the layout and checking how loaded the residents there must be, and he had found the one that looked his best chance. Now he was having to suss out a new block he hadn't tried, but that was ok because he knew what he was doing. No conciereceptionthing-bloke on the desk; that was all he had to watch out for, and once he was inside he could make his selection. Right time of day and with the wind behind him, he might even manage two or three, or the whole block, yeah! This was his big day, the start of his new life. Jez was flying. The sun was shining, the air was early-winter fresh, and he was just high enough to feel it, but not enough to mess it up like he usually managed. Not this time, not again. The Man, that's Jez. The Man!

It took him fifty minutes to walk to the street with the apartment block. It was early afternoon now, but few people were in the street. For the benefit of anyone who might be looking out of a window, he ostentatiously checked a mythical address on the cardboard package and headed towards the front door. Peering through the glass, he reassured himself that there was no official to get in his way, just an area by the lifts and stairs. There was indeed a desk and chair to the side, but it was empty, so nothing to worry about. He didn't even need to tailgate today: he had his tools.

The street was empty, the entrance was empty, nobody was watching him. He inserted the first picklock and held it in position, and then the second. Despite practising on the lock to his own house and room, he suddenly found that he couldn't move a tumbler. Both picks seemed jammed, and he felt the panic rushing up again. Somehow, he stayed on top of it, kept his fingers on the picklocks and didn't run away. Two deep breaths, and he tried again. Still, miraculously, no one was around to see him. Nothing could spot him making his own triumphal secret entry, except for that little red winking light in the corner of the ceiling, spoiling the line of the cornice and pointing towards the door. But he was concentrating on the lock and his fingers, and so completely missed the camera.

Click. Suddenly the tumblers gave it up as a bad job and let him in. He pushed the door open just in time to let a woman behind him squeeze through.

'Oh thank you,' she gasped. 'I was afraid I couldn't get in behind you and would have to rummage for my key. God knows where it is in all this stuff.' And she waved an overfull handbag under Jez's face, laughingly apologetic. 'I've just got five minutes to change and then off out again. No rest, eh? No rest for the wicked!' And she laughed self-consciously again as she pressed the lift button and vanished up to the 1st floor, 2nd floor, 3rd floor, 4th floor, and then stopped.

Not usually famed for his quickness of wit and thought, Jez nevertheless carried out a quick calculation. Someone on the fourth floor was going out in five minutes, say ten to be sure. She was very well-dressed with a comfortable middle-class voice and a handbag full of stuff. Proof that the gods were smiling down on Jez. A gift wrapped up in Christmas paper with a glittery gold bow, that's what she was. His Christmas present, several weeks early maybe, but so what, he wasn't going to turn it down. He turned to the stairs and slowly climbed them up to the fourth floor. He didn't want to go too fast, or she would still be in her flat, but he didn't want to go so slowly that he wouldn't know which one was hers; this was the puzzle.

At the third floor he speeded up so as not to miss her, but the effort reduced him to a coughing fit that set luminous tadpoles swimming behind his eyelids. He recovered at last and made his way more cautiously to the top of the stairs. There were two sets of glass doors, one to the right and one to the left – which should he take? He felt the panic rise again at the prospect of making a choice and once more managed to keep it together. He was King after all, the Man – he would make the right decision.

And sure enough, he was vindicated when he heard the door on the right creak slightly as someone approached it from the other side. He ducked down out of sight, just in time as her footsteps reached the lifts beside the stairs. Luckily for him, she didn't sense Jez lurking. Still muttering to herself what sounded like a checklist of things she needed, she got into the lift and returned to the ground floor. He still didn't know which was her apartment but at least he knew which side it was.

Beyond that door was a short, wide corridor. There were prints of primary colours, odd shapes and occasional figures, hanging every few feet along either wall, prints that Jez couldn't recognise or even understand. If they had pictures as strange as these on the walls, they must be rich. The carpet felt satisfyingly soft under his feet. She was used to luxury. Time for him to share in that!

The corridor was silent. No music came from any of the apartments and there was no sound of anyone moving about or a TV. He had the run of it to himself alone! To make sure, he knocked on the first apartment door and held the package and clipboard ready. There was no answer. He looked up and down the corridor again, just to check, and then retrieved his tools.

He knocked again.

Again, there was no answer and no sound. He tried the handle, just in case, but the door was locked. Once more he unwrapped his picklocks, assessed the size of the keyhole to select the right pair, and began. This time he was calmer, the raking worked smoothly, and in a few seconds the door opened.

'Wow!' was all he managed.

This was not like any room he had lived in, even when he was a child in his parents' nice house. This was large, even though it was an apartment, not a house. His bedsit would easily fit two or three times into the living room. The whole room was light and painted in shades he'd never heard of or seen. The walls each had one picture, similar in style to those in the corridor. The windows were broad and glinting clean with translucent drapes sweeping across them.

There were two modern-looking sofas, a glass-topped table with six high backed chairs. A large television sat in the corner, much bigger than any he'd seen in friends' rooms, yet it didn't seem to shrink the space in any way. On a light wood shelf on the wall opposite the door was a Toshiba music centre, with record player, cassette deck, CD deck and radio, with speakers mounted on all four walls. Beside the music centre was a stand with four or five CDs and beside that, a rack containing over a dozen LPs. He looked through the different albums; the fact that he didn't recognise any of the artists just convinced him further of the quality and wealth of the owner, someone obviously a long, long way above Jez in status.

Standing on the floor against another wall was a partially filled wine rack. And yet, with all these furnishings, the room had so much space. He felt he could have blindfolded himself and walked across the room from end to end, and then side to side, and not bumped into anything. It was completely outside his experience, a home like this. And all the other apartments must surely be the same?

The kitchen was similarly modern, clean, well-furnished and tidy, and the fridge well-stocked. A knife block, toaster and microwave stood on the counter; saucepans and frying pans were in a cupboard next to the cooker – electric, four-ring hob, eye-level grill and oven, all spotless. All Jez had was a microwave and single-ring hob. Why couldn't he have managed somewhere like this?

The bedroom sported a large double bed, tidily made. In the drawer of the bedside table were a box of tissues, a brush and comb, nail scissors, nail file, shoe brush and polish, all clean and unused, and that was it. In the wardrobe hung a number of suits, some unmatched jackets and jeans, shelves with two or three well-pressed shirts and some t-shirts and sweatshirts, equally well-pressed. What world did this guy live in? How did he manage it? And why? Why so many shirts and jackets? Jez only needed one change a week.

The whole apartment smelt of money, lots of money, and owned by somebody with wealth and taste. The trouble was, he couldn't see anything that resembled actual money. He tried every drawer in the main room and the bedroom, but apart from the kitchen drawers and bedside drawer, all were empty; all the wealth was in a form he couldn't take out with him. All he wanted was cash and jewellery, and neither was in evidence. He couldn't carry a television or sound system or modern painting back to his room. He almost cried in frustration. What was the point of being rich if you didn't keep any money around? There were no gold or silver ornaments on shelves and no trophies. Nothing for him!

He started shouting in frustration. He might as well burgle a museum! After all his rehearsal, his panics, his excitement, his fumbling at the lock, his success and then not to be able to take anything away – it wasn't fair!

'Simon? Everything all right, mate?'

A voice from the apartment door broke his preoccupation. He hadn't shut the door behind him when he came in! Idiot! He looked round the corner of the living room to the lobby and saw a tall, well-built man in a suit and tie standing just inside, a worried look turning to anger as he saw Jez.

'You! Come here!' he yelled as he strode towards Jez, who squealed in fright and ran to the other open door which just led into the kitchen. As he got there, the stranger caught up with him and grabbed a mixed handful of shirt and bunched up skin that made Jez squeal even louder. Jez wriggled, trying to break the hold, while the newcomer tried to grip his arm and pull him down.

'Stay still, you thieving fucker!' the man shouted, trying to pin Jez against the wall as he almost managed to slide free. They crashed against the kitchen table and rolled to the floor. Jez's fear brought him to his feet first, and he nearly managed to run from the kitchen, but the man caught his leg, making him stumble forward and clutch at the counter to try and keep his balance. As he crashed down again with the newcomer on top of him, the knife block tumbled down beside him. His free hand scrabbled across the floor, picking up painful scrapes from the scattered blades, while his opponent didn't see him find the handle of one of the knives. Then in a panic, not even aware of what he was doing, Jez swung the knife at the man's body. The yell of shock and pain released Jez from the crushing weight, and he scrambled to his knees, waving the knife and finding his target again and again, terrified that the man would hit him back if he stopped.

At last he did stop, and he took a breath. Lying beside him, gasping and gurgling and with a look of terror, the man bled and bled. Jez stared, horrified, at the amount of blood pouring out of the man, the awful sounds he was making and the pleading way he was looking towards him, hoping for some miraculous help.

'Oh shit, I'm sorry, I'm sorry, I'm sorry, I didn't mean it, honest,' Jez stuttered and then turned and ran from the room, not even noticing the blood that had spurted onto his clothes, his hands and even his face.

He ran to the stairs and leapt down the flights. As he reached the bottom he heard the front door of the building – someone was coming in.

He hid around the corner at the top of the first flight and prayed that they wanted the lift.

They did. There were three of them – a suited man, dressed similarly to Jez's attacker, and a very well-to-do looking casually dressed young couple. There was casual like Jez, i.e. plain neglect and scruffy, and casual that would suit, or even enhance, the most luxurious, rich, swanky setting. These two looked like that.

'The apartment's on the fourth floor, the top. Wonderful views from there, masses of light and space. There's already a lot of interest in it,' he heard the man saying.

'Sorry, I didn't catch your name,' the younger man said.

'Call me Simon, Simon Knight. My colleague, Phil, is already up there. He's been dressing one of the other apartments for a prospective client. He'll come and meet us in there. Ah, here's the lift.'

Jez heard the lift door slide open, then close and the hum as it moved up. As soon as it started, he was down the last set of stairs and running fast away from the block.

He ran and ran, not seeing where he was going, and not seeing anything except the pleading, terrified face staring out of the blood lake, and hearing the gurgle and the gasp. His brain seemed to have shut down while his body, usually so unreliable, ran him back home. It took him two hours, running, walking, stopping every so often to bend over and get his wind back, taking diversions so he couldn't be followed.

He heard sirens in the Holland Park direction and assumed they were for the dead man – he must surely have died by now. But then there were always sirens and blues; they were part of the background ambience of London. As he ran and walked and bent over, his hands clasped to his stitch and his throat raw from panting, he always expected the police to be there, to grab him, to drag him away and lock him up forever. But no one stopped him, despite the blood on his clothes and face. People saw him and stepped aside, wary of what he might be capable of doing.

And all the while as he ran, he muttered through his gasps, 'I'm sorry, I'm sorry, I'm sorry.'

It was dark by the time he got back to his room, and he still hadn't been stopped. It took him no time to fill a needle and find a clear vein. Immediately, he flopped back onto the bed and toppled straight into nightmare-ridden sleep.

When he woke, he remembered that it was not all a nightmare, most of it had happened. He was also in urgent need of a new fix; irrespective of his terror and remorse, his body was shouting for relief. He took out his gear – he still had plenty from his last transaction – and filled the needle as full as he possibly could. As he felt the rush and the elation that followed, he turned suddenly giddy and fell back onto the bed as unconsciousness took him. Just before his vision blackened, he saw through the windows his last glimpse of the top of the blue tower, lit up above the roofs opposite.

Half an hour later, a watcher on the observation point at the very top, the coffee in their hand getting cold, saw with mild interest three sets of blue lights pull up in the distance outside a house in Fulham. They could just make out tiny uniformed stick figures emerging from the cars and rushing at the door. The distance was so great, and the light so poor, that they had no possibility of seeing through the attic window and catching sight of Jez lying on the crumpled bed, his dead face still towards the tower, while the police broke down the door to reach his lifeless body.

CHAPTER 36

Next day, when Gerard went to visit Jenny and Nick, he found two gratifying surprises waiting. The first was that Nick was now officially cleared of any wrongdoing and no further action would be taken. Mr Taylor was with them, having just delivered the news in person.

'So, tell me all,' Gerard said when Jenny whooped the good news almost before he was through the door.

'Just what we knew already,' she said, 'it was always nonsense that he would do anything like that. But …' and again, he saw her draw a breath for the dramatic telling. 'The kids pushed their luck, and that's why the coppers treated him so badly. Incidentally, one has been suspended pending internal investigation for brutality – yay! Anyway, while Nick was waiting in the station (isn't that a song, or something?), those little bastards were being interviewed with their dads present. Well, what with all the abuse scandals going on, with Cleveland, Orkney and what have you, they shouted wolf at him. Yes, they actually had the nerve to say that Nick hit the kid because he wouldn't let him … you know.'

'What! Outside a station, with everyone about? And the police bought that?'

'Erm,' began Nick, 'I'd actually rather you dismissed the whole possibility rather than just picking up on the unlikely time or place it was supposed to happen!'

'Sorry, Nick, of course you wouldn't have, even if it were the bus station not the trains. But even though they don't know you like we do, how could they believe that set-up?'

'Difficult time for the police, now of course,' Mr Taylor interrupted. 'Since the Cleveland and Orkney scandals, it's easy to call "Abuse!" and the police daren't risk the press accusing them of covering it up or ignoring it. In this case, however, a quick check by doctors, and even better, a couple of witnesses whom the officers had failed to spot, showed the whole thing was flawed and would never get as far as a court. So apologies all round, a complaint lodged against the one who trod on your leg, and all done and dusted.' He looked round at them with a satisfied smile, waiting for the applause.

He was duly thanked and congratulated, but before he left, Gerard saw an opportunity.

'While you're here, could I quickly ask a question?'

'Is it one I might need to charge you for, or is it general interest?'

'Ha ha, I'm not sure. Hypothetically, then.'

'Ah, you don't want me to charge you. Go on.'

'If I know of a pimp who is running a string of girls …'

'Gerard, no!' Jenny butted in. 'Haven't you finished with that?'

'Go on,' said Mr Taylor, 'this sounds more interesting than the usual, "My friend has a problem …" query that I get buttonholed with at parties.'

'He is running all these girls and keeping them in line, partly with drugs and more with beatings from some heavies he employs.'

'True,' Jenny intervened again. 'Gerard took a huge beating from him some weeks ago – look, there's still a trace of the bruising.'

'No one will talk, they're all terrified of him – as I am now as well – and so he's getting away with it. What could I tell the police that will close him down if no one will bear witness against him? I mean, vice squad, drugs squad, CID, someone must have the power, surely? But I don't know how to set about it.'

'Mm-mm, quite a story there. Why did he beat you up?'

'Not him personally, but a couple of his heavies.'

'Whichever. Did they tell you it was from this man?'

'They didn't say anything, just ambushed me.'

'Apart from personal revenge, why is this important to you?'

'Because I promised one of the girls that I would rescue her and get her safely away from him. She's young and ill, and if I don't find a way to keep that promise, I'm afraid she won't survive. It's urgent, you see.'

'Let me think. Prompt action is difficult unless the police find him in possession, and for more than personal use. They could arrest him for that, but the odds are that unless other cause was proved, he would be out on bail, and I gather that wouldn't be enough to help your girl. Forgive me, but what is your relationship to her?'

'No relationship, except that I talked with her one night and was horrified by her story.'

'That is not uncommon in London, to be stopped like a wedding guest ambushed by an ancient mariner and be horrified or touched by a tale, resulting in handing over money. Did you give her any …?'

'Yes I did, and I suspect it all went straight to Mahmoud.'

'The gentleman in question?'

A snort from both Jenny and Nick at 'gentleman' confirmed it.

'It wasn't like that, though. I know what you mean, I've been accosted by that sort of beggar plenty of times.'

'And do you give them money, as well?'

'I know they're putting one over on me, but if they tell the story well, I think, well, I'd have paid good money to see that at the theatre, so … And yes, I might give them a couple of pounds for a tale well told. Kate wasn't that sort of girl, though, and it wasn't that sort of story.'

Mr Taylor's eyebrows rose. 'Very interesting – would it be too personal to ask further?'

Gerard listened again to what he was saying, realised what Taylor was thinking and blushed.

'No, I don't mean that … I didn't …'

Nick came to his rescue.

'Gerard is an honourable man – and I don't mean that ironically, he is. Her story came to his attention, and he promised to help, that's all. Don't read any more than the simple facts into this.'

'Fair enough, it's not for me to pry. Although if you do go to the police, they have a very rigorous approach to interrogation.'

'Tell me!' muttered Nick.

'Sorry, of course. But the problem is, you have already cited three separate divisions – drugs, vice and CID. Each one of them would want to run the operation themselves without interruption from the others. So before you even start, there is all manner of delay and squabbling over territory, and the setting up of lines of communication, authority and accountability while the division of responsibility is established.

'Unless, as I say, there is unquestionable proof such as sworn testimony, possession, or proven actual physical assault, whoever ends up running the operation can only use permitted surveillance and undercover means to be able to construct a case to convince the Crown Prosecution Service that a court will convict. That will take a long time if this Mr Mahmoud has as tight a hold as you tell me. And by the time they have managed to obtain the evidence, I'm, mm hmm, afraid that the young lady, from what you say, will have already …' his voice tailed off, the end being unnecessary.

Gerard sat in silence for some moments, looking for an argument to refute Taylor's prognosis. It all seemed too plausible, though.

'So how about Kate? How do we get her away from him if she's too frightened to move?'

'Well, I must stress that I have no experience here myself, but as the, ah, ah transaction happens out of sight, can't you just put her in a car and drive her out of London?'

'But I can't be seen with her, or any of the girls – not to protect me,' he said quickly, noticing Taylor's eyebrows begin their ascent again. 'Mahmoud and his henchmen (there must be a better word, sounds like Bulldog Drummond) know that I want to rescue one, and if they see me talking to any of them, they'll move in and, at the very least, beat and scar her, or maybe worse.'

'It doesn't have to be you, does it? No one you can trust to carry out that part?' and he looked sideways at Nick.

'Not a chance,' said Jenny quickly. 'If you can pull it off, Gerard, I will salaam you, but this one here's had enough trouble and rough stuff. I'm not letting him anywhere near this set-up.'

'Anyway, if Dave, or Farid or one of the others …'

'Dave being …?'

'Sorry, yes, he's one of the bruisers who protects Mahmoud, with Farid. Anyway, my point is that if we do drive her away, I can't be sure they won't see the car, maybe even follow it.'

'I would be surprised if they could react that quickly, but yes, they might at least get the registration number, and that could make you vulnerable. Well, it's not up to me to draw up a plan of campaign for you, but I think that if you are so determined to save her, maybe you could find a team of friends (present company excepted, I know) to manage it. If you don't want me to charge you for advice, I'll leave you to it now. That's a long free consultation you've wangled, but it is much more interesting than a "My friend has a problem"!'

'Before you go,' Nick called. 'Have you heard this one?'

Mr Taylor's expression suggested he knew what was coming, but as it was coming from a client who hadn't yet received the bill, he must take it.

'Go on.'

'Chap sitting in his lawyer's office. "Do you want the bad news first or the really bad news?" the lawyer asks. "Give me the bad news first." "Your wife found a picture worth half a million quid." "That's the bad news?" says the guy incredulously. "I can't wait to hear the really bad news." "It's of you and your mistress."' said Nick and Mr Taylor in unison.

'Ah, you've heard it. Oh well, can't win 'em all I suppose.'

'If you insist, here's one for you,' replied Mr Taylor. 'If you break a mirror, you're supposed to get seven years bad luck. Come to me and I can probably get you off with just five.'

Nick laughed as he showed the solicitor out.

An hour or so after Taylor had left them, the second gratifying surprise appeared. Joe appeared at the front door. His pleasure at seeing Gerard matched Gerard's own.

'I hoped I'd see you while I'm here but didn't like to just turn up on your door, and I don't have a number for you. I'm only here for a couple of days for a conference in Westminster.'

'What about?'

'Oh, just an engineering thing, but there are some interesting new thoughts and tools available. I like to come up to these things, keep up to date and meet old colleagues, you know?'

Jenny didn't need to work hard to persuade Gerard to stay for a meal. He was glad of a chance to talk to Joe again.

'How's George?' he asked, but only got a scowl back.

It turned out that soon after their visit, George had fallen at home and was taken to hospital. They would only release him to a care home, the social workers having deemed his own house unsuitable for him to continue living there alone. The care home he was sent to didn't welcome visitors unless they were close relations.

'He don't have any relations left, poor George, only his daughter in South Africa, and she can't come back for this.' As a result, Joe was no longer able to see George, Annie could no longer shop or bake for him, and he was left in the twilight world of heavily tranquillised residents parked around the edge of a main room with the television on loudly all day and no one talking to each other.

'Bloody awful, but nothing I can do anymore. I don't know how long he'll last in there, but I hope they let us know when he goes. I can arrange a funeral if I can't do anything else for the poor bugger.'

After a short, sympathetic silence while they tried not to give him any platitudes, he asked for their news.

He laughed in disbelief at the idea of Nick attacking a child and was shocked at the idea that children could now just shout 'abuse' and be instantly believed without evidence.

'I know it's happening everywhere, and them creeps who hurt the kiddies deserve all they get, but you've got to have evidence and proof, haven't you, eh? Just a say-so from some child for who knows what reason can't be enough. It's in danger of going like the old witch trials, isn't it? Just accuse, and they must be guilty, no need to prove anything.'

'But how about you, Gerard, what news can I take back to Ann? She's going to want to know how you're doing now.'

'Well, in myself I'm doing a whole lot better than when I first came down to see you, and a lot of that's down to you both. I've still got another big problem weighing on me, but it's outside me, this one, not inside.'

Nick and Jenny exchanged a look and sat back, as Gerard relayed yet again the story of Mahmoud, Dave and Farid, his intervention, Yasser's intervention and the violent consequences of both.

Unlike Jenny, he didn't need to imagine a large hushed audience, or have the urge to prepare or deliver a theatrical version of the story. His way was always to tell the tale unvarnished, plain, and in full. This time he included Mr Taylor's comments and suggestions. He made little mention of Arnold and Yasser and none of Jez, Silke and his other adventures and encounters – rescuing Kate was, at the moment, his only pressing news.

'Well,' said Joe thoughtfully, when he'd heard it all. 'And that's why you came to us all bruised, then? Yeah, you've taken on quite a crusade there, I reckon. Your Mr Taylor's got a good point though, why not just get her into a car and away? Plenty of taxis around, they'd do it.'

'Don't like the idea of a using a taxi,' said Gerard. 'It's involving someone else, maybe putting them in danger, maybe giving Mahmoud a lead to us. Anyway, I can't be sure that the drivers aren't in Mahmoud's pocket. Some of them, anyway.'

'Come on, how big an operator is he? Really? Eh? You make it sound like he's Mr Big, heading up a big organised crime set-up with a team of minders, someone always watching the girls, a fleet of cars ready to give chase at a moment's notice and contacts in the police, taxi service and I don't know where. Is it really that bad? Isn't he just a small-time thug, running a few girls, dealing some drugs, but outside Earl's Court who knows or cares about him?'

'Small-time maybe,' Gerard conceded, 'but he still packs a hell of a punch.'

'Yeah, we want to avoid that I know, but really, once the maid's away from him what is he actually going to do?' Joe asked.

'And what is she going to do?' Gerard said. 'That worries me as well. I can't just drop her in the middle, of, I don't know, Birmingham, Brighton or wherever and expect her to start up a normal life. I thought I could, but no, she'll just be easy pickings for the local dealers there, wherever it may be, and back to square one.'

'Oh dear, Gerard, you haven't changed since uni, have you?' came in Jen. 'Always on the lookout for the waifs and strays. Your problem is you, not other people. Your shoulders are only so big, and your responsibilities are only so broad. You're just as lovable as back then, but honestly, you do make me want to scream sometimes.'

'That's not so fair, Jen,' Nick interjected. 'This is a real girl in real trouble, and from what Gerard says, she's not going to last until Christmas. We both wish he'd never talked to her in the first place, but he did and he's right, he can't do only half the job or she still won't survive.'

'If you don't like a car, what the hell's wrong with using the tube? It's there, handy, and if she's nippy she's at the other end of London on a mainline station to anywhere in the country before they've clocked she's gone. Why is it all such a drama? Are you telling me none of these girls ever catch a tube anywhere, at least once?' said Joe.

'I know,' Gerard sighed. 'I've said that, and friends have said that. We all know, but she won't.'

'Why?'

'Fear, simple as that. A couple of his girls did run like that a few years ago, and he set Dave on them. Then when he got news, he went off after them himself. What happened, God only knows, but all the other girls heard was that they were both killed, very nastily. Since then, no one dares risk it.'

'Who saw the bodies?'

'I don't know.'

'Any pictures, photos?'

'I don't know, but a girl's body was found downriver about three weeks later. They're all convinced it was one of the runaways.'

'Could have been anyone. Plenty of bodies wash up in the Thames, so how does anyone know? P'raps they did get away and this Dave never did see them. Your Mahmoud can't lose face, or he'll lose them all. Tells a lie, they swallow it and bingo.'

Gerard thought. 'It's possible. I never thought of it like that, because I've only heard the story through Kate once and from another friend who'd heard it from a couple of the other girls. He believes it, but more importantly, the girls believe it and aren't going to risk going the same way. He's got them through fear, controlling their money, and through the drugs. There's no way she's got the gumption to catch a tube and follow that through.'

'Right,' said Joe. 'Seems to me you've done a lot of talking and thinking and agonising, and all the while this poor maid is still getting abused and sick and nearer to dying. Isn't it time to do something instead? Nick, Jen, I was going to ask if I could use your phone to talk to Ann, you know, to let her know all's well and that. Would you mind?'

'Of course, you know where it is?'

Joe vanished, leaving the other three looking at each other quizzically.

'I've never heard him say so much in one go,' whispered Jen. 'You've got him more excited than I've ever seen, Gerard.'

'He's got a problem to tackle,' replied Nick, also in a whisper. 'He loves that, it's what he's good at.'

Gerard returned to his flat feeling heartened. After his call to Ann, Joe had come back grinning, and had started working out a plan with Gerard that suddenly made it all possible. Despite Jen's protests, Nick volunteered for a part in it. Everything was still too vague, it needed detailing and called for some recruitment, but for the first time since that foggy night, Gerard saw real hope for Kate.

He walked with a smile up the stairs to his flat, but before he could open the door, Arnold appeared, unusually sombre.

'Gerald? Have you got a mo'? Shelagh's in here too. It's Jez.'

CHAPTER 37

'I saw him just before,' Gerard told Yasser the next morning. 'He must have been on his way there. Honestly, I nearly didn't recognise him, he looked so – normal, respectable, I suppose. Right out of character. Part of his planning, I expect. Some plan! Do you know, he actually broke into the show apartment, of all things? The couple who found the body were on the point of buying it, but obviously … And if he'd gone just one door further along the corridor, he would have hit the jackpot! So typical of him, all intention and no idea how to realise it. I don't mean that to sound callous or indifferent towards the man he killed.'

'Of course not, of course not,' said Yasser, patting Gerard's hand in commiseration. 'How well did you know the young man?'

They were again sitting in a Knightsbridge cafe, away from any of Mahmoud's contacts. Gerard had fallen back into depression at the news of what had happened to Jez. The ridiculousness of the enterprise just seemed to exacerbate the grief he felt so unexpectedly.

'Not so well. I only know that he had been in prison and was an addict with precious little hope. But I don't know, I should have been able to help him. He asked me to help him. That's what I do. I can't even blame Father Holloway for this death.'

'Gerard, my friend, you cannot blame yourself either. You invited him to spend time with you, and he declined. Very sad, I agree, but think of the family of the man he killed. They are grieving their loss far more than anyone else is for this unfortunate young man.'

'My head agrees with you, but just now all I'm seeing is this lost soul dying alone in the dark, in a dingy attic room. Sorry, Yasser, but I'm going to carry this for a while.'

'Good riddance,' exclaimed Nick. 'No one deserved what happened to that agent guy.'

'I know,' Gerard said. 'But Jez wasn't … well, yes he was a criminal, but he was never violent.'

'Tell that one to the guy's folks, won't you? Fifteen stab wounds! Not violent? My arse! I knew you were hanging out with the bohemian and hippy crowd over there, but I never thought you were down with the dregs like that. Good job he topped himself; saves the taxpayer from looking after him in comfort.'

'What do you need?' asked Silke, holding Gerard's hand. 'How are you going to move from here?'

They sat on a bench at the west end of Hyde Park, both wrapped up against the shivering cold.

'What do I need? I don't know. Last night it looked as though it was all turning round – there was real hope of getting Kate away and even bringing Mahmoud down. But now it's the reality of two people dying who didn't need to, and I'm grieving and feeling guilty about the least worthy of the two. God forgive me, that's an awful thing to say about him, but …'

'Yeah, but who's going to disagree with you? Look Gerard, your friend has died, that is true and it can't change. Kate is still trapped, and you can change that, if you all act soon. But you have to bury your Jez first, and I don't mean his body.'

'How?'

'You're the priest. Haven't you helped your people bury their dead? And not just the body in the ground.'

'I suppose so.'

'Oh come on, of course you have. I'm sorry about your friend, and the other guy, but you're alive, your Kate's alive, I'm alive. How did you bury the others? Why can't you try to send your friend on his way, and turn back to the living? What do you need? Your church?'

'Actually, I think yes.'

'Ok, fine. Come along then.' She stood up abruptly and pulled Gerard to his feet. She led the way out of the park, and towards Notting Hill. The trees were mostly bare now, and their feet scuffed small piles of dried leaves as they walked. The sky was a dull pewter, and he felt the chill run through to his bones. He followed her meekly, weakly, all the way to Moorhouse Road and the Church of St Mary of the Angels.

He had never visited here, but she knew her way. He asked in surprise,

'Are you Catholic? Do you worship here, then?'

'My parents were secret Catholics and told me the stories, but as we grew up in the GDR, it wasn't a good thing to boast about too loudly. I never really believed, but I do like coming here to sit sometimes. It is peaceful, and there is something, I couldn't say what. Well, it's comforting, when I need it.'

He nodded and resisted his priestly impulse to assure her that she felt the presence of God. He squeezed her hand, and they both sat in the pews in silence. He was vaguely aware of others in the church, some kneeling and praying. Sightseers were looking around at the stained glass and the statues and peering up at the arched ceiling with its starlit sky. Others were walking towards the altar, bobbing their heads in reverence, some crossing themselves.

A tray of votive candles burned, flickering in the cold air and lit by petitioners asking for healing for friends and family, for forgiveness of some misdemeanour, for help in a job interview, or just as a gesture towards the unknowable.

He sat and watched until the peace of the building reached him, and the cold thawed, both inside and out.

After twenty minutes he stood and walked towards the altar. He knew that in his own church he could step through the wrought iron gates, up the three stone steps and approach the actual altar to perform a Mass. This was not his church, though; indeed, he doubted that the Church was any longer his, although he knew that, like Silke, he could and would come in and share the peace, feel whatever the contact was, and receive some form of blessing. But he wouldn't summon down the body and blood of Christ ever again. Sometime he must return to Derbyshire and tell Father Holloway that he was leaving for good. Not yet, though. Until then he was still a priest.

He knelt in the front pew and for the first time since Jane Conway's funeral, truly prayed. He prayed for the soul of Jez and asked for forgiveness for him and for his victim. As an afterthought, he added a prayer for Kate and for his own strength to help her at last.

In his imagination, he stood behind the altar and performed the Mass for the dead. He knew the words and the motions by instinct and could send his concentration through the form of the rite to picture Jez receiving an absolution, however undeserved Gerard knew it to be. He had failed before in making an intercession, and now, when it was too late for the body, he did his utmost for the soul. He knew that made no difference to Phil and his grieving family, but if there was any truth behind the ancient ritual, then maybe he could steer Jez away from the fate that everyone believed him to be deservedly suffering. In his mind, he was so truly immersed that his consciousness was unaware that his lips moved silently to the words of the Mass, and that his body made tiny movements reflecting the moments that he knelt and elevated the host and raised the chalice.

He knew also that, from a different direction, Shelagh too was invoking her own deities on Jez's behalf. Not devils or demons anymore, but maybe she could make contacts with enough powers to help. Healing was her motivation, so maybe the two of them, from their different directions, could bring Jez some form of relief.

When in his mind he had finished the rite, Gerard crossed himself and stood and lit another candle to put on the tray.

Before he returned to Silke, he thought wryly of Father Holloway and what he would say about this virtual ceremony that he'd performed. For him, every word, every gesture and every genuflection in all of the offices had its due place and must be so strictly adhered to. Any deviation from the form, however minor, was a heresy and to be condemned.

So what? He was no longer bound by fear of Father Holloway. He said farewell to Jez, wished him Godspeed and safe arrival, wherever that may be, and then let him be.

Silke joined him, took his hand again and led him out.

'And how is Jez?' she asked when they stood in daylight again.

'Better.'

'And how are you?'

'Better.' And he smiled. 'Thank you.'

She nodded and said quietly, 'Good. It's time now, I think.'

'Time for what?'

She smiled back at him and shook her head.

'Come along.'

They walked a little further into Notting Hill. He recognised the street that she led him along, with the steps leading up to the front doors; the street where he had followed her that first time he saw her on the train.

She let them into the house – another one broken into smaller apartments, although built as a townhouse for a large family with servants, back in early Victorian days. The interior was warm, bright and recently painted, the original dark staircase replaced with light-coloured wood and carpeted.

Her flat was on the second floor. Smaller than the one that was Jez's and Phil's downfall, and with a more lived in and comfortable feel it seemed to welcome Gerard. Small windows looking out across the street to houses opposite meant that not much bright natural light percolated through, but it was not gloomy.

Unlike Shelagh's room, the walls were decorated with framed pictures. Not fantasy creations but mostly large black and white photographs with some portraits of well-known artists or performers, mostly European, and some of scenes of German towns: Berlin, Rostock, Heidelberg. Gerard recognised the towns from pictures in books from his student days, even though he had never visited the country.

Silke led him into the bedroom and pulled the curtains closed. Although he had known this was where she was leading him, as he walked through the door he felt panicked and utterly inadequate. 'Sin' battled inside him with 'at last'. Another part of him just felt, 'This isn't going to work. I can't.'

'I'm going to give you a massage, you're still too caught up with your friend. I'll help you relax. Lie face down on the bed. Take your coat and jumper off first.'

He obeyed her. As he lay there, he heard her moving about the room, striking matches which his nose and his peripheral vision soon told him were to light incense and candles.

'It's all right, Gerard, let yourself relax. I'm not going to hurt you. Take a deep breath. And as you release it, feel your shoulders ease. Go on. That's good. Now do the same again – and unclench your jaw. Good. And again. Good.'

With clear commands in a slow, quiet voice she did indeed manage to relax him. He lay there with his eyes closed, almost too relaxed he thought, and was aware of her standing beside him, leaning over. She began massaging his shoulders, strong hands finding tension knots and working them, the wings of his shoulder blades, the channels of his spinal column and the muscles along his ribs. Wherever there was tightness, a knot, she worked patiently and deeply.

After she had worked down his back, she stood up straight again.

'All right, take your shirt off now.'

He sat up, and unbuttoned his shirt, still nervous and still unable to look directly at her, but obedient.

At her instruction he lay back down, facedown, and waited for her to resume the massage. He heard rustling and fidgeting beside him, but dared not look. He felt her climb onto the bed as well, straddling his legs, and then the massage resumed. This was a different experience – slower, shallower, more sensual. She worked on his neck, then his shoulders again, down his spine, his left hand side and right hand side. And all the while, he was aware of the smell of the oils on her hands, and he marvelled at the sensation of touch of another's hands on his skin, a sensation that he had not known since infancy.

When she reached his waistband he waited, wondering what would happen. He first felt her kiss his shoulders lingeringly, and then move down his back, following the path her massaging hands had made. He shivered, relishing the sensation so new to him. She moved so that she could lie on top of him, and for the first time in his life he felt breasts pressing against him, and felt the two firm nipples. Entranced, he could only lie there, passively soaking in the experience. No longer afraid, no longer unsure, he learned that all his life he had been so wrong, as had his parents, his Church, and Father Holloway.

She whispered in his ear,

'Now the rest of your clothes.' Again, he obeyed, but now eagerly, no more doubts. She looked at him and grinned. Only now could she hold his eyes and see the change she had brought in him.

'Very good, very good. Now lie on your back. My turn first.' And she climbed on him, impaling herself slowly, not taking her eyes from his.

His education continued through the night, passively learning first, then sharing and then actively dominant, his inhibitions and prohibitions falling away. She taught him sensuality, how to delight a woman, and, as important, how to let a woman delight him. She taught him passion and how to move easily from one style to another, how to read her responses, when to follow her, and when to lead, at last turning the priest into the man.

At six o'clock in the morning on a frosty day with a clear starlit sky, Gerard left the house and started his walk back towards Brompton with a smile that couldn't be wiped from his face, a deeper peace in his heart than he had known for a long time, and a head full of images of delight. As he walked, Father Gerard looked skywards and gave heartfelt thanks to God for his loving gift of sin.

CHAPTER 38

'Something has happened to you, yes?' said Yasser, the next day over their coffee. Rather to Gerard's surprise he had suggested a different venue for their now regular strategy meetings, closer to Brompton this time.

'You are altogether different today. You smile more and look as if you are elsewhere, is that right?'

'Let's just say I have learned some things I never expected to. So yes, something has happened and only good things.'

'Should I ask more?'

'No.'

'Very well then, I wish you joy of your learning. So, you have learned good things, and so have I, although I rather think mine may be a different type of learning from what makes you smile like that.'

'I'm sure yours is different, tell me.'

'You remember I told you that I think I have found an ally? Yes? Well, he is going to join us today, that is why I have chosen here for us. But please, when you see him, listen; do not judge too hastily.'

'Why should I?'

'It will be hard not to, but please, my friend, listen to him.'

'Who is he, Yasser? Do I know him?' From the other's uncomfortable, evasive look Gerard began to guess who this ally might be. His stomach spasmed as he thought back to memories of feet and clubs making contact again and again.

'What have you done?' he stuttered.

'Nothing that will harm us, I promise you. It will all be good, trust me Gerard, trust me.'

'I trust you of course, but him?'

'He will be here soon. He prays at my mosque, he is a strong Muslim, and he despises Mahmoud. He will help us close him down, he will.'

'But why?'

'Like the girls, he is in Mahmoud's power and wants to get free. He wants to leave, but cannot while Mahmoud holds this control. Please, Gerard, listen to him. He will help us, truly.'

'I have no choice, do I? But he mustn't know about Kate. He mustn't.'

'No, I promise. He will help us bring Mahmoud's empire down, but no mention of any of the girls, that's right.'

'When will he be here?'

'Soon. He must be sure that Mahmoud is nowhere in sight first, or the other one, Dave. He is putting himself at risk as well by seeing us. We must trust him.'

'So why so close to his territory? Surely it's more dangerous to meet here.'

'He has little time to spare. Mahmoud will call him soon and want to know why he takes so long to arrive.'

Gerard's euphoria of the night and morning hid away in a cupboard, and his old apprehension took centre stage once more.

'I don't think I can trust him. I know what he's capable of. Suppose he brings Mahmoud and Dave in with him?'

And at that moment of fear, Farid did indeed appear, but alone. He came straight to their table and bowed to Yasser.

'Salaam Alaikum,' he said, and received the response,

'Wa-Alaikum-Salaam.'

He then looked at Gerard and grunted.

Yasser gestured to the chair.

'Please, sit down, join us. This is Father Gerard. He and I are working in this together. We hope that with your help we can bring the whole matter to a satisfactory conclusion. Yes?'

'Hello, Farid,' said Gerard, an attempt at a smile grimacing his face. Farid looked at him once more and grunted again. Then he turned back to Yasser.

'Why is a Christian a part of cleansing Islam in this district?'

'He is not acting as a Christian, but as a man with compassion for the victims, who wants to help them. He is my dear friend, notwithstanding our different religions.'

'"O ye who believe! Take not the Jews and the Christians for friends. They are friends one to another. And whoso among you takes them for friends is indeed one of them,"' quoted Farid.

'I do not take Gerard as a friend because he is a Christian, but because he is a good man. He does not mock or make light of our religion, nor I his. He seeks a good outcome for the benefit of all who live here, especially Mahmoud's victims. If you will not work with us both then I will release you from your promise to help, but I will not forsake his role in this matter.'

Gerard had never heard Yasser speak so sternly as he did at that moment. Farid looked back at him, but without any new favour. Then he spoke quietly in his own language to Yasser, and Gerard was locked out.

The conversation continued for a full ten minutes, but much as Gerard tried, he couldn't tell by tone or body language what was happening. He knew that he was the subject, but his ignorance of the language meant that it was impossible to tell if Farid's argument was contemptuous or angry, or offering to give him the freedom of the city.

At last, Yasser sat back and then turned to Gerard apologetically.

'I am sorry for our rudeness, my friend, but we have had to have a discussion on one or two hadiths, and how the prophet's words

(Blessings and Peace be upon him) may be understood. In addition, Farid has some important requirements if he is to help us.'

'What requirements?'

At last Farid allowed himself to speak to Gerard directly.

'I want to leave this country. It is degenerate, immoral, and it is more and more hostile to good Muslims. Look at how they defend the apostate Rushdie against the justice that has been declared. I listen to another imam in Finsbury. He does not go into bed with the Christians. He is a true Muslim. There is nothing here for such as me. I want to go to Afghanistan. Now that the Russians have been driven out, there are many true Muslims who are faithful to the Prophet – Blessings and Peace be upon him – and I will join them in the mujahideen. I wish to live and fight for Islam, not for the evil like Mahmoud.'

'But why must that be a condition?' said Gerard. 'Why not just go?'

'He has all my money and my passport. If your authorities do not help me, I am trapped here. If I shall give evidence of what I have seen and done, I demand that I am allowed and helped to go there.'

'I will argue your case, Farid. I know a lawyer who might be able to achieve that for you.'

'When will you move against him?'

Gerard hesitated, afraid that this was another trick. He was not at all sure that Mahmoud wouldn't learn everything about this conversation within ten minutes of their leaving the cafe.

Yasser read what was going through his mind. He turned to Farid and quickly gave the answer.

'There are things to do first. One is to approach this lawyer and find out how he can help you. When we move, things will happen too fast if we haven't made the right arrangements first. And there is one of the victims we have made a promise to.'

'Who?'

'I am sorry, but I cannot tell you yet.'

'You do not trust me?'

'I trust you, but the risk for her is too great. I am afraid that Dave or one of the other aides might accidentally learn of her and move against her before we do. I can't tell you yet. But I will tell you, Farid, I am a true Muslim, and never accuse me of not being one. I am imam, I am khatib, and I teach Islam with all my heart. But I will not teach hate, and I will not preach violent acts against our hosts or anyone else. Allah sees all, and He has eternity to punish those who have earned it – I will not sanction anyone who presumes His judgment first.'

Farid sat back with a sulky twist to his lips, but he did not argue further.

'What are you going to do for us, Farid?' asked Gerard.

'I will tell the truth. I will tell the police and the courts of the drugs, the girls, the violence and other things that Mahmoud has done that disgrace our religion and have given you unbelievers a whip to flog us with. I will stand up in court and swear to it on the Quran. But only if they help me fly to Afghanistan immediately. I will not go to one of your prisons for what that man has made me do.'

'The plans are being made, and I promise to argue your needs, Farid. I am not the police, and it is not in my power to promise all you ask, but I do promise to do what I can to persuade them. They are more concerned with stopping the flow of drugs around here than they are in stopping the prostitution. Are you involved in the drugs part?'

'No. Mahmoud and Dave do all that. I just look after Mahmoud and punish anyone he tells me to, anyone who threatens him, or disobeys him.' And he looked hard at Gerard, both of them remembering his punishment.

'He has you and Dave to look after him. How many others does he pay? When it's time to take action, who might we expect?'

Farid puffed and sat back in his chair, looking again at each of them. At last he answered:

'He pays some local taxi drivers, both to drive us where we might need to go, but also to look out for him. The drivers know the girls and let Mahmoud know if they ever see them somewhere outside the area. They might also drive the girls when Mahmoud wants them to deliver drugs to a customer who lives away.'

'What, the girls are his mules?'

'Of course. They make more money for him doing that than just through sex. And sometimes the leaders of the main gang want to give one of us instructions, so the cabs take us there.'

'Ok, so he has some drivers in his pocket. That's important to know. Who else?'

'One or two in the local police, obviously.'

Yasser hissed, involuntarily. 'You were right,' he said to Gerard. 'Sorry, I did not believe you.'

'Do you know which officers he has? We can't risk them warning him before we move.'

Farid shrugged.

'I dunno, he don't tell me or Dave who. We just know we got protection if we got to teach a lesson, or when Dave got to take someone to the river.'

Yasser and Gerard looked in silent horror at Farid. They both knew at once what he meant, and his cold indifference told them as much as they wanted to know about him.

'Right,' continued Gerard. 'As long as we can bypass them, I think it will be possible to persuade them to send you to Afghanistan after the trial. Tell the truth against him, help to put him in prison, and they should lose interest in you. Are you with us?'

He put out his hand for Farid to shake in agreement. Farid ignored the hand, but said,

'I am with you. I shall help, and pray that Allah will forgive me for working with a Christian.'

CHAPTER 39

It was early Tuesday morning as Mahmoud turned down Warwick Road, walking from the tube to his office just below the blue tower. He had no need of the tube as his car would bring him in greater comfort and warmth, and he would never have trouble parking. But with him, Dave and Farid making sure they were often seen leaving and entering the station by different exits, he was less likely to lose any more of his products that way. The girls would be too scared to try escaping by tube.

A month ago it looked like those two religious freaks were going to mess up his operations along the Court, but they seemed to have got the message now. Even after his lesson, the Christian one was still hanging around the area, but as he had a room nearby Mahmoud supposed it wasn't unreasonable. From what Dave and Farid told him, and from what he saw himself, the man had learned his lesson and stopped taking any interest in the girls. The imam? Mahmoud hadn't seen him about much since the other little demonstration, so no worries there.

All the girls seemed to be working ok, but he was worried about one of them, Kate. He knew he'd taken a chance adding her to his stable, being so obviously underage. But enough men liked that, and so far he seemed to have got away with it. Except that these days she was always ill and getting dangerously thin – dangerous, because her appeal was shrinking along with her weight. She made hardly any money for him now, and before long even that little would stop. No, he'd have to cut his losses and let her go soon. He'd get Dave to give her a little night ride down to the river – next week at the latest. And then he'd find someone else for that room, someone who'd give him a decent return on the money he spent hooking them in.

'Got some change, please?' A voice broke into his thoughts, a new voice, from the empty doorway beside him.

He stopped and looked. A new girl he'd not seen before was sitting huddled on a crumpled sleeping bag among torn cardboard and screwed up newspaper. She held out an empty coffee cup from a local takeaway cafe. She had short dark hair, and an accent that was certainly not native London. Mahmoud couldn't yet place it. Her eyes and nose were red from cold at the moment, but she looked potentially attractive. First night on the street? Begging already? Runaway, or too old? No, she was easily old enough not to be living at home, so some other understandable factor had driven her here – just as he was passing too.

He looked at her for a few moments, appraising her and thinking of Kate and the decision he'd made seconds before. He smiled broadly at her, like sun breaking through cloud, and stooped down beside her.

'Of course. Can I help you? My name is Mahmoud.'

'Got any change?'

'Yes, but I can give you more than change. I can help you. Do you have somewhere to sleep?'

'Nowhere I can go back to. I need money.'

'Of course, of course. I can lend you some money, enough for a deposit on a small room somewhere. No, let me give you the money, and then you don't need to worry about it.'

'What you after?' The girl pulled back and eyed him suspiciously.

'Please, you have no need to worry. I work with a charity that helps young people like yourself. Come, let us help you. The streets are not a safe place to sleep, especially now winter is coming. We have some rooms – they're not very big and not as well cared for as we would wish, but at least it will give you an address, and with that you can get yourself work. Come, let me buy you a meal first, then I'll take you to your room.'

As she reached to take his outstretched hand she had a sudden coughing fit and sat back down, hard.

'Sorry,' she rasped, 'it gets cold at night, not good for me.'

'I can give you some – medicine – that will help,' he said, still smiling. 'Come along now, catch my hand. What is your name?'

'Katrin,' she said. 'I'm from Austria.'

As they walked slowly, at the girl's pace, to one of his cafes, he did some more mental calculations. He was going to have to buy food, dope and smack for at least a couple of weeks until she was ready. She didn't strike him as being as green as some of the other girls he had helped. And something about her suggested to him that she might take to this life more readily, which actually meant sooner. So his initial outlay might not be as bad as with the younger ones. At the moment she was attractive enough, with an interesting exotic hint, to bring him in a lot of money – easily enough to make up for what Kate was losing.

Yes, definitely time to sort out the Kate situation. He'd get Dave to make that river trip later today. Why wait any longer? Best to end it all now.

CHAPTER 40

At midday that same Tuesday, winter was treading hard on autumn's tail, the sunny day giving no heat for those out on the streets. Dave was relaxing over a pint when his mobile phone rang, the unusual sound attracting the attention of half the other drinkers there.

'Yeah?' he greeted.

'Dave, where are you?' Mahmoud's voice.

'Prince of T. Why?'

'I need you to do a little disposal this afternoon.'

'Can't do this afternoon.'

'If I say you need to, then you do. Don't you?'

'Nah, not today. Hughie's got a job for me down in Chelsea.'

'Hughie? Oh fuck. All right, how long are you going to be? I need a room empty by this evening.'

'What about Farid?'

'Nah, he's on another job for me at the moment. It would have to be Hughie, wouldn't it! Look, call me when he's finished with you. It's gotta happen today, right? I'll get Ted to stand by for backup.'

'Who is it?'

'Kate. I need her room clear by tonight, so call as soon as you can.'

'Ok.' And Dave hung up, putting his attention back to his pint and *The Sun* newspaper.

Darkness was already falling by four thirty when a grubby white van drove from Aisgill Avenue, making its way to Lillie Road and then to Kenway Road. Dave parked it just along from the building where Kate had her room, and quickly climbed the stairs.

'Oy, get out 'ere, we're going for a ride,' as he thumped the door heavily with his fist. There was silence for ten seconds or so, and then Kate opened it, slowly and fearfully.

'Where we goin'? Is it a delivery? Only I'm meant to be goin' out on me spot soon.'

'Never mind that. Mahmoud wants a word, come on.'

'I need me stuff first, it's nearly time.'

'Too late.'

'No, please, I gotta shoot first. It'll only be a minute. Come on, Dave.'

He was about to say 'no', and then he thought again. After all, if she was full of H when she was found, it would stop any awkward questions or investigations.

''Urry up, we gotta get goin'.'

Soon she was ready, but the drug was already making her drowsy and, cursing her, Dave had to support and simultaneously drag her down the flights of stairs to the van, the doors already waiting open.

At about the same time a car turned from Cromwell Road into Earl's Court Road and travelled slowly in the queue along the street. Inside, Arnold scanned the pavements, looking out for Kate in case she'd optimistically taken an early shift, although he well knew that in her current state she was more likely to miss altogether. Joe let Arnold get on with looking while he kept driving to the slow pace of the traffic, though ready to respond to any instructions.

They'd met for the first time only half an hour before, but Gerard had briefed each of them so thoroughly beforehand that neither felt he was working with a stranger.

'Slow up a bit 'ere,' Arnold said as they drew level with Kenway Road. He peered down the road, then stiffened.

'Quick, turn down 'ere. They've already come for 'er.' And, triggering a blast of angry horns around them, Joe swung the wheel sharply left and accelerated towards the white van parked by Kate's house. A taxi was idling just in front of the van.

As they approached, Dave appeared at the door of the house, pulling Kate by the wrist. Joe braked hard between Dave and the van, and Arnold scrambled out of the door to help Kate, as Joe opened the rear car door wide.

'Put 'er down, mate,' he growled at Dave, who grunted and tugged Kate's wrist hard.

'You, your arse in the van, now!' pushing her down towards the back of the van. When he stood up again he was holding a pick handle in one hand and his housebrick-sized phone in the other. Eyes firmly on Arnold, he muttered into the phone and then threw it back onto the driver's seat.

'In the car, Kate, for Gawd's sake, in the car!' shouted Arnold. He tried to reach her hand, but she was too far in the van's maw. 'Bloody 'ell what a mess. I told you to leave well alone, Gerald, din't I,' he muttered to himself.

'Stay in the van, I said. Mahmoud wants to see you. Now! And as for you …!' And with no other warning Dave swung the pick handle at Arnold's head.

Arnold swayed back out of its way, and as the impetus of the swing carried Dave forward, Arnold stepped in with a heavy right to his solar plexus.

Not expecting any resistance, Dave was unprepared. He grunted and bent over, catching his breath as his stick clattered onto the pavement. Arnold took advantage of Dave's breathlessness to follow up with a hard punch to the nose. Dave collapsed to the pavement, and Arnold immediately stamped on his knee, putting him, screaming, out of the fight for good.

Seeing him on the ground gave Kate enough courage to slip out of the van towards Arnold's protection. The driver of the black cab, Ted, got out and ran towards the fight – Dave's reinforcement.

Immediately, the car door opened, and Joe also stepped out, hands rising into ready fists. Before Ted could get to them, Arnold had hold of the pick handle, and Joe was shaped up ready to land his blow.

Ted looked at the odds, at Dave groaning on the ground, at the stick in Arnold's hands, and decided that whatever he was paid, this might not be worth it. He climbed quickly back into his cab and was around the corner and away in seconds.

'Kate, quick, into the car, while we can.'

'Come on, lass, that's all done now,' said Joe. 'Get in the back, and we're out of here.'

She came out of her terror trance and clambered in.

'Come on, Arnold,' shouted Joe. 'Quick.'

'Get goin' mate,' Arnold shouted back, 'I've got to check this end. Go, go!' and he slapped the car roof.

Joe pulled away fast and accelerated down the road. As he passed the cab waiting by the kerb, it pulled out and stuck on his tail. He couldn't see in the mirror whether or not the driver was radioing in their course, but he wasn't going to take anything on trust.

He wanted Arnold in the car with them to reassure Kate that he wasn't just another kidnapper, but getting clear was his priority now.

He guessed that both Dave and the cab driver knew his number plate by now, and if Mahmoud really did have contacts and lieutenants in the wrong places, they would be identified and spotted before long. More worrying was that the police would also have the number plate and would be more effective at stopping him.

'It's ok, lass,' he called to the back, as he turned onto Cromwell Road. 'We'll soon leave 'im behind and you'll be safe.'

She didn't answer. Joe glanced in the mirror, to see her huddled on the back seat, arms wrapped around her knees, head down and shoulders shaking.

He wanted to be able to stop, to comfort and reassure her, but with the cab on his tail and maybe an interception planned in front, he didn't dare. Now he saw Kate, he understood Gerard's insistence on rescuing her. And now he'd seen Dave, he understood why fear had made him hesitate so long. This was not just a story told in some friends' living room anymore.

He headed towards Hammersmith, but in less than a mile suddenly turned off along North End Road. The mirror showed him that the taxi was still following, and its For Hire light was switched off. As planned, he led his follower into the underground car park in Kensington High Street. Had the cab followed him down the ramp, the next stage would have been trickier to pull off. But as they'd hoped, Ted made the wrong choice. He thought he was playing smart and waited by the exit to catch them as they left.

Joe drove around the levels until he saw the next car waiting with Gerard standing by the door.

CHAPTER 41

'Ok, Kate,' Joe called over his shoulder. 'We're changing cars now. Quick, and get your head down in the back.' As soon as she was out of his car he drove off towards the exit, making sure Ted saw him and could pick up the chase. Gerard held the back door of his car open until she was safely in and then climbed in the front beside the driver. She found herself next to another woman in the back – a woman with wavy hair and pink glasses.

'Hi, Kate. I'm Shelagh. I'm Gerard's friend. Don't be frightened, we're all here to help you.'

'Hello, Kate. And I'm Nick, another one of Gerard's friends,' said the driver. 'We're taking you home where you'll be safe. Can you put your belt on? Then we'll be gone.'

She was too bewildered to argue or question; the abrupt shift and hurry since Dave had hammered on her door was overwhelming, and all she could do was resign herself to go with it. If this was wrong and a trap that ended in her death, so be it. She couldn't fight or save herself now.

'Keep your head down, just in case they're still outside, but I think Joe's drawn them off now.'

'Joe?'

'Yes, Joe. He just brought you here. In the other car?'

'Oh,' was all she managed, and once again she curled up out of sight on the back seat.

When Nick reached the exit he checked quickly, left and right, and satisfied that there was no ambush waiting, set off again westwards, through Greenford and Hillingdon towards the M40.

Once they were out on the main road and were sure there was no pursuit, Gerard turned to Kate in the back.

'I'm so sorry it's taken this long. When we first spoke I thought you'd be free in a few days. But really, it's all right now. We've got about an hour's drive, so try and get some sleep.'

'Sleep? You are joking, aren't you? Where are we going?'

'To a friend's house in the country. There's no danger of Mahmoud and his gang finding you.'

'Then what? I ain't got nothin', no money, clothes, nothin'.'

'They know all that, and they're ready for you.'

'Is this another charity? Like what Mahmoud said?'

'No, nothing like that, honest. Really, Kate, you're safe now.'

She looked as though she wanted to argue, but the after-effects of the day's shocking events were already setting in, and she slumped back into the seat, eyes closed in resignation. Shelagh tried to put an arm round her shoulders, but Kate flinched so violently that she quickly pulled back and made sure there was a clear gap between them on the seat.

'I still don't know how you persuaded Jenny to let you come in on this?' Gerard said to Nick.

'Same way you persuaded Arnold, I expect.'

'Erm, I think you'll find that was me,' said Shelagh from the back. 'I can be very persuasive when I need to be.'

'That's a point,' said Gerard suddenly, 'I didn't see him in Joe's car. Did you see him? Was he in the car with you, Kate?'

'Nah. He stayed behind to keep Dave busy.'

'What?' shouted Gerard and Shelagh together. 'That wasn't the idea. He was supposed to be with us and ride shotgun with Joe in case of trouble,' Gerard added. Memories of Dave's club and feet rushed back to him. 'Dave will slaughter him – he's a brute.'

'No chance, not the way Arnie put him down first,' Kate said in a small voice. 'Dave was trying to force me into his van and Arnie punched him, put him down, then broke his leg. Then he stayed and told Joe to get us out.'

'Broke his leg? How?' Arnold was a big man, but Gerard couldn't imagine him being violent, and certainly not able to put a professional like Dave out of action just like that.

'Sounds like he's met the trouble already then,' said Nick. 'What do we do?'

'Have to keep going, we're too far to go back and help. I didn't even think of that when Joe drove up. I assumed they were there together.'

'I wasn't looking, to be honest,' replied Nick, 'I just watched Kate come over to us. I never realised she was so young and so … Now I see how she, well, the need to help her, got under your skin.'

'But Arnold was supposed to come along as well.'

'Does it matter? He did his bit, he got her to the car and got rid of the opposition. We'll find out what happened when we get there.'

'So he's fighting Mahmoud's heavies by himself, and Joe is in the decoy car on his own. It could get nasty if there are more in that taxi. I've got a really bad feeling now.'

'Don't underestimate Joe just 'cos he's quiet,' said Nick. 'He used to box a bit years ago.'

'Did he? What level? But that won't cut any ice if they stop him – The Marquis of Queensbury's probably just an East End pub to them.'

'This whole thing's his plan, so he'll know what to do. Honestly, Ger, let's concentrate on getting Kate to the house, and then we can worry about the others.'

'And Arnold's no pussy, as you just heard,' chipped in Shelagh. 'For a poet, he can handle himself when he needs to. He's told me a few things about his adventures over the years. Don't underestimate him.' But her voice was less confident than her words.

As Nick concentrated on finding his way through the early evening traffic, leaving London and heading along the A40 towards Oxfordshire, Kate sat upright again, looking out at this new London she'd never been allowed the opportunity to know. And Gerard worried about what might be happening to his friends, while trying to give Kate encouraging smiles.

Progress through the outskirts was slow; Nick and Gerard both kept checking mirrors and windows for any suspicious followers but saw nothing. Joe's decoy had worked for them, but what about Joe? And where was Arnold?

After twenty minutes, Kate whined from the back, 'I need a loo. Can't you stop?'

Gerard and Nick exchanged a glance. Could they stop soon? Was it safe? They'd seen no sign of being followed, but they couldn't be sure.

'Yes,' added Shelagh, 'me too. I think Kate could do with some food as well. Can we pull in soon?'

'There's a service station about quarter of an hour away,' said Nick. 'Just let us get onto the M40 and we can take a break there. Can you manage that, Kate?'

'I dunno. I'll try.'

'Good girl,' said Nick.

'Good girl?' Shelagh exclaimed. 'That's a bit patronising, isn't it?'

'What?' said Nick. 'I'm trying to be supportive here, and I'm driving. What am I supposed to say?' Gerard just smiled to himself and said nothing.

It took twenty-five minutes, not fifteen, to reach the services at Beaconsfield, and as soon as the car stopped, Kate stumbled out and rushed into the building.

'OK,' said Shelagh, 'I'll go and keep an eye on her. Bag a table and we'll get some grub when she's finished.'

'Be quick,' said Gerard. 'I don't trust her not to panic and head off in a lorry somewhere.'

Shelagh mock-saluted him and jogged away after Kate.

Ten minutes later the two joined Nick and Gerard at the food outlet. Gerard raised a questioning eyebrow at Shelagh. Kate just sat down sulkily, not speaking.

'Good call, Gerard,' was all that Shelagh said, nodding.

Gerard went up to the counter, and bought burgers and fries for them all, veggie for Shelagh. It was a rare experience for him and, he imagined, for Nick. They both enjoyed good food and usually eschewed any outlets like this, but needs must.

They sat quietly and ate. He hadn't realised how hungry all of them were now that they'd reached this point, but with the sense of having shaken off pursuit, tension eased and hunger sat up again, demanding to be noticed.

'Another one?' asked Nick, when they'd all finished. 'No, it's all right, Ger, I'll get these.'

He took the orders and brought back the new burgers with coffees for all.

They relaxed even more during the second round and began to talk again. Kate, looking and feeling the outsider, stayed sulky and looked away from them all across the eating area.

'All right, Kate?' said Gerard softly. 'Any problems?'

'I din't think it would be like this. I dunno what's happenin'. What you goin' to do with me?'

'We're getting you right away from Mahmoud, Dave and the others, and taking you somewhere where you can just get yourself better.'

'Then what? What am I gonna do?'

'First things first. We'll get you there safely, get a doctor to you, and you'll be looked after – not the way *he* did, but properly.'

She thought about it for a few moments, then nodded.

'Are you goin' to give me some more money? I couldn't make any this week.'

'Don't worry about that, you won't be short.'

'I can't pay no rent though. And I can't afford to get any stuff. Mahmoud always give it me.'

'We'll sort it for you, don't worry.'

Nick said suddenly, 'Why was Arnold fighting that Dave character, anyway? He wasn't meant to be anywhere around.'

'Dunno, he just turned up in his van and said Mahmoud wanted to see me. Then he attacked Arnie with this pick handle.' Then she smiled, for the first time. 'You shoulda seen the way Arnie put 'im down. Pow! Smack! Stamp! Then 'e got the pick, but we drove off before I saw what 'appened next. 'E was good though. Pow!'

'Why was Dave there though? And why in a van?'

Kate shrugged. 'Dunno. 'E said Mahmoud wanted to see me and took me out of me room. Arnie turned up as Dave was puttin' me in the van.'

Gerard picked up what was in Nick's mind.

'So Dave went and got the van just for you at that moment. Just a coincidence? He couldn't just walk back to Mahmoud with you? Or wait till you were back on the street?'

'I dunno. He just came up and told me to get in.'

'I think we only just did this in time,' Nick murmured to Gerard, who nodded, eyes open in horror at the narrow escape they'd afforded her. Shelagh picked up their exchange and suddenly understood. She reached across the table and put her hand on Gerard's.

'Thank the gods you were all there. But is it safe now?'

'All ok now. Yasser, Silke and Farid will be doing their bit soon, and that's it, we're all clear. The tail will have Joe's number plate of course, but that's sorted too, as long as he doesn't get stopped. We'll be at their place long before he gets there, but Annie knows.'

Nick snapped his fingers in annoyance. 'Stupid! Of course, I should have rung Annie and Jenny and given them a sitrep to reassure them. Just a moment.'

He left the table and took out his mobile phone. They watched as he called the numbers and let them know how the operation was going. He turned his back to them as he spoke, and Gerard guessed that Annie was quizzing him about Kate as well as Joe.

'All done,' he said as he rejoined them. 'It's down to Joe to make his way home and down to us to get cracking again. Another hour or less and we'll be there. Ready?'

'I need the loo again,' said Kate, and headed off. Shelagh looked questioningly at Gerard, who nodded.

'Keep her in sight, she might still make a bolt. Or shoot up again. I don't know which, but don't trust her to walk back by herself.'

'Good for Joe, suggesting we bring Shelagh,' said Gerard. 'Never occurred to me that Kate should have a chaperone. We know she's safe with us, but it didn't occur to me that she might not know that herself.'

'Jen would have known and said so. She wouldn't have come along herself though, I can tell you that!'

'OK, here they come. Next stop, the farm.'

CHAPTER 42

The whole struggle outside Kate's had happened in less than two minutes, and despite the rush hour two streets away, no one seemed to have noticed what was happening.

When Joe and Kate had vanished around the corner Arnold leaned back against the wall and regained his breath. It was a long time since he had had to fight anyone, and his body wasn't as resilient as back then.

When his breathing had returned to normal, he walked across to the cursing Dave, still rolling on the pavement and clutching his knee.

'Ok, mate?' he said. 'Do you need an ambulance or can you walk? I'll give you a hand up.'

'Fuck off,' was the sole reply. 'You are dead, man. Dead man walking.'

'I don't think so. If you're smart, you'll do a runner. Oh sorry, I mean a hobble, don't I? Can you?'

'We know you. You're fucking dead.'

'Oh come on, it's fallin' apart, innit? Get out of it. Let Mahmoud take the fall and get yourself out. Can you stand up? I didn't hear any bones break, but if you can't, I'll get the ambulance. If nothin' else, it'll keep you out the way when the shit hits the fan.'

'If that little cow points the finger …'

'She won't,' Arnold interrupted. 'She's too damn scared to say a word, just like the rest of the stable.'

'Kennels, more like,' muttered Dave. 'Fuckin' bitches, the lot.' A good sign, thought Arnold, despite the abuse. He's calming down a bit at least, even if the menagerie is going from cattle through horses to dogs.

'Whatever,' he said out loud. 'She's safe and away and wants to stay that way. She won't talk, and I know you won't find her, but other people will talk. You bunch of amateurs have upset a lot of ordinary folk round 'ere and I can't rightly think of anyone who wants you to carry on. Word gets 'round that you've let one get away, well, not good for the reputation, is it?'

Dave lay back on the ground, still groaning. Arnold had a sudden thought, the same one that was soon to occur to Nick and Gerard.

'Hey, what was the van for? Why did you turn up in that, just for her?'

'Mahmoud wanted me to …' He paused for just a moment too long. '… take her to him,' he finished lamely.

'And why couldn't Mr Mahmoud come and talk to 'er 'imself, eh? 'E don't live that far away. You don't need a bleedin' van to come 'ere, do you?'

'She's behind with her rent, and stuff. I … persuade his people to keep up to date with all that.'

'Come on, we both know she's too far gone to earn much now. If she's be'ind, she ain't gonna catch up for a long time. She's sick, and she's so skinny now she looks even younger than she is. Not many punters are goin' to go for 'er, so how do you persuade her? Eh?'

Dave stayed silent, and Arnold finished joining the dots that he'd hoped would show a different picture.

'You bastards. You complete, fuckin' bastards. Where were you goin' to do it then?'

'What do you care? Like I said, you're dead too now. You ain't escapin' us.'

'Maybe. So it don't matter if you tell me, does it?'

'There's a place on the river down east, a long way downstream. It'd be days before she showed up, with nothing to tie her to this manor.'

'And she's just a sick kid, and you'd do that. You fuckin' bastards. I've changed my mind, you do need an ambulance.' And without warning he stamped across Dave's knee as he lay there, just as the windows of the street started to reflect the blue flashing lights of the police car that had turned down into the road, its siren drowning the crack that came from the knee, immediately followed by the scream. Arnold stepped back as the car stopped by him and held his hands out to the side in surrender. At the same time the front door opposite opened, and an elderly man on two walking sticks hobbled across the road to them.

'I called you, it were me,' he said to the policemen. 'I see it all – 'e started it,' pointing at Dave, still rolling in pain. ''E swung a pick handle at 'im,' nodding towards Arnold. ''E was trying to snatch a kiddie, I see it. 'E started it all. I'll make a statement.'

At the police station, not far away, Arnold was bundled into a cell while his surprise witness was interviewed. When it was his turn, he said at once,

'I'll not answer or say anything without my solicitor.'

'Who's duty brief?' the senior policeman asked his colleague.

'Nah,' said Arnold, 'don't want a duty man. Get me my solicitor, Mr Taylor. 'Ere.' And smiling, Arnold handed him the business card that Gerard had given him earlier that day – the same card he'd given everyone who had taken part, just in case. After all, no one could tell where the weak link or unexpected twist in the plan would materialise. Mr Taylor was waiting by the phone, hoping that only one of them at most would need to call him, but ready to spend most of the night travelling back and forth if it had all collapsed.

Gerard and Yasser had primed him, and in his turn he had spoken (strictly unofficially) to the chief superintendent of the district. As yet, he had not warned them of tonight's escapade, but they were persuaded into believing him by his story of Mahmoud's management of the girls and the supply of drugs into the area that he controlled. From being a small scale and contained irritation, Mahmoud was now a target for them. If Dave and Farid could be persuaded to testify against him, they were ready to accept this unusual alliance with a defence lawyer, traditionally a member of the enemy camp.

Arnold's intervention, and his surprise witness, offered them the opportunity to prepare a move. Dave was laid up in hospital with a broken knee and a police constable waiting outside the ward. He was going to receive two visitors the next day – a detective inspector from the drugs squad who, after much local wrangling, were given governance of the operation, and then from Mr Taylor who would make him an offer that he really shouldn't refuse.

While Nick drove the others out of London, free from pursuit, Joe was leading Ted's taxi in a different direction, also westerly. He crossed the M25 at Colnbrook, heading towards the M4 while keeping the pursuit puzzled. It wouldn't take him too long to join the others back home, but first he had to lose his tail along the way. He also needed to lose the car before the police stopped him. He knew the Thames Valley Police would have it flagged as stolen on their system, and returning to their jurisdiction now made him vulnerable. He drove carefully, making sure not to draw attention to himself, holding his breath every time he saw a blue flash, or a police car the other side of the barrier. He had no need to worry: the two-vehicle convoy made it all the way to Newbury, where he pulled into the out-of-town supermarket car park, stopped in a sheltered corner and vanished inside the store before Ted could close in and see him.

Joe had a large carrier bag with him and went straight to the toilet, where he changed his coat and put on a pair of glasses and a wig of a very different colour and style from his own hair. He left the store with the stream of other shoppers and then made his way out of the car park to the road where his own car had been waiting for him since that morning. First of all, he crossed to the petrol station near the exit and used the payphone to call his friend and tell him that the car was safely in place with no damage. Hands gloved through the whole adventure, there were no fingerprints on the car to tie it to him, in the unlikely event that the police had tracked him as the 'thief' who had taken it the night before. As he drove off, he saw Ted's black cab still waiting near the decoy, ready to set off again in pursuit. As intended, Ted didn't recognise him and had a long wait in front of him, while Joe himself had a much more leisurely drive home.

He reached his house an hour later, and as he'd expected, Nick's car was in the drive and the house windows were lit up. He rang the doorbell and waited for Ann to answer. Sure enough, he heard the voices inside suddenly stop. Ann opened the door cautiously and looked at him enquiringly.

'Yes?' she asked, as he made no move and stayed silent, trying not to laugh. 'What do you want?'

'All ok then?' he said, and she gaped at his voice.

'Joe? You beast!' and she hit him in the chest, burst into laughter and hugged him.

'What do you look like? What are you thinking? Thank Christ you're safe.' And she pulled him inside where the others were waiting tensely.

'Look what's turned up!' she laughed.

'Well, I didn't want them to spot me in the car park, did I?' said Joe.

'Where did you get all that stuff?' demanded Ann. 'And kill that rat on your head this instant!' and she snatched the wig from him, took off his glasses, and there was Joe, himself again.

He looked across at Kate, feet underneath her on the sofa and looking as tense and scared as she did in his car. Shelagh was sitting on the sofa beside her holding her hand.

'You all right now, lass?' he said quietly. 'It's all done now. Doesn't matter who's in his pocket, we covered our tracks, it's all good now.'

Kate nodded dumbly, still in shock from the last two hours' turmoil and hardly registering who was in the room – Gerard, Shelagh, Nick sitting with Jenny, Ann and now Joe.

Ann had already told her that tomorrow she would see Ann's doctor and then social services; together they could sort out her chest infection, then map out the next moves for her. They could now shut behind her anything to do with Mahmoud and that whole stage of her life.

Exhaustion soon set in, and Ann took Kate upstairs to show her her bedroom. Joe said to the others,

'What now? You staying tonight? Ann's got beds ready in case. You must be pretty knackered after all that.'

'We have to be getting back,' said Shelagh, indicating Gerard and herself. 'It's Jez's funeral tomorrow, and we need to be there.'

Gerard looked apprehensively at Nick, remembering their argument.

Nick shrugged. 'I'm not going to that. Sorry, Ger, it would be hypocrisy for me to pretend to be sorry for that … well, you know what I think.'

'I know,' replied Gerard. 'I doubt many people will show up, but someone should be there to speak for him, and send him off. His life was one massive failure, his death shouldn't be as well. Well, his actual death was, of course, but his funeral at least might …'

'We knew him,' finished Shelagh for him. 'We'll go and see him off. He never did pay me back that tenner, but I won't hold that against him now.'

'Anyway,' she added, looking sideways at Gerard, 'I think our friend here will want to catch up with Silky again PDQ.'

'Silky?' said Ann, coming back into the room in time to hear Shelagh's comment and speaking for everyone, now all staring at Gerard who had turned bright red.

'Silke,' he corrected.

'Well that doesn't tell us much,' said Ann.

'Actually, I think it tells us more than enough. Good on you, Ger, I knew you were up to no good, sneaking off to Earl's Court instead of coming out on the town with me! I always say brevity is the soul of chastity, but you've taken your time, haven't you?'

'She's a friend,' muttered Gerard, 'just a friend. Anyway, she's helping us too, so I need to …'

'Shut up, Gerard,' laughed Shelagh. 'Don't talk her down, or yourself. You want to see her again soon, why not? You've got a lot of time to make up, a good priest like yourself.'

CHAPTER 43

Thursday, and another day of winter sun; the blindest of people could now see Christmas well above the horizon and closing in fast. The sky was clear blue and the trees along the kerbs now completely denuded, letting the sunlight jitter through the bare twigs. It was cold, but bright enough to lift the heart and bring an unsought smile to the lips of unworried folk.

On the twelfth floor of the blue tower, an officer on his break stood at the window looking contentedly at the view. Glancing down to the little residential estate below, he saw a small tableau begin to form.

Two men, tiny figures far below, too small to note their complexion, walked quickly along Aisgill Avenue. Several cars and a plain unmarked van were parked along the kerb; not all were empty. He looked with keener interest now – perhaps something was about to happen.

Mahmoud and Farid, untouched by the sunshine, didn't share an unsought smile; both were clearly unhappy. The world was not on their side this morning, and Mahmoud was not used to that sensation. Farid was more familiar with hostility and mischance, but no more happy with the situation that had started to condense around them. Unlike Mahmoud, he was not taken by surprise, but could not yet show it.

'So where is the bitch now? That's all I want to know. I know where Dave is, but he's no fucking good to me in hospital. Where is she?'

Farid shrugged. 'If Dave couldn't take care of her, then who knows? She's gone, that's all.'

Mahmoud stopped walking and turned to Farid.

'I know she's gone. That's what I'm saying. Why do you think telling me that helps, eh? Moron!' and without thinking, he slapped Farid hard across the cheek. Before his hand dropped down to its normal position, Farid, reacting quicker than Mahmoud could have dreamt, grabbed his wrist and squeezed it tightly, very tightly.

'I help you, I work for you, I look after you,' he hissed, 'but you are not my father, and you are not my imam. You do not ever lay a finger on me.' And he squeezed harder still. Mahmoud turned pale, but did not make any sound. He held Farid's eye and waited. After ten seconds Farid released him and they both breathed again.

'And you do not ever lay a finger on me,' said Mahmoud, quietly, but with strong emphasis. 'I have your passport, and I know enough about you to make you vanish from these streets as if you had never arrived, and only I will know where you are, and the authorities. Now, I want to know what happened on Tuesday and who put Dave in hospital. Where were you?'

'I was at my prayers, where you should have been,' said Farid, 'and before that I was sorting that dealer in Victoria for you. You didn't tell me anything was going on. You didn't tell me to stay with Dave, so how should I know what happened? Tell me now what he was doing for you, then I might have an idea.'

Mahmoud thought for a minute, then sighed.

'All right, I suppose you're right, I didn't tell you. He was supposed to take Kate away. She's become a liability; she's losing me money. I needed her room, so Dave was going to take her to the river. Then next I hear she's gone missing, Dave's been crippled without taking her, you're nowhere to be found, and I've got a new girl for the room and no one's cleared it. The police are all over Dave, Ted hasn't reported to me, and it's all a fucking mess. Who was it? How did they know? And where were you yesterday morning, anyway?'

Farid shrugged. He'd already seen Yasser trying to hide at the corner of the road, and he now tried to move Mahmoud around so that Yasser would be out of his vision.

'I had another job, down in Stepney. Hughie called me and sent me there.'

'Hughie, bloody Hughie again! If he needs you he should ask me! You work for me, not fucking Hughie!'

'But you work for him, so he doesn't need to ask you.'

As they stood talking, Katrin suddenly appeared, but she was not intending to hide. Instead she came straight up to the two of them and broke into the discussion.

'Hey, Mr Mahmoud,' she began. 'I need to tell you, yes? I've applied for three jobs now you've given me that address. I want to thank you, you know?'

Mahmoud immediately broke into his beautiful smile and took her hand as Farid looked on, expressionless.

'Well done, I'm proud of you,' he said. 'You see? We can help you to get your life back on track. But if you will excuse me, I need to …'

'Yes, yes, I can see that, but, please, I need some more of that medicine. Can you give me some, please?'

Mahmoud's smile eased away from his eyes.

'I don't have very much. It's very expensive. If you really need it, I can let you have some in advance, but you will have to pay me back when you are earning.'

'Of course, I understand that, ok. Also, about the room …'

The radiant smile had completely retreated now, its sunshine covered by darkening clouds.

'What about the room? Isn't it better than your doorway? Are you going to complain about all the help I give you?'

'No, no, I don't mean to,' and Katrin came close to Mahmoud, putting a hand on his arm to reassure him. Only Farid noticed what her other hand was doing, and even the entranced watcher on the twelfth floor, staring down at them, failed to see it.

'I'm grateful, really I am, but the room is someone else's, isn't it? Her clothes and things are there, the bedding is filthy and stained, and it's all mouldy in there.'

'I know it's not ideal – the previous tenant left very suddenly on Tuesday without notice, and as your case was an emergency, we didn't have the chance to clear it. Farid here will look after that today, clear her clothes out and give you clean bedding. Don't worry about mould, it's got a roof, hasn't it?'

'Why did she go? What happened to her?'

'Not your business.'

'No, sorry. But can you give me some stuff? I will pay you, really, when I get that job.'

He looked at her, at Farid, and then back at her.

'How much do you need?'

'Enough for a week? I should be able to pay you back then.'

'In a week? I doubt it. But all right, we can work something out for you to pay me back.'

Decision made, the sunshine returned, and he patted Katrin on the shoulder.

'Farid, wait here with our friend. I must fetch the medicine from the office.' And he turned towards a house further down the road.

As soon as he was out of earshot, Farid grasped Silke's shoulder.

'Come back now. Leave it to the police.'

'Not yet,' she said. 'If he turns round and we're gone, he'll know. See it through.'

As Mahmoud approached the house, his office, three cars parked along the kerb opened up to let a number of plain clothes officers out. As he vanished inside the front door, the van disgorged a number of uniforms, complete with a ram, and they all converged on Mahmoud's HQ. At the same time Yasser, as always in his taqiyah and his beige smock shirt, came to join Farid and Silke.

As the police forced the front door, only Yasser saw Mahmoud appear at the rear and run down the garden to escape. Before the others could react, Yasser ran to try and intercept him, soon followed by the police.

Up above in the tower, word had got around that something was happening, and a number of windows on the spur overlooking the small estate were populated.

They watched the pursuers fast converging from three different directions, the newcomer in the middle-eastern dress making first contact. There was a confusion of limbs and activity, with shouts which could be heard at all levels, and then, as the other plain clothes caught up, a figure staggered out of the melee, clutching his stomach, and fell. The fugitive was wrestled efficiently to the ground and secured, while the original two who had stood away from the action rushed to the injured man, kneeling by him and trying to staunch the blood which even those on the upper floors could see spreading out on the pavement.

CHAPTER 44

'I'm going away in January,' said Silke.

'What? How long for?' asked Gerard, looking up at her from the bed. 'Where are you going?'

'The band's been given a tour in Poland. It might extend beyond, it depends on Andrzej, the agent.'

'Well, that's great. Yes, great, well done. Yes, I'm glad for you, good luck.'

She laughed. 'Oh yes, you sound so glad for me, you say it so gloamy? Gloomy? I don't know if it's even going to work, but the guys all believe it and want to go, and I'm not going to be left behind.'

'What about us?' He hadn't wanted to say that but couldn't stop the hurt words stuttering out.

'What about us? Darling Gerard, you know we're not for life. That's not why you chased me over the river. Look, you're not the sad priest anymore, you're better. You're a man and at last you've learned that. "What about us?" You mean, "what about me?", don't you?'

'But I love you.'

'No you don't, not properly. You are in love with having sex with me, and quite right, too. That's not the same, and don't ever think it is, whoever else you meet later. You'll always remember me, but I'm not the only woman in London. Just don't go back to stalking anyone across the river! And feel good when you think of me, I'd like that. But once the band gets to Poland I've no idea what will happen then.'

'So after Christmas I'll not see you again?'

'Maybe, maybe not, we don't know. But there's still a week between Christmas and January. And, we're here now aren't we? And we're not in a hurry yet, are we?' And she lay back down on the bed with him, the dark wig gone and her auburn hair falling across his chest.

'Here's to absent friends.' Nick raised his glass to the full table: Ann, Joe, Gerard, Nick, Jenny, their son James, and Kate. They all followed suit with Kate a few seconds behind the others as she tried to follow the ritual. The Christmas lunch was finished, a triumph for Ann and Joe, with some surprising help from Kate. All her fear and suspicions had been allayed since those first few days at the farm and then the meeting with the doctor and social services.

They were all still in their places at the table, and yet another bottle of wine was draining. Jenny and James were used to Nick's 'absent friends' toast, but it was new to the rest.

As Gerard drank the toast he thought of Silke, Shelagh, Arnold, Yasser, Jez, and even Father Holloway and Mrs Cormac. Some of them would now always be absent.

He wondered who Kate thought of. He saw James throwing covert glances at her and blushing when she caught him. Lucky Jim, he thought, smiling wryly at how Jenny must be reacting inside to that. He's not going to wait until his late thirties to uncover the mysteries. Celibate? No, the word should be 'celebrate!'

Kate wasn't taking too much notice of James. Gwen had stretched out under the table at her feet, repeatedly nudging her for titbits which she tried to discreetly pass under the table while everyone pretended not to notice.

'What's happening with Shelagh and Arnold?' asked Joe. 'Any chance we might see them properly sometime?'

'Arnold's chuffed as anything. His new book is coming out soon, and his publishers are putting it up for a Poetry Society award. He's just hanging out with friends, I think. Having Christmas dinner at one of the pubs and promising complimentary copies to anyone who stands still long enough. Shelagh's spending the holiday time down in Cornwall. I don't know when she's coming back to the house.'

Gerard followed Ann when she went out to check on the hens and round them up. He wanted the chance for a private talk.

'How's it working out with her?' he asked.

'Better than we thought. She's really trying, Ger. Those first days she was so apathetic and resigned, I thought we'd lose her, but once the antibiotics kicked in and the bronchitis lifted, she changed. Gwen helped. She seemed to know Kate was ill and unhappy and spent most of the day lying beside her. Amazing that dog, they've got such a bond now, it's really funny to see. Fair play to her, she helps us as much as she can, but she's still weak, and the detox she's doing is not easy. Still, now she trusts us she wants to pull her weight here and not freeload, so we're both fine with her staying.'

'Well, I'm so grateful to you and Joe for all of it, and Joe for showing us how to do it. Yasser and I were paralysed. We had no initiative and no ideas. We were just stuck with a good intention and nothing more.'

'Not much change there, then, Ger, eh? Always full of good intentions you were. Now it's done, what next? You staying Earl's Court way, or back to the hills and your old parish?'

'No, never that. I'm staying in London. I've got ideas and, yes I know, more good intentions. Nick's helping me with some of them. I'll stay fast where I am for a while. It may be small, but I'm making enough friends locally for it to feel like home. And it's easy to find you here, as well.'

'Well make sure you do, hon. Make sure you do.'

At the end of the afternoon, as midwinter dark was establishing itself again, Gerard made his apologies.

'Are you sure you have to leave?' Ann asked. 'Why not stay over till Boxing Day? You know we've got room.'

'Course he can't,' laughed Nick. 'Silky's waiting.'

'Silke,' he laughed back. 'No, it's not Silke this time, but I promised I'd visit Yasser in hospital this evening. He's stabilised, out of intensive care now and back in the general ward. Thankfully the knife missed his key organs, but he still lost so much blood. Christmas as a date might not mean anything to him, but I'd like to see him, thank him and, well, just see him.' He jingled the keys of his hire car, ready now to say goodbye and leave.

'Well, now you've found us here you'd better be coming back a few times, you hear?'

'I hear you, Ann, and you try keeping me away.'

'And Ger,' said Nick quickly. 'That other matter, your plans. Talk after Christmas? We'll be back home in a couple of days.'

'That would be good, thanks. And James, good to meet you even if we haven't talked much today. Next exeat, perhaps your mum will let me join you both for the day?'

'Sure, be good,' mumbled James, red-faced as Jenny brushed his hair down with her hand and kissed him.

As he was at the door, Kate came up at last.

'What happened with Mahmoud?' she asked.

'He's on remand till his trial, with no bail. Cocaine in his pocket, thanks to Silke, and a big cache of coke, crack, crystal meth and heroin in the house, not to mention attempted murder. Farid and Dave have both been persuaded to testify in return for protection, and deportation for Farid. There were enough witnesses to Mahmoud stabbing Yasser to make sure he goes down. You don't have to testify, nor Silke. They have enough on him without either of you. It really is all over, that part of your life.'

'Is Arnie in trouble for hurting Dave?'

'No, the police accepted self-defence and aren't asking for too much more detail there, just keeping it simple. That lawyer is even better than I realised.'

'What about the others? The other girls? Viv, Jude and the rest?'

'I don't know, I'm afraid. I suspect that someone else will step into his place and it will begin all over again, but as yet, who knows? But how are you doing, really?'

'I'm detoxing at the moment, getting off the stuff. After that's finished, I'll go into rehab sometime in the New Year to try and kick the habit for good. That really scares me. Ann and Joe have been great, and I love Gwen.'

'Will you stay here after rehab?'

'I hope so. Ann and Joe said I could, but I don't want to become, you know …'

'I know, but if you can get a job after rehab, you can always pay rent can't you? And you can help out while you're here.'

'I try to. When I'm not too tired I try to, but at the moment I can't do much.'

'Well. You've earned a break after all that's happened. Good luck, and Merry Christmas!'

'Thank you,' was all she said. But the hug she gave him told him everything.

CHAPTER 45

First week in January, and the shops and offices are coming back to life. Christmas lights and decorations have come down, even though it's not yet twelfth night. Along the pavements, choruses of damp coughs and sneezes provide a counterpoint to the traffic rumbles and siren bursts.

A mix of emotions shows on the faces in the streets and in the shops. There's relief that it's all over for another forty nine weeks, which is marred by a deepening awareness that, despite Shelagh's best efforts on the Yule Solstice, there is still a seemingly interminable period of cold and dark mornings followed by cold and dark evenings, before the promise of spring can be felt and honoured. The cold drizzle adds to the 'So now what?' expression on the faces.

At about three this afternoon, a watcher from the tower is enjoying his impromptu coffee break. The list of the day's tasks have been mostly, and satisfyingly, ticked as complete, and world threats are at a reassuringly low level at the moment. He can't see into Earl's Court Road or the tube entrance, where a middle-aged man wearing a slightly grubby overcoat and worn, unpolished brogues is appealing for help to everyone who passes. Most of them ignore him, more intent on getting into the dryness of the station.

'Excuse me, excuse me, just a moment. Just a second, please?' He's waving a photograph of a pretty teenage girl at everyone, hoping to catch their attention. 'She's my daughter. Someone told me she's around here. Can you help, please?'

But everyone going in and out of the station, dodging the travellers in the opposing tide, is too concerned with catching their train or escaping the wet. No one has the time or patience to stop and tell Kate's father that he's too late, that she has moved on and is a new person now, out of his reach for good.

The watcher drains the last of his coffee and turns back to his desk.

Nothing special happening around here. Nothing to trouble anyone in the blue watchtower.

Back to serious work now.

EPILOGUE

Gerard stood a moment at the front gate, enjoying the warm early summer sunshine on his face before walking up to the front door. Just a few weeks earlier he knew he would have felt the old heavy weight in his stomach, the dread, but not today. Perversely, he was almost looking forward to the encounter.

Mrs Cormac opened the door to him, with a polite smile and greeting, rather than the friendly motherly face she used to show him.

'Good morning, Father Tisserant. Father Holloway's expecting you. In the drawing room, please.'

To have Mrs Cormac look at him like that and speak so formally to him was a jolting reminder of how far he had travelled from his safe days with them.

He waited in the drawing room, awakening memories from previous times – memories of the glass-fronted bookcase that secured all the old, forbidding authorities and the over-polished mahogany table, as dark as the spirit of the rest of the house. French windows opened onto the lush garden with its views of the hills in the background. That view had always been a favourite of his, and he looked hungrily out, re-embossing the detail onto his memory.

'Gerard, my dear boy, welcome! How good to see you again.' And Father Holloway was already in the room, striding towards him, his hands reaching out to clasp Gerard's between his own, his brisk posture belying his years.

Over the sherry that Father Holloway insisted on pouring, he asked the question that Gerard had anticipated in dread.

'And does this mean that you feel ready to come back and pick up your duties again? You certainly look much better now.'

As so often before, Gerard's chain of thought was distracted by the tuft of white hair that always stuck out from behind Father Holloway's right ear. Each time the tuft moved, Gerard was put in mind of a flag waving, 'Beware, heresy here! Beware of Deadly Sin!' This time he had to suppress an urge reach out and smooth it down.

'I do feel much better, thank you,' he replied, 'in all sorts of ways.' He took a deep breath – he was about to unleash one of Father Holloway's most dreaded storms, and he felt himself brace, hoping he could withstand it and stay firm, which he'd never managed to do before.

'The fact is, Father, I mean, well, I've done a lot of thinking, and … well, when it comes down to it, it, you know …'

'You don't propose to return, is that it?'

'Yes, I mean, no, that is …'

'Gerard, just say it, my boy. Just say it.'

'Yes, sorry. I've decided to leave the priesthood, well, the Church.'

The storm rumbled over the horizon, but as yet showed no signs of approaching.

'I did wonder, while you were away. Yes, I did wonder.'

So far, not even a spatter of rain drops or a slight gust of wind. When it did finally break …

'Of course, while you may withdraw, your vows still hold. Your vow of celibacy, for example, is supposed to hold for life and not just for your employment by the church authorities – unless you plan to marry? No, all right then. You will no longer be able to give the sacrament, or say Mass. You may no longer hear confession, but the silence of the confessional is sacred for always – you will never be released from that obligation. Employment is temporary, but the power that was granted you when you took your oath can never be withdrawn.'

'I understand.'

'Do you wish to confess before completing this step? Is there a need for absolution while you still belong with us?'

'I have committed what you, certainly, and probably the Church, would regard as grave sins. But I don't feel in need of absolution.'

Father Holloway looked closely at him, the white tuft waving warnings to Gerard. Still the tempest kept below the horizon.

'Until you tell me those sins I cannot, of course, comment or condemn.' But the deep disapproval was there, rumbling closer to the surface.

'Would it be fair to ask what led you to this, how shall I say, fork in the road? I put it like that because at this moment nothing is irrevocable. You are at the fork, and inclined to take, let us say, the left-hand path, but you still have space to turn and choose to stay on the right-hand one instead. Do you see?'

So once more, Gerard relayed the story of his experiences in Earl's Court. He confined himself to a factual recounting of Kate's rescue and his helping to bring about Mahmoud's fall with the assistance, among others, of Yasser, Shelagh and Silke, and even including his seduction by Silke and his failure to save Jez.

Before he'd finished, Mrs Cormac announced lunch, and he left his tale while they moved next door to eat.

It was a silent meal, and his apprehension of his mentor's coming denunciation rose again. It even robbed him of both taste and appetite, which was a shame, because for him, Mrs Cormac's meals had always been the saving grace of the household, his one shining memory of that time. She would be so mortified to learn how little he enjoyed this last lunch.

'You're probably right,' Father Holloway surprised him as they sat in the drawing room again. Gerard had finished his account of the sabbatical, and now sat back for the denunciation. Although the May sun shone low through the window, he had arranged the chairs, for once, so that neither was dazzled.

'I've thought much about you since your … what should I call it? Breakdown? That sounds an unkind term.'

'It may have been a breakdown, but it didn't feel like I would expect one to feel. I always called it my crisis. Actually it was also a growing disenchantment with the Church and its teachings. Not all the teachings, of course, but an over-strict demand of adherence to dogma. We both know what prompted the final disillusionment.' Now, it must come.

Father Holloway raised an eyebrow at that, then smiled wryly.

'Mrs Cormac's lunch has at least restored your fluency, I see.' He sighed, and scratched with his finger at the arm of his chair. 'You may be right, for all I know. That sad, sad business of Mrs Conway rocked us both, but you even more.'

'It was wrong!' said Gerard sharply. 'We killed her, simple as that. And I can never accept that our Lord ever demanded that of us. What is there in any of the gospels of his life that make us think that? It may have been Paul's view, but Christ himself? It's against everything he taught and practised, but we still did it.' Gerard was fired up now and ready to do battle with Father Holloway's intransigence. But somehow, his enemy was missing.

'I daresay you're not wrong. You were always a better thinker than I.'

'Pardon?!'

'Oh, it's true. I'm very learned, a good scholar, I don't deny. I've studied and absorbed all of these books and can quote all the authorities, but I'm not clever enough to critique them, or argue outside those parameters. And especially not to think through a human problem in its own terms, the way you always do. I've envied that gift, but it frightened me as well.'

'Why frightened?'

'I just see two directions in our life – towards eternal bliss or eternal pain, do you see? And I am so fearful of finding myself on the wrong path that I need a clearly signed and marked road, with handrails to keep me on the one that will avoid eternal pain. When I watch you wrestling with our parishioners' problems and anguish and seeking a way to comfort them, I see you letting go of my handrail and wandering off the marked road. And I am frightened you will find yourself on the painful path and not be able to come back to safety.'

'What is this marked road? What do you mean by handrail?'

'The certainty of these authorities, much cleverer than I could ever be, who have argued the right and safest way to live – to live so as never to displease the Lord. From St Augustine onwards, through St Thomas Aquinas, Loyola, Cardinal Newman, there have been strong injunctions on how we should live and worship, and by staying faithful to these, we should achieve bliss. I know there are contradictions between them, and I am not competent to unpick all the strands. And so my safest course has been to choose the most austere, and follow them, to bring you and our parishioners with me to that bliss.'

'What about ordinary everyday people with ordinary everyday worries? Do they deserve the harshness you impose?'

'Oh, Gerard, here is where you always vexed me. Every time you brought me a problem from a parishioner like poor Mrs Conway, I daren't let myself waver from my narrow path. And I was so afraid of letting you stray on the road to eternal pain that I couldn't let human feelings come into it. Do you think the Lord will understand? I only ever intended to do right by Him.'

The storm had cleared right away, to be replaced by a deep mist that left Gerard thoroughly confused. The monster had somehow metamorphosed, leaving a light shining through the mist, and he knew that soon he would be able to see clearly at last.

Father Holloway spoke again, and Gerard no longer was bothered by the stray tuft behind his ear.

'Your adventure since you left; I cannot begin to imagine how I would have fared. I am always in my head, but at the Temple, we see Christ taking direct action against the moneylenders, and your dealings with this Mahmoud strike me as in the same vein. I do hope that's not blasphemous, or all my rigour is undone.'

This was the nearest that Gerard had ever heard Father Holloway come to making a joke. But then was it a joke or real fear?

'I sometimes regret that I never learned your gift of attraction. In such a short time you drew all these lost souls to yourself. I have never managed that. I need my barrier, I'm afraid.'

Gerard suddenly burst out,

'Do you know how afraid of you I always was? How everything I did or said was interpreted as sin? I never dared relax or even bring you half of the problems that came to me.'

'Yes.'

'And that was right?'

'I thought so then; it was not comfortable, but it was to keep you from the path to eternal pain. Was that so wrong?'

'Do you truly believe God will only reward fear? That Heaven is only open to people afraid of punishment? That it's closed to people who take delight in the sensuous world that He created? Or who seek to help people simply because that is the right thing to do? If his only interest and pleasure is in forcing people to follow His way through fear, what sort of God do we worship?'

Father Holloway walked to the window, agitated.

'As I said, I find it hard to think these things through myself. What is the Lord's gift, and what is the Devil's temptation? What does God want from us but obedience? That is what I have striven for always. And now you give me confusion.'

Gerard sighed.

'I'm not frightened of you anymore. However that came about, it is a gift I'm grateful for.'

'A gift for me too, my boy. You are much easier to be with as you are now. Your old diffidence never truly suited you. Will you change your mind? Will you take up your place again here? Please? I need someone with your view of the world and people to balance my own, let's say, blind certainty. Will you?'

'I'm sorry, but no. I've found my own mission now, and it's outside our Church's certainties and commands.'

'And can you tell me what form this new mission will take?'

'At the moment it's still in embryo, but I want to start a street mission to help people like Kate and the other girls, and addicts like Jez, and the homeless. I want to be able to give them a shelter, a safe place to sleep, to feed them, give them access to medical care and liaise with social services to help. And, of course, spiritual guidance and support, but definitely not evangelical and not as a condition of help.'

'Ambitious and noble, yes. Isn't that the sort of thing that already happens, though? Isn't that what St Martin-in-the-Fields already undertakes?'

'Yes, they do much of that and do a marvellous job. But the problem is vast and still growing. My friend, Nick, is going to help with setting up a charitable status and help me with all sorts of logistical and financial structures. There's a long way to go before it's running and, I pray, making a real change for these people, but that's my vision for it – a street mission. So, I'm afraid that no, the demand is greater in London and the major cities, more so than here, so I shan't return. Yasser and his mosque are also helping and will be a part of it. He's given me so much encouragement and active support, I'm glad to be working with him.'

Gerard looked steadily at Father Holloway at this, waiting for the superior disapproval, but just received a noncommittal nod instead.

'I don't see choosing the mission as a left-hand path, to use your image, but an alternative path. Just not the one we shared.'

'A shame, a shame. I understand, though. Well, before you go, would you do me two favours?'

'Gladly.'

'The first, please listen to some Bach with me again.'

'Of course. I always loved that. First, though, I have a small gift for you. I'm afraid it may not be to your taste, but I would like you to have it anyway.' And he handed Father Holloway, from the bag he carried, a copy of Arnold's volume, *The Toffee King*. Father Holloway looked at it, puzzled, but opened it and read the handwritten dedication on the flyleaf. He gave an uncertain smile.

'Thank you. I will read it at leisure. This is from one of your friends?'

'A very good friend, the first I made there. We met in the National Gallery.'

'And what happened to those other friends from that time? Do you still see them all?'

'Arnold I still see, yes, the author of,' and he nodded in the direction of the book. 'Silke and her band went on tour to Poland at the beginning of the year, but that turned out to be either a fraud or a shambles. In the end they were given just three concerts to play with long gaps in between. They lost more money than they made, and after the first month she stopped writing. I have no idea where she is now. Shelagh, the pagan lady …'

'The witch.'

'Yes, if you like, although she wore that title with pride rather than defiance and certainly not with any malice or malign intent. Anyway, she never came back from Cornwall after Christmas, but joined a group there, down towards Falmouth. Strange, but I miss her more than Silke.

'I still see Kate when I visit Ann and Joe. They've made such a difference to her. She has almost regressed back to childhood, but the one she always thought she should have, with loving parents and a dog she can spoil and take out. She's finished her rehab and is much stronger now, and she's found a local job nearby, as well as helping out at home with the gardens and the chickens. She now counts as a lodger rather than a charity case, and all of them feel better with that. So that story at least seems to have ended well. Nick and Jenny? Well, much as before. I feared they were headed for a break last year, but they're still together. Nick is still stuck in his second adolescence, but as I said, he's giving me valuable help in establishing the Trust which will set up the mission.

'I'm sorry, we are going to listen to Bach together, aren't we?'

Father Holloway relaxed and crossed over to the record player. Gerard was not sure if he was even aware of cassette tapes, let alone the new CDs. *St John's Passion* was already on the turntable, but as always, Father Holloway carefully lifted it off with the lightest possible touch on the edges and dusted it, before replacing it and oh so delicately lifting the arm and placing the stylus. As the much loved music began, it was easy for Gerard to remember the few peaceful hours in a week when they could sit together like this, with no tensions or sense of guilt over an imagined sin.

Gerard was as moved as always by the beauty of the chorale, Bach's writing and the voices. But he noted that the text, which had moved him almost to tears in younger days, now made him uncomfortable. Not quite sceptical, but for the first time in his experience, he felt outside the communion which the words had always drawn him towards. He could listen to it forever, but would never again feel a part of that enclosed world. With that recognition came a sense of confusion – did he feel relief at that knowledge, or loss? He couldn't tell yet, but whichever way his feelings settled, the severance was final.

When the music drew to its quiet close, Father Holloway, as always, lifted the stylus carefully off and replaced the arm, rather than leave it to the automated system. Then, equally carefully, he lifted the record off the turntable, replaced it in its sleeve and put it back in its proper place among the other records. He always did this with the same reverence with which he handled the chalice and ciborium at Mass.

'And now,' he said, after the little ritual of the music was complete. 'Will you join me in a visit to the church, one last time? There's no one else in there, and it's an opportunity to take your leave properly.'

'Very well, but it won't make me change my mind.'

'I know that, but it would please me. You are still in orders, after all. Once I have contacted the bishop and he has issued the order, then you will be free. But remember what I said just now. The power that came with your ordination, the very essence of priesthood – that will always be yours. Come now, your last visit as a serving priest.'

Gerard was not willing, but as he'd done so many times, he acquiesced. His motivation was very different this time, faced with such a different Father Holloway. He was aware of the shift in atmosphere and temperature as they passed through the door, but this time felt no awe or reverence. It was a big, old stone building whose architecture was as familiar as home, but it no longer meant more than that.

He walked slowly around it, studying the stained glass, the wall plaques and the ancient tombs, for the last time.

He once more walked the Stations of the Cross, pausing at each one. Before, each Station had represented for him a stage in the great story, a part of a ritual, and the figures depicted archetypes that his soul had tried to respond to. This time, despite the stylised paintings, he saw at each stage the imperfect humans dealing with their too-human emotions in this awful story. Even Christ was shown as an imperfect human. Wasn't he? Jesus the artisan, not the Christ.

But was he imperfect? His knowledge of His true self and purpose did not prevent His fear in Gethsemane the previous night, nor did it give Him the strength to carry His cross unaided all the way to the execution spot. Did the fear and weakness make Him an imperfect human, or did they actually make Him truly human?

For the first time, Gerard studied these figures with compassion rather than awe, as real people and not just the ciphers in this ancient rite.

Father Holloway watched him patiently on this last tour.

'Come and sit in here one more time,' he said, guiding Gerard to the confessional and opening the confessor's door. 'Sit there for a few moments, and remember all those who came to you for absolution and purging. Give them one last prayer while you still belong to the Church.'

Gerard felt unable to resist this urging, although it was not his wish. He sat in the familiar place and wondered just how much good he had done. Was it Truth, or a comfortable delusion for all concerned? Had Jez sat in this place and asked for help, might he have lived? He didn't hear the curtain open on the other side of the grille, but just heard his old mentor's voice:

'Forgive me, Father, for I think I have sinned.'

ABOUT THE AUTHOR

Malcolm Eva is following the long and distinguished tradition of those who, having retired from useful paid work, have looked for more rewarding but less rewarded activity. This is the first novel that he has published, although not the first that he has written, its predecessors having fallen accidentally into a shredder to the benefit of the reading public.

He has written and contributed to books on systems and business analysis and has recognised that it's now time to complete the work that, many years ago, was his excuse for leaving school teaching.

Two more novels and three novellas are now knocking loudly on the door, pleading to be let out into the world. Patience, they're on their way.

ABOUT THE BOOK

This book took a long time to write, not due to any inherent difficulties, but because various life changes in the middle kept putting it on hold. And then major changes in the world, which would have been irrelevant if I had actually finished it when intended, confused me as to what direction it should take.

Its genesis lay in three unconnected incidents: the first was seeing the marvellous Bob Pegg, a Yorkshire singer/songwriter, in Oxford in 1978. One song that he sang that night lodged an earworm in my head: The Priest Loves the Dancer and the Dancer loves the Drummer. Long after I had forgotten the story wrapped around that chorus, those two lines stuck with me. Then six or seven years later I was working in Earl's Court, yes, in that same blue tower, and living nearby in a hotel while a house purchase kept getting held up, nearly collapsing, and after three months finally completed. One morning as I was walking to work, a line dropped into my head from nowhere, 'Father Gerard thanked God for his loving gift of Sin.' I had no idea who Father Gerard was, or how or why he sinned, but it immediately brought back Bob Pegg's chorus, and I knew that I had to create something out of these two fragments. The third happened soon after when, one very misty evening, I was accosted by a teenage girl while on my way back to the hotel, with the call, 'Business?' My reaction was Gerard's initial response, 'Sorry, no thank you!' and a scuttle back to my shoebox room.

I started planning the book from then on, but new jobs, new relationships, fracturing relationships, new homes, and the repetition of that whole cycle, kept getting in the way, and in the late

1990s I put the whole thing on the shelf (well, actually, onto some floppy disks). I never forgot about it, and it stayed at the back of my mind. Then early in the new millennium came 9/11 and the world I had been writing about changed, especially attitudes to the likes of Yasser. I gave up then and thought that it would just end up as a promising unfinished work at the back of the drawer.

Soon after Covid had in its turn upset the world, I re-read it and thought that it did have legs, and I should work on it once more. My dilemma was to either make it a period piece, set in the 1980s or 90s, or make it part of the current disturbed twenty-first century world. I settled for the former, and after a number of rewrites following feedback on its first and second drafts, it is here in your hands and, I hope, in your head too.

If you have, thank you for reading it.

ACKNOWLEDGEMENTS

My thanks for honest feedback on initial drafts to my stepson, Tom Welch, and Dea Parkin and her team at Fiction Feedback, and to Katherine Frances for some scrupulous copy editing and proofreading.

Thanks to Karina Gabner for the cover artwork. Thanks also to Megan Sheer, of Sheer Book Design, for the layout of the book and for helping me through the publication process.

Grateful thanks to Bob Pegg for allowing me to make his chorus my epigraph. The song, 'The Priest, The Dancer and The Drummer', later found its way onto his CD '*The Last Wolf*' – very highly recommended!

Thanks to my lovely wife, Rosie, for patiently putting up with my vanishing upstairs into the world around Brompton and Kensington day after day.

Printed in Great Britain
by Amazon

51890252R00184